Praise for
North! Or Be Eaten

"Peterson deserves every literary prize for this fine book. It is obvious that his musical talents have been put to good use as his use of words, plot, and narrative read like a well-scored film script. A very fine book, by a very fine writer and future talent. Amazing—thrilling and well worth reading again and again."

—G. P. TAYLOR, *New York Times* best-selling author of *Shadowmancer* and The Dopple Ganger Chronicles

"Toothy cows are very dangerous. Andrew Peterson convinced me and shivers run down my spine at the very thought of meeting a toothy cow face to face. The author spills characters like Podo and Nurgabog onto the page, then weaves a tale of danger that holds the reader captive. Believe me, you will relish being held captive by this master storyteller. But be sure you don't get caught by the Stranders. Those people just ain't civilized."

—DONITA K. PAUL, author of *The Vanishing Sculptor*

"In a genre overrun by the gory and the grim, Peterson's bite-sized chapters taste more like a stew of Gorey (Edward) and Grimm (the Brothers). *North! Or Be Eaten* is a welcome feast of levity—and clearly a labor of love. Andrew Peterson has awakened my inner eight-year-old, and that is a very good thing."

—JEFFREY OVERSTREET, author of *Auralia's Colors* and *Cyndere's Midnight*

"An immensely clever tale from a wonderful storyteller—filled with great values and even greater adventure!"

—PHIL VISCHER, creator of *VeggieTales*

"Thrills, chills, spine-tingling mystery, and lots of smiles. It's not easy to combine heart-pounding danger with gut-busting laughs and make it work, but Peterson pulls it off. For readers who want nonstop action infused with powerful, life-changing themes, *North! Or Be Eaten* is a must-read."

—WAYNE THOMAS BATSON, best-selling author of The Door Within Trilogy, *Isle of Swords,* and *Isle of Fire*

"Andrew Peterson is a gifted storyteller, scene painter, and wordsmith who takes you on a rollicking white-water ride of adventure. Readers of all ages are sure to find *North! Or Be Eaten* worthy of a big mug filled with a favorite beverage and a cozy nook near a crackling fire for hours on end. Here there be tales within yarns within stories. Listen, reader, bend your ear, but keep an eye peeled lest the dreaded Fangs of Dang be near!"

—R. K. MORTENSON, author of *Landon Snow and the Auctor's Riddle*

NORTH! or Be Eaten

NORTH! or Be Eaten

**Wild escapes.
A desperate journey.
And the ghastly Fangs of Dang.**

ANDREW PETERSON

THE WINGFEATHER SAGA BOOK TWO

WATERBROOK
PRESS

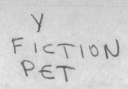

Y
FICTION
PET

NORTH! OR BE EATEN
PUBLISHED BY WATERBROOK PRESS
12265 Oracle Boulevard, Suite 200
Colorado Springs, Colorado 80921

The characters and events in this book are fictional, and any resemblance to actual persons or events is coincidental.

ISBN 978-1-4000-7387-0
ISBN 978-0-307-44666-4 (electronic)

Published in association with the literary agency of Alive Communications Inc., 7680 Goddard Street, Suite 200, Colorado Springs, CO, www.alivecommunications.com.

Published in the United States by WaterBrook Multnomah, an imprint of the Crown Publishing Group, a division of Random House Inc., New York.

WATERBROOK and its deer colophon are registered trademarks of Random House Inc.

Library of Congress Cataloging-in-Publication Data
Peterson, Andrew.
    North! or be eaten : wild escapes, a desperate journey, and the ghastly Fangs of Dang / Andrew Peterson.—1st ed.
        p. cm.—(The Wingfeather saga ; bk. 2)
    Summary: Jealousies and bitterness threaten to tear apart the three Igiby siblings, heirs to a legendary kingdom across the sea, just when they must work together to battle the monsters of Glipwood Forest, the thieving Stranders of the East Bend, and the dreaded Fork Factory.
    ISBN 978-1-4000-7387-0—ISBN 978-0-307-44666-4 (electronic) [1. Brothers and sisters—Fiction. 2. Adventure and adventurers—Fiction. 3. Fantasy.] I. Title.
    PZ7.P4431No 2009
    [Fic]—dc22

                                    2009015368

Printed in the United States of America
2009

10 9 8 7 6 5 4 3 2

For Aedan, Asher, and Skye.
Remember who you are.

Contents

NORTH! or Be Eaten

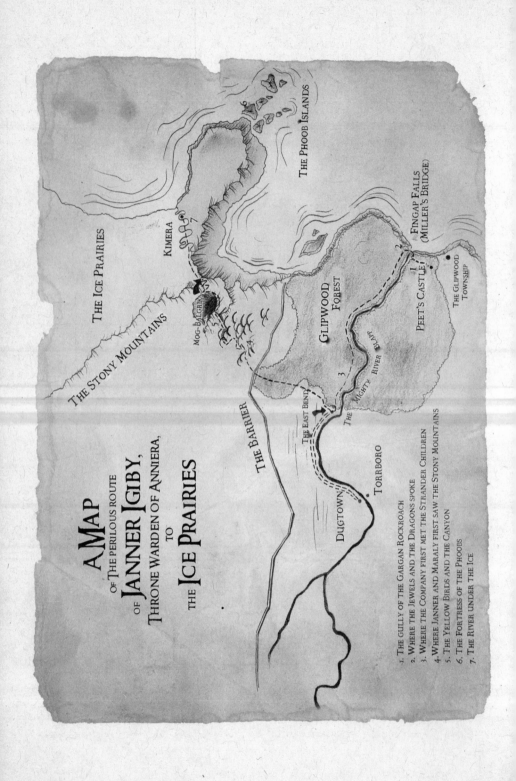

A MAP
OF THE PERILOUS ROUTE
OF JANNER IGIBY,
THRONE WARDEN OF ANNIERA,
TO
THE ICE PRAIRIES

THE ICE PRAIRIES

THE PHOOB ISLANDS

FINGAP FALLS
(MILLER'S BRIDGE)

KIMERA

THE STONY MOUNTAINS

MOG-BALGRIK

GLIPWOOD FOREST

PEET'S CASTLE

THE GLIPWOOD TOWNSHIP

THE MIGHTY RIVER BLAPP

THE BARRIER

THE EAST BEND

TORRBORO

DUGTOWN

1. THE GULLY OF THE GARGAN ROCKROACH
2. WHERE THE JEWELS AND THE DRAGONS SPOKE
3. WHERE THE COMPANY FIRST MET THE STRANDER CHILDREN
4. WHERE JANNER AND MARALY FIRST SAW THE STONY MOUNTAINS
5. THE YELLOW BIRDS AND THE CANYON
6. THE FORTRESS OF THE PHOOBS
7. THE RIVER UNDER THE ICE

The Lone Fendril

TOOOOTHY COW!" bellowed Podo as he whacked a stick against the nearest glip-wood tree. The old pirate's eyes blazed, and he stood at the base of the tree like a ship's captain at the mast. "Toothy cow! Quick! Into the tree house!"

Not far away, an arrow whizzed through some hanging moss and thudded into a plank of wood decorated with a charcoal drawing of a snarling Fang. The arrow protruded from the Fang's mouth, the shaft still vibrating from the impact. Tink lowered his bow, squinted to see if he had hit the target, and completely ignored his grandfather.

"TOOOOOTHY— oy! That's a fine shot, lad— COW!"

Podo whacked the tree as Nia hurried up the rope ladder that led to the trapdoor in the floor of Peet the Sock Man's tree house. A sock-covered hand reached down and pulled Nia up through the opening.

"Thank you, Artham," she said, still holding his hand. She looked him in the eye and raised her chin, waiting for him to answer.

Peet the Sock Man, whose real name was Artham P. Wingfeather, looked back at her and gulped. One of his eyes twitched. He looked like he wanted to flee, as he always did when she called him by his first name, but Nia didn't let go of his hand.

"Y-y-you're welcome…*Nia.*" Every word was an effort, especially her name, but he sounded less crazy than he used to be. Only a week earlier, the mention of the name "Artham" sent him into a frenzy—he would scream, shimmy down the rope ladder, and disappear into the forest for hours.

Nia released his hand and peered down through the opening in the floor at her father, who still banged on the tree and bellowed about the impending onslaught of toothy cows.

"Come on, Tink!" Janner said.

A quiver of arrows rattled under one arm as he ran toward Leeli, who sat astride her dog, Nugget. Nugget, whose horselike size made him as dangerous as any toothy cow in the forest, panted and wagged his tail. Tink reluctantly dropped his bow and followed, eyeing the forest for signs of toothy cows. The brothers helped a wide-eyed Leeli down from her dog, and the three of them rushed to the ladder.

"Cows, cows, cows!" Podo howled.

Janner followed Tink and Leeli up the ladder. When they were all safely inside, Podo heaved himself through the opening and latched the trapdoor shut.

"Not bad," Podo said, looking pleased with himself. "Janner, next time you'll want to move yer brother and sister along a little faster. Had there been a real cow upon us, ye might not have had time to get 'em to the ladder before them slobbery teeth started tearin' yer tender flesh—"

"Papa, *really*," Nia said.

"—and rippin' it from yer bones," he continued. "If Tink's too stubborn to drop what he's doin', Janner, it falls to you to find a way to persuade him, you hear?"

Janner's cheeks burned, and he fought the urge to defend himself. The toothy cow drills had been a daily occurrence since their arrival at Peet's tree house, and the children had gradually stopped shrieking with panic whenever Podo's hollers disturbed the otherwise quiet wood.

Since Janner had learned he was a Throne Warden, he had tried to take his responsibility to protect the king seriously. His mother's stories about Peet's dashing reputation as a Throne Warden in Anniera made Janner proud of the ancient tradition of which he was a part.[1] The trouble was that he was supposed to protect his younger brother, Tink, who happened to be the High King. It wasn't that Janner was jealous; he had no wish to rule anything. But sometimes it felt odd that his skinny, reckless brother was, of all things, a king, much less the king of the fabled Shining Isle of Anniera.

Janner stared out the window at the forest as Podo droned on, telling him about his responsibility to protect his brother, about the many dangers of Glipwood Forest, about what Janner should have done differently during this most recent cow drill.

Janner missed his home. In the days after they fled the town of Glipwood and arrived at Peet's castle, Janner's sense of adventure was wide awake. He thrilled at the

---

1. In Anniera the second born, not the first, is heir to the throne. The eldest child is a Throne Warden, charged with the honor and responsibility of protecting the king above all others. Though this creates much confusion among ordinary children who one day discover that they are in fact the royal family living in exile (see *On the Edge of the Dark Sea of Darkness*), for ages the Annierans found it to be a good system. The king was never without a protector, and the Throne Warden held a place of great honor in the kingdom.

thought of the long journey to the Ice Prairies, so excited he could scarcely sleep. When he did sleep, he dreamed of wide sweeps of snow under stars so sharp and bright they would draw blood at a touch.

But weeks had passed—he didn't know how many—and his sense of adventure was fast asleep. He missed the rhythm of life at the cottage. He missed the hot meals, the slow change of the land as the seasons turned, and the family of birds that nested in the crook above the door where he, Tink, and Leeli would inspect the tiny blue eggs each morning and each night, then the chicks, and then one day they would look in sad wonder at the empty nest and ask themselves where the birds had gone. But those days had passed away as sure as the summer, and whether he liked it or not, home was no longer the cottage. It wasn't Peet's tree house, either. He wasn't sure he had a home anymore.

Podo kept talking, and Janner felt again that hot frustration in his chest when told things he already knew. But he held his tongue. Grownups couldn't help it. Podo and his mother would hammer a lesson into his twelve-year-old head until he felt beaten silly, and there was no point fighting it.

He sensed Podo's rant coming to an end and forced himself to listen.

"…this is a dangerous place, this forest, and many a man has been gobbled up by some critter because he weren't paying close enough attention."

"Yes sir," Janner said as respectfully as possible. Podo grinned at him and winked, and Janner smiled back in spite of himself. It occurred to him that Podo knew exactly what he'd been thinking.

Podo turned to Tink. "A truly fine shot, boy, and the drawing of the Fang on that board is fine work."

"Thanks, Grandpa," Tink said. His stomach growled. "When can we eat breakfast?"

"Listen, lad," Podo said. He lowered his bushy eyebrows and leveled a formidable glare at Tink. "When yer brother tells ye to come, you drop what yer doin' like it's on fire." Tink gulped. "You follow that boy over the cliffs and into the Dark Sea if he tells you to. Yer the High King, which means ye've got to start thinkin' of more than yerself."

Janner's irritation drained away, as did the color in Tink's face. He liked not being the only one in trouble, though he felt a little ashamed at the pleasure he took in watching Tink squirm.

"Yes sir," Tink said. Podo stared at him so long that he repeated, "Yes sir."

"You okay, lass?" Podo turned with a smile to Leeli.

She nodded and pushed some of her wavy hair behind one ear. "Grandpa, when are we leaving?"

All eyes in the tree house looked at her with surprise. The family had spent weeks in relative peace in the forest, but that unspoken question had grown more and more difficult to avoid as the days passed. They knew they couldn't stay forever. Gnag the Nameless and the Fangs of Dang still terrorized the land of Skree, and the shadow they cast covered more of Aerwiar with every passing day. It was only a matter of time before that shadow fell again on the Igibys.

"We need to leave soon," Nia said, looking in the direction of Glipwood. "When the leaves fall, we'll be exposed, won't we, Artham?"

Peet jumped a little at his name and rubbed the back of his head with one hand for a moment before he spoke. "Cold winter comes, trees go bare, the bridges are easy to see, yes. We should grobably po—probably go."

"To the Ice Prairies?" asked Janner.

"Yes," said Nia. "The Fangs don't like the cold weather. We've all seen how much slower they move in the winter, even here. Hopefully in a place as frozen as the Ice Prairies, the Fangs will be scarce."

Podo grunted.

"I know what you think, and it's not one of our options," Nia said flatly.

"What does Grandpa think?" Tink asked.

"That's between your grandfather and me."

"What does he think?" Janner pressed, realizing he sounded more like a grownup than usual.

Nia looked at Janner, trying to decide if she should give him an answer. She had kept so many secrets from the children for so long that it was plain to Janner she still found it difficult to be open with them. But things were different now. Janner knew who he was, who his father was, and had a vague idea what was at stake. He had even noticed his input mattered to his mother and grandfather. Being a Throne Warden—or at least *knowing* he was a Throne Warden—had changed the way they regarded him.

"Well," Nia said, still not sure how much to say.

Podo decided for her. "I think we need to do more than get to the Ice Prairies and lie low like a family of bumpy digtoads, waitin' fer things to happen to us. If Oskar was right about there bein' a whole colony of folks up north what don't like livin' under the boot of the Fangs, and if he's right about them wantin' to fight, then they don't need us to gird up and send these Fangs back to Dang with their tails on fire. I say the jewels need to find a ship and go home." He turned to his daughter. "Think of it, lass! You could sail back across the Dark Sea to Anniera—"

"What do you mean 'you'?" Tink asked.

"Nothin'," Podo said with a wave of his hand. "Nia, you could go home. Think of it!"

"There's nothing left for us there," Nia said.

"Fine! Forget Anniera. What about the Hollows? You ain't seen the Green Hollows in ten years, and for all you know, the Fangs haven't even set foot there! Yer ma's family might still be there, thinkin' you died with the rest of us."

Nia closed her eyes and drew a deep breath. Peet and the children stared at the floor. Janner hadn't thought about the fact that he might have distant family living in the hills of the Green Hollows across the sea.

He agreed with his mother that it seemed foolish to try to make such a journey. First they had to get past the Fangs in Torrboro, then north, over the Stony Mountains to the Ice Prairies. Now Podo was talking about crossing the *ocean*? Janner wasn't used to thinking of the world in such terms.

Nia opened her eyes and spoke. "Papa, there's nothing for us to do now but find our way north. We don't need to go across the sea. We don't need to go back to Anniera. We don't need to go to the Green Hollows. We need to go north, away from the Fangs. That's all. Let's get these children safely to the prairies, and we'll finish this discussion then."

Podo sighed. "Aye, lass. Gettin' there will cause enough trouble of its own." He fixed an eye on Peet, who stood on his head in the corner. "I suppose you'll be comin' with us, then?"

Peet gasped and tumbled to the floor, then leapt to his feet and saluted Podo. Leeli giggled.

"Aye sir," he said, mimicking Podo's raspy growl. "I'm ready to go when the Featherwigs are ready. Even know how to get to the Icy Prairies. Been there before, long time ago—not much to see but ice and prairies and ice all white and blinding and cold. It's very cold there. Icy." Peet took a deep, happy breath and clapped his socked hands together. "All right! We're off!"

He flipped open the trapdoor and leapt through the opening before Podo or the Igibys could stop him. The children hurried to the trapdoor and watched him slide down the rope ladder and march away in a northward direction. From the crook in the giant root system of the tree where he usually slept, Nugget perked up his big, floppy ears without lifting his head from his paws and watched Peet disappear into the forest.

"He'll come back when he realizes we aren't with him," Leeli said with a smile. She and Peet spent hours together either reading stories or with him dancing about with great swoops of his socked hands while she played her whistleharp. Leeli's presence seemed to have a medicinal effect on Peet. When they were together, his jitters ceased, his eyes stopped shifting, and his voice took on a deeper, less strained quality. The strong and pleasant sound of it helped Janner believe his mother's stories about Artham P. Wingfeather's exploits in Anniera before the Great War.

The only negative aspect of Leeli and Peet's friendship was that it made Podo jealous. Before Peet the Sock Man entered their lives, Podo and Leeli shared a special bond, partly because each of them had only one working leg and partly because of the ancient affection that exists between grandfathers and granddaughters. Nia once told Janner that it was also partly because Leeli looked a lot like her grandmother Wendolyn.

While the children watched Peet march away, a quick shadow passed over the tree house, followed by a high, pleasant sound, like the *ting* of a massive bell struck by a tiny hammer.

"The lone fendril,"[2] said Leeli. "Tomorrow is the first day of autumn."

"Papa," said Nia.

"Eh?" Podo glared out the window in the direction Peet had gone.

"I think it's time we left," Nia said.

Tink and Janner looked at each other and grinned. All homesickness vanished. After weeks of waiting, adventure was upon them.

---

2. In Aerwiar, the official last day of summer is heralded by the passing of the lone fendril, a giant golden bird whose wingspan casts entire towns into a thrilling flicker of shade as it circles the planet in a long, ascending spiral. When it reaches the northern pole of Aerwiar, it hibernates until spring, then reverses its journey.

Room Eight
of The Only Inn
(Glipwood's Only Inn)

After it flew over Peet's tree house, the lone fendril's shadow passed over Joe Shooster, proprietor of The Only Inn (Glipwood's only inn), as he lay pinned face-down in the dirt, fighting back tears. From the front door of the inn, Joe's wife, Addie, watched in horror. Her hands covered her mouth to stifle a scream as the Fang drove his boot harder into Joe's back.

The day was bright and blustery. The wind drove leaves and tumbleweeds through the streets to collect in the nooks of the town's battered buildings. A few weeks ago, the Glipwood Township had been wrecked by a mighty storm that descended on Skree like an apocalyptic stomp of the Maker's boot. Ferinia's Flower Shop had lost its roof, and rain flooded the building. Some structures had been flattened, leaving parts of Glipwood in rubble. Others, like The Only Inn, Books and Crannies, and the town jail, survived, sad reminders of the town that once lay quiet and peaceful at the edge of the cliffs.

Joe grimaced and managed to speak. "No, my lord, I have seen nothing of them. I swear it."

The Fang cracked Joe's head with the butt of his spear—hard, but not hard enough to render him unconscious. A cry slipped out of Addie's mouth, and the Fang whipped his head around and fixed her with a cold look. Joe felt the Fang's cold, damp tail drag over him as the Fang stepped across his body and climbed the steps to the inn's front door. Addie screamed as the Fang burst through the swinging doors and seized her by the back of the neck.

"You, then, sssmelly woman," the Fang growled, covering his snub nose and retching.[1] "Look old Higgk in the eye and tell him if you've ssseen or heard from the Igibys or from that nassty man who used to run the bookstore, Oskar Reteep."

Addie went pale and trembled, unable to speak or take her eyes off the long fangs jutting out of the creature's mouth, oozing venom.

"That one's useless, Higgk," called another Fang who watched happily from the street. "See what it does when you bite it."

"Aye!" called another. "That's what the poison in yer teeth is for, ain't it?"

Joe Shooster pulled himself to his knees and clasped his hands. "Please, lords! Don't hurt my Addie. She knows nothing. Nor do I, and I swear to it." Joe tried to keep his voice steady, but seeing his wife's pale face so close to the Fang's teeth made it impossible. "Please."

The Fangs of Dang derived much pleasure from watching Joe and his wife squirm and began to chant for Higgk to bite the woman. Higgk grinned and opened his mouth. His fangs lengthened, and tiny streams of venom squirted from them, criss-crossing Addie's blouse with steaming, hissing burns. Addie's eyes rolled backward, her eyelids fluttered, and Joe prayed that she would be unconscious when the Fang bit her. She went limp and sagged in the creature's grip.

A long whistle came from deep within The Only Inn. Joe dimly recognized it as the teapot on the stove in the kitchen.

Addie's eyes fluttered. "Tea's ready," she slurred, and in a flash of inspiration, Joe leapt to his feet.

"Wait!" he cried.

"What?" Higgk barked. "Have you sssuddenly remembered the whereabouts of the Igibysss?"

"No, lord, but if my Addie is gone, who will cook you booger gruel? No one else in Skree can make a pot of it like Addie Shooster. And what about midgepie? And clipping-topped gullet swanch?"[2]

Higgk hesitated. The other Fangs stopped their heckling and cocked their heads sideways, considering Joe and Addie in a new light. Except for the whistle of the teapot,

---

1. Addie Shooster was in fact quite fragrant, by human standards. Her cooking was lauded in Glipwood as the finest in Skree, and when she didn't smell like roast and totatoes or cheesy chowder, she was careful to apply flower petal perfume in copious amounts to her neck and arms. This perfume is likely the scent to which the Fang referred.

2. Joe remembered Nia Igiby's bargain with the late Commander Gnorm to prepare him a maggotloaf weekly. Not only had it rescued her children from the town jail and the Black Carriage, but it had bought them a degree of immunity from the Fangs, who were too lazy to cook for themselves and who valued such meals nearly as much as gold and jewelry and murder.

there was silence. Joe wiped his hands on his apron and met his wife's eyes. She took some strength from him and said, "M-my critternose casserole is dreadfully good, sir."

"Fine," Higgk said.

He released Addie, and she fell to the ground in a heap. Joe rushed over to her and placed a kiss on her forehead.

"Ugh," said the Fang. "If I don't have a plate of that critternose casserole by sundown, I'll finish what I started." The Fangs hissed and snarled and chuckled their agreement. "If you learn anything about Reteep or the Igibys and you don't tell Higgk, no amount of food will save your smelly ssskins."

Joe and Addie hurried to the kitchen, where they set to work concocting a critternose casserole, the name of which Addie had invented on the spot. She sent Joe out to round up as many rodents as possible so she could begin the work of removing their little black noses.

Joe kissed her and thanked the Maker they were both still alive. "I'll be back soon, love," he said.

He hung his apron on the back of a chair and pulled on his boots but hesitated with his hand on the doorknob. Joe peeked out the window that opened on to the back courtyard. He saw no Fangs.

Instead of going outside, Joe tiptoed up the kitchen stairway to the second floor of the inn. He paused at the top and stared at a hallway lined with doors.

He listened. He heard faintly the raucous Fangs in the streets. He heard the creak of the old building and the gusty wind outside. Joe stole down the hallway to room eight and eased the door open.

Room eight contained a neatly made bed, a wash basin on a chest of drawers, and a desk, each piece of furniture simple but sturdy. Joe moved to the window and paused, looking out at the wreckage of Glipwood with a pang of sadness. Below the window lay what remained of Shaggy's Tavern. The stone chimney stood like the trunk of an old petrified tree, the ground littered with planks, broken stools, and shattered bottles.

Wincing at the creak of his footsteps on the wooden floor, he crept to the chest of drawers and slid it away from the wall. Behind the bureau was a small doorway. Joe looked around one last time and ducked inside, pulling the chest back into place behind him.

The doorway opened on to a cramped room lit only by a tiny window in the ceiling. The light was weak, but after a moment Joe's eyes adjusted, and he could see the plump figure shivering in the bed.

"Hello, old friend," Joe whispered.

The man stirred and tried to sit up. A blood-soaked bandage adorned his large belly.

Joe put a hand on his arm. "Don't sit up. I have to step out for a bit, but I wanted to check on you first. Do you need water?"

The man on the bed tried in vain to flatten a lock of white hair against his balding head. "I'm...parched," he said, "to paraphrase the wise words...of...Lou di Cicaccelliccelli."

"I'll take your word for it," Joe said with a smile, pouring a cup of water from a pitcher beside the bed. He lifted it to Oskar N. Reteep's mouth. "I'll be up later to change your bandages. Do you need anything else?"

Oskar swallowed the water with a grimace. "A few more books would be splendid, if it's not too much trouble."

Joe looked at the stacks of books in every corner of the room. "I'll do my best," he said. "Rest. I'll be back tonight. It's nice that you're able to talk again, Oskar."

"Yes," Oskar wheezed. "And Joe, there's much I need to tell you. Zouzab... beware—" He broke off in a fit of coughs.

"It's all right. There will be time to fill me in on everything later." Soon Joe would have to tell Oskar that his little companion Zouzab was gone, probably killed by the Fangs. He didn't want to burden the old man with more grief.

Oskar leaned back and fell asleep immediately. As bad as he looked, he had come far in the weeks since Joe found him bleeding on the floor of Books and Crannies. The day the storm came, Joe and Addie had spent the better part of the afternoon maneuvering him into the inn. No Fang reinforcements had come since the night before the storm, when Podo and the Igibys fled to Anklejelly Manor to escape the hundreds of Fangs that had come for them. Joe still wasn't sure what became of the Fangs that night, but it seemed that someone, or something, had killed them all.

When the Shoosters emerged from their hiding place the morning after the battle, it felt as if the world of Aerwiar had ended. Dark clouds roiled in the sky above the deserted town, and the streets were clogged with the dust, bones, and armor of countless Fangs. Soon Shaggy emerged from the tavern, and the Shoosters felt great relief at his appearance. They had been neighbors for decades and were the only members of the Glipwood Township who chose to stay rather than flee to Torrboro or Dugtown the night the Igibys fought their way out of the Black Carriage.

But then the one friend the Shoosters had left was taken from them.

One afternoon a company of Fangs tore through Glipwood on their way north from Fort Lamendron. From a second-story window of The Only Inn, the Shoosters watched helplessly as Shaggy pushed a wheelbarrow of firewood across the street. When the Fangs saw him, they pushed him to the ground and one of the lizards sank its fangs into Shaggy's leg.

The Fangs left as quickly as they had come, but by the time Joe and Addie raced to Shaggy's side, he was already dead. The Shoosters wept as they buried their friend in the Glipwood Cemetery at the southern end of Vibbly Way. Joe scavenged the SHAGGY'S TAVERN sign from the building's wreckage. It bore the name of the tavern and an image of a dog smoking a pipe. Joe placed it at the head of Shaggy's grave after carving, in his finest lettering, the inscription "Shaggy Bandibund, an Exemplary Neighbor and Friend."

Now the Fangs were back, demanding to know the whereabouts of Reteep, Podo Helmer, and the Igiby family, and Joe had no idea why. Oskar had mumbled a great deal in his sleep about the Ice Prairies and the Jewels of Anniera, whatever those were, but Joe Shooster was merely the proprietor of The Only Inn. He didn't know about such things and didn't care to. He just wanted Oskar to recover and things to somehow go back to the way they were before the Fangs set foot in Skree.

If the Fangs wanted Oskar, then Joe Shooster knew the right thing to do was to keep Oskar hidden. When the old man's wounds were healed, Joe would figure out what to do next. In the meantime, he had to be careful. As Joe had just seen with Higgk the Fang, it wasn't just Oskar's life in danger but his and sweet Addie's as well. He hated to think of harm ever coming to her.

Joe bid Oskar farewell with a pat to his leg, and Oskar grunted in reply. Joe listened at the back of the chest of drawers for a long moment before sliding it aside and creeping out from behind it. He scooted the chest back into place and froze.

What was that sound? Movement from the window behind him? A sheen of sweat swept over Joe's body, and his mind raced. As casually as possible, he removed a handkerchief from the pocket of his vest and dusted the top of the chest. He hummed to himself as he moved from the chest of drawers to the desk and risked a glance at the window.

A face stared back at him.

A small figure with delicate features and a patchwork tunic perched outside the window of room eight. His eyes were piercing and cold, and they froze Joe in his tracks.

"Zouzab!" Joe said aloud, glad and confused to see the little fellow. Oskar would be pleased his friend was still alive.

He waved at the ridgerunner, who nodded in reply. The little creature was probably worried about his old master and would be a great help to Joe and Addie as they nursed Oskar back to health. Joe placed the handkerchief back in his pocket and slid the window open.

"Welcome, Zouzab!" he said, as the ridgerunner skittered through the window like a spider. "It's good to see a familiar face in Glipwood."

"Greetings, Mister Shooster," Zouzab said. His voice was thin and brittle—not like a child's, but not like a man's either.

Joe patted the little man on the head, failing to notice the look of disgust that flashed over Zouzab's face when he did so. "I suppose you're wondering about Oskar, aren't you?" He smiled at Zouzab, happy about his good news.

Zouzab's eyes widened almost imperceptibly, and he nodded. "Yes, Mister Shooster, I'm most concerned for his…health."

"Well," Joe said and then remembered Oskar's words just a few minutes ago: *"Zouzab…beware."*

Joe had assumed Oskar wanted to warn his little friend to beware of the Fangs— but now he wasn't so sure. He detected something sinister in the way the ridgerunner studied him.

"Oskar…" Joe faltered.

Zouzab took a step forward.

"Well—I haven't seen him. Not since the day before all this chaos descended on Glipwood. Have you?" Joe cleared his throat, removed his handkerchief, and busied himself with dusting the rest of the furniture in the room, tightening the sheets, and fluffing the pillow, acutely aware of Oskar's presence on the other side of the wall. He prayed the old man wouldn't wake up or snore.

Joe opened the door to the hallway and paused at the threshold. "Would you like to come with me? I have twelve more rooms to dust, and it's terribly exciting work, I assure you. Otherwise, you're welcome to leave the way you came in."

Zouzab watched him in silence, like a cat about to spring. The two stood in room eight for what felt to Joe like an eternity before Zouzab looked over the room one last time, bowed, and leapt lightly to the windowsill.

"Good-bye, Mister Shooster," Zouzab said, and in a flutter of patchwork, he was gone.

Joe crossed the room on trembling legs to close and latch the window. Then the silence was shattered by a loud burst of flatulence from Oskar's secret room.

Zouzab's head appeared in the window.

"Excuse me," Joe said with a shrug.

The ridgerunner narrowed his eyes, wrinkled his nose, and was gone.

3

Two Plans

Janner's and Tink's excitement had evaporated.

Boys sometimes forget that before one leaves on an adventure, if at all possible, one must pack. There are situations in which packing is secondary—such as escaping a burning building—but if there is time to plan and arrange and discuss before leaving, then it is a fact of life that grownups will do so. When children say it's time to leave, they mean, "It's time to leave." When grownups say so, they really mean, "It's time to begin thinking about leaving sometime in the near future."

After Nia's pronouncement, she and Podo proceeded with the day's chores as if a monumental decision had not been reached at all. The next day, the children chopped firewood, washed clothes and blankets, fetched water from the creek, and prepared meat to be salted and dried while the grownups planned, arranged, and discussed.

That evening after dinner, Nia and Podo unrolled an old map to work out their route to the Ice Prairies. They agreed to travel south to the edge of the forest, then west along the border until they reached the road to Torrboro. At Torrboro, they would travel south and west again in order to skirt the city and avoid the Fangs concentrated there.

"Three days west of Torrboro, the Mighty Blapp River ain't so mighty. It's wide but shallow enough to ford," Podo said. "And the Fangs should be scarce there."

"What about the Barrier?" Nia said.

"What's the Barrier?" Janner asked.

"I reckon you wouldn't have heard of it. It's here," Podo said, and he ran his finger across the map. "The Barrier is Gnag's best attempt to keep Skreeans from doin' exactly what we're tryin' to do. It's a wall that runs the length of the southern border of the Stony Mountains. It's patrolled by Fangs night and day. A few years after the Fangs took over, some folks realized the Fangs didn't move too fast in the cold, so a lot of Skreeans fled north. 'Course, most of 'em died. Fangs are slower in the cold, but they can still fight, and they can still bite. Especially when those they're after are women and children and men without weapons. Gnag's answer was to construct the

Barrier. It doesn't keep everyone out—it's a lot of wall to patrol, see—but it does its job well enough that the masses don't try an' run off. Oskar told me that if you're west of Torrboro and your company is small enough, you can find a breach in the wall and slip through unnoticed. That's what we aim to do."

"And Peet says he can get us through the mountains," Nia said.

"As long as he don't wake up some mornin' with his crazy head screwed on sideways and walk us off a cliff," Podo said. "Or into a crevasse or a nest of bomnubbles."[1]

"Nugget's not afraid of bomnubbles," said Leeli proudly. Below, Nugget barked at the sound of his name. Janner didn't want to tell Leeli that even Nugget might be an easy kill for a bomnubble.

"We'll need twenty days' supply of provisions," Nia said.

"Aye, which means we should plan for thirty," Podo said.

"Why?" asked Janner.

"Because, dear, you never know what might happen," Nia answered. "Journeys like this seldom go as planned."

"How did you come up with that number, though?" Janner asked. "It'll take twenty days to travel to the Ice Prairies?"

"Well, it's about two days to Torrboro, then three days past that to ford the Blapp, and—you know what, lad?" Podo said gently.

"Sir?"

"It'll be easier for me to just show you than to explain it. We've got a lot to sort out, and when ye get the journey under your feet, you'll learn more than I can tell ye now. Understand?"

Janner sighed. "Yes sir."

Nia and Podo moved the discussion to the other room and left the children with a long list of assignments from their T.H.A.G.S.[2] to keep their minds occupied until bedtime.

As the Igiby children settled in for a bedtime story from Podo, Oskar N. Reteep struggled to read by the fading light that drifted through the window in the ceiling of his

---

1. Bomnubbles! Woe!

2. Three Honored and Great Subjects: Word, Form, and Song. Some silly people think that there's a fourth Honored and Great Subject, but those scientists are woefully mistaken.

secret room. He squinted through his spectacles at the last few sentences of a book titled *The Anatomy of an Insult*.[3]

"Daft old hag," Oskar muttered as he tossed the book aside. It landed on a heap of other books in the narrow space between the bed and the wall. "Wouldn't know a good insult from a digtoad."

Oskar remembered falling asleep before he could warn Joe about Zouzab. He doubted the little traitor was still around, but Joe and Addie should know the ridgerunner was in league with the Fangs, just in case.

Oskar was dreadfully hungry and suspected he had slept for more than a day, though without a visit from Joe, he couldn't be sure. He also felt stronger. He had crossed a threshold in his recovery and could now speak without coughing.

He grimaced as he leaned forward and swung his feet to the floor, one hand placed gingerly on the bandage wrapped around his torso. Early that morning, by the light of his lantern, Oskar had found he was able to stand and even shuffle around the small space afforded by his quarters. He was excited to demonstrate this for Joe at his next visit, but to Oskar's disappointment and mounting concern, Joe never showed. He had heard none of the familiar bumps and voices from the kitchen or common room. All day he had read and reread books, trying to quiet the nagging fear that something was wrong.

Every day, Joe or Addie had changed his bandages, brought him water and food, and when Oskar was lucid enough to listen, they spoke to him in hushed voices about the Fangs and the Igibys and Podo. Oskar was careful not to tell them the true identity of the Igiby children. The less they knew, the better.

At first, his concern was only for the Shoosters. Now he was thirsty, his stomach growled, and he was beginning to consider the seriousness of his own situation. He doubted he could yet care for himself or even squeeze through the small door on his own, and the thought of starving or dying of thirst in his hidden room made it seem like a tomb. He wondered if some day years from now, someone would discover his skeleton lying on the bed, surrounded by books. He wondered what book he might be reading when he finally breathed his last, and determined to grab a good one as soon as he sensed the end coming so that whoever discovered him would know he had good taste in literature.

---

3. By Helba Grounce-Miglatobe, a well-known psychologician who claimed to have been ridiculed unduly as a child and as such was an expert, according to her book, in the field of "meanery and insultence."

Oskar removed his spectacles and cleaned them with the corner of the bed sheet.

He replaced his spectacles and adjusted a long tendril of hair so that it draped across his head. Oskar was no more able to admit defeat than to admit he was bald as a boulder. He looked at the small doorway on the opposite wall. His wound had stopped bleeding, but he was in no condition to crawl through the little door. He chuckled at the thought that his sizable belly might prove more of a hindrance than his stab wound.

His musings on his girth and its bearing on his escape were interrupted by a scream that worked its way through the wooden walls of the inn. Oskar tensed. The scream trailed off and gave way to the muted snarls of Fangs. The old man's lips moved with whispered prayers as he looked desperately around his shadowy cell, wondering what to do. He gathered his strength, took a deep breath, and stood. Stars filled his vision, and he heard another scream. It sounded like Addie.

Oskar made his way to the door one painful step at a time, cursing his weight, his wound, and the Fangs of Dang with insults heavily influenced by his recent study of Helba Grounce-Miglatobe's book. He reached the door and placed a hand on the wall to steady himself, breathing heavily and noticing with a stab of panic that new blood stained his bandage.

He lowered himself to his knees with great effort and placed a shoulder against the back of the chest of drawers that served as his door. The sounds of struggle coming from outside the inn were clearer now, and the Fangs weren't just snarling, but laughing.

He had no idea what he would do once he made it out of the room, but his instinct demanded he do *something*. He didn't know the right course of action, but clearly the wrong one would be lying in his bed and listening to the sounds of his friends being captured—or killed—by the Fangs.

Oskar heaved with all his might, and the chest of drawers slid out of the way.

Wincing at the pain in his chest, he crawled to the open window and gasped. Shaggy's Tavern was a ruin of broken planks. Across the street, what was left of Ferinia's Flower Shop sat broken and sad as a trampled lily. Beside it, to his relief, Oskar's own Books and Crannies still stood, just as Addie Shooster had assured him it did, intact except for a strip of wooden shingles missing from the roof.

Oskar's shock at the battered state of the Glipwood Township turned to dread when he spotted the source of the screams.

A team of black horses stood harnessed to the Black Carriage. But it wasn't the Black Carriage Oskar had seen the night Podo Helmer and Peet the Sock Man battled the Fangs. This carriage was longer and sleeker, and was, to Oskar's horror, more frightening to behold than the other. Instead of one chamber, there were several horizontal compartments just big enough for a man, as if the carriage were a wagon bearing a stack of iron coffins turned on their sides. Long spikes rose from the top of the carriage, creating a fortlike enclosure where two Fangs perched with crossbows.

Joe Shooster lay motionless in the street. A cluster of Fangs surrounded him and jabbed him with the butts of their spears. Another Fang clutched Addie's arms behind her back and pushed her down the steps from the jail. One of the Fangs on top of the carriage turned a switch, and the lowest of the horizontal doors clanged open. Two of the Fangs dragged Joe to the carriage and threw him in. Addie screamed as they forced her into the box above Joe's. The Fangs slammed the coffin doors and laughed as the hooded driver whipped the horses and drove the carriage out of sight.

Then a conversation drifted up through the window.

"That was fun," said a Fang standing in the street below.

"Aye. Nothin' like the squirmin' and the screamin'," said another wistfully. "Wish there was more of it these days. Been standin' around in thisss town for days with nothin' to do but pick at me scales."

"Won't be long afore we have some action," said the first.

"Eh? What do you know that I don't?"

"The ridgerunner says the Igibysss are in the forest."

"Imposssible."

"Why?"

"Because the cows woulda swallowed 'em up by now."

"Nah. They're with that socky fella. The mean one. He ain't afraid of the toothy cows. The ridgerunner says he's got bridges all through the trees. Says they're livin' in a tree house."

Oskar's eyes widened, and he smiled in spite of his pain. The Igibys were alive!

"Livin' in a what?" said the Fang.

"A tree house."

There was a pause.

"What's a tree house?"

"Don't know. Sounds familiar, though. Something about it gave me an odd sorta sick in me gut."

"Well, we'll find out tomorrow. Tonight the rest of the troops arrive; then we're movin' into the forest to find 'em. Leavin' tomorrow after first feeding. Catch 'em by surprise."

"No," Oskar breathed.

Then his strength snuffed out like a candle, and he collapsed to the floor of room eight, unaware of the small puddle of blood that gathered beneath him.

4

Appropriate Words from Ubinious the Whooned

The next morning after breakfast, Peet the Sock Man returned to the tree house, carrying a skinned and gutted cave blat over his shoulder. He mentioned casually that there might be a pack of horned hounds hot on his tail, at which point Podo roused Nugget to be on alert. As Peet pulled himself and the cave blat carcass up through the tree house door, the howl of a horned hound curled through the air, and Nugget bounded into the woods after it.

Janner and Tink sat cross-legged on the floor of the tree house, trying their best to attend to their T.H.A.G.S. though their minds spun with excitement about the journey ahead.

Tink was busy sketching the Igiby cottage from memory at his mother's request. She said they might never go back to Glipwood, and wasn't it nice that Tink had his father's sketchbook to peruse so he could see bits and pieces of his family's past? At eleven years old, Tink wasn't able to imagine passing his sketchbook on to anyone, let alone his own children. But he liked to draw, and Janner knew he had a vague sense of the value of archiving his work, of telling his story with the pictures he made.

Janner focused on his journal, trying to describe the intense anticipation he felt over the impending journey to the Ice Prairies and his frustration at having to wait around while preparations were made. Leeli sat in the crook of a fat tree limb, memorizing lyrics from a book of songs.

Janner heard Nugget bark and looked out the window to see the dog returning from the deeper forest, carrying the limp body of a horned hound in his mouth. Nugget was so gentle with the children that it was hard to imagine him attacking anything, but the giant dog was capable of killing more than just horned hounds. He and Peet had faced an assault of hundreds of Fangs of Dang and survived without a single wound that Janner ever saw.

At the base of the tree, Peet was hard at work, digging a hole to bury a chest full of his journals. There were too many to carry, and he didn't want them to fall into the Fangs' hands. He yelped when Nugget dropped the dead hound atop the pile of dirt beside the hole and shooed the great dog away.

"Hounds are bad flavor! Bad tastiness in your stew and worse on your books."

Nugget whined and dragged the hound back through the trees.

Just as Janner dipped his quill into the ink bottle and resumed writing in his journal, Nia's voice called from below.

"Boys, come down. I need you to try on your packs."

Janner and Tink tossed their books aside and clattered down the ladder.

Nia stood with her back to a pile of odds and ends and regarded her sons with her arms folded. She had spent the last few weeks working diligently at sewing packs out of Peet's old blankets and a few animal skins piled in the corner of the tree house and now handed each of the boys a completed backpack covered with flaps, ties, buttons, and compartments.

Janner slung it onto his back. He knew they'd need food, but he didn't know what other supplies a long journey required.

"Here's the book your father gave you," Nia said, placing it in Janner's pack. "I've wrapped it to keep it safe. And you'll need these." She handed him Tink's sheathed sword, pointing out the leather ties with which to lash it to his brother's pack.

The packs grew heavier and heavier as Nia filled them with necessary items: a box of matches, an oiled tinderbox in case the matches ran out, satchels of dried meat, packets of salt, a coil of rope, a folding knife Nia had scavenged from the weapons chamber of Anklejelly Manor, and the extra tunic and breeches. Nia lashed Janner's unstrung bow and a quiver of arrows to the side of the pack opposite the sword; then she did the same for Tink.

Nia stepped back and narrowed her eyes at the packs on her sons' backs. "The packs will suffice," she said with a nod. Then her eyes moved to her sons, and Janner moaned. "But your appearance will not. Come on."

Nia subjected Janner and Tink to a painful scrubbing. It felt to Janner like his mother intended to rub the skin from his bones. Then she set to work on their hair. Using one of the folding knives she'd placed in their packs, Nia sawed at their hair, grunting and tugging until locks of Janner's and Tink's shaggy hair lay in clumps at their feet.

When Nia was satisfied, she retrieved a looking glass and held it up. Janner looked at himself with surprise. In the harrowing weeks since they had first rescued Leeli from Slarb, a lot had happened. Janner could see it in his own eyes: a look of gravity, a

maturity that he hoped might someday become wisdom. He handed the mirror to
Tink, wondering if his little brother would notice the same thing of himself.

Instead Tink immediately made the goofiest, ugliest face he could muster and
burst into laughter. Leeli encouraged it with laughter of her own, and Tink went on
for several minutes, inventing silly faces and laughing until he couldn't breathe. Hard
as he tried, Janner couldn't help grinning at his brother's antics, and he noticed their
mother smiling too.

Behold, Janner thought, *the High King of Anniera. Maker help us.*

His thoughts were interrupted by a strange sound in the forest.

Janner peered into the trees, wondering if it was his imagination. After weeks in
Glipwood Forest, he had come to recognize the shriek of the cave blat, the gribbit of
the bumpy digtoad, the horrible moo of the toothy cow, and the wail of the horned
hound. Peet had even taught Janner and his siblings about the various birds that sang
in the boughs and how to tell which ones were hostile, which were mischievous, and
which were singing dirges for fellow birds that had been gobbled by a gulpswallow.

But this sound was different. It was almost human. Janner took quick stock of his
family to be sure everyone was present, and to his increasing alarm, all were.

"*Shh!*" Janner clamped a hand over Tink's mouth. "Hear that?"

"Mmmf," Tink replied.

The sound got louder, now accompanied by the faint *kshhh-kshhh* of snapping
twigs and brush trampled underfoot. Podo and Nia heard it too. They all stood, heads
turned, listening. Nugget whined and paced back and forth until Leeli hushed him.

Finally, the voice echoing through the timbers grew near enough that the words
became clear.

"In the words of Ubinious the Whooned, 'Run, Igibys! If you're out
there, run! They're coming!'"

5

A Traitor in the Trees

Oskar Noss Reteep bounced and jiggled atop the bewildered donkey like jelly in an earthquake. He held the reins high in the air and had long since lost any hope of his feet finding the stirrups. His spectacles dangled from one ear, and a magnificent swath of white hair, attached just above his ear, lifted from where he had pressed it to his head and flew behind him like a flag of surrender.

Janner nearly came out of his skin when he recognized his old employer. The last time he had seen Oskar, the old fellow lay dying on the floor of Books and Crannies, urging him to flee. On that last, awful night in the Glipwood Township, amidst the horror of the Fang battle, Zouzab's betrayal, and the family's escape to Anklejelly Manor, Janner had assumed Oskar was dead. To see him alive came as a shock, but it turned quickly to joy. Janner smiled as Reteep bounded toward him, making such a racket that flocks of wrenchies perched in the trees cawed and flapped away.

"Janner!" Podo's voice found its way through the thoughts in Janner's head. "BOY!"

Janner snapped out of his daze and realized that of all the Igibys, he was the only one standing still. He gasped when he finally realized what Oskar was bellowing.

"RUN, IGIBYS! IN THE WORDS OF—"

Before he could finish, the poor donkey—whether from fatigue or because he could no longer bear the indignity of such a jiggly rider—went down. Oskar's eyes bulged as he soared through the air toward the clearing where Janner stood. He flew with a surprising grace, hair trailing behind, spectacles dangling, his mouth forming a perfect O as the reins, still firmly in his grip, snapped taut and flipped the round man over to land on his back at Janner's feet.

The donkey brayed.

Oskar lay on the ground, blinking, surprised he wasn't dead.

"Janner! My boy, I'm glad to see you. I came as fast as I could." Oskar winced and placed a hand on his side as Janner helped him to his feet. The old man's middle was wrapped with bloodstained bandages.

"I don't know how you're alive, Mister Reteep, but I'm glad," Janner said.

Podo descended the ladder from Peet's castle with a bundle on his back, while Nia and Leeli gathered food supplies and shoved them into various packs. Tink dropped Peet's leather-bound journals one at a time from a tree house window; Peet caught them and piled them atop a rectangle of coarse fabric spread out on the ground.

"That's all of them, Uncle Peet!" Tink called.

Peet nodded, folded the canvas over the books, and heaved the pile into the hole he had dug.

"Oskar! How much time do we have?" Podo barked.

"Oh dear." Oskar brushed himself off. "Not more than a few minutes. I tried to sneak away, but they saw me, and there are hundreds of them. Hundreds!"

A new sound drifted through the woods. A horrible sound, like nothing Janner had ever heard. Part moan, part growl, it was clear it came from something large. Even Nugget whined. He bounded to Leeli and pressed his great furry body against her, whether to protect her or to be protected, Janner wasn't sure.

"And that's the other thing," Oskar said gravely.

"Eh?" Podo heaved a supply-laden pack over his shoulder. "What's the other thing?"

"Trolls." Oskar shuddered and wrinkled his nose.

Trolls? A shiver of fear coursed through Janner. He had never seen a troll, though Pembrick's *Creaturepedia* depicted several troll races, all of which were formidable and ghastly to behold.

His heart skipped a beat at the look of worry that flashed over Nia's face. She was serene in the worst of circumstances, able to grow icy cold even as the heat of danger rose. But when the troll's growl-moan sounded again, closer than before, her face wrinkled in a way that made her look old and tired, though only for a moment.

Podo looked hard at Oskar, then nodded. "Well, whether it's trolls or Fangs or me Great-Granny Olaraye comin', we're getting out of here fast. Janner, get that donkey over here and tie what ye can to the saddle. Tink!"

"Yes sir," Tink said from behind Podo.

"Help yer sister with her things, then have yer bow and arrow ready. You ride on Nugget with her and shoot at anything you're sure you can hit. Be *sure*, understand? Arrows are precious."

"Yes," said a papery voice just above them. "Arrows are precious. But they'll do the Igibys no good, I'm afraid."

Zouzab Koit perched high in the overstory and looked down on them with an expressionless face. Oskar sputtered, so enraged that he could think of no one to quote.

"You!" shouted Podo, his face already reddening for the torrent of curses about to burst from his mouth.

But before he could say a word, Peet the Sock Man screeched and leapt impossibly high, swinging himself into the boughs where Zouzab crouched. Zouzab skittered away, blowing his high-pitched whistle as Peet pursued. In a flurry of whirling branches and falling leaves, the Sock Man and the ridgerunner were out of sight, leaving Podo and Oskar trembling and speechless. Their anger was interrupted by another troll call, then another whistle blow, not far away.

"No time! Move!" Podo said.

While Janner pulled the tired donkey to its feet, Nia pushed the dirt into the hole where Peet had stashed his precious journals. She threw a pile of leaves atop the fresh dirt and spread them around to conceal it.

"Papa, where will we go?" Nia cried as Podo rushed up the ladder to the tree house.

"Don't know, lass! North, I reckon," he called over his shoulder. "We can't go south now, like we planned."

"But—but there's nothing north but the river. We'll be trapped!"

"Ah!" Oskar said. "There's a bridge. A way across…" He doubled over and coughed. Janner rushed to his side to steady him.

Podo climbed down the ladder in a blur, carrying an armful of dried meat, which he shoved into his pack. "We're fools to stay here a toot longer. Hurry!"

"Here." Nia tossed Peet's leather satchel to Janner. "Tie this to the donkey, then get your things. Go!"

"Mama, Mister Reteep is hurt," Janner said. "Where's the water from the First Well?"

"I don't know, son. Artham had it. We'll have to give Oskar some when we get far enough away from the Fangs." She turned to Oskar. "Can you make it? Can you ride?"

Oskar nodded, wheezing.

Janner's sword, lashed to the side of his pack, thunked against his hip when he threw the pack over his shoulders and reminded him how heavy and real and dangerous swords—and the situations that called for them—were. The growl-moans of the trolls grew louder, and Janner could hear the faint *thud-thud-thud* of marching feet.

Leeli sat astride Nugget, her hands on the tufts of black fur that gathered at the sides of her dog's great head, her newest crutch slung with twine over her shoulder.

Tink sat just behind his sister with his bow ready. Nia held the tired donkey's reins and ran a soothing hand along its jaw. When Oskar tried to mount the donkey, it fixed him with a surly eye and brayed.

"All right, lads and lasses," Podo shouted, "we're off at a quick pace, hear?"

"But Grandpa, what about Uncle Peet?" Leeli asked.

Podo lowered his voice and spoke without looking his granddaughter in the eye. "We ain't waiting fer him. No time. He'll catch up."

"But—"

"After them!" snarled the faint, unmistakable voice of a Fang of Dang.

Janner saw a green, scaly face appear in the tree-choked distance, then another, and another. Podo took hold of Nugget's collar and led him at a run, deeper into Glipwood Forest.

6

The Gully Rim

Through the forest they ran. Behind them, like an invisible storm blowing through the trees, came the howls and moans and stomping feet of the Fang army. The donkey needed no prodding from Janner to quicken its pace. Peet the Sock Man was nowhere to be seen, but his screech occasionally cut through the darker sounds behind them.

Podo drove them onward, and even with his peglegged limp, he had to check his speed to allow the rest to keep up. Janner and his mother ran with the wild-eyed donkey between them, and Oskar huffed and wheezed in the rear.

As they ran, Janner looked over his shoulder and saw a line of Fangs weaving in and out of the trees, and among them, three lumbering trolls, which broke fat limbs like twigs. Janner felt a combination of horror and fascination and wished he could somehow stop the pursuit so he could get a better look at one of the smelly hulks.

"Janner, watch where you're going," Nia said, and he just had time to dance around a small tree. Ahead, Nugget trotted beside Podo, choosing his path with care so that Leeli was safe from low branches. With each troll bellow, Nugget's ears flattened against his head and he whined.

"*Shh,* boy," Leeli said, leaning forward to speak in her dog's ear.

Tink sat behind Leeli with his bow at the ready.

"Tink, can you see them?" Janner huffed.

"Yeah, I see them," Tink answered, trying to hide the worry in his voice. "They're getting closer. Grandpa, they're getting closer!"

"Aye, I hear 'em, lad," said Podo. "You just keep that arrow on the string."

Janner tried not to look back, but he couldn't help himself. He saw even more Fangs and trolls, close enough that he could make out looks of vicious glee on their faces. He could also smell them. A sharp, bitter odor polluted the air, and with the smell came memories of Slarb, of Gnorm and the Black Carriage, of cold, damp Fang flesh. With the memories came deep and overpowering fear. Since Oskar had burst into the clearing, Janner had felt tension and urgency—but now that he remembered

Horned Hound

The horned hound bites. It also chews and eats and can stab with its pointy horn. Petting is not recommended. Like the toothy cow, it is drawn to—and driven mad by—the smell of fire.

From Pembrick's *Creaturepedia*

the iron grip of a Fang claw and the ooze of venom from a Fang tooth, he was truly afraid.

"Oskar!" Nia cried.

Janner saw the old man stagger, teetering like a pile of dishes about to collapse. When Oskar reached out to steady himself on the nearest tree, Janner saw with alarm that the old man's hand was bright with blood. Oskar's knees buckled, and he crumpled to the ground.

Podo rushed back to his friend and pulled him to his feet.

"Janner, make room!" Podo ordered. Janner shoved the bedrolls and supplies from the donkey's back and with Podo's help heaved Oskar onto the poor beast. The old man lay on his stomach, draped over the saddle like a game animal freshly killed. His eyelids drooped, and his face was pale and clammy.

"Tink!" Leeli screamed, and Janner turned to see a new reason to fear. A horned hound burst from the ranks of the charging Fangs and barreled toward them. It wore a collar, and its face and body were decorated with black war paint.

Tink sat frozen on Nugget's back.

"SHOOT!" Podo roared.

Tink blinked twice and came back to himself. He drew the bow and loosed the arrow, and the hound collapsed in a burst of leaves.

Podo didn't need to give the order to run like mad. Nugget leapt into motion so fast that Tink nearly toppled from his back. Nia ran beside the braying donkey and steadied Oskar, who moaned as he jiggled along.

The way was difficult. The forest north of Peet's tree house rose and fell in steepening hills. Now and then they had to skirt around treacherous gullies, dried riverbeds tangled with fallen trees.

From the top of a long slope, Janner saw the Fangs were no more than an arrow shot away, and two more of their horned hounds sprinted toward the Igibys. Tink loosed another arrow and missed. As he hurried to draw another arrow from the quiver, Peet swooped down from the trees with his talons bared, killed the hounds, and disappeared into the leaves again.

Janner knew Peet was no match against so many Fangs, but his sudden presence was like a cool wind on a hot day. A Throne Warden of Anniera occupied the space between the Igibys and their enemies.

Peet's appearance had a surprising effect on the Fangs as well. Janner couldn't see much, but he sensed the space between himself and the Fangs increasing. Though they numbered in the hundreds, the Fangs hung back, wary eyes on the branches above.

Suddenly Janner found himself skidding down a steep bank. Podo had led Nugget into a deep gully and was halfway across the depression, amidst old branches, brown leaves, and rotting tree trunks. The trench stretched a long way in both directions, so they had no choice but to cross it.

The donkey stopped dead in its tracks on the rim of the slope. Janner pulled at the reins while Nia pushed from behind, but the animal wouldn't move. Its eyes were fixed on the gully floor, its nostrils expanding and contracting like a beating heart.

If Janner had not been running in fear for his life, he might have remembered what Pembrick's *Creaturepedia* had to say about such gullies in Glipwood Forest; he might have thought to warn his family before they scrambled down into the tree-clogged floor. If Janner hadn't been thinking about the Fangs and trolls snarling through the woods behind him, he would've suggested firmly that the Igiby family find a way *around* the gully, even if it added hours and miles to the journey.

If Peet the Sock Man, so familiar with the dangers of the forest, had been with them and not fending off the Fangs and trolls and horned hounds, he would've most emphatically suggested that the Igiby family *not* descend into the hole.[1]

But they did.

---

1. From Pembrick's *Creaturepedia:* "Avoid the gullies and sinkholes of Glipwood Forest at all costs. It is commonly known that the gargan rockroach sets its trap in such places. But the gargan rockroach lying in wait beneath the leaves and limbs gathered at the bottom of the gully is only one of the dangers to the oblivious gully crawler. The sweet scent emanated by the female gargan rockroach sends some animals into a temperbolic trance and draws them irresistibly to the waiting rockroach. It is not uncommon to find gathered in the gully any number of deadly creatures trapped and awaiting the gargan rockroach's return from deeper in the earth where it tends its young."

7

Monsters in the Hollow

Nugget stood at the bottom of the gully with one great paw atop an old rotten tree trunk, Leeli and Tink on his back. Nia slid down to join them while Podo and Janner, halfway up the slope, tugged at the donkey's reins. Janner scrambled to the rear of the donkey and pushed with all his might, but it did no good. The fear-struck beast brayed and whipped its head in defiance. It had no intention of going any farther.

"Come on, you stubborn old clomp chomper!" Podo yelled.

"We need you to come just a little farther," Leeli's voice called sweetly from across the gully. "That's it. Come on!"

The donkey's ears moved forward at Leeli's voice, and its braying ceased. It took one halting step forward. Podo arched an eyebrow at Leeli, who smiled in return. Janner risked another look behind him as he slid down the gully slope.

Peet the Sock Man had dropped from the trees and stood before the line of wary Fangs with his arms folded across his chest, his back straight, his chin thrust out, and his eyes closed. He reminded Janner of Mayor Blaggus when he conducted the Glipwood Township Orchestra.

Then a troll emerged from the Fang front lines. It was the first clear look Janner had at one of the creatures, and he understood why Nia and Podo looked so worried when Oskar mentioned them. The troll's legs were short and stout, but the creature still stood twice as tall as a man. Its torso and arms bulged with muscle and veins; a tiny head with a sprout of gray hair peeked out from between its shoulders. The troll's eyes were hidden in the shadow of its bony forehead—a forehead matched by a bony jaw that looked strong enough to batter down a castle gate.

The beast gripped an iron-studded club in a fist the size of a wheelbarrow. It held the club above its head for a moment, then growled at Peet (in a moanish sort of way) and slammed it down. The ground vibrated, and pebbles shook loose from the bank where Janner stood. The donkey lost any courage Leeli had awakened and backed away.

"Grandpa!" Janner cried. "We have to leave it!"

They scrambled out of the gully, lowered Oskar from the donkey's back, and draped his arms over their shoulders.

The troll slammed its club into the ground again.

Peet still hadn't moved. He stood petulant and motionless, buying the Igibys precious time just as he had on their escape to Anklejelly Manor. When Janner and Podo reached the bottom of the gully where the others waited, Janner took one last look up at the terrified donkey. He felt sorry for it and wondered if the Fangs would put it to work or if they would eat it.

Then he saw, dangling from the donkey's saddle, Peet's satchel.

Janner ducked out from under Oskar's arm and skittered back up the slope. The trolls and Fangs had inched closer to where Peet now skipped in circles and whistled to himself. The man was as brave as he was crazy, and the Fangs didn't know what to make of it. Janner tried to untie the straps that bound Peet's satchel to the donkey, but they wouldn't loosen, so he tore it open to grab what he could. He dug through a bundle of journals tied together with twine, a hammer, one old boot, a live mouse, and a leather flask—the water from the First Well.

Janner gasped. He tucked the flask into the side pocket of his pants and leapt back into the gully.

But something was wrong.

Nugget should have crawled up the other side by now, but he stood motionless in the bottom of the gully. Leeli pleaded with her dog to awaken from his trance. Tink had dismounted and stood in front of Nugget with his hands on the sides of the big dog's face, calling his name.

Nugget responded with a lazy whine.

Then Tink screamed and struggled with something at his feet. Janner scrambled over fallen limbs to his brother before anyone else had time to react. When he saw the source of Tink's distress, Janner screamed too.

From a space between two dead limbs on the gully floor—which Janner now realized wasn't a floor at all—a milky-eyed head emerged. Its nose was moist and wide, its snout long like a horse's but stouter, and two yellowed fangs jutted down from a mouth full of crooked, sharp teeth: a toothy cow, trapped below them in a gargan rockroach den. What they thought was the gully floor was more like a giant brushpile hollowed out from below.

Within the cow's mouth was Tink's left foot, a foot that would've been removed from his body and well on its way to the beast's digestive system had the cow not been sluggish in the fog of the rockroach's gassy trap. The toothy cow's eyes oozed a yellow fluid and rolled around in a drowsy fashion as it worked Tink's ankle deeper into its maw.

Janner pulled at Tink's leg, but the cow's smaller teeth were angled inward.[1] If the cow had been fully awake, Janner was sure Tink would be yet another member of his family with only one working foot.

Podo appeared with his sword drawn and whacked at the monster, but the cow's head was only partially visible through the opening in the branches, and he couldn't do enough damage to release Tink's foot from it's mouth.

The commotion jarred Nugget out of his trance. The great dog barked and tensed his body, taking in the situation as if he had just woken from a dream. When Nugget saw the cow, he pounced at the opening in the floor, which nearly sent Leeli flying from his back. When he landed, the patchwork of branches where they stood shifted and revealed more of the toothy cow's head.

The brothers and their grandfather looked at one another long enough to share the realization that they were about to fall—and then they did.

Nugget crashed to the ground. Leeli landed in the soft fur of her dog's flank, and Janner, Tink, and Podo followed, head over heels, slamming into the leafy floor of the gargan rockroach's den.

Janner was disoriented but realized that in the fall, Tink's foot had slipped loose from the cow's jaws. Then he saw the fear on Podo's face. The old pirate looked past Janner at something that froze him like a statue.

The den was crawling with monsters.

---

1. To prevent prey from escaping. It is but one of the many deadly features of the Skreean toothy cow. See illustration, *On the Edge of the Dark Sea of Darkness*, 288.

8

A Thorn of Contempt

There were four toothy cows; a hissing, flapping family of cave blats; a horned hound, wounded so that it stood on only three of its legs; and a diggle staggering about, flashing its quills. Piles of animal bones littered the floor, and the skulls of all manner of forest creatures gazed at the Igibys.

"Don't move a muscle, lads," Podo whispered. The toothy cow that had been sucking Tink's foot leaned against the side of the enclosure, breathing heavily, a sick rattle in its throat. The animals were sluggish, but Janner could see that beneath the daze brought on by the rockroach's gas, the beasts were fierce and hungry.

"Wake up, Nugget!" Leeli took his paw in her hands and shook it. "Nugget, please!"

Nugget lay where he had fallen, a heap of black fur. The dog panted, his eyes glazed, like he was lazing by the fire on the verge of happy sleep. The rockroach's poison was stronger here. Leeli scooted to Nugget's head, heedless of the beasts so near, and called his name again.

Tink sat on the ground and gagged at the cow slobber on his foot. His shoe and the bottom of his pant leg were wet, dripping, and smelly enough that an eager band of flies already buzzed about.

Nia called through the hole above them. "Boys! Leeli! Are you all right?"

"Aye, lass, they're fine!" Podo said, not taking his eyes off the congregation of animals. He lowered his voice. "Boys, draw your swords, and do it slowly."

Janner rose with care, tugging Tink up by the strap of his pack.

"Ewww," Tink moaned at the *splootch* that sounded when he put his weight on the wet foot.

Is he really more worried about his wet foot than the situation we're in? Janner thought with a flash of anger.

When Janner drew his sword, Tink overcame his disgust and drew his own. The two boys stood side by side, just behind Podo. The horned hound shook its head, and its eyes regained some energy. It seemed to be willing itself to attack, to come awake long enough to wreak some violence before the rockroach ended its life. The toothy cows mooed and shook their mighty flanks to wake from their stupor.

The horned hound growled. Its lips curled back in a snarl, and a tendril of drool dangled from one of its longer teeth. It took a wobbly step forward and happened to put its leg in the path of the drunken quill diggle. The diggle hissed and arched its back. Three quills the length of a forearm sprang from the diggle's back and lodged in the horned hound's neck.[1]

The hound pounced on the quill diggle. The cave blats squealed and hopped about, the cows mooed, and finally, Nugget came back to himself. He yawned and scratched behind his ear with one of his giant rear legs.

"Nugget, wake up!" Leeli cried, and wake up he did—but only enough to stand, yawn, and stretch. The cows and the cave blats circled one another. They crashed into the walls and loosed a shower of leaves and twigs.

"We can't climb out without leavin' Nugget here to die," Podo said. "He'd never be able to climb through the hole we made in the ceiling. See that?" Podo pointed his sword at a patch of light on the far side of the gully, beyond the animals. "Where the floor slopes up? When I tell ye to, head that way and hack a hole in the ceiling big enough for Nugget to follow!"

Janner spotted a speckle of sunlight breaking through the branched roof. The animals blocked the way. Before Janner could wonder about Podo's plan, his grandfather cried out and leapt into the fray, sword whirling.

"Now!" Podo screamed.

The old pirate swung his sword, pushing the cows, the hound, the diggles, and the blats aside. The animals turned on Podo as one, jaws clacking and eyes oozing.

"Tink," Janner screamed, "get Leeli onto Nugget, *now!*"

"What?"

"Now!"

Tink winced but obeyed and flung his sister atop Nugget. Janner tugged the dog forward, into the chaos where Podo fought the beasts.

"Tink, don't just stand there!" Janner shouted. "You heard what Grandpa said! Cut a hole in the ceiling! If you're a king, then *act* like one!"

---

1. Quill diggle quills have little poison. Their main function is that of defense, though diggles have been known to attack in groups in order to fell larger animals. The quill diggle has, of course, very sharp teeth.

Quill Diggle

The Skreean quill diggle is only dangerous if it bites or flings its quills. It is ordinarily shy of humans but has been known to be lured close enough for petting. Its needlelike quills and squishy face make petting most unpleasant, however.

From Pembrick's *Creaturepedia*

Tink froze. He looked at Janner as if he had just been slapped, then sprinted through the fray as fast as only Tink could sprint. He crawled up the far slope of the gully and hacked at the branches of the ceiling.

Tink's hesitation didn't last long—half a heartbeat—but in that tiny space of time, a multitude of bitter thoughts roared inside of Janner, all of them aimed at his brother like arrows. *Behold,* he thought again, this time without a trace of humor, *the High King of Anniera.*

Just as Janner hurried Nugget and Leeli past Podo and the toothy cows, light poured in through the hole in the ceiling. Tink had made it through. He sheathed his sword and tore the branches away.

Janner scrambled to the dog's rear and pushed, trying not to think about the sound of Podo's struggle just behind him. Leeli leaned forward and closed her eyes as Nugget burst through the hole and bounded up the far side of the gully.

Janner clapped Tink on the back. "Go!" Tink climbed through the hole. *No hesitation this time,* Janner thought. He turned and shouted, "Grandpa, come on! We're out!"

It was at this moment that Peet the Sock Man leapt from the rim of the gully at top speed, his arms spread wide like wings. Janner watched his uncle with awe.

His socks had long since fallen away in shreds, cut to pieces by the talons at the ends of his reddish forearms. Peet's white hair trailed behind him; one of his eyebrows lay flat and low, the other arched like a curl of smoke; and in Peet's eyes blazed a single purpose: *Protect. Protect. Protect.*

What struck Janner most about his uncle in this moment was not the graceful leap through the air or the deadly, mysterious talons, but that amidst all the danger and panic, Artham P. Wingfeather's gaze was fixed on *him* with what Janner knew to be a fierce affection.

There in the gully of the gargan rockroach, with toothy cows below and Fangs of Dang approaching, Janner felt safe.

But only for a moment.

Podo screamed. As Peet alighted on the tangle of branches at the edge of the hole, Janner spun around, expecting to see that the toothy cows had bested Podo after all. But the cows were gone.

Or, they were mostly gone.

The upper half of a toothy cow disappeared into the mouth of—*what?* Janner saw his unshakable grandfather shaking, retreating on trembling legs toward the opening where Janner stood.

From the darkness at the rear of the den, the gargan rockroach emerged.

9

The Gargan Rockroach

Long, spindly legs reached out of a hole in the rear of the den and waved around like a cluster of shiny black broomsticks. They were attached to what looked like a cross between a cricket, a beetle, and a slug.

The rockroach's back was rounded and hard but plated so it could wriggle and bend, and its sheen gave it the appearance of being moist or sweaty. Beneath the dome of its armored shell was a face with four beady eyes—two large ones above two smaller ones, all attached to the head by stems. The rockroach's mouth looked just like a human mouth puckered up to kiss, except for the spidery mandibles that surrounded the lips and wriggled, clacking together like the sound of marbles spilled on a wooden floor.

Janner gasped as its mouth stretched open and gobbled up a full-grown toothy cow. The cow mooed helplessly as it was worked deeper and deeper into the rockroach's maw by the hundreds of little black mandibles. Janner couldn't bear to watch. He turned away as the cow's head disappeared and the moo was cut short.

The horned hound hopped on its three good legs toward Janner, not to attack him but to escape the giant insect. The gargan rockroach gathered itself and heaved its bulk the rest of the way out of the hole, revealing itself to be as long and thick as a house. With its spindly legs, it snatched up the horned hound and swallowed it with a great, hissing slurp.

Peet the Sock Man sprang through the hole in the ceiling and landed in a feline crouch. The rockroach turned its four black eyes on Peet and wiggled toward him. Podo roared and raised his sword. Peet rolled away from the rockroach's grasping broom-handle legs just as Podo brought his sword down on one of them with all his might. The sword clanged and bounced off the leg, but the rockroach was startled and backed away just long enough for Podo to leap past it, toward Janner.

Peet crouched in the far corner of the den among a pile of animal bones. He lifted a bone the size of a club and whacked at something in the pile. The quill diggle and the family of cave blats wobbled out, clearly in a panic but slowed by the rockroach's poisonous vapor. The rockroach tossed the quill diggle into its mushy black pucker.

Thinking the rockroach was going after the cave blats next, Peet broke away from the corner. But the rockroach ignored the blats, leapt forward, and barred Peet's way with its front legs.

"Lad, we've got to get out of here!" Podo cried, dragging Janner by his shirt collar. Janner saw his uncle in the shadow of the gargan rockroach, ankle deep in bones, and imagined poor Peet's bones lying on the floor among them.

"No!" Janner cried, wrenching himself from his grandfather's grip. He had seen how useless Podo's sword was against the rockroach's armor, but maybe if he could get close enough to stab the creature near its head, he could find a weak spot.

Janner forced himself forward on trembling legs until he stood a few feet from the rockroach. It braced its many legs against the wall on either side of the Sock Man, enclosing him in a sort of cage. The creature's insect face was expressionless, but it seemed to enjoy toying with its prey. The puckered mouth opened and closed as the mandibles that surrounded it clacked only inches from Peet's face.

Janner moved as close to the rockroach's head as he dared and drew his sword. Behind the stems that held the creature's bulbous eyes, he saw a hole large enough to stab, a break in the armor where he could bury the blade into soft skin. He closed his mind to the smacking sounds, the squeals of the cave blats, and Podo's frantic cries behind him, and thought only of driving his sword into the gargan rockroach's neck so that his uncle might survive.

Janner struck. The blade slipped down, past the leg joints, behind the eye-stems, and into the dark hollow where Janner hoped soft flesh lay unprotected—but his sword clanged into something hard as stone.

There was no soft spot. His elbow vibrated and his grip on the sword faltered. One of the rockroach's legs knocked Janner across the den. He landed on his back and felt the wind burst from his lungs. He felt a dull pain in his hip, probably from a rock or bone on the floor of the den.

The rockroach released Peet and with a great clicking skittered toward Janner.

Everything seemed to slow down. Janner saw Peet leap from the corner and run toward him. The gargan rockroach's black eyes flicked sideways at Peet, but it didn't turn from its path. As Peet passed beneath the hole in the ceiling, an enormous hand—a troll's hand—reached down, seized Peet by the hair, and lifted him through the hole, his feet churning, his claws scratching uselessly at the troll's massive fist.

The rockroach hunkered over Janner, widened its awful mandibles, and stretched open its squishy black lips. Janner was surprised he didn't feel more panic. He lay on his back, watching the terrible beast with a sort of fascination and surprise that *this* would be how he died. He also felt a dull irritation at the rock causing such discomfort to his hip.

Then Janner realized with a grim smile that it wasn't a rock at all. It was Peet's flask of water from the First Well.

While the rockroach gloated over him, Janner wondered what would happen if he drank the water, though he had no real physical wounds that needed to be healed. Then he wondered what would happen if the rockroach drank the water, and before he realized what he was doing, Janner removed the flask from his pocket, opened it, and flung it into the rockroach's mouth.

Wisps of steam rose from the droplets that sprayed across the beast's face as the flask spun through the air. Then the flask was gone, buried in the depths of the monster's belly where the toothy cows, a horned hound, and a quill diggle had so recently gone. The beast reeled backward. Its legs and mandibles wheeled at blinding speed, and steam rose from its mouth like smoke from a chimney.

A hand grabbed Janner's shirt and dragged him backward. All at once, Podo's cries broke through and rattled Janner's ears.

"—NEVER SEEN SUCH THWAP-NOGGINED FOOLISHNESS! JANNER WINGFEATHER, MOVE YER FEET!"

Janner snatched up his sword and scrambled through the hole, then up the north slope of the gully with Podo close behind.

Janner and Podo crested the top to find Oskar lying on the ground, unconscious. Nia and Tink stood beside Leeli and Nugget, looking not at Janner but at the opposite side of the gully.

Janner turned and saw, gathered at the edge of the slope, too many Fangs to count. Their swords were drawn, arrows nocked, spears raised. Some watched the Igibys with smug looks, and some eyed the hole in the floor of the gully. Among the Fangs were four trolls, so tall that their heads brushed the leaves and branches of glipwood trees. On one troll's hulking shoulder sat Zouzab Koit and another ridgerunner, both of whom appeared quite pleased with themselves. In another troll's smelly grip, Peet the Sock Man squirmed and squawked and shook his head in panic.

"That's them," said Zouzab.

A Fang at the front of the line nodded.

"One word from me," it shouted, "and the troll will sssqueeze the life from Artham Wingfeather."

10

The Mighty River Blapp

The Fangs and trolls gathered on one side of the gully, the Igibys on the other.

"You know as well as I do that Peet would rather die than let you have these kids," Podo called across the span. The Fangs of Dang parted so that the troll clutching Peet could move forward.

The troll's hands were enormous. The three fingers and one thumb on each hand were the length of one of Janner's arms and twice as thick. With one hand, the troll gripped Peet around the waist, pinning his arms to his sides, and with the other, it covered Peet's head so none of his face was visible. A tuft of Peet's white hair peeked out of the top of the beast's fist. The troll looked like a child holding a doll.

"That may be true," said the Fang, "and if he'd rather die, who am I to ssstand in his way?"

The Fang motioned to the troll, and with a grunt, the troll tightened its grip. Peet stiffened. His legs strained downward and his toes pointed at the forest floor.

"Stop!" cried Leeli.

Her voice was a bright, beautiful sound. She nudged Nugget forward so that he stood with his great paws at the edge of the gully. Her back was straight, and she seemed to Janner more angry than afraid.

"You let him go right now!" So earnest and commanding was her voice that for a moment the trolls and the Fangs appeared to consider her demand.

"Leeli, stay back," Nia said.

"You may be the Song Maiden of Anniera, young one, but you have no power here," said Zouzab. At the ridgerunner's mention of the Shining Isle, a chorus of snarls erupted from the Fangs.

The leader of the Fangs glanced at one of the archers, who nodded. In the silence of the wood Janner heard a faint sound, like trees creaking in the wind—the tightening of bowstrings.

Peet began to struggle, his cries muffled by the troll's hand over his head. The Fang archer eased his scaly head sideways along the sightline of the arrow and squinted one eye shut.

The arrow was trained on Podo.

Janner's mind spun. He knew that at a word from the Fang commander, the archers across the gully could send a hundred arrows flying at them. But if the Fangs wanted them dead, he realized, they'd be dead already. Gnag wanted the Jewels of Anniera, and he wanted them alive, though Janner had no idea why.

"Grandpa, get down," Janner said in as firm a voice as he could muster.

Whether because Podo sensed the same thing as Janner or because he submitted to some new authority in his grandson's voice, he dropped to the ground behind Janner. A chorus of angry hisses slithered across the distance between the Fangs and the Igibys, and Janner saw there had been more than one arrow aimed at his grandfather.

"Mama, get behind me," he said.

"Don't be silly," Nia whispered. "It's too dangerous."

"I think they're afraid to kill us," Janner whispered. "Gnag wants us alive, but I don't think the same goes for you and Grandpa and Oskar. Please, just get behind me."

Nia shot a fiery look at the Fangs across the way and ducked behind Janner. Tink sidled backward and hid behind Nia.

"No, Tink!" Janner said through gritted teeth. "Stay up front. They don't want to shoot us, just the grownups."

Tink let out a nervous laugh and hopped up again. "I knew that. I did."

Janner nearly snorted with laughter in spite of the danger, but then he remembered the way Tink had hesitated in the rockroach den, and his laughter fizzled away.

Nugget and the Igiby children stood like a rampart in front of the three adults.

The Fang commander watched them with interest for a moment, then burst into laughter. The other Fangs joined in, and even the trolls boomed what must have been chuckles of their own. Janner's cheeks burned with humiliation.

"Where do you think you'll go, fools?" the Fang asked. When he spoke, the laughter died away. "Do you think you can ssstand there forever, while your elders cower behind you like kittens?" At this, Podo's chest rumbled. "And what will you do when this silly ssstandoff is over? In a matter of minutes we'll be across this gully and you'll be bound and beaten. Where will you go? To the river? Will you swim across the Mighty Blapp and not be stabbed by the daggerfish or drowned in the rapids?"

Janner's skin crawled with embarrassment. The Fang spoke the truth. For these

few moments, Podo, Nia, and Oskar were safe behind the children, but what would
they do when the Fangs advanced? Janner could hear the faint rumble of the river's
rapids in the distance, but what would they do when they reached it? The Fang was
right. They were caught, and nothing could be done.

"Ah!" the Fang continued. "And what about this skinny fellow? Will you let
Mooph here squeeze him like a fruit? No, I think you're finished, Wingfeathers. Gnag
the Nameless has thingsss for you to do."

"Janner," Tink whispered. "Janner, the rockroach. Look."

From the hole in the floor of the gully, a tendril of steam rose, and in the shadows, a deeper darkness writhed. A tremor shook the ground and sent pebbles and
twigs rattling down into the rockroach den.

*If a little water from the First Well made Nugget as big as a horse, what did a whole
bottle of it do to the rockroach?* Janner wondered.

He looked across the gully at his uncle in the troll's fist. What would Peet do? Peet
was the true Throne Warden of Anniera. Would he suggest that Janner, Tink, and
Leeli give themselves up after all that had been done to keep them alive and safe from
Gnag the Nameless?

Janner didn't think so.

Then he made a choice.

"Back up," Janner whispered. He grabbed Tink's elbow and Nugget's collar and
edged them backward.

"Janner, what are you doin'?" Podo asked. "We're out of options here, lad. Oskar's
at the end of his rope, and the Blapp's the only thing we're running to."

Oskar yawned and sat up. "To the contrary," he said. "I've had quite the refresh-
ing nap. And as I said earlier, I recall…" He adjusted his spectacles and looked north.
"Podo, old boy, have you heard of Miller's Bridge?"

"What are ye talkin' about, Reteep? This is no time for a history lesson!"

"In the words of—"

"In the words of Podo Helmer, we're stuck! Best we turn ourselves in and hope
for a way out when the Maker affords one."

"What's Miller's Bridge?" Tink asked.

A memory surfaced in Janner's mind, the image of a map of Skree from a history
book he had studied only a year ago. Where the Mighty River Blapp poured into the
Dark Sea of Darkness lay Fingap Falls. In parentheses below the words "Fingap Falls"
was written "Miller's Bridge, Second Epoch." Janner blinked, and the picture in his
mind vanished.

"Back up!" he said again. Then he called to the Fang commander, trying to keep his voice level. "We'll be going now. This has been a nice visit. Please give our regards to Gnag the Nameless when you see him."

The Fang commander saw the Igibys moving away and snarled. Janner looked at his uncle in the grip of the troll and was terrified he had just cost Peet the Sock Man his life. The Fang commander stomped away from the gully and gave the troll an order. Janner's breath came in short gasps, and his eyes squeezed shut of their own accord. He couldn't bear to watch the troll kill his uncle.

But he heard no scream, no sounds of struggle. Janner pried open his eyes to see that the troll that had been holding Peet was gone. He had no time to consider this, however, because the Fang commander's voice rang through the forest.

"AFTER THEM!"

"Run!" Janner said, and he spun around and pulled his mother to her feet. Tink and Podo helped Oskar up and draped one of the old man's arms over Nugget's back. The other arm went over Podo's shoulder, and the dog and the pirate ran after Tink with Oskar between them. Janner and Nia took up the rear.

Behind them, the Fangs poured into the gully. Janner heard the wooden ceiling give way beneath their weight, then the screams of the Fangs, the bellows of the trolls, and above it all, a bloodcurdling chatter—the clicking, clacking, insectile racket of the gargan rockroach.

Janner risked a look behind him and beheld a shiny black nightmare bursting above the rim of the gully. The gargan rockroach had tripled in size. The domed back of the giant bug rose like a hard brown bubble, and its churning legs were like many-jointed spears, stabbing and clawing at the Fangs. Just as Janner tore his eyes away from the carnage, a troll wheeled through the air and slammed into a tree as if it were nothing more than a toy.

They ran and ran. No one spoke. No one asked about Miller's Bridge. The only sounds were their heavy breathing, troll screams echoing through the forest, and the steady roar of the Mighty Blapp growing closer with every step they took.

"It won't be long before the Fangs get past that thing," Podo said between breaths.

Janner knew the Fangs would be at their heels before long, but a few minutes was better than nothing, wasn't it? At least they were still free, even if they were running for their lives.

Then he remembered Peet. Maybe in the confusion of the gargan rockroach's attack, Uncle Artham had found a way to escape.

Oskar stumbled, and his arms slipped from Nugget and Podo. "I'm all right, I'm all right," he said, wincing as Podo pulled him back to his feet.

They stopped. Everyone but Leeli was winded and pale from running. Nia walked a little way ahead and looked north, her hands on her hips.

Podo took hold of Janner's shoulder and cleared his throat. "Ye didn't save any of that water from the First Well before you threw it at the rockroach, did ye? Oskar here could use a drop or two."

"No sir," Janner mumbled. He hung his head, half sorry and half angry that he was about to get a lecture for something that had saved their lives. He stared at the ground, painfully aware that the rest of the family was looking at him.

But Podo didn't lecture. He lifted Janner's chin and looked him in the eye. "You did good, lad. Kept your head back there. I'm proud of ye." He patted Janner's back. "It's just like Ships and Sharks, ain't it? Always a way out."

"Not always," said Nia, who stood at the top of a rise not far ahead.

When Janner reached her, he saw that they had come to the end of Glipwood Forest. Below them, writhing through a mass of wet boulders, lay the white, angry waters of the Mighty River Blapp.

11

The End of the Road

So what's this about Miller's Bridge?" Tink asked.

They stood at the crest of a hill and looked down at the impassable mayhem of the Mighty Blapp.

Oskar's side had stopped bleeding, but the old man was near exhaustion. He had been running since that morning, first stealing the Fangs' donkey from the stable behind Ferinia's Flower Shop, then driving the donkey north and into the perils of the forest, only to be forced to run when he finally reached his friends. He dabbed his forehead with a handkerchief and tried to smile. It was a weary, gaunt smile that made Janner fear for his mentor's life even as it made him love the kind old fellow even more.

"It's so old that it might be a legend," Oskar began. His legs buckled and Janner rushed to his side to hold him up. "Oh dear."

"I think I remember seeing it on a map," Janner said. "It's a bridge—at Fingap Falls."

"Fingap Falls!" Podo sputtered. "Blubber and porridge, how could there be a bridge at that awful place? I went there as a boy, and it was all cloud and thunder, a thing to make yer stomach curl up into yer throat. No. Absolutely not. We can't go east."

"Why not?" Nia said. "We can't go west. The forest stretches for miles and miles, and Maker knows how many cows we'll meet, even if the Fangs don't catch us."

"But—but—Fingap Falls is too close to the Dark Sea. Might fall in." Podo crossed his arms over his chest as if that ended the conversation.

"Papa, if there's a bridge, and it's a short walk from here, we might make it across before the Fangs even know it's there. They might even assume we went west. I think we should listen to Oskar and Janner."

"Listen, lass." Podo lowered his eyebrows at her. "There comes a time when you have to choose between death and capture. I'd rather die than let these slithers tie me down, but we've got these youngsters here to think about. You saw the way those Fangs held back when the kids stood in front of us. Those lizards don't want to kill 'em. Or they do, but they're afraid to for fear of Gnag the Nameless. Maybe they stand a better chance of survival if we turn ourselves in. Maybe—maybe Gnag won't turn out to be as bad as all that."

Nia raised an eyebrow.

Podo waved a hand in the air. "Aw, that's not what I mean. I'm just sayin' that if the Fangs don't aim to kill 'em, maybe that's better than bein' hurled over the edge of the falls and into the sea."

Tink nodded. "I think he's right, Mama. I don't want to die." He gulped. "And I *really* don't want to die from falling over the cliffs."

"Thank ye, lad. Glad you have some sense in your head."

Nia was so upset she couldn't speak. Janner hated seeing his mother and grandfather at odds. When Peet was around, the two men argued constantly, but this was different. This was deeper than an argument. This was a decision that meant more than peace between two people—it was the difference between life and death for all of them.

Janner didn't know what to think. If they gave themselves up, at least they were still alive. As long as the Jewels of Anniera remained, the throne of the Shining Isle stood a chance of being restored. But if they died, whatever plans Gnag had for the children would be thwarted, which had to be a good thing.

"We can't just let them take us," Leeli said. "Would King Esben—would Father—have chosen capture over death? He chose death, didn't he? He could have escaped the castle, but he chose to risk his life for, well, whatever it was in the castle that he needed to protect."

"Grandpa, we might make it," Janner said. "Maybe there *is* a bridge."

"But what if there isn't?" Tink asked, shifting the weight of his backpack.

"There's a bridge," Oskar said. "There has to be, old friend. Ships and Sharks, remember?"

"FINE!" Podo roared, then quickly took control of himself. "Fine. Maybe there's a bridge. Oskar, if ye say there's a bridge at Fingap Falls, it's to the falls we go. Move! We've wasted precious time."

Nugget had no problem bounding from boulder to boulder. Tink leapt from rock to rock, trying in vain to keep up with the dog and his sister. The Mighty Blapp rushed with increasing frenzy as it neared the falls. The air was thick with a mist that soaked the Igibys and Oskar, but it smelled clean and sharp.

They picked their way over the rocks as the bank rose, so steep that Janner worried it would be impossible to find a safe way down to the bridge, if it existed. The other side of the Blapp looked no different—wet boulders and shale that sloped up to a tree line. He knew from maps that the river evenly divided Glipwood Forest. Beyond the forest in the north lay the Stony Mountains and then the Ice Prairies. He had always dreamed of seeing more of Aerwiar, but he never imagined it would be on the run from Fangs, trolls, and horned hounds.

"Look!" Leeli cried.

She and Nugget stood a stone's throw ahead of the rest, where the river took a sharp turn to the right and seemed to course straight into a towering cliff and disappear.

"I see it!" Leeli said. "Fingap Falls, and then the sea. It's beautiful!"

At these words, Podo bowed his head and closed his eyes—in prayer or worry, Janner couldn't tell. The old man's mouth drew down at the corners, and his nostrils flared. The youth he had gained from the water from the First Well was gone. Janner now saw a tired old man in wet clothes, gray-white hair dangling from his head in stringy locks. Podo's eyes opened and looked right at him. They stared at each other for a moment, then Podo winked, forced a smile, and pushed on to the next boulder.

Behind them, Janner heard the growl of a troll and the howl of a horned hound.

He pulled his mother to the next boulder and kept hold of her hand as they hurried on. Podo helped Oskar, while Tink kept close to Leeli and Nugget. Janner was glad to see that Tink turned around every few steps to be sure his bow wasn't needed.

Finally, they rounded the bend in the river and beheld, far below, a plume of rainbow-lit mist, the hissing cloud that churned up from Fingap Falls. The river was split by jagged, towering crags into hundreds of roaring courses that tumbled downward in white madness. Far beyond and below the mist lay the wide, silent gray of the Dark Sea of Darkness.

Such a view demanded that the company stop in its tracks. They huddled together, sopping wet and weary. If Janner had been able to read minds, he would've learned that each of them had the same thought: with the Fangs behind and the falls ahead, it seemed certain the river would kill them. It would suck them in and hurl them into the cold black Deep.

Tink stood in front of his grandfather, trying to be heard above the roar of the falls.

"What?" yelled Podo.

"I said, I don't see a bridge!" Tink shouted.

Tink was right. The idea that there had ever been a bridge at Fingap Falls struck Janner as ridiculous now that he could see the place with his own eyes.

"What do we do?" Janner cried.

"We go!" said Leeli. Wind whipped her hair across her face, and she looked at the sea with a familiar look of fierce determination.

Podo's face, however, was ashen. He stood with a steadying hand on Oskar's shoulder, and his eyes shot every which way but toward the sea. The two men were a pitiful sight. Oskar's belly was wrapped in bloody bandages, and the top of his head glistened with moisture. Water and sweat dripped from Podo's eyebrows. Their shoulders sagged, and their mouths hung open. It was unfair that two old men—two *good* men who ought to be sitting by the fire with their feet up and their bellies full—clung to each other on the banks of the Mighty Blapp with death before them and death behind.

"Grandpa," Leeli said. "I can see the sea from here, and it's not dark at all. It's wide and terrible and beautiful. We're supposed to go that way. I don't know why, and I know I should be afraid, but there's something...*right* about it. Something about the size of the ocean, about the way it stretches out forever and flat—it makes me want to sing."

It seemed a silly thing to say, but Leeli's eyes were steady. She angled her chin and pulled her hair from her face so that the wind blew it out behind her. Podo smiled at his granddaughter and nodded. Janner looked beyond the mist but saw only the ocean and felt nothing other than a dizzy shiver in his stomach at how far below the falls it lay.

Nia placed a hand on Nugget's collar, took a deep breath, then led the dog and Leeli down the rocky incline toward the falls.

A great crash split the air.

Just behind Janner, a boulder the size of a horse exploded into flinders of stone. Janner looked up and saw a troll peering over the edge of the bank from among the trees. Then several Fangs appeared, and soon the tree line above the riverbank teemed with them.

Arrows clattered against the rocks around Oskar and Podo. Janner screamed at Tink, and they moved closer to the old men. The arrows stopped for the moment, but Janner saw the Fangs conversing and pointing at Nia. She stood near Leeli, but not so close that a good archer would have much difficulty avoiding the little girl and hitting the mother.

Podo waved and shouted at Nia to stay close to Leeli. The Igibys hurried along a stretch of shale that ran parallel to a foamy pool at the edge of the river. From the corner of Janner's eye he saw the shapes of fish as long as his arm swimming in the shallows.

"Get back from the water!" he cried as they ran. No one heard what he said, but they looked where he pointed and moved as far from the edge as possible.

Janner looked back to see two trolls skidding down the bank, jarred by the larger boulders and grinning so wide that he saw in each of their mouths two squarish front teeth with a generous space between. With much less grace (though that is hard to imagine), the Fangs tumbled down behind the trolls as chaotically as if they had been pushed from above—which was probably what had happened. The trolls found their feet, brushed themselves off, and set after the Igibys at a trot just as the first of the Fangs reached the bottom.

When the trolls passed the shallow pool, schools of daggerfish leapt from the water. Their needle-sharp noses burrowed deep into the trolls' coarse flesh. The trolls wailed and yanked out the fish even as more leapt from the water, and Janner was sick at how close he and his family had been to the same fate.

Everyone hustled nearer to the falls but Tink, who stood staring at the rocks.

"TINK!" Janner yelled.

Tink had one eye squinted shut and his head cocked sideways. He eyed the bank above the falls the same way he studied a tree he was about to draw.

"What are you *doing*?" Janner screamed. He yanked Tink's arm so hard that his brother stumbled and fell.

"Ow!" Tink cried as he leapt back to his feet.

"Tink, they're right behind us!"

"Do you think I don't know that?" Tink said through clenched teeth, charging ahead of his brother.

"Then what were you doing?" Janner snapped.

Tink didn't answer.

The boys skidded to a halt when they reached the others, who had come to the end of the road. They stood at the brink of a cliff. Below was a whirling murk of mist.

To the left sped the river, angry, white, and cold.

To the right, the steep wet slope of shale and boulders rose and disappeared in gray mist.

Behind them, the trolls and Fangs advanced.

"There's no bridge, is there?" asked Janner.

"Not anymore, son," said Nia. "If there ever was a bridge, it's gone."

12

Thunder, Spray, and Stone

So this is the end," Janner said.

Nia smiled and pushed a lock of damp hair from his eyes. "I'm glad we tried."

Janner rested his head on his mother's shoulder, surprised he could find any amount of comfort when their situation was so bleak, all because he was near those he loved and who loved him.

Then he thought of Tink. Janner rounded on him and jabbed a finger in his brother's chest.

"What were you doing back there? All day we've been in danger, but you keep standing around! Is this a game to you?"

"I wasn't standing around! I saw something—"

"Oh, stop it," said Leeli. "Now's not the time." She leaned forward and rested her head between Nugget's ears. The dog whined and wagged its tail. "Why aren't they coming?"

"Because they know we're trapped, lass," said Podo. "Look."

The Fangs gathered at the bottom of the bank and ordered the trolls back. The Fangs seemed worried that the children might somehow get pushed over the falls in the fight if they advanced too quickly, so they proceeded with caution. More Fangs appeared, and they organized themselves into ranks. Meanwhile, the trolls knelt like children at the river's edge and ran their fingers through the speeding water. When daggerfish leapt, the giggling trolls batted them out into the rapids.

"Where do we go now?" Oskar asked.

"Nowhere," said Podo with a deep sigh. "We stand and fight." He drew his sword. "We fight, and we don't give up until the water's lapping at our toes, eh? If something terrible happens and us old codgers don't make it through this, then you kids stay together, hear? Fight with yer teeth if you have to, but *stay together*. I don't know what old Gnag has planned for you, but you just trust the Maker and…and do like your father would have you do. Do like me and yer ma would have you do. Don't just follow your heart. Your heart will betray you."

"Tink, where are you going?" Janner asked. Tink was ten steps or so away, picking a path around a boulder that seemed to hover in the fog. "Tink!" Janner yelled, growing angry again.

"I told you, I thought I saw something," Tink said without looking up. "An outline in the rocks, like someone had started to draw some stairs or a path down from the tree line but never finished. Look!" He kicked at some loose stones.

All Janner could see was more rock.

Tink rolled his eyes and brushed some more of the shale away. "Steps," he said.

The squared hunk of rock was worn smooth from years of erosion, but it was clearly man-made, as wide as a sword length and cut from the bedrock.

"I don't see what you're so happy about. How does a step or two get us past the Fangs?"

Tink pointed below the cliff where the others gathered, and Janner understood. He saw buried beneath the pebbles and slate the faint outline of more steps, cut into the face of the cliff. Even now that he knew they were there, he had to squint and use his imagination to see the stairs, and he wasn't sure anyone but Tink would have spotted them.

Janner laughed and clapped Tink on the back. "Stairs! Tink found stairs!"

The steps probably led to another dead end, but knowing their final stand wouldn't be there on the bank, that it wouldn't happen for a few more minutes, made Janner giddy.

While Podo lowered an eyebrow and Oskar raised both of his, Nia, Leeli, and Nugget sprang to where Janner and Tink stood. Nia saw the steps at once. She gasped, kissed Tink's forehead, and led Nugget down. Janner, after giving Tink a look of apology, followed his brother down. Podo and Oskar went last. In moments they disappeared below the lip of the cliff and into the mist.

The stair was treacherous, no more than a narrow ledge cut into the wall of rock. The wall curved away from the bank and seemed to lead straight into the waterfall, while on the right the ground fell away and vanished into the void below.

Over the noise of the falls, Oskar and Podo could be heard just behind Janner and Tink, huffing and grumbling things like "blasted wet clothes" and "my spectacles are so fogged up I can hardly see a thing" and "speed up, ye old bag, they won't be far behind."

Just in front of Janner, Nugget kept as close to the wall as possible, his tail between his legs. The ledge took them behind a rush of water, a passageway of thunder, spray, and stone. When they emerged, the stair descended more sharply into the mist.

Nugget stopped, and Janner bumped into the dog's rear.

"What is it?" he called to Nia and Leeli as he squeezed past Nugget.

"The steps end here," Tink said, pointing at a fall of white water hissing through a gap as wide as the lane that led from the Igiby cottage. Had it been a stream in the forest, they might've jumped across with little trouble.

Janner crept forward and stuck his hand into the rushing water, and it was jerked downstream as if someone had slapped it. There was no way they could wade or swim across without being swept away.

"What's holdin' us up?" Podo asked from behind Nugget.

Janner turned to answer and saw Fangs descending the steps behind them.

"Grandpa!" he cried.

In one fluid motion, Podo drew his sword, spun around, and put an end to the nearest snake man. It took a few moments for the second Fang in line to understand what had happened, but when it did, it snarled and waved its sword at Podo.

"Hurry!" Podo roared, parrying a blow and kicking the second Fang over the side. Another was close behind.

"Tink, can you make it?" Janner yelled.

"Make what?"

"The jump! It's our only chance. Can you do it?"

"But then what? What about Oskar? What about Grandpa?"

Janner's temper flared again. "I don't know! Even if you're the only one who makes it over, that's better than all of us being caught! Can you do it?"

Without another word, Tink backed up, took a deep breath, and jumped. He landed on the other side of the gap and rolled to a crouch.

"Leeli, can you get Nugget to jump over?" Nia shouted.

"I think so," Leeli said. She leaned over and whispered into Nugget's ear.

"Here, boy!" Tink called. He clapped his hands and whistled.

Janner saw Podo struggling with another Fang, this one wielding a spear. Podo danced back from the point of the spear and bumped into Nugget's rump. Nugget yelped and leapt to the other side of the gap.

"Good boy, Nugget!" cried Nia.

"Mama, you're next," Janner said. "Go!"

Nia grabbed Janner's elbow. "No, son, you should—"

"Go!" Janner screamed, and Nia went. She was thin and strong, but her feet didn't reach the other side. Nia landed with her waist at the edge, her hands flailing to find purchase on the rock. Her legs disappeared into the rush of water and whipped her sideways.

"Mama!" Leeli screamed.

Tink grabbed her hands and pulled with all his might, but he could feel his mother slipping away. Nia didn't scream. She clenched her jaw and set her gaze on her son and daughter, her eyes burning into them so that veins stood out at her temples.

Nugget took a fold of Nia's blouse in his teeth, lifted her from the rapids, and set her down. She rolled onto her back, gasping.

Janner wasn't sure what to do next. He knew he could make the jump, but what of Oskar and Podo? Someone would have to hold off the Fangs to allow the others to escape, and if Nia had barely made the leap, then Oskar was certain to perish.

Janner drew his sword.

He wanted to be strong and brave enough to push past Podo and fend off the Fangs so that his grandfather could escape, but he knew he was no match for the Fangs. Though they had shown themselves poor fighters, they were still venomous and strong. Much had happened in the weeks since the Dragon Day Festival—he had helped Podo defeat Commander Gnorm, and he had grown used to the heft of a sword—but he was still only twelve.

Janner told himself he wasn't being cowardly—he was being realistic. Gnag wanted the Jewels of Anniera, not Podo or Oskar. Wouldn't it be right to escape while he could? Wouldn't Oskar and Podo tell him to do the same?

He looked back through the mist and saw Tink, Nia, and Leeli watching, none of them sure what to do. Podo raged on, cursing the Fangs amidst the clang of swords and the rumble of the Mighty Blapp. Oskar pressed a hand to his wounded side and sank to the ground.

Janner stood between those he loved with his sword drawn, wavering between two terrible choices: flee and hope Podo could hold off the Fangs long enough for him and his siblings to make their way across the falls—if indeed there was a way—or throw himself into a fight he couldn't possibly win.

Then Janner remembered his uncle. He saw in his mind the way Peet the Sock Man had soared through the air into the rockroach gully with that fierce look in his bloodshot eyes.

Protect. Protect. Protect.

Janner was no longer just Janner Igiby of the Glipwood Township. He was Janner Wingfeather, Throne Warden of Anniera, protector of the throne, and protector of those whom he loved. He imagined Peet—Artham Wingfeather—hair jet black, eyes clear, sword arm strong. Artham reminded him that royal blood pumped through his veins, royal not just because of ancestry but because of the love of those who had gone before him and laid down their lives for him.

A battle cry rose up from within him like a fountain. He pulled Oskar to his feet and half-carried him to the water's edge.

On the steps above, another Fang appeared beside the one with the spear and aimed a crossbow at Podo. Just before it fired, Podo seized the end of the spear and slammed one Fang into the other, knocking them both over the edge. The bolt shot away into the mist. Before the old pirate had time to catch his breath, two more Fangs emerged from the fog. Podo groaned.

"Tink! Help Leeli down!" Janner ordered. "Nugget, come here! Here!"

With a whine, Nugget hopped back across the gap.

"Come on, Mister Reteep," Janner said. "I need you to get on Nugget's back."

"Oh my," wheezed Oskar. "I don't think this is a good idea, young Janner. In the words of the poet Shank Po, 'I'd rather not. What else have you got?'"

Janner smiled in spite of himself. "Come on, sir."

He pulled Nugget's head to the ground, and the dog's body followed. Oskar limped over to the giant dog and fell upon it gracelessly. Nugget whimpered and strained to his feet beneath the weight of the big man. Oskar wrapped his arms around Nugget's neck.

Nugget, strong as he was, had never carried anyone as large as Oskar. The dog nosed at the edge and whined at Leeli. She smiled and clapped her hands twice.

The dog crouched, flexed the great muscles of his legs, and sprang. He landed well, but Oskar lost his grip and tumbled off onto the ground.

Janner turned to Podo.

"Lad, ye better go! Old Podo's not got much left in 'im. You've got to get safe away!" Podo thrust the spear at another Fang. "I'm in a good spot. No more than two can attack at a time. Somebody's got to stay here and hold 'em off."

Janner saw the reason in Podo's plan. It made sense.

He stepped past Podo and raised his sword. He wasn't sure how to place his feet or hold his weapon for the coming attack, but he knew that if Artham Wingfeather, Throne Warden of the Shining Isle, could see him now, he would smile.

13

Miller's Bridge

Janner never had a chance to swing his sword.

The two Fangs at the steps retreated into the mist and left Janner and Podo dumbfounded.

"Come on, lad!" The old pirate wasted no time scrambling down the steps. He skidded to a stop at the edge of the rushing water. Without being told, Nugget hopped across again and crouched so Podo could climb on. The giant dog barked and carried him over.

Janner was the last to cross.

They pushed on, still unable to see more than a few yards ahead. The rock ledge widened and allowed them to move at a quicker pace. Then, above the rumble of the falls, came the familiar, chilling sound of the troll growl-moan. Beneath it was a vibrating *thud-thud-thud*, as if the river had a beating heart. Janner realized the troll was running down the steps behind them.

"Hurry!" Janner screamed. He moved to the front of the procession to find Tink taking the first step down another narrow length of stairs.

"I'm hurrying!" snapped Tink. "I just can't see what's ahead!"

Janner barreled down the steps past Tink, hoping they didn't end abruptly as the last ones had, or his momentum would carry him straight over the edge. Immediately the mist lightened. Sunlight broke through in places, and he caught sight of blue sky.

Janner's heart pounded in time with the *thud* of the troll footsteps. "It's clearer down here!" he called over his shoulder. "We might be getting close to the other side!"

The others descended the steps as quickly as they dared. Janner kept an eye on the mist behind them, waiting for the trolls to emerge.

The air changed from a featureless fog into wisps and curls stabbed with sunbeams. The sky was fully visible above, but below lay only mist, so it seemed they were walking on a cloud.

Then with a *whoosh* of wind, the mist spun away for a heart-stopping moment.

The eternal gray of the Dark Sea of Darkness yawned before them. Here the plateau of Skree was twice as high as the cliffs of Glipwood. The tiny whitecapped waves were invisible at this height, and the horizon curved downward to the north and south, which made Janner wonder if the books he had read were right after all in their claims that Aerwiar was as round as the moon.

At last Janner saw the final cusp of Fingap Falls and realized with a snap of despair that they had only begun to cross the giant river. Where the Blapp poured over the edge and into the sea, the river divided into a score of channels, all of them as wide as rivers themselves, spreading out like foamy veins before they careened into the Dark Sea.

But the waters made one last stop on the way down.

A shelf of rock jutted out and caught the falls like an open hand, forming a shallow lake in its palm. At the far edge of the shelf rose stone towers like giant fingers curled upward, and the white waters slipped between them and merged again as they fell. Between each of the towers stretched what looked from this distance to be a paper-thin span of rock.

Miller's Bridge.

Janner could see that it had been built by a far greater civilization than his own. The towers were worn by thousands of years of weather and water, but it was clear they were no natural formations. *Someone built this,* he thought, and he felt very small. And he understood why the bridge was so little known; only those foolish enough to descend the stair into the mist would ever get close enough to see it.

Then, as quickly as the mist had been whooshed away by the gust of wind, Janner's thoughts were scattered by an earsplitting roar behind them.

Podo turned to face the troll.

The creature loomed over them, squatting on a boulder the size of a house. It had come from another direction, Janner realized, probably leaping through the mist from boulder to boulder so that it could cut the family off or at least surprise them. While Podo had been watching the stairs behind, the troll had been approaching from above. After a dumb grin at the Igiby family, the beast gathered itself and leapt from the rock.

"Run!" Podo bellowed.

Heedless of the dizzying height, Janner grabbed Nugget's collar and sprinted down the steps, which angled away from the cliff wall and narrowed.

What had been a ledge was now a bridge held up by stone turrets. The way was still wide enough for two to walk abreast, but the fall on either side made the going precarious. Nugget followed Janner only because of Leeli's constant assurance, and

Janner wondered more than once whether the ancient bridge would support the giant dog's weight. He prayed it would, even as he hoped it collapsed beneath the troll.

The troll landed on the ledge with a crash that sent vibrations through Janner's feet. Just behind him, Nia struggled down the steps as quickly as she could with Oskar limping beside her, an arm around her shoulder. Tink took the rear with Podo and inched down the stairs backward with his bow trained on the troll. Janner reminded himself again that if they survived, he owed Tink an apology and a great deal of praise.

The troll stopped where the ledge became the bridge. The brute cocked its head sideways and scratched at its sprout of hair, then hammered a fist on the bridge. Pebbles shook loose and vanished into the water below, but the bridge held. A second troll joined the first, and they appeared to be conversing, their big, lippy mouths flapping at each other in earnest. Janner wished he could hear what kind of language they spoke, and if he hadn't been running for his life, he would've laughed at the thought.

They reached the first of the towering fingers of the shelf. The top was a flat area no larger than the Igiby garden, big enough for six humans and one giant dog, but not by much. From here Janner could see the whole of Fingap Falls above and behind: the network of waters pouring between the rocks, slamming into carved boulders and scattering again, gushing down through the misty air to the palm of the rock shelf, where the water gathered into what looked like a boiling lake before it slipped between the towers and into the Dark Sea.

The shelf jutted out from the cliff so that when Janner looked down he felt that he was floating. He saw only white water, and below, the gray sea. All the world was water.

Each of them, even Nugget, was out of breath. Their arrival at the first tower seemed something of an accomplishment, and the trolls hadn't yet ventured onto the bridge, so they silently agreed to stop for a moment's rest. Nugget bore Leeli at the center of the huddle. She sat with her back straight, one hand stroking Nugget's neck, the other shading her eyes as she gazed out at the horizon with a calm that mystified Janner. Tink held Nia's hand and rested his head against her arm, looking like the tired little boy he was.

Janner clenched his jaw. He wished he was back in the Igiby cottage, lying in the bunk below Tink, laughing with his brother about some silly thing. Their lives in Glipwood hadn't been ideal, but standing on a rock amidst the clamor of Fingap Falls wasn't ideal either. Even T.H.A.G.S. seemed better than this.

Podo cleared his throat and spat into the Dark Sea. Janner saw that his grandfather trembled, facing the sea with what looked like defiance. Podo's sword was drawn as if the ocean, or something in it, was about to attack.

"Hadn't we better go?" yelled Oskar, leaning wearily against Nugget's flank. "They're coming."

All eyes turned to the ledge far behind them. The two trolls clung to the stone wall so that the long line of Fangs had room to cross the bridge in single file.

With a deep sigh, Podo turned away from the sea and shook his head as if waking from a dream. "Tink, how many arrows do you have left?"

"Twenty, maybe twenty-five."

Podo squinted at the Fangs crossing the span. "Aye. That'll help, for a little while at least. What about you, Janner?"

"Sir?"

"Arrows. Have ye got any?"

"Yes sir. I had thirty-two when we left." Janner loosed the cords that bound his bow to the pack and nocked an arrow.

"Don't waste any time, lads. They've no place to hide, and ye might give us time to get across. When those lizards are close enough to make you nervous, turn an' run like mad. I'd tell ye that it's time to be men," Podo said, "but I can see you already know that."

Janner drew his bow and aimed at the nearest Fang.

Podo and the others moved across the narrow bridge to the next tower. The bridge wasn't long, but with the Dark Sea yawning thousands of feet below them, the going was slow. Nia tugged at Nugget's collar while Podo and Oskar followed, wind whipping their hair and clothes.

The Fangs were halfway across the span to where the boys stood. Tink released his bowstring and sent an arrow whizzing through the air.

14

The Last Tower

The first Fang in the long line jerked and tumbled from the bridge. Janner shot next and watched with disgust as his arrow arced through the air and disappeared into a fall of water. When Tink's second shot felled another Fang, he looked sideways at Janner with a hint of a smile.

Janner took careful aim and missed again. On the third shot he finally hit his target. *Twenty-nine arrows left*, he thought, wondering how many Fangs were strung along the ledge and back up to the riverbank. Hundreds?

Thanks to Tink, the Fangs fell steadily from the stair bridge and the line advanced no farther. The Fangs were agitated, but they had to know that sooner or later the arrows would run out, and they weren't shooting back. The Fangs wanted them alive. As long as the lizards didn't change their minds, the boys were the safest defense against the creatures. Janner glanced back at the rest of the company and saw that they had reached the second tower and were edging onto the next bridge.

Tink's bow twanged, and another Fang tumbled into the roiling water. To his surprise, Janner saw that the front of the line was farther away than it was before.

"It's working!" Tink cried.

The Fang in front waved its sword and shouted at the line, trying, Janner guessed, to get them to move back. Two Fangs tripped in the clumsy retreat and fell screaming into the water.

"Why are they retreating?" Tink asked.

The Fang in charge beckoned to the trolls, but the trolls shook their heads. The Fang pointed at Janner and Tink and brandished its sword at one of the trolls. The troll shook its head again, but with less certainty. Finally the other troll nodded and released its grip on the wall. The other followed suit, and the two beasts stepped to the edge of the long stair bridge that led directly to where Janner and Tink knelt.

Janner gulped. Surely the bridge was too old, too fragile to support the weight of the giant creatures.

But the ancients knew what they were doing when they constructed Miller's

Bridge. The two trolls inched their way to the center. Janner prayed the bridge would collapse, but it didn't. When they saw the bridge would hold, the trolls grinned stupidly and picked up their pace.

Tink loosed a shot at the first troll, but the arrow glanced off its skin.

"Come on!" Janner said, pulling Tink to his feet. The Igiby boys fled, and the trolls bounded after them. The beasts closed the distance with every stride while the Fangs followed at their heels.

Far ahead, the others neared the bridge that led to the fifth and final tower. *And what then?* Janner wondered. *What happens when there's nowhere left to run?*

Just as the boys reached the bridge to the third tower, the ground shook. The trolls were only a few feet behind, and one of the beasts had pounded its fist on the tower floor.

Tink sped ahead of Janner, arms and legs pumping, but with the awful sound of the trolls' huffing and puffing so close behind, Janner was able to keep up with his brother for the first time in his life. Podo stood at the edge of the farthest tower and frantically waved the boys on. Janner saw fear on his grandfather's face. Podo drew his sword and sprinted toward them with a scream stretched across his leathery face.

The distance whizzed by in a blur of slick stone, white water, and slate sea. Janner could feel the *thud-thud-thud* of the trolls' footsteps just behind him. He felt a distant sense of relief at the sight of Nia and Oskar picking their way up the slope of the north riverbank. At least *they* had made it. If only there were a way to stop the trolls and Fangs from crossing, they'd be safe—for a while anyway.

Podo stopped in the center of the final bridge as the boys approached him, but he wasn't looking at them. His fiery eyes were trained on the troll at their backs. Podo raised his sword and arched his back, straining every muscle in his barrel chest.

"Tink, duck!" Janner screamed.

In midstep, both Igiby boys hunkered over and sped past their grandfather on opposite sides. Janner felt his right foot slip from the edge of the bridge and saw the dizzying surface of the sea directly below, but his momentum carried him to the tower, where he stumbled and fell. Janner turned in time to see the sword leave Podo's hand and spin through the air toward the oncoming troll.

The sword buried itself in the beast's neck. The troll widened its tiny eyes in surprise and tumbled forward as it clawed at the sword hilt with clumsy hands. Podo danced backward on the bridge to dodge the beast as it collapsed. When it slammed into the bridge, the skill of the ancient builders was put to its final test—and failed.

A mighty shudder sent rocks plummeting to the water below. The dead troll lay motionless, the blade of the sword peeking out from between its shoulders. The other troll, standing just behind its dead companion, howled and beat its chest. In its anger it was unaware of what became immediately clear to Janner, Tink, and Podo: the bridge was about to fall.

A thrill shot through Janner like a bolt of lightning. *We might make it! If the bridge collapses, we just might make it!*

More rocks broke loose from the quaking bridge. The second troll cut its roar short when it realized at last what was happening. Fangs congregated on the tower behind the troll, growling and peeking around it to see what was wrong.

Janner got back to his feet and ran with Podo and Tink across the last tower. On the far side, Nugget carried Leeli down the steps from the tower to the gentle north bank, where Nia and Oskar waited. Leeli dismounted into Nia's embrace.

Janner's heart rose at the sight of his family, then sank when he turned to see that the bridge had not yet fallen. The troll stepped over its dead companion and made its way across the damaged bridge. It roared and flexed its mighty arms.

Please, thought Janner. *Please let it fall.*

With a great *crunch,* the bridge shifted and sank a few hands lower. The Fangs that congregated on the tower grew agitated as more stones tumbled away.

Podo shook his fist at the troll. "Come on, ye monster! Take another step!"

The ground trembled again, and the troll's little eyes shifted from the bridge to the sea. But again, the rocks settled.

The troll's fearful look became a wicked grin. The Fangs snarled and clanged their swords. To Janner's horror, the troll leapt the final distance and landed on the tower only a few feet in front of them. It raised itself to its full height and roared so loud that the falls themselves were shamed.

Janner felt a tug at his pack.

"I'll be needing this, laddie," Podo said as he drew Janner's sword. "Though I don't think me sword-throwin' trick will work twice in one day." He looked down at Janner with sad eyes. "Now you be a good man. You lead this family to safety, like I know you can." He kissed Janner on the top of his head. "Never stop fightin' for 'em, hear?"

The troll took another step forward. With a heavy sigh, Podo raised his sword and strode to meet it.

Tears filled Janner's eyes, and he thought about protesting, joining Podo in his final stand—but he had no sword. Podo had taken it. He thought about using his bow but knew it would do no damage. All he could do was obey his grandfather's final command: *"You lead this family to safety."* Podo would only last moments against the troll, but it was all he could give.

Janner blinked away his tears and turned. He had to honor his grandfather's sacrifice by getting his family away and keeping them free from harm for as long as he could.

Leeli screamed. Her shrill voice cut through the air like a thousand silver arrows. Janner just had time to leap out of the way as Nugget, no longer carrying Leeli, bounded up the steps.

The giant dog gave a bone-rattling bark when it reached the tower, then sprang through the air, past a bewildered Podo, and slammed into the troll like a boulder into a barn door.

The troll staggered back, trying in vain to shield itself from Nugget's teeth, which snapped and bit and tore at the troll's arms and neck and face. The troll lost its balance and teetered, slow and heavy like a felled tree.

It crashed into the bridge with such force that the towers on either side trembled, and Janner saw one of the Fangs lose its footing and fall. The bridge that had stood for a thousand years crumbled into a thousand pieces.

Nugget sprang off the troll as it fell and landed with his upper half on the opposite tower where the Fangs gathered. His back legs scrabbled at the side of the rock but found no purchase, while above him the Fangs battered his face and front paws with their swords and spears. Nugget bit and barked and growled. Fang after Fang screamed and fell from the wall as the dog struggled, but more Fangs appeared, with more weapons and more determination to push the dog from the tower.

Janner felt a sob rise from his gut and tear from his lips, and then came the sound of Leeli somewhere behind him, screaming Nugget's name. She had crawled up the steps to the tower with a look of pale shock on her face.

Nugget twisted a Fang's leg in his mouth and pulled the creature from the wall. Wounds covered his face and forelegs. He turned his great, shaggy, bleeding head and looked at Leeli. She crawled past Janner, sobbing, reaching for her dearest friend across the empty space where the bridge had been.

Nugget barked one last time, a big, gentle sound that echoed off the stone and water of Fingap Falls. Janner saw a change in Nugget's face at the last jab from a Fang spear, a tired but contented look that made him believe the brave dog would fall to the sea happy, knowing he had saved Leeli from harm one last time.

And then Nugget was gone.

15

A Song for Nugget the Brave

Janner didn't watch him fall. His eyes closed so that the wet stone beneath his hands, the cold wind, the howls of triumph from the Fangs, his little sister's wailing were all he knew.

Podo lifted Leeli over his shoulder and carried his granddaughter away, dragging Janner by the shirt collar as he went. Janner's eyes opened, his vision blurred with tears. He ran down the steps behind Podo, noting with detachment the looks of confusion and surprise on Nia's, Tink's, and Oskar's faces.

They climbed the bank slowly, dragging heavy hearts. No one uttered a word, no one looked back to see if the Fangs had found a way to cross the gap.

After a long, winding climb over gravel and boulder, the Igibys, Podo, and Oskar reached level ground. Soft green grass stretched before them for a short distance before the trees of the forest gathered into a green wall. They stood in a clearing roughly the size of the Glipwood Township, an oasis of open space surrounded by glipwood trees.

The area was littered with large stones, but they weren't the rounded boulders of the falls. They were squared, stacked in places, and overgrown with weeds. Beneath the grass, the trail they followed up from the river became a cobbled roadway, the stones the ruins of a cluster of buildings.

Leeli fell to the grass and wept.

"I'm afraid to say it," Podo said hoarsely, "but we might be safe. Look."

Janner and Tink stood beside Podo and looked down. From their vantage point they saw all of Fingap Falls arrayed before them. To the right flowed the white water of the Mighty Blapp, snaking into the mist of the upper falls. Below it jutted the shelf that caught the waters in its giant palm. The bridges spanning the five towers looked as thin as ribbons. At the fourth, of course, there was no longer a bridge, and the surface of the tower was clogged with the tiny movements of Fangs in retreat.

Janner could hardly believe he had just crossed such a precarious distance; in fact, he could hardly believe such a place existed at all.

He turned to see Oskar and Nia lift Leeli and walk her to a stone bench. Nia held Leeli's head to her chest and rocked to and fro while Oskar patted her back. Leeli cried.

Janner remembered the day at the cottage when she thought the Fangs had killed Nugget. She had cried little and soon grown silent. That had been far more worrisome to him than the way Leeli now wept. She seemed older, no longer shocked that such a thing could happen in the world but heartbroken because it had. Her tears struck Janner as the right kind of tears.

Tink sat on the ground with his back to the stone bench and absentmindedly pulled weeds from the cracks between cobbles. Podo knelt in front of Leeli on his good knee.

"Leeli," he said gently.

Hair stuck to her wet face. Her cheeks were splotchy red, and her chin quivered. She reached for her grandfather and hugged his neck, crying harder than before. Podo lifted her and carried her some distance away, whispering and patting her back with his big, callused hands.

Janner plopped to the ground beside Tink, and the weariness of the day fell on him like a blanket. He leaned his head back on the stone and looked at the sky. White clouds slid across the deep blue dome, peaceful as a sigh. His eyes drooped shut, and wind tickled his face and the hairs on his forearms. The rockroach den, then the trolls, Peet's capture, the foggy despair of the flat beside the river, the dizzy sight of the Dark Sea, the troll breathing at Janner's back—and Nugget.

He opened his eyes and looked at the sky again. Where was Peet now? Janner was afraid for him but felt sure Peet was still alive. He had survived terrible things for years, and something about the way Zouzab watched him from the troll's shoulder made Janner believe Gnag wanted the Sock Man alive for some reason.

For a long time they sat among the ruins. Podo and Leeli finally came back to where the others rested, and though her face still bore the weight of her sorrow, Janner could see that his sister was *present*. Her eyes didn't stare into nothing. They saw the situation, grieved for it, and faced it.

As Janner drifted to sleep, he was aware of Nugget's absence; no giggles from Leeli; no big, whiny yawns; no sense of safety knowing that, whatever lay in wait for them in the shadows, at least this huge, happy monster was on their side.

Janner woke with a start. Dusk approached, and the clearing lay in cool shadow. Leeli slept on Nia's lap. Oskar lay on his back, hissing with pain while Podo worked to remove the old fellow's bandages. Tink assisted Podo with a sick look on his face. Janner wondered for a moment where Nugget and Peet were, until he remembered with a shiver that the day hadn't been some awful dream.

"Hold on now," Podo said. "I'm almost finished. Tink, hand me the knife, eh?"

Tink passed a small knife to his grandfather, who used it to cut away the clotted bandage.

"There," Podo said, eying Oskar's wound. "It's not as bad as I thought. Hardly a scratch, ye big baby! We'll get you wrapped up again, and in a few days I wager you'll be good as before."

"Which wasn't all that good, if you remember," said Oskar. "In the words of Izikk the Slapped, 'I'm round as the moon and just as big—ouch! That hurt!'" Oskar laughed and turned his tired eyes on Janner. "Miller's Bridge, my boy! Can you believe it? A legend proved true. A lot of that going on these days, it seems. Lost jewels, heroic deeds. I tell you, seeing the way you Igibys—Wingfeathers, rather—manage to survive makes me dare to believe the old stories are true after all. All those epics about mighty victories and brave kings. If I live long enough to sit at a desk again with a quill and parchment, I'll tell about this day. I'll put it down so that a thousand years hence some lad will read of the day Janner Wingfeather charged the Fangs of Dang beside his stout grandfather or how young King Kalmar's skill with the bow drove an army of Fangs to retreat."

Janner and Tink blushed.

"Don't forget Nugget," said Leeli. She was awake now, leaning against Nia.

"Of course, my dear," said Oskar. "I'll write of brave Nugget, whose bark shook the trees, Nugget, whose love for Leeli Wingfeather sent him flying to meet a troll twice his size, whose might shattered Miller's Bridge and saved the Wingfeathers from a Fang horde."

Janner braced himself for more of Leeli's tears, but she didn't cry. She worked her way to her feet and rummaged around in her pack for her ancient whistleharp. "Mama, will you get my crutch? I want to see the ocean."

Leeli limped to the precipice above the bank and sat. She took a deep breath and looked out over the Dark Sea of Darkness with a smile. The sky in the east blushed at the coming darkness. Leeli brought the whistleharp to her lips and played.

Janner and Tink joined her and stared out at the sea, her song conjuring images of Anniera, feelings of home, of fire in the hearth. Then the song changed. It took on a sad tone, the notes bending upward like the croon of a lonely bird, and Janner knew Leeli was playing for Nugget. She poured her heart into the song and filled it with everything she felt.

Suddenly, like a dream hovering at the front of his mind, Janner could *see* Nugget. The image swirled like a reflection in a pot of stirred water, gathering itself into clear, moving pictures of little Nugget running through the pasture, fetching a ball, wagging his tail as Leeli stooped to hand him a hogpig bone. The images hovered like smoke from a pipe, scene after beautiful scene of Nugget in all the stages of his life.

Janner shook his head and looked at his brother. Tink saw it too. He smiled with wonder, staring at the empty air before him, waving his hand before his eyes to see if the picture would scatter.

Janner closed his eyes and still saw the images sifting in the blackness, in and out of focus, but always there, changing with the melody Leeli played. Janner opened his eyes again and focused on the falls beyond the image. He could see through it if he wanted, but as soon as he paid attention to the song again, the image thickened.

Then something changed.

16

The Jewels and the Dragons

A deep sound shook the air, a sound Janner had heard before but couldn't place. He looked left and right, expecting something to emerge from the trees, wondering for a moment whether he was hearing things that weren't really there. But it wasn't his imagination.

Oskar sat up and said, "Ah!" Nia smiled, hurried to the cliff, and looked down at the ocean. Podo, however, groaned and shook his head, then crossed to the far side of the clearing and into the forest. Janner had no time to wonder at this because by then he'd seen them.

The sea dragons.

Far below, the dragons danced on the surface of the ocean, tiny, glimmering worms on a gray floor. Their voices rang through the air, across the great distance and over the roar of Fingap Falls. The dragon song mingled with Leeli's, and the music pulsed with joy and then sadness.

Janner blinked with wonder when he focused again on the images swirling before him. He no longer saw Nugget but a spray of giant waves, then something red and gold—the dragons. He had only ever seen the creatures from the heights of the cliff, but now he could see them as if he floated just above the surface of the sea, a stone's throw away.

They were as beautiful as they were fearsome. Their bodies shimmered with metallic scales that swirled with color. The dragon closest to him glittered orange and gold, like the strikes of a thousand matchsticks, but its winglike fins cycled between shades of blue. Its head was sleek and graceful, perfect for slicing through the water, and its eyes—big and deep and serene—sent a chill down to Janner's toes, because it was suddenly clear the dragon *knew* it was being watched. The eyes rolled back, and translucent lids slid over them as the dragon opened its mouth and sang. Teeth lined its mouth, but not in the crooked, yellow way of the Fangs or the toothy cows; these were straight and bright and sharp as needles.

Janner pushed his mind through the image and looked again at his brother and sister. Leeli's eyes were closed, and though she smiled, tears wet her cheeks while she played. Wind stirred Tink's hair, and he stared at the empty air before him; his eyes flicked back and forth as if studying a drawing that hung a few feet before his face.

The song changed to a gentle hum, and Janner turned his mind again to the floating image. A dragon rose from the waves bearing something black on its back, nestled between its fins. It was Nugget.

The other dragons wheeled into formation around the one bearing the great dog, their long, graceful necks still arched as they sang. They brought their noses close to Nugget's wet, battered body. Together they lifted the dog into the air so that he appeared to float atop the streams of a fountain, and then they bore him below the surface.

To Yurgen's crypt where heroes lie, said a voice in Janner's mind. It whispered and screamed and sang at the same time.

Leeli's song came to an end, and Janner ached for her to keep playing. Whatever power the song had awakened in the three Wingfeather children would leave a terrible emptiness when it was gone.

She must have sensed some new thing approaching, because she paused only for a moment. She played another tune, low and dark, with a melody that gave Janner a feeling of danger. The image thickened again and hovered just over the waves. The dusk had deepened, so the figure that lifted from the water was difficult to see. It was another dragon, but Janner knew it was ancient, even by a dragon's standards. The other dragons had twisted and danced, but this one was still, unbothered by the giant waves lapping at its sides. The others had shimmered, but this one was gray and lightless except for the pale shine of its eyes.

He is near you, young ones.

Janner trembled, but he wasn't afraid; the voice wasn't evil.

"Keep playing," he whispered to Leeli. She looked unsettled but nodded and continued.

Tink's eyes were wide and full of fear, like he was staring at a ghost. Janner was about to ask Tink what he saw that frightened him so, but the voice spoke again.

He is near you. Beware. He destroys what he touches and seeks the young ones to use them for his own ends.

"Who?" Janner whispered, not sure if the dragon could hear him. "Gnag the Nameless? Who?"

We have been watching, waiting for him. He sailed across the sea, and he is near you, child. We can smell him.

Janner's heart pounded. Gnag the Nameless was near? Janner had never thought of Gnag as anything but a scary name, an evil, featureless being. Could it be that Gnag had arms and legs and crossed the Dark Sea like anyone would, on a boat? Janner wasn't sure if the thought made Gnag the Nameless more or less frightening, but he *was* sure that if Gnag was nearby, they had no time to rest, no time to sit on the cliff listening to the dragons. They had to get as far away as possible.

The dragon sank beneath the waves. Leeli's song ended, and she lowered the whistleharp to her lap with a sigh.

Janner rubbed his eyes and shook his head, still not sure whether or not he was dreaming. "What just happened?" he asked.

"I don't know," Tink said, "but they're taking Nugget to a cave."

"How do you know that?" Leeli asked in a quiet voice.

"I'm not sure. They showed me. I saw them carry his body deep into the sea and into a cave, where they laid Nugget on a pile of rocks. The cave was full of bones, and the bones were covered with some kind of markings. Writing, maybe."

"I asked them to take care of Nugget," Leeli said, "with my song. I told them who he was, what he did for us."

"I can't remember what they looked like anymore," Janner said.

Tink stared out at the horizon. "I can still see them. Their fins—did you see the fins? They were huge. Eight sea dragons. Three silver, two reddish gold, an orange, and a blue. Then that last one—the old gray one." He paused. "And I saw other things, Janner. Awful things." He shuddered.

"What? What did you see? Was it Gnag the Nameless?" Janner asked.

"Gnag? No…I don't know." Tink shook his head and closed his eyes.

A short distance away, Nia cried out. "Where's your grandfather? Papa!"

Podo emerged from the trees. The old man was winded, his limp more pronounced than usual as he made his way toward them. His eyes were downcast. "Boys, set up the tent. It'll soon be too dark to see."

"Grandpa, something weird just happened," Janner said. "The dragons—"

"Tent! Now!" Podo snapped.

Janner's cheeks burned. What had he done to deserve that? If Gnag the Nameless was nearby, then it made no sense to pitch a tent. They had to get away or at least hide.

"Grandpa," he said, and Podo fixed him with a blazing eye. Janner resisted the urge to cower and apologize. He had to say *something*. He stood up straight and clenched his fists. "Grandpa, the dragon spoke to me."

Podo's face was hard. "Aye?" he rumbled after a moment. "And what did the dragon *say*, boy?"

"It said that Gnag the Nameless was near. It said he had sailed across the sea and they could smell him. It said, 'Beware.'"

"Gnag the Nameless." Podo snorted. "A sea dragon said Gnag himself was close by. Is that what you're tellin' me?" The old pirate crossed his arms and raised an eyebrow.

Janner pointed at Tink and Leeli. "Ask them! They heard it too! Or—they didn't exactly hear it, but—but they saw things and felt things. Didn't you?"

"Yes sir," Tink said. "I saw them. Up close."

"And I felt them, Grandpa," Leeli said.

Podo and Nia exchanged a glance, and Podo waved a hand in the air. "Well, did the sea dragon also tell ye that his whole race is a bunch of scaly liars? Did he tell ye that they manipulate and confuse for the thrill of it? Sea dragons watch the doings of men with a wicked eye and would just as soon see you run off the cliff as run from Gnag the Nameless."

What? Janner thought about the rush of emotions he always felt on Dragon Day. The sea dragons were frightening, fascinating, even haunting—but not evil. It was Leeli's song that had beckoned them, and *Leeli* certainly wasn't evil. And then there was Nugget's body. The dragons had carried him away with such care—there was nothing evil about that. But how could Janner argue with a pirate? Podo knew more about everything than Janner, especially the sea.

"That's what it said. I just—I just thought you should know," Janner said quietly, unable to meet Podo's eyes. If he had looked up, he would've seen that Podo wasn't able to meet his eyes either.

"Boys, see to setting up the tent like your grandfather told you," Nia said after a moment. "We can talk about the sea dragons in a little while. Gnag the Nameless or not, we all need a meal and a rest. Maker only knows when we'll have another."

"Food?" Tink asked.

Nia nodded. "We'll eat the dried diggle that Artham made us."

"Food," Tink repeated.

17

An Ally in Dugtown

The tent took the boys longer to raise than they would've liked. Janner had a hard time focusing on the task at hand because he kept looking over his shoulder at the dark wall of trees, half-expecting Gnag the Nameless to leap out and gobble them up. The sun was down and stars flickered in the east by the time they finished. The air cooled, and with the constant wind curling up from the cliffs, the family and Oskar gathered in the crowded tent for warmth as much as for companionship.

"Let's see to that meat," Tink said. "I'm so hungry I could eat a boot."

"But first we should have some light," Oskar said.

"Mister Reteep, we can't," Janner said. "Fire draws the critters out of the forest, remember?"

"You're quite right, lad. But that's not true of *all* fire." Reteep removed something from his pouch and asked Janner for a match. Oskar held in his hand a round, greenish candle. "Snotwax, my boy. We can't smell it, but most animals loathe its odor. Look." He pointed at an insect buzzing madly for the opening in the tent flap, then placed the candle on the grass between them and smiled.

Nia removed several strips of dried diggle meat from her pack and passed them around. It wasn't much, but they were all grateful.

"I hope Uncle Artham's all right," Janner said between bites.

"Me too," Nia said. "But I'm sure he's been in worse places than a troll's fist. Now, tell me about what happened with the dragons."

"I'll be outside," Podo grumbled under his breath. "Oskar, you wanna come?"

"Goodness no," Oskar said. "I find the whole business quite fascinating."

Podo grouched his way out of the tent, and Janner told his mother about what he had seen, heard, and felt.

"You saw this too?" Oskar asked Leeli, adjusting his spectacles.

"No sir," Leeli said. "I didn't see much of anything. Lights and fuzzy shapes, really. But I...*felt* something. Like my heart had an invisible arm that reached out and touched something in the dragons." Leeli's cheeks turned red. "I know that doesn't make sense."

"It felt like you were connected somehow? Is that it?"

"Yes—connected. I couldn't hear words, exactly, but I could feel their thoughts, like when you rub your eyes and you see colors and shapes like fireflies. And the shapes told me things. I couldn't quite understand them, but Janner could."

"'To Yurgen's crypt where heroes lie,'" Janner blurted. "I just remembered, the dragons said that before they carried Nugget under. That must be the cave Tink saw. Some sort of dragon burial ground, I guess."

"Astounding," Oskar whispered. "Janner, have you read of Yurgen?"

"No sir. Sounds familiar, though."

"He was king of the dragons, long ago," Oskar said.

Janner closed his eyes and flipped through the pages in his mind. "In the First Epoch. I didn't know his name, but I remember the story. He sank the mountains, digging into the earth to try to find…what was it?"

"The *holoré*," Oskar said.[1]

"That's right—the healing stones. He needed them to save his wounded son, right? But he never found the stones, and he dug so deep that the mountains collapsed—"

"The Sunken Mountains," Tink said. "I never knew that."

"Which is why I always tell you to read more," Janner said.

Tink rolled his eyes.

"I always assumed it was just a legend," Oskar said.

"It's no legend," Podo mumbled from just outside the tent.

They were all silent as the tent flap opened and Podo crawled back inside. He settled in the far corner at the edge of the candlelight.

"I've sailed through the Sunken Mountains, and a sadder place you'll never see. Aye, sea dragons are ancient critters. One look into their eyes and ye feel yourself fallin' back in time. There's more to 'em than pretty songs and long teeth. They *know* things." Podo shivered and closed his eyes. "They *remember* things."

---

1. O holoré lay thee low
   Holoél dark in the Deep
   Down beneath the earth you go
   Go holoré fast to sleep

   Rise again holoré now
   Spring abundant holoél
   Render green the dying bough
   Raise the rock where Yurgen fell
   (See Book One, page 52.)

"If they know so much, what makes you certain it lied about Gnag the Name-less?" Janner asked carefully.

"Because, lad, if Gnag was nearby, we'd all be dead."

The candle flickered. No one moved. Janner's skin crawled with invisible bugs. Finally Oskar cleared his throat. "They remember things, do they? Well, I do too." The old man forced a smile, trying his best to clear the creepy air. "I remember read-ing in an old book that there was once an alliance between the sea dragons and the kings of Anniera." Janner looked to see if Tink was listening, but he was busy search-ing his lap for stray crumbs. "This was two epochs ago," Oskar continued, "so I thought it was just a legend. After tonight? I'm not so sure. Perhaps your mother knows more than I do, children. She was the queen, after all."

Nia shrugged. "Esben mentioned the sea dragons once in a while, but it never seemed of much importance. I heard talk of the old days, when the young dragons were hunted."

Tink looked up from his search for crumbs. "They were hunted?"

"It was a terrible thing, and it was a long time ago," Nia said. "I don't know any-thing about an alliance."

"Ah! But you didn't know anything about Miller's Bridge, either, highness," Oskar said happily. "I'm going to read the old books much more carefully from now on, I'll tell you that. In the words of Bimm Stack, 'I've an idea! Attend closely to me and you might find your shoes.'"

Everyone in the tent, including Podo, looked at Oskar with great confusion, try-ing to sort out what the quote had to do with old books. Oskar took another bite of his dried meat and scratched his belly.

"So what do we do now?" Janner asked his mother.

"Why don't we ask your grandfather." She turned to Podo. "Papa, what do we do?" she asked in her queen voice, the voice she used when she was tired of talk and ready for action. Even ornery old pirates sat up straight when such a voice was directed at them.

"If the Fangs send a message by crow to Torrboro, I reckon we've got a day, maybe two, before they set to patrollin' this side of the river. For now, we ought to bunk down and sleep. Tomorrow we'll head north, though I don't know quite how. Once we get past the Barrier—*if* we get past it—the lands between here and the Ice Prairies are unknown to me. The crazy old Sock Man was the only one of us who knew the way." Podo looked out at the night through the flap of the tent.

"There's an ally in Dugtown," Oskar said.

"What ally?" Podo asked.

"His name is Ronchy McHiggins. He's a fine chap and has been my contact for many years. Runs a tavern called the Roundish Widow that serves the finest sailor's pie I've ever laid mouth on."

"Mmm," Tink said.

"He cooks it with a sprig of honeybud, and the mashes atop it are copiously peppered and garlicked. Seven vegetables are mixed with goat crème and—"

"Can we trust him?" Nia asked.

Oskar cleared his throat and eyed his diggle meat with disdain. "I hope so. He's the one who introduced me to Gammon."

"Who's Gammon?" Janner asked.

"Gammon's the leader of the rebellion in Kimera," Podo said. He seemed more alive now that they had the beginnings of a plan.

"Kimera's in the Ice Prairies," Nia told Tink before he could ask.

"Gammon's the one who helped me smuggle the weapons to Anklejelly Manor," Oskar told Janner. "An imposing fellow, strong and cunning. He'd have to be to survive all these years. I met him in Torrboro not long after the Great War," Oskar continued. "He saw my cart heavy with crates of books and convinced me to help him. I was so surprised to find anyone with the mettle to defy the Fangs, even in secret, that I agreed. I carried weapons Gammon collected from the rubble of Skree. We hid them in crates beneath old books and soon amassed all the weapons you found beneath the manor. Gammon has weapon chambers like that all over the continent, waiting for the day when the Skreeans will use them."

"Well, what's he waiting for?" Tink asked. "If the weapons are in place, then why not fight back now?"

"Because he isn't ready. As I said, he's cunning. His followers trust him explicitly and believe he knows what he's doing. It's a good thing he's on our side," Oskar said, "because with his charisma and strength, he would be a formidable enemy. Each time I met him, I found myself hanging on his every word. A trustworthy fellow, though, I'd bet my books on it."

"And ye think this McHiggins fellow at the tavern can help us?" Podo asked.

"I think so. He's Gammon's main contact in Dugtown. If anyone can find us a guide over the Stony Mountains to the Ice Prairies, Ronchy McHiggins can. His sailor's pie, as I said, is *delicious*."

Podo thought for a moment, then nodded. "Aye. Sounds like our best option. 'Course, there are Stranders to think about."

"Ah. The Stranders," Oskar said.

"What are Stranders?" Janner asked.

Podo and Oskar exchanged a glance.

"Better we worry about the Stranders tomorrow, my boy," said Oskar. "The day's been long enough." He blew out the candle, careful not to let any of the wax spill, and the company slept.

Janner's last thought was a prayer for safety for his uncle.

But Peet was not safe.

18

Old Wounds and New Healing

Peet couldn't move his arms or legs.

The troll tromped southward, dragging Peet with a length of rope like an ox with a plow. Peet, wrapped tight from head to toe in chains, was jarred and battered by every root, stone, and pothole in the road. He drifted in and out of consciousness, and every time he woke, he saw Zouzab and the other ridgerunner perched on the troll's shoulders, watching him with wicked pleasure.

He remembered the gargan rockroach's terrible clacking the day before. Just as Zouzab had ordered the troll to retreat from the gully, Peet caught a glimpse of the Igibys and Oskar fleeing north. Though he had screeched and thrashed, the troll held him fast, so tight that his vision blurred and everything went black. When he awoke it was night, and he was wrapped in chains like a moth in a spider web.

"You'll be glad to know that your precious 'jewels' have escaped once more," Zouzab had said. He sat cross-legged by a fire and shoveled a handful of sugarberries into his mouth, then passed the basket to the other ridgerunner. The red stains around their mouths looked like blood.

Peet had stared at the ridgerunners without speaking, partly because the chain wrapped around his face made it hard to breathe, and partly because he couldn't figure out whom the ridgerunner was talking about. His mind was a muddled mess.

Jewels? I love the jewels, but what—I remember! The children! Who escaped? The children, yes. Good. What were their names again? I can't remember their names. Hungry and thirsty. Arms hurt. I shouldn't have left him. I didn't mean to. I didn't want to, but I left him. Oh, Maker! What have I done?

Peet's mind filled with shadows and feathers and a wail that echoed through dank corridors. He was dimly aware of the ridgerunners watching him from the fire as he thrashed and whimpered in his chains, but they seemed a world away.

What have I done? I abandoned him. No!

A rustle of feathers, deep in his mind, and he knew no more.

Now it was a new day and his mind was clearer. He knew his name, the Wingfeather children's names, and where they were taking him. The road rose and fell over gradual hills and was well worn by Fangs. The light in the east told him he was heading south.

To Fort Lamendron.

He screamed.

The ridgerunners laughed.

As Peet screamed on the road to Lamendron, morning birds chirped in the clearing where the Igibys slept. Cold blue light crept through the slit in the tent door.

Janner stretched, forcing his eyes open and shaking the cobwebs from his mind. To his left, Podo snored so loudly that Janner wondered how it hadn't woken him sooner. Oskar didn't snore, but with every long exhale of breath, his lips made a windy *pfffffhhhhhh*.

Janner propped himself on one elbow and rubbed his eyes. In the faint light he could see Tink asleep with his head on Podo's leg and Leeli curled up beside Nia with her backpack cuddled to her chest the way she used to hold Nugget. Janner crept from the tent.

The clearing was soft with dewy mist. Chunks of rubble rose out of the fog like gravestones, but the effect wasn't unpleasant. He had been awake for many sunrises before, but never so close to the cliffs that he could watch the fiery ball lift itself from the sea. He walked through wet grass and sat with his feet dangling over the cliff.

The Dark Sea of Darkness wasn't dark at all at this hour. Feathery clouds at the edge of the world glowed orange and savage yellow. Birds wheeled in the bright air far below.

Janner thought of his life only weeks ago, in the dregs of summer, when hay needed baling, the hogpig needed feeding, the garden needed weeding, and life was boring. So much had happened to the Janner he used to be. His life had been in danger countless times. More tears had been shed in these last weeks than in his whole life before. Nugget was dead, the Glipwood Township ravaged. Before, he lived under the oppression of the Fangs of Dang, but now he was on the run from them.

Then he thought of his father, Esben, and remembered the picture of him sailing on his twelfth birthday, an image Janner considered the essence of freedom. He thought about the royal blood in his veins and about the long-gone glory of his kingdom.

He had been too busy to think much about the real Anniera. It hovered in the distance of his best dreams but remained a dream only. It was hard to believe it actually existed, that across these very waters a home awaited him. A real island where there had once been real towns, where there stood a real castle—the castle where he was born. Janner ached to see it. He remembered the words of his father's letter: *"This is your land, and nothing can change that."* He imagined lying in the warm wind of a heathery slope, eyes closed so he could feel the heartbeat of his land.

He was only twelve, but he knew enough to realize that the way before him would be hard. *Is it worth it?* he asked himself. Was it worth losing his old life in order to learn the truth of who he was and who he was becoming?

Yes.

Like the pluck of a stringed instrument, the first edge of the sun broke loose and poured light over the world.

The rest of the company was awake, grateful for the promise of a proper breakfast. Podo, who had assured the family that in daylight a small fire would be safe enough, sat on a rock rearranging the bacon that sizzled in the frying pan. With his other hand, Podo absentmindedly scratched at the stub below his knee where the rest of his leg had once been.

Janner knew that at night his grandfather often unbuckled the harness that bound the wooden peg to his leg, but it was rare to see him in broad daylight without it. It was unsettling to see him now, vulnerable and—

"You're starin' like you've never seen me stubby leg before, lad," Podo said, squinting at Janner.

"Sorry," Janner said. "It's just—why won't you tell us how you lost it?"

"Oh, I will, lad. One of these days." Podo took a deep breath. "It's not a fun story for yer Podo to tell, but I'm startin' to think I should dig it up sooner rather than later. There's things you lot should know."

"What things?" Tink asked quietly. Janner thought he saw Podo and Tink exchange an odd look, and the old pirate's eyebrows bunched together like a cloud at the front of his head.

"Can we just eat breakfast?" Leeli asked.

"Aye, lass. That's a fine idea," Podo said, and Tink looked away.

"Oskar, how's your wound?" Nia asked.

Oskar blinked at the mention of his name. His gaze had been firmly placed on the sizzling bacon. "It's fine, dear. Much better after a good night's sleep." He placed the arm of his spectacles in the corner of his mouth. "You know, from the moment I first laid atop old Nugget, I felt something happening. The wound…warmed up somehow, in a quite enjoyable way. This Water from the First Well—you don't suppose it gave Nugget some healing power, do you?"

"I had a dose of the stuff too," Podo said. "Did the wound feel different when you were leanin' on me?"

Oskar thought for a moment. "No, I don't remember that it did."

"But we only gave you a drop, remember?" Tink said. "Uncle Peet gave Nugget too much."

"Hmm." Oskar frowned and tore the bloodied bandage away to reveal a bright red scar on his belly.

"It's gone," Leeli said.

"A final gift from dear Nugget, young princess," Oskar said with wonder, and Leeli beamed.

"So when do we leave?" Tink asked after gulping down two strips of bacon. His lips and cheeks shone with grease. "You said we had a day before the Fangs started patrolling the north bank of the river. Shouldn't we get moving?"

"Aye, lad. We should." Podo winked as he cinched the strap of his peg to his thigh and thumbed the buckle rod into a well-worn hole. "Now you're thinkin' like a king."

Tink gulped and looked away.

Janner decided it was time to apologize. "Tink, I'm, uh, sorry I yelled at you yesterday. You didn't deserve that."

Tink shrugged and poked at the fire with a stick.

"We wouldn't have made it without you, you know. Out of about thirty arrows, I only hit, what, three Fangs? I'm a terrible shot."

"You *are* a terrible shot," Tink said with a smirk.

"I don't know much," Janner said, "but for what it's worth, I think—I think you're going to make a fine king."

Tink's grin vanished. "Thanks. I hope so," he said quietly. He left the fire and started taking down the tent.

Janner looked at the others. He had done his best to apologize and had even gone one step further with a compliment. "What was that all about?" he asked under his breath.

"Just let him be," Nia said. "He'll be fine."

The tent was rolled and tied to Podo's pack, and in minutes the company was ready to go. After all that had happened the day before, Janner felt ready for anything. His pack had lost its stiffness and hung from his shoulders in a way that fit him. He had wielded his sword in battle, and its weight no longer burdened him but gave him courage. He recalled the heft of the bow in his hand, the tension and release when he drew it and loosed the arrows. The calluses on his palms felt good, and he imagined his hands one day being as tough and capable as Podo's.

"Say the word, King Kalmar," Podo said with a slight bow of his head.

Tink looked like a mouse in a trap.

Then he loosed a belch that rivaled one of Podo's, and in a fit of laughter, the company set off into the forest.

19

Ouster Will and the First Books

All day the company traveled through the wood, and except for the persistent worry that around every tree hid a toothy cow or horned hound, the trip was oddly enjoyable.

Janner relaxed for the first time since they had left Peet's castle, as if a cold river inside him was finally in thaw. Still, the words the old gray dragon had spoken haunted him.

"He is near you. Beware."

It occurred to him that the dragon hadn't actually *said* Gnag the Nameless was nearby. But who else could it have meant? Who else would *"seek the young ones to use them for his own ends"*? The dragon probably meant the leader of the Fangs at Miller's Bridge. Or it might have been talking about Zouzab Koit—but why would a little ridgerunner be of any concern to the sea dragons? Podo was probably right—the sea dragon was lying, manipulating Janner for the fun of it. But somehow that didn't seem right either.

With every step they took toward Dugtown and away from the sea, Janner worried about the dragon less and enjoyed the beauty of the forest more. They saw no sign of toothy cows or horned hounds, and only spotted one cave blat when it skittered behind a distant tree. Janner wondered why the animals on the north side of the river were so scarce. He thought about the old days in Skree, before the war, when Podo and Oskar said the dangerous creatures of the forest were kept in check by rangers and the people could travel where they pleased. The forest was a peaceful and lovely place when one wasn't running for one's life, and Janner began to understand anew what had been lost when the Fangs invaded.

"Mister Reteep?" he said. "Is it true that Gnag the Nameless only came to Skree because of us? because he wanted the Jewels of Anniera?"

"Yes and no," Oskar said after a moment. "It's true he sent his armies here because he thought you had come this way, but he would have come anyway, sooner or later. Don't blame yourself for what happened in Skree."

"But why would he have come, if not for us?"

"You remember your history, don't you, son? How many times did a wicked man come to power and suddenly find his kingdom too small? The Praxons did it in the Third Epoch. The Shriveners did it when Tilmus the Bent took the throne, and look what happened to the Furrows of Shreve. There's nothing left but the Woes, a terrible waste where there was once a garden the size of an ocean." Oskar stepped over a fallen branch. "No, when a king forgets who he is, he looks for himself in the rubble of conquered cities. He is haunted by a bottomless pit in his soul, and he will pour the blood of nations into it until the pit swallows the man himself."

Janner shuddered. That deep, hungry darkness scared him because he felt it too, though he found he wasn't afraid of falling into it, not when he thought of his family. It was as if, between himself and that inner darkness, there were many arms reaching out to catch him, arms like the branches of a tree, there to break his fall and give his hands and feet purchase.

"That's why Anniera was strong, lad," Oskar continued. "The Throne Warden protects more than the High King's flesh. He protects his soul by reminding him at every turn what is good and noble and true in the world. The Throne Warden protects not just the king but the kingdom as well. It is his job to remember and to remind. And sometimes, as you have seen, it is his job to sound the horn of battle and swing his blade for those he loves."

"Do you think Uncle Artham is all right?"

Oskar nodded. "Aye. If he's survived this long, it's either because of his wits or because Gnag the Nameless wants him alive, as he does you. Perhaps it's a little of both. No, I'm certain Peet the Sock Man will show himself again someday. He's no ordinary man, you know."

"He's definitely not ordinary," Janner said.

"That's not what I mean," Oskar said. "It was said that Artham P. Wingfeather shone with Eremund's Fire.[1] The wicked fled before him, and for all the years he and your father occupied Castle Rysen, peace and joy ran deep as a river."

---

1. Eremund was a Throne Warden in the year 54 of the Third Epoch. When the High Queen Nayani, his little sister, was kidnapped by Symian pirates, he passed through many trials to bring her home. He sailed past the edges of all maps in pursuit of the pirates and years later returned with the queen at his side. His courage was rare, even among Annierans, and it was said that his eyes were golden and shone in the dark like candles. Several books detailing his exploits are preserved in the Grand Library at the Castle Rysen. See *The Eremiad*, translated by Hureman Perdus, Symar House Publishers, 345.

"I remember my mother saying that all the maidens in the kingdom had their eye on him," Janner said.

"That's what I've read. Did you know they wrote poetry about him?"

"Really?"

"It's true. Let's see,..." Oskar tapped his chin with one finger. They walked in silence for a few moments; then Oskar cleared his throat and began.

> *All children of the Shining Isle, rejoice!*
> *A hero strides the field, the hill, the sand*
> *With raven hair and shining blade in hand.*
> *The wicked quake when lifts the Warden's voice!*
>
> *So fleet his mount and fierce his mighty band!*
> *So fair his word and fine his happy roar*
> *That breezes o'er the Isle from peak to shore!*
> *So tender burns his love for king and land!*

"Who wrote that?" Tink asked.

"I don't know," Oskar said. "I found it in a book of Annieran poems. Very valuable."

"Her name was Alma Rainwater,"[2] Nia said. "She was a good friend of mine. We always thought she would marry your uncle. We hoped she would. But she never made it out of the castle."

"I'm sorry, highness," Oskar said. "I know Anniera only through books. Walking with you through this wood is like a children's story come true."

Nia smiled. "You have no need to apologize, Oskar. Remembering Alma is good for my heart. Do you know any more of her poems?"

Oskar recited every strand of Annieran poetry he could remember.

The company stopped for lunch, and since they had seen no animals bigger than a meep, Podo risked a fire.

"See this?" he said, indicating an oak with limbs that dipped almost to the ground. "If the fire attracts anything too big for us to handle, we'll climb that tree until it's safe to come back down. Any problems with that plan, Reteep?"

---

2. Though little known outside of the Shining Isle, Alma Rainwater was one of many Annieran poets whose work was hailed as revolutionary because it rhymed and followed a strict form called *ba-dum-ba-dum pentameter*.

Oskar pushed his spectacles to the bridge of his nose and eyed the tree. "Ah! Well! Let's see…I can't think of any forest creatures more dangerous than a toothy cow or a hound that are known to be good climbers. Of course, there could be snakes or snickbuzzards—we *are* closer to the mountains now, though not much. And then there are bugs. Stinging bugs like the—"

"All right, then. That's the plan."

Janner and Tink fetched firewood while Leeli and Nia rummaged through the packs to find pots and pans and the spices needed to make the dried diggle meat taste more like a pot roast. Once the fire was crackling nicely, they sat around it with nervous eyes on the forest. Since the underbrush was sparse, it was possible to see trees an arrow shot or more away, which was good, Janner thought, because it would be easy to see anything coming. But it also made him feel like he was being watched.

For a long time they sat and ate (too long, Podo insisted), and the conversation led to the three gifts the children had received from Anniera. Leeli and Tink showed Oskar the ancient whistleharp and the sketchbook. He fussed over the whistleharp, his eyes wide and boyish as he recalled to himself its significance in Annieran history. Oskar was speechless as he tilted the pages of their father's sketchbook into better light and gazed at them through his spectacles. His eyes gleamed with emotion.

"*Anniera,*" Oskar whispered as he looked at pictures of the Shining Isle drawn by the High King himself. It was the closest he had ever come to seeing that fair country with his own eyes.

Finally, Janner removed the big, leather-bound book from his pack.

"Fascinating!" Oskar breathed. He reached for the book like a child reaching for a dollop of candy.

"Grandpa says it's one of the First Books," Janner said.

"Aye," said Podo. "I heard it was among the treasures of Anniera but never laid me eyes on it until the night we fled the castle."

"What are the First Books, anyway?" Leeli asked.

"There are many legends, young princess," Oskar said. "One is that the Maker himself wrote them and gave them to Dwayne—he was the First Fellow, you know—as a gift for the care and governance of Aerwiar. The Books taught Dwayne the ways of wisdom and guided him as he reigned throughout the First Epoch, which was, they say, about five thousand years ago. Another is that Dwayne and Gladys—she was Dwayne's wife—wrote the First Books together and that they're a record of their time ruling the world. Another theory is that the First Books were written by Will, their second son, who caused all manner of problems."

"Problems?" Janner asked.

"He was called Ouster Will in the histories," Nia told him. "Here in Skree we have the Black Carriage to scare children while they lie in bed awake. When I was a girl in the Green Hollows, it was stories of Ouster Will that made us shiver in our sheets. They said the ghost of Ouster Will made your house creak in the night, that Ouster Will was the spidery feeling on the back of your neck when you walked through the woods alone."[3]

Janner's skin crawled. Tink drew a hand across the back of his neck and shivered.

"Ouster Will is as dead in the ground as me Grandpappy Helmer," Podo snorted. "You and your ghost stories."

"I'm not saying I *believe* them," Nia said. "I'm saying Ouster Will was a bad man—bad enough that there are still scarytales about him thousands of years after he died. Why do you look so nervous?"

Podo grunted.

"Where was I?" Oskar asked, patting the big book in his lap the way a mother pats a baby.

"The First Books," Janner said.

"Ah. Other legends say Ouster Will wrote the First Books. They say he learned many secrets of Aerwiar, secrets the Maker gave to Dwayne, intended for the king and the king alone."

"What kind of secrets?" Leeli asked.

"Well, over the thousand years that Dwayne ruled—"

"A thousand years?" Tink's eyes widened.

"Yes. Maybe more. And during his long reign, he guarded the First Well carefully. The well stood at the center of the city, and Dwayne administered its healing waters to the sick and wounded. And Dwayne himself, without meaning to, lived longer than anyone else." Oskar glanced at Podo. "It's a long story that we don't have time to tell right now, but it's enough to say that Will overthrew his father—killed him—and stole the throne, intending to wield the power of the First Well for his own ends. There are some who believe the First Books were Ouster Will's record of the secrets he discovered."

Janner looked at the book in Oskar's lap with wonder and dread. He wanted to believe the Maker had written it (though that seemed impossible), or that Dwayne, whom Janner had always pictured as a kind old man, wrote it. He shuddered at the

---

3. For a sample of a Hollish poem about the dreaded Ouster Will, see Appendices, page 328.

thought that Ouster Will, some villain from the shadows of history, was the author of the book entrusted to him.

Oskar jiggled with delight as he opened the book. "This writing. Do you know what language it is?"

"No," Nia said. "Like Papa, I never saw the book until the day we fled. I gathered that Esben had it, but I didn't know where he kept it hidden. He spent much of his time with Bonifer in those last days."

"Squoon," Oskar said, looking over the top of his spectacles at Nia. "I know that name."

"Bonifer Squoon!" Janner blurted. "I remember that name too." He closed his eyes. "*This is the Journal of Bonifer Squoon, Chief Advisor to the High King of Anniera, Keeper of the Isle of Light. Read this without my permission and I will pound your nose.*' Was he Esben's—er, Father's—chief advisor?"

Nia and Podo exchanged a glance. "Yes," she said. "How did you…?"

"His journal was in the bottom of the crate from Dang," Tink said. "The one we unpacked for Mister Reteep just before I found the map."[4]

"I read it," Oskar said. "In fact, I was reading it when I heard you and Peet fighting the Fangs in front of the jail that night. I assumed it was a forgery or some kind of fiction from Anniera, a children's book perhaps, fashioned to seem like the real thing for the purpose of feeding young imaginations. But you say this Squoon was truly the advisor to the king?"

"Aye, and Squoon was the type to tell you that he'd pound yer nose, that's for sure," Podo said. "Not that he would've ever actually pounded it. He was much too cowardly for that."

"So I was in possession of the chief advisor to the High King's journal. Right there in Books and Crannies, but now gone forever," Oskar sighed. "In the words of Vilmette Oppenholm in her essay on the decline of free cupcakes, 'How awful.'"

"I wonder how that journal ended up in Skree," Nia said to herself. "Where did you say you found the crate from Dang, Oskar?"

"In Torrboro. Over the years I've come across several crates of its kind, probably loot from ships the Fangs pirated between here and Dang. It was a nice surprise, but not unheard of. The journal, of course, had I known it was authentic, would have been a great deal more than a surprise to me."

"What was in it?" Nia asked.

---

4. See map in Appendices, page 329.

Oskar thought for a moment. "Nothing that interesting. No mention of first names that I remember—only 'the king' this and 'the queen' that. He wrote of his trips to and from Dang. He seemed to do a lot of that, supervising shipments and trade routes and such. Odd work for a king's advisor, especially since he was an old fellow. But I thought little of it, since I believed the journal was a piece of fiction."

"I remember he spent a lot of time abroad," Nia said.

"So he was a busy old feller. What does this have to do with the book?" Podo said with a trace of annoyance. Janner could tell he was itching to move on.

"Bonifer and Esben spent much time together in those last days," Nia explained. "I heard them talking about the First Book more than once. That's all I know about it."

"The letters look like Old Hollish, the ancient language of the Green Hollows. Do you remember that from your youth, highness?" Oskar asked Nia.

"I studied Hollish when I was a girl, but no one speaks it anymore. *Old* Hollish is another thing altogether." She narrowed her eyes at the writing in the book and tilted her head from one side to the other. "Try this," she said, flipping the book around. "There. I can't read it, but it's definitely some version of Hollish."

"Ah!" Oskar said. "I see it now, too." He studied the cover and binding of the book. "This isn't the original cover. Whoever replaced it, however many years ago, didn't know the language either and placed the new cover backward. What we thought was the first page is actually the last. See?"

It all looked the same to Janner, but it was fascinating nonetheless.

"I think, highness, with what I know of languages and what you remember of Hollish, we might be able to translate this." Oskar looked at Nia eagerly.

"I don't know," she said. "There's a reason these books were hidden. A reason they haven't been translated before."

"But highness, there must also be a reason the book has been preserved all these years."

"And a reason Father wanted me to have it," Janner said quietly.

"We really need to get a move on," Podo said, kicking dirt over the fire. "I know ye'd like to sit all day and have a nice discussion about old, upside-down languages, but we've got a long way to go."

The crunch and snap of breaking branches echoed through the forest.

Janner and Tink leapt to their feet, drew their swords, and took their places on either side of Podo, forming a fierce wall of protection in front of Nia, Leeli, and Oskar.

A toothy cow, bigger than any Janner had ever seen, lumbered toward them.

"The tree!" Podo yelled. "Now!"

Seconds later, they were safe in the swooping limbs of the glipwood oak, looking down at the giant beast as it limped around the trunk of the tree. Blood dripped from its teeth. The cow's milky eyes rolled, wild and unable to focus.

"Look!" Leeli pointed at a spear that hung from its right shoulder.

The cow gurgled. Its eyes fluttered, and with an ignoble shudder, it crumpled to the ground and died. After a moment of silence, the company climbed down the tree.

"I'm glad she was injured," Podo said as he wrenched the spear from the cow's side, "or we might not have had time to get clear."

Tink squatted near the cow's head and poked at it with a stick.

"So there are Fangs nearby," Janner said, eying the bloody spear.

"No, lad," Podo said. "This ain't a Fang spear. Far too fine a weapon for that. This explains why we've not seen any critters before now." He threw the spear aside and wiped his hand on his breeches. "Stranders."

"*Now* will you tell us what a Strander is?" Tink asked.

"Aye," Podo said darkly. "Thieves and killers. If they're around, we need to move, and fast. The sooner we get clear of the forest, the better."

20

In the Hall of Lamendron

That evening as the sun set on Skree, the troll flung Peet to the floor of the great hall at Fort Lamendron. Torches flickered on the walls. The Fangs at the perimeter of the room hissed at the chained figure writhing on the floor in front of the throne.

Zouzab and the other ridgerunner slunk to the foot of the dais and bowed. "Greetings, General Khrak," said Zouzab.

Just behind the ridgerunner, Peet lay on his back and stared at the high ceiling. For the moment, his mind worked properly, and he remembered everything. The troll had dragged him for a night and a day from the forest, through the Glipwood Township, and down the long road to Fort Lamendron. Peet ached from every jarring inch of the journey.

He found some satisfaction in the fear in the Fangs' eyes when they looked at him. They had good reason to be afraid. If he were free of his chains, he could put an end to every beast in the room. Just to be sure, Peet flexed his muscles. The Fangs sank back, but the chains held fast.

"I see you've captured the Throne Warden," said Khrak.

Zouzab nodded.

"Excellent. Gnag will be pleased. But I don't sssee the children."

"The jewels," Zouzab said, then paused.

"Speak, creeper!" Khrak hissed.

"The jewels have…escaped. Again."

Khrak's face was unreadable. Peet grinned. Zouzab glanced at the rafters of the hall and the high windows, probably in case he needed to make a quick getaway. Khrak had a reputation for being more ruthless than the average Fang, which was saying something.

"I could tell you all the details about how your Commander Higgk's incompetence led to their escape," Zouzab continued, "but the important thing is not that they escaped."

"And what *isss* the important thing?" asked the general in a menacing voice.

"The important thing, General Khrak, other than the capture of the Throne Warden, is that we listened as the mother and grandfather planned and discussed, and we know where they're going."

"Ah. And where isss that?"

"The Ice Prairies."

"Kimera?" Khrak asked.

"Yes, my lord. They know of the force gathered there, and the leader, a man named Gammon. They know that the Fangs, mighty though you be, cannot endure the harsh cold, so they believe it is safe there."

"Safe, eh?" said Khrak to a nearby Fang.

"Aye, General," said the Fang with a snicker, "perfectly ssssafe."

The Fangs in the hall burst into laughter.

Peet broke into a sweat. Had Gnag figured out a way to protect the Fangs from the cold? He had to find a way to tell the children!

He strained and twisted, sensing Khrak's eyes on him, and then his mind grew muddy, and he forgot where he was, who he was, who the children were. He became little more than a chained animal.

When the laughter died away, the Fang on the throne stepped down from the dais and stood over Peet. Its tongue flitted out and tickled the air only inches from Peet's face.

"I know exactly what to do with you, Artham Wingfeather," said the Fang, and at his name, Peet's mind cleared a little.

"D-don't send me back," Peet stammered. "P-please…"

"Back to Throg?" Khrak said with a wicked grin. "You don't want to go back to the Deeps of Throg? Why, I'm sure Gnag the Nameless could find you a place in the dungeon. Your old cell, perhaps? The one with the excellent view, as I remember."

Peet wept and shook his head.

Khrak straightened and looked at him with disgust. "Stop whimpering. It's the Phoob Islands for you, Wingfeather. We'll let the Grey Fangs try to…*make* something of you. Take him to the docks!"

21

Podo's Nightmare

As the sky grew dark and the forest grew darker, Podo called a halt. There had been no sign of Stranders and no more toothy cows in the six hours since lunch.

"Can we have another fire?" Leeli asked her grandfather sweetly.

Podo sighed. "No lass, I'm afraid not. Not at night. If we want light, it'll have to be of the greenish sort."

After a cold, silent meal by the light of the snotwax candle, Podo set up the tent near a good climbing tree and stood watch while Tink and Janner huddled over the ancient book in Oskar's lap. Now and then the old bookseller beckoned Nia over and held the candle so that she could see the page. She gave him her best guess about the sound or meaning of a letter, then returned to her spot next to Leeli.

Janner was sore and tired, but his mind whirled with questions long after Nia blew out the candle and the others fell asleep. He wanted to know why Podo, who had seemed so happy during the weeks at Peet's castle, was now so irritable and distant. He wanted to know what about the Dark Sea gave the old pirate pause. He wanted to know what had happened to Peet the Sock Man. He wanted to know why his father had left him this giant, timeworn book written in a language nobody remembered. He wanted to know who the Stranders were. He wanted to know what Gnag the Nameless could possibly want with him and his brother and sister. Janner's mind was as tired from thinking as his legs were from walking, and he finally felt himself drifting to sleep, floating into the dream realm like a boy on a boat.

"I'm sorry," said a voice.

Janner sat up, not sure if he was dreaming. After a moment the fog in his brain thinned, and he remembered where he was. He heard the snores and deep breathing of the others, crickets outside the tent, and an owl somewhere in the distance.

"I'm so, so sorry," came the voice again. It was Podo.

"Grandpa?" Janner whispered. There was no answer. He crept to where Podo lay. By the faint light in the tent, he could see that his grandfather's eyes were closed, his mouth slightly open. "Grandpa, you're dreaming," Janner whispered.

"No excuse, lords…I'm sorry. I didn't know. Ye must believe me," mumbled Podo, on the verge of tears. Whatever he was dreaming about was awful. The owl hooted again, and Janner thought about lying back down and leaving Podo to his dream, but then the old man's mouth drew down and he moaned.

"*Grandpa!*" Janner whispered again, this time with a hand on Podo's shoulder.

Podo's eyes opened. One of his stony hands shot up and caught Janner by the throat, but Podo came to himself and released him just as quickly.

"You were dreaming," Janner gasped. The two looked at each other in silence while Podo's breathing slowed.

"Outside," the old man whispered.

They crept out of the tent and stood in the living silence of the forest. The stars were so bright that the leaves cast shadows. Podo removed his pipe from his pocket, packed it with tobacco, and lit it without saying a word. The chill in the air seeped through Janner's clothes and set him shivering, but the smell of the pipe smoke was warm and comforting and conjured memories of the Igiby cottage and the hearth.

"Dreaming, eh?" said Podo.

"Yes sir."

"What did I say?"

"You said there was no excuse, that you didn't know. And that you were sorry."

Podo drew long on his pipe and blew the smoke out slowly. "Aye," he said to himself. "That I am."

"What for?" Janner asked timidly.

"For things I done a long time ago. Things that ain't been paid for yet."

"But you won't tell me what."

"I reckon not. Not yet, at any rate."

Janner wanted to press him but could tell from the tone of his grandfather's voice that it would be better to leave it alone.

"Back to bed, lad. I've a feelin' in me bones that tomorrow our little holiday walk through the forest is comin' to an end."

"How do you know?" Janner asked with a yawn.

"The trees are sparser. Can't hear the river anymore, which means it's leveled out. And that means we'll run into the Stranders that put the spear to that toothy cow. If they can kill one of those critters, you can bet your boots they'll make quick work of us."

"Have you ever seen them before?"

"Aye. I grew up here, remember. Long before Skree was such a dangerous place. Ma and Pa traveled often to Torrboro to buy seeds for farmin' or sell hogpiglets if we had any extra. 'Course the inns in Torrboro were a pocketful too expensive for the likes of a Helmer, so we'd take the ferry across the Blapp to Dugtown, where my folks could afford a room. In Dugtown things weren't near as pretty, but they were a lot more fun to a stinker like me." He laughed to himself and blew out another puff of smoke. "More than once I tore off from me parents and found myself in all manner of trouble with the seedy types in Dugtown. More than once those seedy types turned out to be Stranders.

"See, lad, Dugtown is a city of criminals, mercenaries, vagabonds, and adventurers. If it's trouble you're lookin' for, that's where you'll find it. But there are some types that even Dugtowners can't abide. Some criminals can steal yer underwear right out from under your clothes, but they wouldn't think to hurt ye. But others steal more than just yer possessions; they'd pick yer pocket *and* cut yer throat, just for fun. Dugtown is a rowdy place, but the folk that live there have a sense of what's right and proper, even if it's as slippery as a daggerfish. If the Dugtowners call you unfit for society, then you're a bad one indeed." Podo chuckled. "You get banished from the city, and you scrounge yer livin' along the river, scrapin' to survive among a whole society of murderous curs. The worse you are, the farther along the strand of the Blapp ye end up."

Janner was wide awake now. "So tomorrow we're going to run into them? The Stranders?"

"I'm afraid so. This far out, they'll be the worst of 'em."

"They sound as bad as Fangs."

"Aye." Podo hugged Janner and sent him back to bed. "Worse, even."

Janner sneaked back into the tent and lay awake until dawn. He watched his grandfather through the crack in the tent flap, pacing and puffing his pipe as the sky outside went from black to dark blue to chilly white. Leeli lay curled up next to Nia, still hugging her pack. Her thin blanket had slipped off, so Janner pulled it up to her chin.

Oskar choked on one of his monstrous snores, and Tink's eyes fluttered awake. "Janner?" he said in a sleepy voice.

"Yeah?"

"I don't want to be a king."

Janner almost asked Tink what he meant but stopped himself. He knew exactly how his little brother felt. "It's okay. I don't much want to be a Throne Warden either."

"You don't? But you're so good at it. You don't hesitate. You always seem to know what to do."

"That isn't how it feels," Janner said. "Don't worry. I'm sure you'll—" *You'll what? Would Tink really make a good king?*

"What?" Tink asked, propping himself up on an elbow.

"I'm sure you'll do fine. I don't think either of us is cut out to be a king or a Throne Warden yet. I think we're supposed to be studying our T.H.A.G.S. and playing handyball and reading books. But if that's true, then it's also true the Fangs aren't supposed to be in Skree, our father's supposed to be alive, and Leeli's supposed to have two good legs."

"But it is what it is," Tink said.

"It is what it is."

"What are we going to do?" Tink asked.

"Today? We're going to leave the forest. Podo says we'll probably run into the Stranders."

"No, I mean after that."

"Well…Dugtown. Then the Ice Prairies, hopefully."

"After that?"

"I don't know." Janner felt a snap of irritation in his chest. Usually he asked the questions and worried over the future. For once, at least this morning, Janner was content to let things happen as they would. "Anniera, maybe?"

"But it seems so…impossible, doesn't it? I mean, do you really think Gnag the Nameless and the Fangs and the trolls will just let us have it? Or am I supposed to be the king who leads—what, an army of rebels against these monsters? Janner," Tink said quietly, "I don't think I can do it. I just want to be left alone, like it was in Glipwood, before everything happened."

"It's too late for that, Tink. Besides, remember what Oskar told us about the Skreeans? He said they were miserable deep-down, that their lives weren't really lives at all anymore."

"It felt like a life to me. I was happy in Glipwood, as long as we stayed clear of the Fangs. I mean, we had the cottage, the Dragon Day Festival, zibzy with the Blaggus boys, stories by the fire—hot meals! And now look at us!" Nia stirred and mumbled something in her sleep, and Tink lowered his voice. "We're sleeping in a tent, Nugget's dead, Peet's—who knows what happened to him. My back hurts! I don't like carrying this pack around." Tink sat up and hugged his knees. "I just don't want to be a king."

Janner sighed and closed his eyes. He missed Glipwood too.

Then he thought of Anniera. He remembered the picture of his father on the boat. He remembered the tug in his heart when he heard the dragons singing, the way he felt the previous morning when he saw the sun glide from its grave in the Dark Sea.

Was it worth it? *Yes.*

"Glipwood is gone, Tink."

Tink closed his eyes.

"We can't go back."

Tink sighed. "I know."

"You know what I want? I want a long string of days like yesterday, when we walked through the forest, listening to poems about Uncle Peet, laughing together. No swords or bows or Fangs. I want to rest. But I'm afraid that we won't be able to for a long, long time—not until we make it to Anniera. Until we make it home. If we have to fight to make it there, I'm willing to do it. And if I have to pull you by the collar, you're coming with me. Look." Janner pulled Esben's sketchbook from Tink's pack, flipped it open, and held it in the light that crept through the tent flap. "See this picture? The lawn below the castle wall, where the people are sitting by the shade tree?"

"Yeah. I've looked at it a hundred times."

"That's a *real* place. And it's ours. And I'm going to *wallop* you at zibzy on that lawn some day."

Tink smiled. "I'll be the one doing the walloping. I'll always be faster than you."

Janner told Tink that he loved him, and Tink said that he loved Janner too, but not in the way a husband and wife might. Janner punched Tink in the shoulder, and Tink punched him back. Just to be sure he believed him, Janner jabbed Tink in the ribs, and they both laughed hard enough to wake everyone but Oskar, who snorfled, smacked his lips, and rolled over.

Podo thought it would be funny to strike the tent with Oskar still sleeping in it, so after a quick breakfast of dried fruit, Janner and Tink helped Podo pull the stakes and lift the center stick that held the canvas aloft. They laughed and whispered to one another as they raised it like a giant umbrella and exposed Oskar to the sunlight, and still he snored. When the tent was rolled and lashed to Podo's pack, there was nothing left to do but rouse Mister Reteep. Leeli nudged his shoulder, and his only response was a slight shift in the tone of his snore. Nia joined Leeli and prodded Oskar on the other side. Soon they were rocking him back and forth so hard that Podo, Tink, and Janner doubled over with laughter. Oskar snored and scratched at his belly.

"Mama," Leeli said.

Nia wiped a tear from her eye, still laughing along with Podo and the boys.

"Mama," Leeli repeated.

"What is it, dear?" Nia asked, trying to contain herself.

"Who is that?" She pointed to the trees just over Nia's shoulder.

Two mean eyes set in a dirty face regarded the Igibys and Podo.

"I'm a Strander, that's who."

22

The Stranders of the East Bend

The Strander stepped from behind the tree.

She was a girl not much older than Janner, covered from head to foot with black dirt that made her eyes and teeth bright. Tattered clothes hung from her skinny frame. In her hand was a dagger, and the way she held it made it clear she knew how to use it.

"Seen me cow?" the girl demanded. "Got 'er good just yesterday, and she run this way. If ye ate 'er, I'll carve ye up and bring ye back to camp in a sack."

"Nobody ate your cow, lass," Podo said, stepping forward.

The girl hissed and brandished the knife at the old man. "I ain't yer lass," she spat. "And you'd best not take another step forward or I'll put an end to one of ye before ye have time to notice I'm gone."

Podo held up his hands. "You throw that knife and nobody's tellin' you where the cow is. We don't mean ye any harm, so why don't you ease up and tell us your name. Mine's Podo. Podo Helmer."

"Don't care who ye are. Just want me cow."

Podo and the girl engaged in a glaring contest that, to Janner's surprise, the girl won.

"Fine," Podo said. "The toothy cow's a half day's walk behind us. You'll find the remains of a campfire we were foolish enough to light, and yer cow—or what's left of it—is nearby."

The Strander girl narrowed her eyes at Podo and considered the information. "Right." She nodded. "I believe ye. Now drop your weapons."

"Don't get too big for yer britches, lass," Podo rumbled. "Nobody's droppin' any weapons—"

The girl threw the knife so fast that Janner hardly saw her move. It thunked into something wooden, and he saw with shock that it was embedded in Podo's peg leg. The girl had already drawn a second knife and stood ready to hurl it at Leeli.

"Enough!" Podo said with his hands in the air. "We'll give ye our weapons, all right? No need to do anythin' drastic."

"Good. We'll take yer packs too."

"We?"

Without a sound, more children appeared from behind trees and swung down from branches, each of them fierce as a horned hound and ready to kill. The Igibys backed into a huddle around the still-snoring body of Oskar N. Reteep.

Without warning, Oskar sat up, spouting the sounds of Old Hollish letters, and declared he had unraveled another piece of the linguistic puzzle. He fumbled for his spectacles, placed them on his nose, and said, when he saw the gang of dirty children, "Good morning."

"We'll be takin' you lot with us," the girl said. "Banikon! Take five others and find the cow. Bring back as much as ye can carry. Hurry it up."

Without a word, one of the boys chose five children, and they slipped into the forest as silent as shadows.

The remaining Stranders—Janner counted eleven—gathered the Igibys' packs and weapons and rifled through them, pocketing food and matches and whatever else they fancied. To Janner's relief, they showed little interest in the First Book, the whistleharp, and Tink's sketchbook.

When the girl was satisfied the packs were sufficiently plundered, she tossed them back to the Igibys. Then she approached Podo with a wary eye and yanked her dagger from his peg leg. "Come on, then. Camp ain't far."

At a nod from Podo, the Igibys and Oskar followed. If Podo was taking orders, then these Strander children were dangerous indeed, Janner thought.

They varied in age and size. Some were boys and some were girls, though the girls carried themselves like no girl Janner had ever seen. He was certain that, girl or boy, the Strander children were all deadly accurate with their daggers.

Whenever Podo or Nia tried to communicate with the Igiby children, the girl leader hissed and waved her knife. Leeli bore up like the princess she was, hurrying along on her crutch without complaint, and to the Stranders' credit, they allowed Podo and Janner to take turns carrying her on their backs from time to time.

Within the hour, Janner smelled smoke and spotted signs of a camp not far away. Several figures around the fire stood and peered into the trees at their approach. They were filthy, bedraggled, and seemed content to be so. Janner could see the Mighty River Blapp not far away, wide and quiet.

"Have you got it?" asked one of the men.

"Yes and no," answered the girl. "May we come near?"

No one said a word. Janner glanced at his family and saw fear on all their faces, except Podo, whose jaw was set and whose eyes glinted like hot metal. The Strander children stood in silence around the Igibys, looking back and forth between the man at the fire and the girl.

"And who've ye got with ye?" asked the man.

"Don't know. Found 'em not far from here."

"And you found the meat, did ye?"

"I already said I did."

The man at the fire tilted his head, in anger or admiration, Janner couldn't tell. "All right, then. Come near."

The Strander children slipped in among the adults. If they had parents, it didn't show; none of the children hugged or greeted anyone. They stood near the fire with half-hidden smiles and held out their hands to the flame.

"So where's the food, Maraly?" the man asked the girl.

"On its way. Sent Banikon with a company to fetch it. Found this lot sleepin' not far from here. Had weapons, they did."

Another of the children dumped the swords, knives, bows, and arrows to the ground.

"We don't aim to stay long," Podo said. "You can keep the weapons and whatever supplies ye like."

The man approached. A long beard hung from his face in matted locks that looked like a cluster of dead brown snakes. He wore his hair tied back, revealing a high, dirty forehead with a jagged scar across it.

"Listen," Podo said. "We don't want to trouble ye. We're headin' to Dugtown, and we'd like to be on our way."

The dirty man straightened to his full height, a hand taller than Podo, and looked down into the old pirate's face. "You'll be on your way when I say ye can be on your way. Move over to the fire and make yourselves comfortable. There's much to be done."

He turned away and barked at his clan. "Tie 'em up!"

The other Stranders rushed forward. They pushed and tugged, laughed and spat at the Igibys as they moved them to the fire and tied their hands behind their backs. The Igibys sat on a bench near the fire while the Stranders went about their business, either punching one another in the shoulder in some kind of game, sharpening daggers, or making awful faces at the children to see if they could make them cry.

Janner admired Tink's restraint. He knew his little brother could make ugly faces with the best of them, but he chose to stare at the fire instead. Two of the men erected a spit above the fire, flashing black-toothed grins at the children. Janner noticed hundreds of bones in the dirt around the fire pit, some of them tiny fishbones, some of them as long as his arm. It explained why the animals in the forest had been so scarce. He saw the skulls of bumpy digtoads, toothy cows, and daggerfish half buried in the ashes and dirt. There were no human skulls, but with the hungry way the Stranders looked at them, he wouldn't have been surprised.

"They didn't tie our ankles," Tink said quietly, "but I suppose it's no good trying to run away, is it?"

"No, son," said Nia. "They know these woods. We wouldn't stand a chance."

"We could fight," Leeli said. "Or *you* could fight. I wouldn't be much help. But if you could get your hands free, the weapons are right over there."

"I appreciate the notion of fightin' as much as anyone," said Podo, "but as long as they don't mean to cook *us* on the spit, I think we'll do best to take things slow for now."

They sat that way for hours, uncomfortable, hungry, and thirsty. The presence of the Blapp a short distance away acted as a constant reminder that they hadn't had anything to drink since breakfast.

When at last the sun set, the Strander children returned with the toothy cow. They had cut the meat from its bones and carried it in sacks, which they dumped out on a canvas beside the fire. Like flies to old food, the Stranders gathered around the flames. The man with the beard appeared with a barrel, and the Stranders cheered. The two men who had erected the spit skewered hunks of toothy cow meat and hung them over the fire, where they steamed and hissed, producing a surprisingly delicious smell.

"Might as well let ye have a bite and a swallow," said a voice just behind the Igibys. "It might be yer last." The leader of the Stranders freed each of their hands, then leaned over Podo. "Ye seem the type that'll know this to be true: if you try and run, we'll kill you and toss yer bodies into the Blapp. Understand?"

Podo looked like he wanted to punch the man in the nose, but he nodded.

"Good," the Strander said.

The girl Maraly appeared with a basket of odd-sized bowls and cups, filled them with liquid from the barrel, and passed them around. Janner sniffed the drink in his bowl. It smelled sweet and warm, but he wasn't sure he wanted to try it. He heard a slurping sound on his right and turned to see that Tink had already finished off his cup.

"What does it taste like?" Janner asked.

"It tastes wet. Who cares? I was thirsty." Tink held out his cup for more. Maraly looked to the shaggy-bearded man, who nodded, and she refilled Tink's cup.

The Stranders were laughing and clapping and telling stories just like the Dug-towners that came to Glipwood on Dragon Day, and, as on Dragon Day, Janner found it hard not to like them for it. They seemed not to have a care in the world.

When the meat was declared done, two men removed the skewer from the fire and passed it around. The Stranders tore the brown, juicy meat from the stick and devoured it like dogs, smacking and sucking their teeth in a way that disgusted Janner and made him hungry. He couldn't believe toothy cow meat could smell so good.

Tink held his hands over his stomach and sat with his mouth half open, watching as the skewer made its way around the circle. Tink moaned when the skewer finally reached him, tore off a hunk of meat, and gobbled it up.

The leader turned to his clan and raised his voice. "Stranders!"

"Of the East Bend!" they answered.

"Quick hands! Long beards!" he cried.

"And sharp daggers!"

"No law!" shouted the leader.

"No law!" They raised their cups and roared with laughter.

"Now then, clan," the man said, raising a hand, "it's time we got to know our new friends. My name is Claxton Weaver. I'm a thief, a wanderer, and a swinger of steel. I don't like Fangs, I don't like strangers, and I don't like rules. These are my people, and this is my camp, and we'd just as soon toss ye into the river as let ye have another scrap of our meat. So you'd better think of somethin' that ye have or somethin' you can do for me that'll help me understand why I should let ye keep breathin'."

The Stranders' good cheer vanished, and they scowled at the family. Oskar stopped midchew and looked up at the man. Leeli, Nia, and Janner froze as well. The only sound was Tink's lips smacking as he ate his meat, aware of nothing but his hungry belly.

Podo considered the man for a moment and said, "Aye. Well. We've got food. We've got weapons, as you can see. I'm willin' to let ye have the lot of it if you let us go safe and hale, Claxton Weaver." Then the old pirate's voice deepened and his nostrils flared like a mad horse's. "But if you decide that's not enough, then ye need to know that my name's Podo Helmer, and I roved the Strand before you were born, with the likes of Growlfist and the Pounders. Don't look so surprised, laddie. I crept the West Redoubt with Yule Borron by the light of the Hanger Moon. I've sailed the Mighty Blapp a hundred times, from here to the edge of the map, and I can fight with hands, teeth, and even me eyebrows if it comes to it. Do you understand what I'm sayin'?"

Claxton Weaver stood aghast, his face so wretched and alarming that even Tink stopped chewing his meat. Nia pulled Leeli close. Janner's body tensed, and he wished his sword were at hand because he feared he would soon need it. The Stranders around the fire sat still as stone.

Podo stood and looked into Claxton's eyes. "But listen here, Weaver. I can see you rule this bend in the river. I'm old and one-legged, but I'm no fool. If it's strangers ye don't like, then save it for the next ones that scrape into yer bend. I'm as much a Strander as you are, I'm no Fang, and I've offered you everything we have. If that's not enough, then me boys and I'll fight like dragons." Podo took a step nearer the tall man. "And *you're* the first one I aim to lay me teeth and me bushy eyebrows on."

Janner's skin prickled with pride, and he curled his fingers into fists. He knew they were nothing like Podo's weathered hands, but they would have to do.

Claxton's eyes flitted to Janner and Tink, then Oskar, considering Podo's threat. "Ye crept the West Redoubt?" he asked. "Really?"

"By the light of the Hanger Moon."

Claxton's eyes narrowed and burned with a cold light. Such a fierce look passed between the two men that Janner cringed, as if all the darkness in each man's soul poured out and fought a great battle in the space between them. It wasn't clear who won, but Claxton appeared satisfied that Podo was at least a worthy enemy, if not a comrade.

The tension faded from the bearded man's face, and he smiled. "Then I've found a reason to allow ye to live, Podo Helmer. You're gonna tell us a tale—an account of the Strand in the days of yer youth. Me clan and I will sleep tonight with the thrill of old stories in our bones." Claxton's smile vanished and he lowered his voice. "But if what ye have to give ain't good enough, old man, then it'll be the Blapp or my blade for you and your company. We Stranders can fight like dragons too, remember." Claxton turned to his clan. "Can't we?"

The Stranders bared their teeth and hissed. In one deadly motion, the men, women, and children around the fire drew their knives, ready to leap over the fire at Claxton's order.

23

Growlfist the Strander King

Podo stood before the Stranders, shifting his weight from his good leg to his stump and back again. Claxton sat on a log in the center of his clan, his arms folded across his chest. The Igibys and Oskar gathered behind Podo. The fire had burned down to a steady red glow that turned the air the color of a bad dream.

"Podo Helmer," Claxton said, "proceed."

Janner looked at his grandfather in a new light; it seemed the old man had no end of secrets. But as much as Podo hated his past, and as much as Janner hated to imagine his dear grandfather running with such a wretched band, there was a chance it might save all their lives. He knew his grandfather had a story in mind, but he had serious doubts that Claxton and his hissing, knife-wielding people would turn them loose no matter how rousing the tale.

Podo closed his eyes for a moment and took a deep breath before he began.

"Stranders! I stand before you with but one leg, me hair white with age, and me belly full of yer good meat. This fire here burnin' low sends me thinkin' about Growlfist the Strander King on the night I first met 'im."

The Stranders murmured and nodded their heads.

"Aye, I met 'im, all right. Fierce he was, and a full head taller even than Claxton here. It was said his eyes were so mean he could cook a fish just starin' at it, and I'm here to tell ye it's true. Saw 'im do it any number of times.

"Many years ago I was fishin' in a bend of the Blapp not far from here, bobbin' in a boat with a bucket full of redgill, when I saw a dark parade wend its way down from the north hills. Filthy they were, and a cloud of dirt hovered above 'em like a storm set to burst. Indeed, lightning cracked from the dirt cloud, and a miry thunder rolled. *Stranders!* I thought, and I shivered in me boat."

The Stranders cackled with pride.

"I'd never seen 'em up close—not *real* Stranders, mind you. Some of those closer to Dugtown *call* themselves Stranders, but you at the East Bend know the men from the girls, don't ye?"

The clan snarled and laughed and pounded fists on knees, including the girls, Janner noticed, Maraly loudest of all.

"Well, I'd been driftin' for a few days. I knew folks this far downriver could only be dangerous, and to tell it straight, that's why I floated as far as I did. Danger was nothin' for Podo Helmer, scrabbly and young as I was.

"Then a voice comes tearin' at me from the tallest man I ever saw. He was the eye of the dirt-storm, and the Stranders around him swirled like the wind. 'Come near!' he commanded in a voice deep as the river, and my boat fairly paddled itself across the current to where Growlfist the Strander King stood. The nearer I came, the more fearsome was his appearance. Teeth like clamshells, a jaw like a tree root, a shaggy beard as brown and muddy as a bumpy digtoad's hind feet."

Again, the Stranders muttered their approval.

Podo continued. "I stood before Growlfist on both me feet—this was before I lost one, see—shaking like a belcher's belly. I'd seen tall men before, and dirty men too, but there was none wickeder than the Strander King, and I told him so. He asked by whose permission I was fishin' redgill in his waters, and I told him straight: nobody's. He bent so close to me face that I could see the fleas in his beard.

"Then I did somethin' so foolish and so desperate that I can't remember deciding to do it. If I'd stopped to think, I never woulda tried. Now, you Stranders know this, but for the sake of me family here what don't know yer ways as well, I'll tell you the Stranders are a slimy bunch."

Janner expected the clan to be angry at this, but they carried on with their usual backslapping agreement.

"Slimy as the bottom of the Blapp!" Podo said.

"Aye!" they cried.

"And if there's anything a Strander respects, it's someone as slimy and wretched and thievin' as themselves, eh?"

"Aye!" they cried again, louder.

"So ye want to know what Podo Helmer did?" he cried.

"Aye!"

Podo lowered his voice to a near whisper. "I picked Growlfist's pocket."

The Stranders stared at him open-mouthed. Even Claxton looked surprised.

"Ye picked *what*?" Maraly asked.

"Picked his pocket. Picked it right there on the banks of the Blapp with all his clan watchin', and they didn't see a thing. I'm mighty swift when I've a mind to be, and I decided that me only chance was to prove to Growlfist the Strander King that I was fit to ride in his company."

Podo let the silence reign for a few moments, relishing, as he always did, a tale well told.

"What did ye steal?" someone asked.

"The only thing I could lay me fingers on. Stole his pone."[1]

At this, the Stranders gasped.

"Didn't know what I'd done at the time, of course. It was right there in the front pocket of his breeches—a golden bird no bigger than a baby's fist. Growlfist had me by the collar with his dagger at me throat, all his clan laughin' and beggin' him to put an end to me. But before he did, I said, 'Growlfist, if you kill me and throw me in the river, you'll lose yer wee golden bird.' The Strander King patted his pockets and narrowed his burnin' eyes at me as I raised the trinket to his face—and winked."

"You winked?" Claxton said, now as lost in the story as the rest of his clan.

"Aye. Old Growlfist's eyes opened as wide as his mouth, and he started laughin' so hard it scared his clan as bad as it did me. Something unnatural about a man as wicked as Growlfist laughin' like that. Stopped his clan dead in their tracks, and we all stood there wonderin' what he would do."

Podo paused, his hands out, palms open to the night sky. "Growlfist set me on the ground, hit me so hard in the face that I still have proof"—Podo turned his right cheek into the fire glow so that all could see the finger-length scar along his cheekbone—"and welcomed me into the clan. Snatched his pone right back, and since he was the mighty Growlfist, nobody challenged it. Wasn't long before I was runnin' with the Pounders, and not long after that, Sharn the Torr sent his troops to try and clean up the Strand."

"And you crept the West Redoubt," said Claxton, the suspicion back in his voice.

"That's right."

"Well, old man, it's a good story. I'll give you that." Claxton stood and stretched. Janner's blood went cold, because it was clear from Claxton's swagger that Podo's story hadn't satisfied him—or if it did, he was unwilling to admit it. "But not good enough,

---

1. In Strander culture, the leader of the clan carries at all times a small item of significance to him or her, called a *pone*. If another Strander manages to steal the pone, he or she becomes the new clan leader as long as it remains in his or her possession. Of course, should a Strander fail in an attempt to steal the pone, the clan leader is free to apply whatever punishment is deemed appropriate or enjoyable.

Podo Helmer, because I don't believe a word of it. No man could've picked the pocket of Growlfist the Strander King with his whole clan watching. *I'm* the finest thief in Skree—once in Dugtown, I snicked the shoes right off a feller, and he didn't even know it till he got home—but not even I could've slipped the pone from Growlfist the Strander King."

Claxton drew his dagger. Just as Podo tensed to spring at the clan leader, Leeli cried out. A Strander held a knife to her throat. Podo closed his eyes and trembled with rage. Janner's heart pounded. The Fangs were evil to the bone, but these people were worse somehow. Other than their dirty appearance, they didn't look so different from Dugtowners—or from Glipfolk, for that matter. He was used to the Fangs being evil, but not ordinary men and women.

"Clan!" Claxton cried. "Podo Helmer, the fat man, and the woman will be sleepin' sound at the bottom of the Blapp tonight! The children we'll keep, of course."

The Stranders surged forward with knives drawn and teeth bared. They tore Nia away from Leeli. Oskar breathed a deep sigh and hung his head as they pulled him to his feet.

But Tink worried Janner most. His brother stared at Claxton with an odd look, not of fear or worry, but—was it fascination? admiration? Even as the Stranders jerked Tink to his feet, his eyes stayed on the tall, bearded brigand, and Janner's eyes stayed on Tink.

One minute Podo had held the Stranders in thrall with his tale, and a breath later the Igibys, Podo, and Oskar were surrounded and firmly in the grip of the clan again. Weaponless, with no leverage, no money for a bribe, it felt to Janner that they had finally reached their end. There were far too many of the smelly men, women, and children to fight, and unless Podo had another trick in his brain, the Jewels of Anniera would soon be caged and their guardians would be in the cold black depths of the Mighty Blapp.

24

Quick Hands and Quicker Feet

In the midst of the clink of knives and the cackle of black-toothed men and women, Janner heard a wonderful sound. It was a sound he had known for as long as he could remember, one that never failed to bring a smile to his face and a warm fire to his belly.

Podo was laughing.

His laugh was like the sound of trees bending in the wind, the bubbling of a river where the mill wheel spins. All the tension in Janner's neck and face eased away, and he laughed too. Leeli giggled.

Nia glared at her father. "And *what* is so funny?"

Podo struggled to control himself. "I just wanted to thank you all. Ye've been very kind and generous."

Everyone, Strander and Igiby alike, was confused.

"What are ye blatherin' about, old man?" asked Claxton.

Podo breathed out the last of his mirth, then looked into Claxton's face and arched a bushy white eyebrow. "I said I wanted to thank you all. Yer generosity is very great. It's so thoughtful of you to weigh me down so that me trip to the river bottom is as swift as possible. Didn't know Stranders had it in 'em to have such compassion on those they mean to murder."

Podo winked at Janner, then reached inside his shirt and removed an iron cup. He dangled it from his finger, and the way the Stranders' eyes followed its motion back and forth as they struggled to understand struck Janner as one of the funniest things he'd ever seen. He snorted and covered his mouth.

"That's me cup," said an old man in the back.

"Is it?" Podo reached into his shirt again and removed a shiny dagger.

Claxton snatched it away. "Which one of you oafs does this belong to?"

A woman with a patch over one eye raised her hand, and Claxton hurled it to the ground at her feet.

Podo reached into his shirt again, his eyes atwinkle, and removed a handful of coins, two green-jeweled earrings, a bigger knife, a bracelet made of snail shells, and a toy boat. One of the children rushed forward and tore this last item from his hand. On and on this went, and just when Janner was sure Podo had no more folds in his clothes in which to conceal the things he had taken, out came another necklace or box of matches or an iron arrowhead.

With each new revelation, the Stranders oohed and aahed and gave Podo more and more of their respect. Even Claxton's face softened a little as he stood with his arms crossed, his eyes and Podo's still locked in contest.

"Finished?" he asked.

Podo made a show of patting his shirt and breeches, then nodded. "Aye, that's it."

"Well, then. This has been a fine display, Podo Helmer. It's shown what fools inhabit the Strand." He glared at the shamed faces of his clan. "I must admit, I'm inclined to believe ye might have crept the West Redoubt, and maybe even met Growlfist himself."

Janner smiled. Podo had clearly bested Claxton and shown himself worthy of the Stranders' esteem, if not their friendship.

"But *no* man picked the pocket of Growlfist the Strander King," Claxton said, his voice booming over the camp, "and no man picked mine. Let your last breath be a drink of the river, and let me clan remember to keep watch when strangers enter the fold. Take the children to the cages and their keepers to their grave."

The blood ran from Janner's face.

But the Stranders hesitated. Murderers and thieves they may be, but they didn't like the idea of drowning such a one as Podo Helmer, who struck them as a Strander if ever there was one.

"Maybe we can just toss the woman and the round one in and let the peg leg live," Maraly suggested. The Stranders nodded.

Claxton's jaw clenched. He glared at the girl for a long moment and looked as though he might strike her, but he took a deep breath and said, "That may sound like a good idea, but listen close! He may have a story or two in his pocket, but I say he's too womanly sweet to these children and the miss. Pickin' pockets is easy, but his eyes ain't shadowy enough for our kind. And here on the Strand we *live* by shadows, clan! We roam the woods and slay Fang and farmer, we steal and rove and let no man tell us where's where and what's what! We've no use for lyin' old men or their companions."

Claxton knew how to stir the muck in the Stranders' hearts. They jittered and hissed again.

"The children we'll keep," he said, "but these three are only good for daggerfish food. I'm the head of this clan, and that's what I say."

As one, the Stranders leapt upon the old pirate. Podo fought, but they were too many, and he disappeared beneath a pile of swinging fists and kicking legs. They bound his arms with rope and stood him up again. Strings of white hair clung to his sweaty, angry, trembling face. It was hard to believe that only moments ago, his rumbling laughter had filled the air.

The Stranders bound Nia and Oskar, both speechless, and Claxton nodded at Maraly. She marched away with a shout, and the Stranders pushed the adults out of the firelight and toward the river. Janner, Tink, and Leeli watched in stunned silence as they were taken away.

"Wait!" Janner pleaded. "No! We just want to pass through! This isn't fair!" He felt a blinding pain on the side of his face and found himself on the ground, blinking away tears.

"Quiet, boy, or I'll hit you again," Claxton muttered.

As hard as he tried, Janner could think of no plan, no ideas that could stop what was happening. He wished Peet would come swooping in to save them as he had done so many times before. He wished Nugget were still alive.

Lying on the ground, Janner saw the hem of Leeli's dress, orange in the glow of the fire. He saw the leather slipper on her good foot and the way her bad foot curled in on itself, the toe of the slipper rubbed bare where it dragged along the ground.

Beyond Leeli's feet, he saw Tink's, and his heart skipped a beat. Tink's toes wiggled inside his boots, and his right foot occasionally twisted back and forth in a way that made a circle in the dirt. Janner had seen his brother do this countless times, always just before he broke into a sprint during a zibzy game or when they played Ships and Sharks with Podo.

Tink was about to run.

Tink was fast, of course—probably faster than any of the Stranders—but even if he managed to get away, he had nowhere to go. North was the Barrier. South was the river. East was the Dark Sea. He might run west, toward Dugtown, but he wouldn't last long without Podo—or Janner, for that matter. What did he plan to do, alone in the wilderness?

Janner had to stop him. They stood a better chance together, and Podo and Nia had always urged the children to stay together at all costs.

As usual, Janner fumed, *thinking only of himself.*

Leeli pulled Janner to his feet. "You all right?"

"I'm fine," he whispered, shaking his head clear of the pain from Claxton's blow. "But I think Tink's about to—no!"

Janner tried to grab him, but it was too late—Tink broke away, bumped into Claxton, and leapt past the fire.

Janner couldn't believe his little brother could be so selfish, so reckless. He wished he were free just so he could wrestle Tink to the ground and teach him a lesson with his fists. Was he really going to leave them all behind?

"Coward!" Janner screamed, aiming all the anger in his heart at his brother's back. It felt good to say it, and he hoped it echoed in Tink's ears with every step he took away from them.

But before the word died away, and before Claxton and the Stranders had time to react, Tink sprang onto a bench on the far side of the circle and spun around.

"STOP!" he yelled in a voice much deeper than usual. His eyes were wild with panic, shooting from Claxton to the Stranders to Nia and the others in the darkness beyond the firelight. For a moment his eyes rested on Janner with a look of sadness and confusion.

"If…" Tink said in a quavering voice, "if you k-kill them, you'll never…"

"Never *what*?" Claxton leapt across the fire in a whoosh of bright sparks and clutched the neck of Tink's shirt. Tink gulped and squinted one eye shut. "I'll never what?" Claxton repeated. "I'm sick of all the talk and the stories and the threats. This is *my* clan, *my* bend in the river, and I'll draw my blade on whoever I want."

"D-draw what blade?" Tink asked with a smile that worked its way through all the terror on his face.

"What blade?" Claxton narrowed his eyes. "Why, *this* blade—" He reached for his dagger and choked.

"*This* blade?" Tink produced a dagger from his sleeve and held its point just below Claxton's ear. He gripped it with a steady hand and looked calmly into the big man's eyes.

The Stranders gasped. Janner's jaw went slack. He had just called his brother a coward, and yet there he stood, face to face with a murderer. Janner wanted to hide his face in shame.

"He took Claxton's own blade," the Stranders said.

"That's not all!" Tink said. He reached into his shirt and withdrew a tarnished medallion on a chain. It dangled from his fist and sparkled in the firelight.

More gasps and murmurs issued from the Stranders. "The pone! He took Claxton's pone!"

Quick as a cat, Claxton twisted Tink's wrist so that he dropped the dagger. He flung Tink to the ground, picked up the knife, and snapped it back into its sheath.

"And I'll have me medallion back," he said, snatching it away. He turned a nervous eye on his clan. "Did ye see that, East Benders? Never have I seen such grum in a boy. Picked me own pocket, right here in front of me Stranders! Now the way I see it, I could either flay him here and now or make an ally of a young man who may someday find great renown along the Strand. I hate to put an end to such a promisin' future."

He pulled Tink to his feet and clapped him on the back. "Now, how did the old man's story go? Let's see. He picked the golden bird from Growlfist's pocket, Growlfist laughed, and then...ah, yes!"

He struck Tink in the face so hard that the boy flew over the bench and landed in the shadows beyond it.

"Tink!" Leeli screamed.

Claxton laughed darkly. "Never try to game with Claxton Weaver, boy."

Then something happened that would be talked about on the Strand for a hundred years.

From where he lay in the shadows, Tink flung a dagger at Claxton, and the handle struck him on the back of the head. Janner didn't know how Tink had done it, but he'd stolen the dagger a second time. Claxton, with a look of great confusion and a knot sprouting on the back of his head, crumpled to the dirt, unconscious.

The Stranders cheered and rushed to where Tink lay. They stood him up and brushed him off, chattering about his quick feet and quicker hands.

Maraly offered him a wad of damp cloth for his bloody lip and sat him on the bench. "Me dad's had that comin' for a long time," she said, and she kissed Tink on the cheek.

His ears turned red as sugarberries, and he grinned so wide that his cheeks stuck that way for an hour.

Nia, Oskar, and Podo were freed and ran back into the circle. They hugged the children and fussed over Tink, and Janner's stomach ached with the shame of what he had said—and even worse, of what he had thought.

A bent old woman in a filthy dress pushed through the crowd and poked Tink in the belly with a cane. Her face was warty and caked with mud, and she wore her hair in a grimy bun on top of her head. The Stranders fell silent.

"Ye've taken down Claxton Weaver, head of the East Bend, boy," she said. "We were all growin' weary of Claxton. The fool's me son, and that's all that's keepin' him alive right now. You should know he'll be after ye when he wakes, and aimin' to kill. But don't fear. I've a mash of slugroot that'll keep this old mudbeard in bed for a few days at least. We Stranders won't abide a clan leader dumb enough to let his dagger be swiped twice in one night." She whacked Claxton in the leg. "If there's anything we in the Strand have always liked, it's a good tale and a quick hand, and you're so fast even I didn't see you swipe the dagger that second time. Hmph. Didn't have it for long, but the lad got his pone, didn't he, clan?"

"Aye!" the Stranders cheered.

"What's yer name?" she asked.

"Kalmar." Tink straightened. "Kalmar Wingfeather."

"Kalmar," the old woman said, and she spat. "Hmph. Well then, you and yours'll have no shelter, but the fire is yours if you like." Then she hobbled over to Podo and squinted up into his eyes. "Podo Helmer," she said, jabbing him with the cane. "You're not as handsome as ye used to be, old man. But me heart is still yours if ye'll have it."

25

Tackleball in the Fog

Nurgabog?" Podo asked, flabbergasted.

"Aye. It's me." The old woman smiled, and her leathery, wrinkled face creaked in protest. The Stranders whispered and pointed like they were seeing some rare animal for the first time. "I never thought I'd see ye again, but here ye stand, as ugly as a dig-toad and naught but one full leg—and still I want to kiss you a thousand times."

"Nurgabog, dear, it's fine to see ye," Podo said, backing up a little. "Why didn't you say somethin' when we first showed up? If you didn't plan to toss us in the river at all, it might've saved us a fat lot of worry."

"I let 'em tie ye up because half of me heart would be happy to see you thrashing in the Blapp while ye sank! You left me fifty-five years ago without a word—and that was when I still had me teeth!" She sighed. "But the half of me heart that still wants to smooch won out, I reckon. I wouldn't have let 'em kill my sweet Podo."

"Thank ye, Nurgabog. You're as pretty as ever ye were."

She answered with a whack of her cane. "Don't you lie to me, old man! I know I'm ugly as a riverweed! Now listen. We Stranders of the East Bend will offer you a few days' rest on account of Kalmar Wingfeather's quick hand and your fine looks fifty-five years ago—on one condition."

Podo winced.

"I want one deep, satisfyin' kiss from yer grizzled lips, Podo Helmer. Been waitin' for it long enough."

Nurgabog hobbled forward, closed her eyes, puckered her lips, and waited. Podo took a deep breath, leaned closer, and gulped. It was like watching someone about to eat a rat. Stranders and Igibys alike stood rapt and silent. Janner clamped his eyes shut and heard a long, wet kiss, then Nurgabog's girlish sigh.

The Stranders burst into applause as Nurgabog tottered away. Podo wiped his mouth with his forearm and watched her go with a look of fondness, sadness, and nausea. The clan dispersed, nodding at Tink as they passed. They paid no more mind to the Igibys than to the dirt in their teeth.

Bumpy Digtoad

The bumpy digtoad has been known to attack humans, though never yet fatally. Victims of a digtoad attack complain of the "squishy, flootchy feeling" of having a sticky tongue violently flapped upon them. Since the bumpy digtoad has no teeth, its bites are said to feel to the victim like being "gummed like a dumpling in an old man's mouth."

From Pembrick's *Creaturepedia*

Tink swaggered over with a hand to the wound on the side of his head.

"Amazing!" Janner said. "That was *amazing*."

Tink shrugged.

"Listen." Janner took his brother by the shoulders. "I'm sorry. Sorry I called you a coward. Sorry I doubted you."

Tink toed at the dirt, took a deep breath, and nodded. "It's okay."

The knot in Janner's stomach unraveled. He hugged Tink as tight as he could, and he didn't care that Tink was too shocked to hug him back.

"So how did you do it?" Leeli asked. "How did you steal the pone?"

"I noticed Grandpa slipping the coins and knives from the Stranders as soon as we got here," Tink said. "You can tell from the way their clothes hang whether there's anything tucked in there and if it's simple to snatch. It's easy, really."

"Ha!" Podo said as he approached. "Easy as pickin' a totato from the vine, ain't it, lad? I tried to get somethin' from Claxton but couldn't get close enough to 'im. Do ye realize what you did back there, Tink?"

"Picked the clan leader's pocket?" he said.

"Aye, but ye didn't just snag any old thing. You got his pone! Do ye know what that *means*?"

"I guess not."

"Don't let it go to yer head, but it means that for now, you're the clan leader. The boss of this bend in the river." Podo beamed with pride. "*My* grandson."

Tink's face went pale. "Oh no. Do I have to do anything? What am I supposed to do?"

"Not a thing," Podo chuckled. "We'll be leavin' soon enough, and they'll choose another leader. Besides, a clan leader ain't in charge of anything. He does what he pleases, and the rest of the clan has to do what he pleases too. Bein' a clan leader ain't about havin' responsibility—it's about havin' none at all."

Two Stranders appeared and dropped the family's packs to the ground.

"Old Nurgabog told us to put everything back," one of them said.

"Our thanks," Podo answered.

The Stranders left the Igibys free to sit around the fire and inspect their packs. Janner found his old book, his tinderbox and matches, his folding knife and his bow, his dried meat and mirror. As far as he could tell, his belongings were all accounted for.

"It's all here," Nia said. She turned to her father. "You never told me you ran with the Stranders."

"Why didn't you tell us?" Tink asked.

"Because it's not somethin' I'm proud of," Podo said. "Just because it makes for a good story doesn't mean I wouldn't go back and change it if I could." He looked at Nia. "There's much I ain't told ye, daughter, and much I don't mean to ever tell."

With that, Podo lay down with his hands under his head and closed his eyes, and soon, beside a warm fire under the cool stars, they were all fast asleep.

Janner woke to a world shrouded in fog.

It draped the ground, creeping up from the river and collecting in eerie pools around tree trunks and depressions in the land, coursing between the rickety buildings that made up the settlement of the clan of the East Bend. The structures were made of planks and shutter boards, leftovers from the ravaging of Skree at the end of the Great War. They reminded Janner of Peet's tree house, but unlike Peet's castle, these buildings were shabby and unkempt, constructed without imagination or care. Stranders slept in or near the shacks, nothing for their beds but dirt, no pillows but their dingy hair and dirty arms. Beyond the shacks, deeper in the fog, squatted the cages.

Janner could see nothing inside them, and the iron gates hung open. The Strander children had been so timid when they approached the camp the night before. *May we come near?* the girl Maraly had asked, and they hadn't approached until Claxton gave his permission. Why were the children so careful around the adults? And where were their parents?

Then he realized Tink was gone. The rest of the company lay fast asleep by the ashes of the fire, but Tink was nowhere to be seen. Janner scrambled to his feet.

In the trees to his left, he heard voices, then a giggle. Tink appeared out of the fog at a trot, holding a leather ball under his arm. Janner breathed a sigh of relief and waved. Tink waved back, put a finger to his lips, and vanished into the fog again.

Janner tiptoed away from the fire and followed Tink into the fog. Before he had taken two steps, Maraly materialized out of the mist like a ghost. Janner gasped and braced himself for a fight—the girl had a wild, mean look in her eyes.

Out of the fog flew the ball Tink had been carrying. It smashed into the side of Maraly's head, and she staggered sideways, scooped up the ball, and disappeared into the fog again, whispering, "Kalmar! I'll get you. You can't outsmart Maraly Weaver."

Janner shook his head in disbelief.

Sounds of struggle came from the left, and he followed them through the fog until he found Tink and Maraly tumbling about on the ground, struggling for the ball that lay just out of reach. Janner strolled over and picked up the leather ball, and instantly found himself in the middle of the fight.

Maraly Weaver fought dirty. She clawed and hissed, snapped her teeth and punched. She socked Janner in the gut, and he doubled over, gasping for air and angry she had turned a friendly game into a fight. But he wasn't in Glipwood anymore. This was the Strand, and if he didn't want to get a little hurt, then he shouldn't play.

Neither of the Igiby boys matched Maraly for meanness, but they got used to dodging her attacks. The three played tackleball until the fog lifted and the camp awoke. It was the most fun Janner and Tink had had since that last zibzy game with the Blaggus boys on the morning they explored Anklejelly Manor.

Podo stoked the fire and prepared a breakfast of oatmeal and diggle strips. Janner plopped on the stump beside him, winded, wounded, and filthy from tackleball.

"Good morning!" Oskar said with a puff of his pipe. Janner's old book was open in the old man's lap, and beside him on a stump were a few pieces of parchment and an ink bottle. "I've been working on this since I woke. The language isn't so different from Old Hollish after all. Look." He held out a piece of parchment on which he had scribbled several lines.

"What does it say?" Janner asked.

"A fine question, lad. A fine question." Oskar's face fell. "I'll have to ask your mother. I can't remember much of Old Hollish other than the look of the letters. All I'm doing is sorting out the new letters from the ancient ones. Once I have a page finished, your mother and I will set to work translating it."

"Made a friend, have ye?" Podo asked as Tink sprinted past the fire with Maraly at his heels.

"I guess so," Janner said. "Tink has, at least."

"We'll eat some breakfast and then tread on. Every day we're out here, the Fangs have more time to widen the search. It's taken us longer to get to Dugtown than I thought it would, and the Ice Prairies aren't gettin' any closer."

Leeli and Nia returned from the river, their hair and faces dripping wet.

"The shoal was safe, then?" asked Podo.

"No daggerfish, and it was right where your old sweetheart told us it was," Nia said.

Podo rolled his eyes. "Nurgabog gave me this." He held up Claxton's pone medal-

lion. "Said if we ran into any more trouble from Stranders between here and Dugtown, the pone would give us safe passage. Claxton's a feared man, she says."

"Feared by everyone but Tink," Leeli said.

"Aye, lass. He did good last night, didn't he?"

Tink lurched past, hugging the ball to his chest while Maraly clung to his back
and pounded on his ribs.

"If we don't run into any trouble," Podo said, "we'll reach Dugtown by dark. Nurgabog told me where to find a river burrow."

"What's that?" Janner asked.

"A Strander hideout. We can stay there while we make arrangements in Dugtown to get past the Barrier and up to the Ice Prairies. The Stony Mountains'll be too
cold for Fangs and too rugged for travelers. All we'll have to fend from will be the
snickbuzzards."

"And the bomnubbles," Oskar said.

"Aye, and the bomnubbles."

"They're a terrible breed," Oskar said. "Nigh impossible to kill. I remember reading in Pembrick's *Creaturepedia* that—" He broke off at a glance from Podo. "Er, I'm
sure we won't see any. Probably not real anyway."

When the smell of oatmeal and diggle strips reached Tink's nose, he dropped the
tackleball without a word, plopped down at the fire, and smacked his lips.

"Boys, wash your hands," Nia said, and she told them how to find the safe shoal.

The brothers squatted at the sandy shore and dipped their hands in the water.
Before them the Mighty Blapp slipped past on its way to Fingap Falls; the opposite
shore was lined with the trees of Glipwood Forest.

"I like Maraly a lot," Tink said.

"She's, uh, nice, I guess. A little rough, don't you think?" Janner asked.

"Not *that* rough."

They washed in silence for a moment.

"She told me I'd make a good Strander," Tink said.

Janner laughed. "You'd make a terrible Strander. You're too smart for them.
Besides, you're no thief. You're no killer, either. You're the High King of Anniera,
remember?"

They walked back to the camp in silence.

26

Along the River Road

You need to leave," Nurgabog said. "Things have changed." She stood before Podo, her freckled hands folded over the handle of the cane. She pursed and unpursed her lips so that her whiskery chin bobbed up and down like a cork in the water.

"Is Claxton awake?" Podo asked, wiping a dollop of oatmeal from his lip.

"No, ye fool. Claxton's curled up in his shack like a sick kitten. The Fangs are comin'."

Podo dropped his bowl and leapt to his foot. "Where? When?"

"From the North Road. The Barrier's not far from here, and one of our scouts said he seen a gang of 'em comin' this way. They weren't due for several days yet, and now we've got to scramble to get ready for 'em. You need to scat. Take the River Road. Ye'll see Stranders aplenty but no Fangs. Things are gonna happen in the East Bend that neither you nor your family should see." Nurgabog smiled a crooked smile. "That kiss last night was the closest me withered heart will find to goodness before I meet the Maker and all his wrath, I fear."

With a tap of her cane, Nurgabog declared the conversation over and hobbled away. The Stranders were busy strapping on their sheaths and sharpening daggers. They cast nervous glances at a road that stretched north toward the wooded hills. The Strander children, including Maraly, were nowhere to be seen.

"Something bad is going to happen," Leeli said.

Podo sensed it too and dumped the grease from the skillet and thrust it into his pack without wiping it down. "Janner, Tink, get ready. Hurry!"

Oskar passed the old book to Janner and gathered his ink bottle and parchment, careful not to smudge the fresh ink. Janner's and Tink's packs needed only to be strapped shut and swung over their shoulders. As soon as Nia finished gathering the bowls and cups from breakfast, Podo took a last look around the fire and nodded.

"Keep up, lads and lasses. You too, Oskar. We're gonna be off at a trot for a while, and it won't be fun."

"Wait!" Tink said. "I need to say good-bye to Maraly."

"No time for that, lad," Podo said.

"But—"

"No time!"

Podo struck off in the direction of the river, and the others did their best to follow. "Maraly!" Tink cried over his shoulder. "Good-bye, Maraly!"

But neither Maraly nor any of the Strander children were anywhere to be seen—just filthy men and women who poured out of the camp with daggers drawn and nefarious smiles stretched across every face.

As they descended the slope to the river and the camp of the East Bend disappeared, Janner heard a final, chilling cry ring out from Nurgabog Weaver: "READY THE CAGES!"

Conversation was a waste of precious breath, so they moved in silence. If Leeli ever had reason to miss her dear Nugget, it was now. Podo moved at a merciless pace along the road that followed the river. He looked back occasionally to be sure the children were keeping up, but he never slowed. Leeli hopped along with her crutch faster than Janner had ever seen. Her wavy hair rocked back and forth with every lurching step, and she stumbled often, but she needed no encouragement to get away from the Strander camp as quickly as she could.

Oskar didn't run, exactly. He shuffled along with his arms pumping and his belly bouncing, but his feet never quite left the ground. His flap of hair had given up altogether on covering his baldness and trailed behind like a sad wisp of smoke. Oskar hadn't had this much exercise in years, but he was determined not to slow down the company. *Wshhh-a-heeesh-a-wshhh-a-heeesh* went his breathing, like the sound of someone sweeping a floor.

Janner was so unsettled by the Stranders at the camp, the strange disappearance of the children, and the coming of the Fangs that he was afraid to look back. The sea dragon's warning came to his mind: *he is near you.* What if Podo was wrong and the dragon was telling the truth? Gnag the Nameless could be slithering into the East Bend even now. The hair on the back of his neck rose.

If Tink felt the same fear, Janner couldn't see it. After his call to Maraly went unanswered, Tink's face had darkened. He ran beside Janner without taking his eyes from the muddy road.

The rise and fall of the land gradually settled into a flat, grassy bottomland, a wild green in contrast to the muddy road and the gray-brown course of the river. After hours of running, helping Leeli to her feet, running again, slipping in the mud, and so on, Podo stopped so suddenly that Nia thudded into him.

"Down!" he hissed, motioning for them to duck. They were too tired to question it and plopped into the mud like a slop of wheezing hogpigs.

Podo didn't appear winded in the least. "Stranders ahead," he whispered, pointing at a stand of trees in the distance. "They've not seen us yet, but they're bound to any minute. Nia, I hoped to put this off as long as possible, but it's time to put on our disguises."

"Disguises?" she repeated.

"Leeli, you too. It's got to be done."

Podo scooped up a handful of mud and smiled. Nia's eyes shot from the mud to Podo's face and back to the mud, and before she could stop him, he smashed it into her hair. She sputtered and struggled for words but none came. Podo, Oskar, and the children didn't bother to hide their enjoyment as they covered her from head to toe with mud. Leeli came next. She clamped her eyes shut and grimaced while they smeared her with the muck, but in the end she was laughing. When Nia and Leeli looked as grimy as any Strander, Nia had her revenge on Podo, smiling savagely as she caked his face and hair.

When Podo was satisfied the company was sufficiently filthy, he nodded. "Now you lot just keep quiet. I know how to speak like one of 'em, and besides, as ye saw yesterday, it's usually the clan leader who does most of the talkin'. Just stay behind me and try to look mean."

They had been running with little rest for half the day, and Janner was glad for Leeli's sake that Podo led them at a walk. They veered off the road and crossed the green bottomland to the trees so there would be no question that they intended to enter the Strander camp. When Podo approached, three men rushed forward, hissing and swinging daggers. Podo stood his ground and held Claxton's pendant in the air.

The Stranders stopped in their tracks a few steps away.

"That's Claxton Weaver's pone, but you ain't Claxton Weaver," one of them said suspiciously.

"No, I ain't," Podo said. "But I got his pone all the same, so if you're wise, ye'll let us tread on without trouble."

The three men considered this in silence.

"Tell us how you swiped Claxton's pone. If we believe ye, we'll let you traipse the Middle Bend. Aye?"

Podo glanced at Tink. Janner wondered if the story that an eleven-year-old boy had not only thieved Claxton Weaver's pone but had twice stolen his dagger and conked him unconscious with it would be more believable than something Podo might make up.

"Truth is," Podo said, stepping aside and pointing at Tink, "this young feller swiped it. Pulled it clean out of Claxton's tunic just last night in the East Bend. Left Claxton so befuddled that he didn't notice the boy swiped his dagger too."

The Stranders raised their dirty eyebrows at Tink. "This boy swiped the pone?"

"Aye," Podo said. "Ask him if ye like."

One of the men narrowed his eyes and stepped forward. Tink stood still as a fence post.

"You expect us to believe that you're the one that lifted the pone, boy?"

Tink gulped and nodded. Podo reached for his dagger.

The Strander grinned and slapped Tink on the back.

"Then I reckon you're none other than Kalmar Wingfeather," he said. "You can come near anytime, lad. Got word from one of the East Benders that Claxton Weaver was finally knocked from his heap. Well done, young feller. Claxton had it comin' for a long time. Tread on, then."

The Stranders slipped into the trees and were gone.

"Tink, you're famous!" Janner said, and Tink smiled from ear to muddy ear.

"Blast," Podo said. "Now the whole Strand knows yer name."

Tink's smile faded. "I didn't mean to give him my real—my *really* real name. I didn't want to tell him my name was Tink, and Kalmar was all I could think of. Sorry."

"It isn't such a bad thing, my boy," said Oskar. "The name Wingfeather may not be widely known in Skree, but there are those who know enough of Anniera to recognize it. Seems to me that if word spread the King of Anniera was alive and loose on the Strand, why, Skreeans will relish the news! And it'll make the Fangs none too happy."

"I reckon that's true," Podo said, and he winked at Tink. "*Let* the Fangs know High King Kalmar swiped the pone of Claxton Weaver. But if the word's spreadin' this fast, we've got to get movin'. We need to find the burrow by dark."

27

A Bruise on the Back
of the Land

Podo had to show Claxton's pone to three more Strander clans that day, each less threatening than the one before. Only the first clan showed any sign of having heard the rumor of Kalmar Wingfeather's quick hands, but Podo assured Tink the tale would ride the tongues of storytellers for a few years at least and the details would double and triple in size. Tink laughed, but Janner could tell something was on his mind.

The closer they drew to Dugtown, the worse the road got. Everywhere Janner looked he saw potholes and broken wagon wheels, abandoned shanties, stray dogs with missing legs or eyes or fur. Mud caked everything and sucked the color from the world. Mud splattered up from puddles in the road and dried on Janner's arms and neck so that he felt like he was made of clay.

After they encountered the last group of Stranders, the Strand changed. What had been grassy bottomlands became worn-down farmsteads, sagging fences, and hogpigs snorting in muddy fields. Before, they traveled alone but for the occasional Stranders, but now scrawny chickens squawked across the road, and poor, sad-faced men and women stood in silence and watched the Igibys pass with dull interest. The Wester Strand, as Podo called it, was a listless place, a string of shacks as bent and bony as the people who dwelt there. The water crept downstream so flat and slow that it seemed less like a river than a long, narrow lake.

Podo nodded to himself and announced they were clear of the Stranders.

"Then this is Dugtown?" Leeli asked.

"No, lass. We're close, though." He lowered his voice. "These poor folk live along the Strand but aren't so mean yet that they're willing to make their beds with the clans farther east. They're content to try to make their way by plantin' seeds and raisin' beasts. Too poor to live in Torrboro, too honest to scrape by in Dugtown, not yet vile enough to throw in with the Stranders. They live their lives with a mighty sorrow."

As the company moved on, most of the mud farmers—as Podo called them, though not without pity—ignored them, but some stood up from the fields where they were unearthing stones in the way of the plow, or stopped hammering a rotten plank to a rotten structure with a rusty nail, or peered out their windows to watch the Igibys as they passed.

"Has it always been like this?" Leeli asked.

"No, lass, not always," Podo said over his shoulder.

"But for far too long," Oskar said, "that's certain. For many years the Stranders have made trouble along the river. These poor, tired folk have suffered between the indifference of the elite in Torrboro and the hostility of the ruthless in Dugtown and the Strand."[1]

"Someone should do something," Leeli said quietly.

"What would they do?" Janner asked. "It seems like the whole world is as awful as it is here."

"Things weren't this bad in Glipwood," Tink said.

"No, but it didn't take much to tip the scales," Janner said. "In just a few days, the town was deserted and the Fangs moved in. Everything in Skree is as bad as it is for these mud farmers. It's just that here we can see it for what it is."

Out of the corner of his eye, Janner saw a smile on his mother's face. She and Podo's eyes met, and he sensed he had done something that made her proud. He thought back to the way he felt in Glipwood on Dragon Day, when Oskar had first helped him see the sadness beneath the merriment. None of the visitors to Glipwood laughed from the belly; none of them smiled except in defiance of the way they really felt. Only Armulyn the Bard was able to muster any true feelings of joy, and Janner had noticed that for himself and for the people who listened to his songs with such

---

1. Long before the Great War, the Stranders and the Dugtowners had made a mess of things, mainly because the Torr Dynasty chose to ignore them. Sharn the Torr made an attempt to clean out and restore order to the Strand, but the Stranders were fierce fighters and, without the honor of soldiers, were all but impossible to defeat in battle. For years the war was waged. Sharn and Growlfist the Strander King agreed to a temporary truce during the Battle of the West Bend. Shortly after, Growlfist and his Pounders breached the battlement of the West Redoubt in the middle of the night and assassinated the highest ranks of the Torr army—a dishonorable action even by Strander reckoning, but effective. Though Growlfist lost most of his men, the loss to Sharn and his soldiers was greater. The army from Torrboro retreated and left the citizens of Dugtown to deal with the Strand on their own. See *A History of the Blapp (Sordid)* by Grindenwuld Hollisra (Blapp River Press, 401).

desperate attention, the joyful feelings the songs brought to the surface always came with tears. Theirs was a burden too heavy to be lifted by songs alone, however fine the melody.

"Someone should do something," Leeli said again, this time in a feisty tone. Everyone knew better than to challenge her. She was right.

Podo stopped at the top of a gradual incline. To the right stood another cluster of tired buildings. Chickens chattered and pecked at the dirt, and a fat rooster perched on the roof of one building. An old man snored on the porch, a wad of rags his pillow. Behind the house stretched a fallow field bordered at the rear by a stand of scrub trees. To the left and down the slope coursed the Mighty Blapp, which was now anything but mighty.

Then Janner saw why Podo had stopped.

"What is it?" Tink asked as he approached. "Oh."

"Aye, that's Dugtown," Podo said. "I've not seen it for a great many years."

The city lay in the distance like a bruise on the green land. The shacks on either side of the River Road grew in number and were absorbed into the sprawl of Dugtown. Janner knew Dugtown was big, but his imagination hadn't prepared him for this. His stomach crawled at the sight of so many streets and angles in such disarray. Buildings stood three and four stories tall, constructed at odd angles, as if each level were an afterthought.

At some unknown signal, a ringing of bells erupted from the city—first one, then a few more, then what seemed to be thousands of bells clanged like a swarm of invisible, metallic bats rushing into the night. Above the buildings, Janner saw hundreds of wooden towers, rickety and thin, scattered across the city like ugly weeds sprouted from ugly grass. At the sound of the bells, a fire was lit on the platform at the top of each tower. The flames rose as high as a man, and on each of the towers nearest them, Janner spied a figure standing watch. A city lit by a hundred giant torches should have been beautiful, but it looked to Janner more like something from a scarytale.

"Is that Torrboro?" Leeli asked, pointing at the other side of the river. Janner pulled his eyes from the terrible sight of the nearer city and was relieved to see the fine, soaring walls of Torrboro in the distance. The Palace Torr crouched near the river like a giant animal. The tallest tower was the tail, and the palace walls bulged and curved to give the impression of the animal's legs and bulk—

"A cat?" Janner asked.

Oskar chuckled. "A *kitten*, to be precise. You'll see the same theme repeated often in Torrboro's architecture. A most unfortunate obsession of the Torr Dynasty, I'm afraid. In the words of Verbichude Yay, the famed art critic, 'Ugh. Might they have thought of something else?'"

Torrboro shone in happy contrast to Dugtown. Its wide, paved streets wound in graceful curves, and the majority of its buildings were of pale, creamy stone.[2] At the river front were many boats moored to docks, and Janner detected the movement of what must have been thousands of people bustling to and fro. The mass of people and activity thrilled Janner. He didn't get the same claustrophobic, sinking feeling from Torrboro as he did from Dugtown.

"Why can't we go to Torrboro instead?" Janner asked.

"Because the Fangs are thicker there," Podo said. "See that palace? That's where General Khrak resides. The meanest Fang of them all."

"He commanded the invading armies," Oskar said. "He's shrewd—not your ordinary brute Fang. He's probably sitting in the palace right now, trying to figure out how to get his claws on the lot of us."

"Aye, which is why we're not headed that way," Podo said. "It's easy to get lost in Dugtown, and that means it's easy to hide. The Fangs are in Dugtown plenty, but they're not there so much to patrol as to carouse. They like the taverns and the filth and the shadows. They're there for fun, and so they're not as like to interfere with a traveler on the street unless they have to."

Janner saw movement on the road ahead. "Grandpa, look."

"Eh?"

Janner pointed.

Podo sucked in a breath. "Fangs!" he said. "Follow me!"

He bolted into the house where the old man slept on the porch. Chickens scattered. Oskar, Nia, and the children hurried after Podo into the shadowy old building. The old man stirred and muttered a few garbled words but kept sleeping.

Once inside, Janner could see nothing. He could hear Podo's familiar *tap-clunk* and his raspy gripe: "Been so long I can scarce remember how to find the…"

Janner heard the rattle and clomp outside of armored Fangs on the march. It didn't sound like a large unit, but it was enough to make him tremble.

"Papa, they've stopped," Nia whispered.

Podo ignored her, grumbling to himself.

The harsh sound of a Fang's voice came from outside, and the old man on the stoop woke with a grunt.

---

2. The color of buttermilk, a favorite potation of kittens.

"Grandpa, they're right outside," Tink said.

"*Shh!*" Podo said, and then, so quietly Janner could barely hear him, "Step down. Easy, that's it, honey. Oskar, ye'd better pretend you're one of those Torrboro kittens and tread lightly, ye hear? Good. It's not far down." Then Janner felt Podo's strong, sure hand on his shoulder. "Down we go, boys," he whispered.

The wooden steps creaked as the family and Oskar moved down into darkness, but not loud enough to alert the Fangs, who questioned the old man on the porch. Podo pulled the trapdoor shut above them. He removed his pack in the darkness, fished about inside for a match, then lit it.

They stood at the foot of a stair in a damp cellar. *The Fangs aren't the smartest creatures in Aerwiar, but even the dullest of them would know to search the cellar,* Janner thought. For some reason, though, Podo didn't look worried. He ran his fingers along the seams in the stone wall, still mumbling to himself. The match died out and the cellar went black again. Footsteps thumped somewhere in the house above them. When the second match hissed to life, Podo's face appeared in the yellow glow, his eyes wide, holding a finger to his lips—unnecessarily, since the Igibys and Oskar already stood silent and terrified.

Podo crept to another wall, still feeling the stones for something. Fangs clunked through the house while others taunted the man outside. Then Janner heard a click, and in a corner of the cellar floor, another trapdoor swung down, spilling the dirt that had covered it and revealing the first few rungs of a wooden ladder. Podo used the last seconds of the match light to point down. As quiet as mice, they all crept down the ladder into what Janner guessed was the Strander burrow.

At the top of the ladder, after Podo clicked the trapdoor back into place, he tugged a string that dangled from the top rung. As Podo later explained, the string wound through a hole in the stone floor, behind a beam in the cellar wall, and up to the ceiling of the cellar, where it was attached to a mechanism that released a pan of dirt through a grid of holes.

With a muted *poof,* the dirt landed atop the conspicuous square of the trapdoor and concealed it.

The Fangs who leapt into the cellar a moment later were certain they caught the sharp scent of a match recently struck, but it was a mystery they couldn't solve, as the old man on the porch swore again and again that he had seen no one enter the house.

28

O Anyara!

Janner climbed down the ladder in complete darkness. Not more than three rungs above, he heard Podo's boot scrape wood, then a subtle *clop* when the peg leg reached the next step. Below was the sound of Tink's heavy breathing, and below that, Oskar N. Reteep's whispery grunt with each step down: "Oh dear. Oh dear. Oh my. Oh dear."

Finally, Janner sensed the long, square shaft widening, and Oskar's voice came from not far below. "Ah! In the words of Keeth Yager when he consumed a bucket of henmeat soup, 'I never thought I'd reach the bottom!'"

Leeli's snicker in the darkness was so pleasing it nearly shed a light of its own. When Janner's feet touched the ground, he was surprised to find a floor of loose sand. Podo struck another match, and the yellow light illuminated their surroundings.

They stood in a chamber the size of the Igiby children's bedroom, bare of everything but a lantern on the floor beside the ladder. The walls were a yellow, crumbling rock, the same color as the sand on the floor. Podo lit the lantern and made a quick search of the area before he was satisfied that, for the time being at least, they were safe. The family removed their packs and sat in a circle.

"Oy! That was a close one." Podo sighed as he eased himself to the ground.

"Do you think they were looking for us?" Janner asked.

"Aye."

"How long do we have to stay here?"

"Don't know."

"Long enough to eat, I hope," Tink said.

"But not so long that this filth attaches to my skin permanently," Nia said, picking clumps of dried mud from her cheeks. "You men can sit around in your stink all year if you like, but Leeli and I would rather not."

"Food! Food would be a fine thing right now," said Oskar. "Well said, young Kalmar." Oskar rummaged through Nia's pack and passed out strips of dried diggle meat, a hard loaf of bread, and the canteen of drinking water.

As he chewed the tough meal, Janner longed for a steaming pot of cheesy chowder or pot-roasted henmeat, and though he didn't want to admit it, he wished he were clean of the mud disguise as well.

Leeli hummed as she chewed her meat and picked absently at a clump of dirt in her hair, unconcerned with the state of the food or her person. As usual, Janner noticed, she bore an odd contentment with their situation. Ever since Nugget had fallen to the sea—or, more specifically, ever since Leeli's song had created that odd, dreamlike connection with the sea dragons, Leeli had floated through the journey with a strange calm.

"I think we should rest," she said with a yawn. "I'm sleepy. And Grandpa?"

Podo grunted and raised his eyebrows at her.

"Thanks for taking care of us." She leaned over to kiss him on the cheek and wrinkled her nose when she couldn't find a clean spot. Podo sat still, his eyes big and shiny, and when instead of a kiss she placed her tiny hand on the side of his face, the old pirate's mud-stiffened face cracked into a smile so wide that bits of dried dirt fell away and revealed clean skin beneath.

They all agreed rest would be a good thing, so the family and Oskar lay on the dirt floor and slept.

In the morning, or what Janner assumed was morning, he woke to find Oskar hunkered over the First Book in the lamplight. He hummed to himself and looked as happy as Janner had ever seen him. When he saw Janner was awake, his eyes brightened.

"Lad! Come look at this."

Janner yawned, stepped over Tink's snoring body, and sat next to Oskar. The old man placed the big book in Janner's lap.

"I've made much progress. You see these characters? I think they're music notes. I won't know for sure until your sister has a chance to try it out, but this might be a melody from the First Epoch! And I've translated the first few pages. Look at this word. The swoop on this letter indicates a change in tense, much like Old Hollish. But Old Hollish expresses the tense with a—" Janner smiled weakly, uninterested at the moment in swoops and old languages. Oskar chuckled. "You're right. Tedious stuff. Especially first thing in the morning. Here's the point." He removed his spectacles and placed them in the corner of his mouth. "The book is a narrative, as far as I can tell. I don't know who wrote it, but it was someone who was there when it all happened."

"When what happened?" Janner asked, waking up a little.

"When the First Kingdom—Anyara—fell. It tells the story of what happened—what *really* happened to the first city, where Dwayne and Gladys ruled for most of the First Epoch."

"Anyara? I've never heard of it."

"Neither had I until I started nosing around in your book, my boy." Oskar donned his spectacles again with a wink. "But it sounds a lot like another kingdom we both know, doesn't it?"

Janner tried to think past the sleep still in his brain. "Anniera?"

"That's right."

"So Anniera sits where the First Kingdom used to be?"

"Well, that's my guess. It's hard to say. But listen to this first paragraph:

Anyara tall and green, my beloved land,
gone to gray and ash now.
My fists are sore
from beating the ground.

Anyara! Dwayne and Gladys dead beneath the mountain,
all the music still and silent, all the enemies revel and curse,
all the world a broken thing,
a broken thing.

Rise again, mountain, burst again, spring,
grow again, crop and seed and arbor,
love again, heart inside me.

Or, Maker, let me die and weep no more.
O Anyara! My land! My land!
When Gladys bore a second son, the end began,
and if you listen,
I will tell you.

"It's terrible," Janner said.

"Yes," Oskar said quietly. "But that's not all. It goes on to say the kingdom was… *protected*. I'll have to ask your mother to be sure I'm translating it correctly. The power to save Anyara lay 'beneath the stones'—whatever that might mean—and whoever wrote this book was the last soul left to tell the secret. I'm not certain, but I believe that somewhere beneath Anniera, probably beneath the Castle Rysen, where your family made their home, was a room, perhaps. A chamber or tunnel of some kind, known only to the High King. I'll know better once I've had more time to translate. But if there *is* a chamber, if there is some secret there that can protect Anniera..." Oskar looked over his spectacles at Janner. "That could be the reason your father risked his life to get you this book."[1]

Janner stared at the lantern flame, his mind overwhelmed with information. It was hard to believe that beyond the walls of this dark burrow existed a world like the one Oskar described, a world of kings and powerful stones and dark enemies. It was even harder to believe that Janner was tangled up in that world like a dragonfly in twine. Suddenly he wanted nothing more than to climb the ladder and breathe fresh air, Fangs or no.

"Oskar," Podo said from the shadows at the perimeter of the burrow. He was a vague form leaning against the stone wall beside the ladder.

Oskar heard the danger in the old pirate's voice. "Eh, old friend?"

"You heard what Nia said. There's only one thing that needs to be in Janner's mind, and that's to make it to the Ice Prairies. No long-lost kingdom, no silly stories about magic stones and forgotten secrets. We both know that stuff is no more real than the groanin' ghost of Brimney Stupe."

"But the ghost *was* real, Podo! Or—the *story* of the ghost was real. My wind contraption just added a little terror to the tale."

"I'm in no mood to ninny with ye. We both know there weren't no ghost."

"No, there wasn't a ghost, but the story of the ghost was as real as you and I. And the story of the ghost came from somewhere, didn't it? Brimney himself was real, or else who built Anklejelly Manor?"

Podo rumbled.

"Fine, fine," Oskar said. "In the words of Phinksam Ponkbelly, 'I don't want to poke a snickbuzzard in the gobbler.' All I want is for young Janner *Wingfeather* here to know who he is and where he came from."

"And all I want," said Podo, "is to get these kids and their mother someplace they can live out their years in peace. Anniera is sacked and gone. There's no more an Anniera than there is an Anklejelly Manor. It's a dead island, as dead as snakeskin, and

---

1. For more from the First Book, see Appendices, page 326.

that's what these young *Igibys* will be too if they get ideas in their heads about kings and stones and secrets. It's ideas like that that landed us in this hole. If ye'd kept that fool map hidden better, we might be blowin' smoke rings at Shaggy's Tavern right now."

Oskar stared at the floor. When he spoke, his voice was little more than a whisper. "Do you know how many heirs to the throne of Anniera exist in the world? *One.* And he's snoring on the floor at your feet. Peet the Sock Man is likely dead, or he'd have found us by now, which leaves exactly one Throne Warden in all of Aerwiar. Leeli here is the first Song Maiden in generations." Reteep raised his eyes to Podo's. "I tell you, old friend, I'd rather be stuck here in a Strander burrow than blowing smoke rings in Glipwood, where the Fangs spit and howl and kill our spirits. At least we're here because we *choose* to be. We're here out of bravery and not cowardice.

"You sailed the seas and ran with the Stranders and did Maker knows what else in your sea-storm of a life. All I've ever done is read about such things. And here I sit in a cave with all that's left of the Wingfeather clan—the stuff of legends, Podo! And legends don't hide beneath the ice just so they can grow old and die with a fat belly and a bald head—not that my head is bald. My hair is full and flowing. I've always prided myself on it."

Podo rolled his eyes. "What's your point?"

"Well, it's just…wherever you take us, be it the Ice Prairies or the belly of a gargan rockroach, these children should know who they are. At all costs, they should remember who they are."

Hearing Oskar call him and his siblings 'the stuff of legends' gave Janner goose bumps, but it also gave him a shiver in his stomach. He had read enough stories to know that legends became so by great suffering and great feats. Janner didn't want to suffer, and he wasn't sure he was brave enough or smart enough to accomplish anything legendary. But he couldn't deny that he desperately wanted to know more. He could've listened all day to Oskar's theories about the fall of Anyara, knowing it could be a history of his home, of the kingdom where his father once ruled. Janner shook his head at the wonder of it.

"Pah," Podo said. "It's time to go."

Oskar's face fell, and he closed the book while the old pirate woke the rest of the family.

29

T.H.A.G.S. in the Strander Burrow

How will you know if the Fangs are gone?" Nia asked. She stood at the foot of the ladder, peering up into the shaft.

"We don't need to worry with that just yet, lass," Podo said. "Watch this."

He limped over to the ladder and ran a finger along a seam in the rock. With a *click*, another hidden door appeared, this time in the wall behind Janner.

"Who made all this?" Janner asked.

Podo grinned. "Stranders are rotten to the core, but that doesn't mean they're not smart as foxes. Used to be I could get from here clear under the Blapp to Torrboro and never once see the light of day nor a drop of water. Tunnels run under both cities like hollow roots, all cut by brigands over the epochs so they could steal and escape without a trace."

"And nobody knows about the tunnels?" Tink asked, bending over to peek into the darkness beyond the door. His eyes were wide and curious, and Janner knew if he and Tink had been alone, his brother would have already disappeared into the tunnel like a dog on the hunt.

"Nobody but the Stranders. It's been a long time, but I think yer Podo can make his way deep enough into Dugtown for our purposes." Podo looked at Oskar. "You say this Ronchy McHiggins fella lives on the river side of town?"

"Yes. The Tavern of the Roundish Widow is near the river, on Riverside Road, just a few blocks east of the ferry. It's been years, but I'm sure I can find it."

Podo nodded. "The tunnel should get us close. The streets of Dugtown are too dangerous fer me in broad daylight. Might be recognized. I'll get you as close as I can and wait in the tunnel while you find yer man." Podo turned to the others. "You four stay here."

"Grandpa, please let me come with you," Tink begged. "I'll be quiet, and I'll do exactly as you say."

"No, lad. There's not much to see in these tunnels but rock and dirt and worm droppings. Ye'll be as safe here as anywhere, and Oskar's the only one who really needs to go."

Tink sighed. Janner wasn't happy about staying either, but not because he was eager to go tunneling (though that *did* sound like fun). The walls and ceiling of the burrow seemed to be closing in on him, and he couldn't shake the feeling he was in a tomb.

"We won't be long, Nia. An hour to find Ronchy, assumin' he's still there, Oskar will make the arrangements, then another hour back here. If all goes well—and it seldom does—we'll be back by lunch." Podo winked at his daughter. "Save me some of that tasty bread, eh?"

"Just hurry back." Nia forced a smile. "And bring a bucket of water with you. I may never get this dirt off."

"Janner, you're in charge."

Janner nodded, trying his best to act like a Throne Warden.

Podo disappeared into the doorway without another word. Oskar adjusted his breeches well over his belly in preparation for tunnel travel, rubbed his hands together with excitement, then ducked through the door after Podo.

The children and Nia stared at the tunnel for several moments, as if Podo might reappear, having changed his mind about the whole thing.

"T.H.A.G.S.," Nia said.

The three children looked at her in disbelief.

"Tink, work on a sketch of Fingap Falls and Miller's Bridge. Leeli, it's probably a bad idea to make too much noise in here, but you can practice your whistleharp fingerings, and we'll try and sort out the notes in the First Book. Janner, much has happened in the last few days that needs written about."

When the children realized their mother was serious, they plopped down in the dirt and set to work on their schooling by the light of the lantern. Once Janner remembered the welcome feel of the quill in his hand and heard the *skritch* when he formed letters on the parchment pages of his journal, the walls of the cave retreated. He sank into the writing and was swept along the river of his memory of the last few days. The escape from the gargan rockroach. Podo's strange fear of the sea. The race along the narrow spans of Miller's Bridge.

Nugget. Poor, brave Nugget.

The sea dragons! Janner smiled and felt a thrill in his belly. He described the metallic shine of the dragons' skin, the sense of thunderous power behind their eyes, like dark clouds heavy with rain, and mingled with that power a kind of deep knowledge. But then there was also an odd feeling of—

Janner couldn't think of the right word. He looked up from his paper to see Tink hunkered over his sketchbook, his tongue poking out of the corner of his mouth.

Fury.

That was the word. Something more than just anger, something far beneath the surface that had lain silent for an age and waited for its moment to erupt. Even stranger, Janner wasn't afraid of the fury, because it seemed directed elsewhere. He felt that if it were unleashed, he wouldn't be *safe,* but he at least stood a chance of escaping it. He pitied the target of the dragons' ancient wrath.

He still heard the dragon's voice in his mind and remembered every word: *"He is near you, young ones. He is near you. Beware. He destroys what he touches and seeks the young ones to use them for his own ends. We have been watching, waiting for him. He sailed across the sea, and he is near you, child. We can smell him."*

Janner shivered. He was sure now that either the dragon had lied, as Podo said, or it meant someone other than Gnag the Nameless. If Gnag were nearby and knew where the Igibys were, the Fangs would've captured them long ago.

Hours passed, and even Nia knew the children couldn't work on their schooling forever. She declared a recess and ordered the children to repack their supplies. Janner and Tink took great pleasure in inspecting their belongings. They laid out their bows, took inventory of the few arrows they had left, removed their swords from their scabbards and cleaned them as best as they could without water to spare. Leeli cleaned her little mirror, dusted off the whistleharp, and took stock of the remaining food, which she wrapped carefully in cloth, then tied with twine.

When everything they owned was returned to the backpacks, cleaned, counted, and well packed, the children and Nia sat in a circle around the lantern and waited.

And waited.

They ate a meager lunch at what they estimated to be noon, chewing in silence and taking small sips from what remained of the water in the canteen. Then they waited.

And waited.

Finally, just when the boredom began to turn to worry for Oskar and Podo, they heard voices from the tunnel door.

"Told you this was the right way, ye luggard!"

"You and I both know you chose the *other* turn! As the impeccable cartographer Conrad Tottingtown declared, 'Nobody listens to me!'"

"Not true, Reteep. I can't *help* but listen to ye. You've been squawkin' like a goose for hours now!"

"Oh dear."

When Oskar and Podo emerged from the darkness and straightened, the children rushed forward and assaulted them with hugs.

"Ronchy's going to make the necessary arrangements this evening," Oskar said once he and Podo had eaten a few bites. "He said we should return at midnight and the guide would be waiting in the alley behind the Roundish Widow. He said if we had come three days sooner, Gammon himself could have smuggled us north. He was in Dugtown to meet with other members of his force."

"You're sure you can trust him?" Nia asked.

"My lady, I find it hard to believe that a man capable of making such delectable sailor's pie would be of much danger. Oh, the pie!" Oskar patted his squishy belly.

"I don't see what choice we have, lass," Podo said.

"What do you think, young Wingfeathers?" Oskar asked.

Janner and Tink were taken aback. Did Oskar really want to know what they thought? The way Nia, Oskar, and even Podo looked at the three of them told Janner they did.

"Uh," Tink said.

"Well," Janner said.

"Yes," Leeli said. "Whatever happens, even if Mr. McHiggins isn't trustworthy, we can't stay here, and we can't go back." She looked at the adults with her wide, innocent eyes.

"The Song Maiden of Anniera has spoken," Oskar said gravely.

And the matter was settled.

The day passed in a slog of boredom.

After Oskar woke from a noisy nap, he and Janner set to translating more of the old book, occasionally asking Nia for whatever help she could give. She surprised herself at the amount of Old Hollish she remembered, and page after page of translation piled up beside Oskar on the burrow floor. At first Janner was fascinated by the narrator's sad account of the fall of Anyara, the invading armies, the lists of numbers of fallen soldiers, and the positions of lines of battle and encampment. But after several pages the writer settled into an agonizing accounting of dates and numbers and the lineages of heroes who fell or conquered this enemy or that. It was all very confusing and seemed excessively unimportant, with the exception of occasional lines of great understatement.

"On the fourth day of Secondmoon, in the year 1235 of the First Epoch, Boron son of Nam descended from Mount Flimkhar and fought a giant kamril for seven days, defeating the monster with the knuckles of his right fist."

"What's a *kamril*?" Janner asked.

Oskar shrugged. "Nia?"

"I don't remember. *Kamril*…it sounds like *kamaral,* the Hollish word for "bird." A giant bird, maybe?"

Leeli and Oskar did their best to decipher the music notes but had little luck. Though she played softly, when she fingered the notes the way she thought it was written, the song was so terrible that they all covered their ears.

On and on Oskar worked by the light of the oil lamp while Tink returned to his sketchbook and Leeli and Podo conversed, until Janner fell asleep with his head on the old man's shoulder.

"It's time," Podo whispered.

Janner had been dreaming about the sea, a fine dream about wide blue skies and a skiff cutting through the water. He was sad to wake. The burrow was just as dark and drab as ever. The promise that they would soon emerge from the tunnels into Dugtown beneath a starry sky gave Janner a tingle of excitement, however, and he quickly stretched and shouldered his backpack.

"It's about time you lot woke up," Oskar said, donning his spectacles and leaning against the wall in an attempt to look spry and rugged. He was becoming quite the adventurer, Janner thought. The old man adjusted his lock of muddy hair and clapped Podo on the back.

Podo rolled his eyes. "Ready?"

"Yes sir," Janner said.

"Shut the door behind ye, lad," Podo said.

They ducked into the tunnel.

30

Sneem's Last Words

The door clicked shut, and Janner turned to see Podo's lantern bobbing around a bend in the tunnel. The ground was no longer dirt but smooth stone. The walls of the tunnel were far enough apart that Janner could barely touch them with the tips of his fingers. The passageway descended gently, and now and then Janner sensed other tunnels on his left and right. Podo took so many turns that Janner wasn't sure he could find his way back to their burrow if he had to.

After a long, musty hour of walking, Podo stopped, face to face with a bearded rag of a man. The man gripped a dagger in his fist and pointed it at Podo's chest. Podo had a dagger of his own trained on the Strander's belly. The man carried a sack over his shoulder, probably spoils from a thieving run.

"Where from?" the man growled.

"The East Bend," Podo growled back.

"Claxton Weaver's clan?" the man asked.

Podo pulled Claxton's pone medallion from his shirt and waved it in the man's face. "It ain't Weaver's clan no more."

"Ah," the man said with a nervous smile. His eyes flicked to the children. "Then which one of these lads is Kalmar? I'd like to meet 'im."

With a nod of permission from Podo, Tink stepped forward timidly. "I'm Kalmar."

The man winked. "Heard ye ran circles around Claxton, whackin' him with a switch till his pockets was empty and his bootstrings was tied in knots. Well done."

"Well," Tink began.

"Traipse on, then," Podo interrupted. The man gave Tink a quick nod, then slipped away into the darkness. "Everyone all right?" Podo asked with a tender eye on Nia and Leeli. "Good. We're almost there."

He led them into the next passageway on the left. After a few steps, they climbed a stone stairway until they came to what looked like a dead end. But in Strander tunnels it seemed there was no such thing as a dead end. Another hidden door slid open, and the company emerged into another round burrow with a dirt floor and a ladder that disappeared into a chimneylike opening. For a moment it felt as though they had traveled in a great circle.

"Now listen," Podo said, "and listen close. This ladder empties into the cellar of another house, but with one big difference. Dugtowners still live in this one. We're just below the heart of the city, and the folk what live in this house likely haven't a pinch of an idea there's a burrow in their cellar. We've got to creep like snails through this house lest we wake the tenants and they scream bloody terror. Earlier today we were lucky they weren't home, but more likely than not they'll be here, and they'll be sleepin' lightly. No Dugtowner can afford to sleep too deep, or they're like to wake up in an empty house."

"But if there's a way into their cellar, why don't the Stranders just steal everything anyway?" Janner asked.

"Some of the folk in these houses know about the tunnels and let the Stranders come and go as long as they get a share of the loot. Other folk don't know, and the Stranders like it that way. If they stole too much from a tunnel house, the owner might get suspicious, find the door, and seal it off. It's happened plenty. I don't know if these people know about the tunnel or not, but we're not gonna find out. We're gonna creep. Understand? Good." Podo extinguished the lantern. "Stay close."

Janner came last again, feeling his way out of the trapdoor and onto the sandy floor of the cellar. All he could hear was the careful breathing of the rest of the company. Podo eased the trapdoor closed with a thump, and Janner heard a scraping sound as Podo concealed the door with loose dirt.

"Come on," Podo whispered. "Like snails."

Janner tiptoed behind Tink, grimacing in the darkness at every tap of Leeli's crutch, every scrape of every foot on the stairs that led out of the cellar and into the house. Podo eased the door open and waved them on through a kitchen not much different from that of the Igiby cottage: four chairs and a table sat in the center of the room, a black iron stove squatted against one wall, and a shelf held stacks of plates, bowls, and canisters of spices and oils. Someone lived here, had dinner here, laughed over their meals here. Did they know Stranders slipped through the shadows while they slept?

When the family and Oskar clustered at the front door, so still and silent that Janner believed he could hear his own heartbeat, Podo put a hand on the doorknob and turned it slowly. The door creaked open, and he bustled everyone outside, then eased the door shut behind them.

Only when Podo breathed a deep sigh of relief did Janner and the others relax.

They stood in front of a nondescript wooden house, if it could be called that. It was a wooden, two-story structure, not filthy but far from clean. As far as Janner could see in both directions, the houses on either side of the road were similar. Narrow walkways were all that stood between each dwelling. No plants hung from the eaves, no paint adorned the walls; just gray building after gray building. The road was rutted and muddy. Rats and hackerels skittered in the shadows, trying in vain to avoid patches of orange torchlight.

Janner looked up at the nearest of the torch towers. Far above, a figure squatted on the platform beside the iron bowl where the bonfire raged. He hunkered like a vulture at the edge of the stand, peering down at the streets, a black shade against the whirl of flame. Not far away stood another tower with another fire and another figure, this one pacing.

The figure on the nearer tower straightened and turned, and Janner's heart leapt into his throat. The silhouette on the tower had a tail and the unmistakable stooped posture of a Fang of Dang.

"Aye, lad. I see 'im," Podo whispered. "Everyone stay here until he turns the corner. Then follow me."

They stood with their backs to the house, where the shadow of the roof's overhang hid all but the outermost tip of Oskar's belly. When the Fang made his way to the far side of the blaze, Podo burst into a run. He kept close to the houses, careful to stay under the cover of the overhangs while the others did their best to follow. Podo skidded to a halt at a wide cross street.

At the corner of the cobbled street stood a sign that read GREEN BLOSSOM AVENUE. The buildings here were brick and stone, three and four stories tall, with wide windows displaying meats and cheeses and tools for sale.

Oskar wiped his brow and looked up and down Green Blossom Avenue. "We turn left here. Toward the river."

But before Podo took his first step, a company of Fangs marched around a corner two streets away. "Back! Back!" he rasped.

In the bustle of seven people—one of them quite large—trying to reverse direction, Leeli lost her footing and fell. Janner tugged her to her feet and dragged her back.

"I'm sorry! I'm so sorry!" Leeli whispered.

"*Shh*, honey! It's not yer fault!" Podo said.

"But—" Leeli said.

"Leeli, it's okay," Janner said.

"But—" she repeated, and Podo shushed her again.

He pushed them into the narrow corridor between two buildings. All Janner could see was Podo's sweaty shirt and the old planks of the houses on either side. Louder grew the sound of marching Fangs. Janner closed his eyes, praying they would march on and the sound would fade to silence.

But the Fang company halted. Janner held his breath.

"My crutch," Leeli breathed. "I tried to tell you."

Podo hung his head.

One of the Fangs barked an order, and a set of footsteps came nearer. Janner waited for the moment when the scaly face would appear. Podo would kill it before it even knew what it had seen, but then the other Fangs would be after them. With so many Fangs on the torch towers and marching through the streets, Janner knew they wouldn't escape for long.

"A ssstick or something," the Fang said. It stood just around the corner from where they hid, so close that Janner could smell it. The Fang in the street growled something unintelligible, and the nearer Fang answered, "A crutch? Not sure what a crutch is, sir. Ssseems like I used to know…. Yes sir. Sorry, sir. I'll bring it."

The Fangs resumed their march. The family waited a long time before they eased from the corridor.

"I'm sorry, Grandpa," Leeli said with tears in her eyes.

"Hush, lass." He stroked her hair with his gnarled hand. "It's me who's sorry. If a Song Maiden of Anniera tells ye somethin', you listen." Then he added in a quieter voice, "No matter if she's a Song Maiden—if your sweet granddaughter tells ye somethin', you listen then too. Come here." Podo handed his backpack to Oskar, then boosted Leeli onto his back.

When he was sure the Fangs were gone, Podo led the company south on Green Blossom Avenue. The cobbled road was littered with horse droppings but otherwise clean. Tall buildings loomed over the street, their windows dark and covered in a layer of dust and grime. In the windows were various wares and merchandise for sale: sacks of grain, crude statues bearing dresses and coats with stiff dignity, bird cages, and forks and spoons.[1] Janner spotted a storefront that boasted one simple, beautiful word—BOOKS—and pointed it out to Oskar.

The old man shook his head and scowled, "Peddlers and crooks," he said. "Wouldn't know a good book from a bad tooth."

---

1. Knives, of course, were prohibited.

The family kept close to the buildings, careful to stay out of the glare of the torch-light. At each cross street, Podo checked the towers, and then they sprinted out of the shadows from one side to the other. It seemed that any moment another regiment of Fangs would leap from behind a building.

But finally Oskar whispered, "This is it."

They stood at the intersection of Green Blossom Avenue and another wide street called Riverside Road. Green Blossom crossed Riverside and sloped down into the black expanse of the Mighty Blapp. More tall brick storefronts lined the north side of Riverside Road, but on the south along the riverbank stood wooden boathouses bordered by docks and bridges. The wind changed, and a sharp odor filled Janner's nose.

"Ah, the sweet smell of jarp and redgill from the riverboats," Podo said with a sigh. "Been too long since I filled me belly with fish."

Tink moaned with longing and put a hand on his stomach while Janner fought the urge to gag.

Far across the river, Torrboro lay in darkness. All that could be seen of the Palace Torr or any of its surrounding structures was a wink of torchlight reflected on the surface of the river.

"Look," Oskar said, pointing down the street to the right. A series of wooden signs hung from the row of buildings and creaked in the waterfront wind: BILLY BUTTON'S APPARELLRY, TOBACCO FOR PIPES (YOUR WIFE WILL LOVE IT!), LUCKY ROCKS. Another shingle depicted an impossibly fat woman in a black dress, weeping, a handkerchief over her mouth and nose. THE ROUNDISH WIDOW, the sign read. ALE, COMFORT, AND SAILOR'S PIE. The Igibys huddled in the doorway of a shoe repair shop, and the sign above their heads read A PLACE FOR FOOTS.

Just across the street, a torch tower rose from behind the boathouses, and Janner didn't need to look to know a Fang stood at the top, watching the street for movement.

"Well," Podo whispered.

"Well," Oskar echoed, donning his spectacles with a flourish. "In the words of the great warrior Triliban Plubius the Bruised, 'Whether crushed or sheltered by the Maker's hand, 'tis beneath it we go, from breath to death.'"

"Aye," Tink said.

"On the far side of the Roundish Widow there's an alleyway," Oskar whispered. "Ronchy said to meet him there at midnight, and Maker only knows how late we are."

At that moment they heard a great many *clangs* that echoed faintly off the distant walls of Torrboro.

"It's one o'clock," Podo said.

"An hour late," Nia said.

"But he'd wait for us, wouldn't he?" Leeli asked.

"I hope so, little princess." Oskar smiled, then looked at Podo. "Ready?"

Podo took a deep breath and risked a peek at the torch tower. "No sign of the Fang. He must be on the other side."

Then from the foot of the tower that sprouted from the quay side came the grating snarl of a Fang, so close that even Podo sucked in a breath.

"Sneem!" it said. "I'm comin' up!"

"Glag! About time," answered Sneem's voice from far above. With much hissing and puffing, the Fang called Sneem skittered down the ladder in plain sight not a stone's throw away. When it reached the base of the tower, hidden behind the boathouses, the two Fangs exchanged a harsh greeting, and then the other Fang appeared above the boathouse roof, climbing the ladder.

Sneem emerged from between two boathouses directly across the street, wiping soot from its face. Janner's heart skipped a beat. The Fang walked straight toward them. It was only one, but one was all it took to alert the others. Maybe the Fang wouldn't see them. Maybe its eyes were still dim from standing so long at the bright fire and it would walk right past the Igibys. Maybe Tink's stomach wouldn't growl and Podo wouldn't burp and they would make it safe to the alleyway where help awaited.

"Sneem!" called Glag, now on the tower platform.

Only a few steps from the cobbler's door, Sneem stopped and turned. "Eh?"

"Forgot to tell you. Word has it he's back."

"The Florid Sword?" Sneem asked.

"Or whatever he calls himself. He was spotted on the west side of town already tonight, so be wary."

"Bah! Let him come. I'll skewer him like a daggerfish."

After a moment Glag said, "Do you mean, *you're* the daggerfish doing the skewering, or do you mean you'll skewer him like *he's* a daggerfish that you're trying to stab in the river?"

Sneem cocked his snaky head sideways to sort out the question. "Either way, the Florid Sword gets skewered, don't he?"

"I sssuppose," said Glag, "but it might be harder to stab him if he was swimming about in the water like a daggerfish. Them are fast. But if *you* was the daggerfish, you'd just leap out of the river and jab him, right?"

Sneem thought about this for a moment, then said, "I'll get 'im. Like a fish."

Please keep talking, Janner thought. *As long as they're talking, Sneem won't turn around and see us. Maybe they'll go back and forth like this until dawn, or until Peet appears to rescue us, or until the Fang curls up and goes to sleep right there in the street.*

And who is the Florid Sword?

Podo tapped Janner's shoulder and mouthed the words, *"Be ready."* He slid Leeli from his back and carefully drew his sword. Janner and Tink did likewise, wincing at every creak in the leather of their packs as they moved. Maybe if they were quick enough, Sneem wouldn't have a chance to sound the alarm.

The Igiby boys and Podo moved quietly in front of Nia, Leeli, and Oskar. The three shining blades extended beyond the canopy shadow, floating in the torchlight as if in the grip of ghosts. Janner was afraid but eager to see Sneem's surprise when he turned to find three figures with bright blades leaping—like daggerfish—from the shadows.

The Fang on the tower bid farewell, and Sneem waved with the nearest thing to friendliness Janner had ever witnessed among Fangs.

When Sneem turned around, he took a single step and stopped. But he wasn't looking at the Igibys. His black eyes were aimed at the rooftop above them.

"The Florid Sword!" Sneem cried.

Those were his last words.

31

In the Alley of the Roundish Widow

The Florid Sword leapt from the roof of the cobbler's building, bounced off the canopy, flipped through the air, and landed graceful as a cat behind Sneem. He wore a black cape, black boots, and black gloves, and had black hair that hung to his shoulders. Everything about him was black as coal, including his mask. The whites of his eyes shone. He thrust his narrow sword and put a grisly end to the Fang. Janner caught the white flash of his teeth when the man smiled.

"To be sure, Sneem, thou fiend, the Florid Sword hath run you through like unto a bolt of iron lightning piercing the watery depths of the Mighty Blapp, may she run wide and muddy all the days of mine own life! Flayed by my blade! Aha!"

Glag sputtered in outrage from the tower platform. The Florid Sword spun, and his cape whooshed in a graceful circle. He unslung a bow from his shoulder, notched an arrow, and let it fly. First there was a *thonk,* then a moan, then the sound of Glag's body crashing through the roof of the boathouse.

"And thou!" cried the Florid Sword as he slung his bow over his shoulder again and glared at the hole in the roof. "Glag, the fallen foul fool! Fah!" He straightened and flourished his cape, then yanked his blade from Sneem's limp body and wiped it on a patch of the creature's leather armor.

Podo, Tink, and Janner never moved. All three of their mouths hung open. Janner made out a bright red symbol on the front of the man's black shirt. An F and an S curled and swooped like thorny vines across his chest.

The Florid Sword set his bright gaze on the Igibys. "And who on this coal black night art thou?"

"I'm Podo Helmer. This is my family."

"Helmer. Family. Words, nothing more! And more words I have for you. Three of them: The Florid Sword! I am he! Aha!"

Fang footsteps thudded in the distance, louder with each step. The Florid Sword grabbed Sneem's scaly ankle with both hands and dragged him toward the river without another word.

"What was that all about?" Tink asked.

"The Florid Sword," Podo said with admiration. "Never heard of him."

"I've heard talk of a hero who swoops down from rooftops," Oskar said, "who foils the Stranders when they're up to no good and takes great pleasure in upsetting the Fang rule in this part of Skree. I've never heard him called the Florid Sword before, though."

"Well, who is he?" Nia asked.

"Nobody knows."

Janner caught himself smiling. He imagined climbing the buildings, bounding from rooftop to rooftop in a black disguise, Fangs in pursuit.

"Look," Tink said.

The man in black was barely visible in the shadows of the riverside docks, but after a faint splash, the bright red emblem on his chest reappeared as he approached the Igibys again. Janner and Tink were so enraptured with the mysterious hero, they nearly forgot that a Fang regiment was drawing near.

"Be thou gone, friends! Take cover!" the Florid Sword cried. "'Tis well after midnight, and thou shan't be spared if thou art snared!" The swordsman waved, bowed grandly, and sprinted up the center of Green Blossom Avenue.

Podo sheathed his sword and boosted Leeli onto his back, then bustled everyone down the street to the Roundish Widow. Just as Oskar said, between the tavern and the next building lay a narrow alleyway.

Janner was first into the shadows. Old crates were strewn here and there, along with a pile of cracked dishes and a bucket of rusty nails. Two figures stood, startling Janner so badly that he nearly tripped. He blinked, unable to make out any details in the darkness. The figures—men—made no further movement and didn't speak.

When Podo trotted up with Leeli on his back, Oskar broke the tense silence.

"I can't see clearly, old friend. Is that you?"

"It is," came the answer. The voice croaked like a digtoad.

"Ah! Good! I'm sorry we're late."

"It's nothing. I'm glad you're safe. The Florid Sword is about tonight. He's got the Fangs alert and unhappy." Janner heard fighting in the distance.

Podo pushed forward and extended his hand. "Podo Helmer. Ye must be Ronchy McHiggins."

The man nodded. Janner's eyes adjusted to the gloom, and he saw that Ronchy was a small man, much smaller than his voice suggested. He wore an apron covered with grease and handprints. It was too dark to see much about his face other than that his hair was slicked back and his moustache, wider than his head, curled out like the antennae of a grasshopper.

Podo turned to the other man. "And who're you?"

"I'm Landers. Migg Landers. I'll be your guide to the Ice Prairies." He was nearly as tall as Podo and at least as strong. Like Oskar, he was mostly bald, but unlike Oskar, he didn't bother trying to hide it. "Been there many times myself, and I can't imagine why you'd want to go. But Ronchy here says you can pay. You *can* pay, right?" His voice was smooth and careful; something about it bothered Janner.

"Aye. We can pay," said Podo.

Landers held out a hand and waited.

For a moment, Podo didn't move. Then he grunted and said, "Oskar, me pack if you please."

Oskar handed the pack to Podo, who opened it and removed a pouch without taking his eyes from Migg Landers.

"This should be plenty."

"Skreean coin or gold?"

"A little of both. More gold than gray."

The man poured a few of the coins into his hand and inspected them, then nodded and tucked the pouch away. "Fine. That'll be all, Ronchy."

"Oskar, you'll be fine with Migg here," Ronchy croaked. "He's one of Gammon's men. He'll get you and your friends safe past the Barrier."

"Thank you, old friend," said Oskar.

Then Ronchy McHiggins looked straight at Janner. His eyes moved to Tink, then to Leeli, then back to Oskar. "It's true?" he asked.

"Yes," Oskar said. "It's true, Maker help us."

"Aye." Ronchy turned to go. "Maker help us."

He opened the side door to the Roundish Widow and stepped through. The door lock clicked into place behind him.

"Remove your packs and settle in. We'll be here for a while," said Migg Landers.

"Why?" asked Podo.

Migg took a threatening step forward so that he and Podo stood nose to nose. "For starters, old fella, don't question Migg Landers. If I tell you to put on a dress and dance a whirl, you'll do it, no questions asked. Since you and I are new acquaintances, I'll not give you a pounding this time."

Janner was shocked at the unwelcome change that had come over their guide, but he also felt a little sorry for him. Landers was under the mistaken impression that Podo Helmer was too old to be any trouble.

Podo stood tight as a bowstring, his bushy eyebrows low and angry, but he held his tongue. After a moment, he smiled a whiskery smile. "I understand, young fella. We'll do as ye say."

"Good. To answer your question, pappy, we can't go anywhere till the next bell tolls and the Fangs change their guard. That means you've got an hour to bide. So doff your packs, plant yourselves on the cobble, and keep quiet while I check the street."

Podo nodded. As Landers walked to the alley opening and peeked around a corner, Podo motioned for the boys to drop their packs. "It's going to be a long trip, lads," he said. "We need him, and if he has to feel like he's the king of the heap, then I'll keep me smelly mouth clapped shut for now. It ain't a battle worth fightin'. Speakin' of the king of the heap," Podo said, removing Claxton's pone from around his neck, "this belongs to you." He tossed the medallion to Tink.

Outside the confines of the alley came the steady *clop-clop-clop* of marching, the bark of commands, and the crack of whips in the distance. *Was Dugtown always this way or only when the Florid Sword was up to his mischief?* Janner wondered. It would've been better if the caped hero hadn't chosen this particular night to carouse, yet Janner was glad to have seen him in action. He relished the thought of a common Dugtowner—a cook or a woodsmith, perhaps—donning his disguise in some secret cellar chamber and then creeping into the streets to fight the Fangs of Dang.

"I don't like the idea of traveling all the way to the Ice Prairies with someone as mean as him," said Leeli as she settled herself on the ground.

The family and Oskar sat in a circle behind a stack of crates, their backpacks in a pile beside the back door of the tavern.

"Don't worry, lass," Podo said. "Once we get past the wall, I plan to teach Migg Landers a lesson on respectin' his elders." He craned his neck to see over the crates. "What's he doin', anyway?"

Migg Landers stood at the entrance to the alley, peeking around the corner at Riverside Road. Something wasn't right. Janner tried to ignore the tickle in his stomach, a sense of warning he couldn't explain. Migg Landers wasn't an admirable man, but from what Oskar said, Dugtown had a great shortage of admirable men. Ronchy said he could be trusted, so what else could they do?

Tink fidgeted with the pone, chewing happily on a strip of diggle meat. The adults spoke in whispers, and Janner gathered they were discussing their food supply,

guessing at how long their journey might take—things he would have found interesting if not for this nagging worry at the front of his mind.

Then he realized something had changed. The streets were silent. The drone of
marching Fangs, the pop of the whips—all gone.

"Grandpa!" Janner whispered. "Something's wrong!"

Podo glanced at the alley entrance and froze. The look on the old pirate's face was
enough to tell Janner that his feelings about Migg Landers were correct.

"LANDERS, YOU TRAITOR!" Podo bellowed. This image of Podo would stay with
Janner for a long time—this stout old mast of a warrior, eyes ablaze, the muscles in
his shoulders and neck tight as sails in a storm.

Leeli screamed so long and loud that every Fang and Dugtowner within an arrow-
shot of the alley must have heard.

"Ronchy, no!" Oskar groaned. "How could you?"

Janner turned, dreading what he would find at the entrance to the alleyway,
though from the bitter stench in his nostrils he already knew.

"I thank you kindly for the coins, old man," Migg Landers said with a grin.

Behind him hissed a wall of Fangs, swords bared, teeth dripping, scales glinting
yellow in the torchlight.

Then, to Janner's horror, a Fang leapt forward and sank its teeth into Migg Landers's shoulder. The big man screamed, shuddered, and crumpled to the ground in a
heap.

"Nowhere to run, Igibysss," said the Fang.

32

Ronchy McHiggins Makes a Discovery

The Fangs had learned by now not to give Podo Helmer time to think. They rushed forward, their swords trained on Podo and only Podo. Janner heaved the pile of crates into their path. The Fangs batted and hacked the crates away and pushed forward.

Janner was certain Podo would leap into the fray and fight to his death rather than allow the Fangs to capture his grandchildren—and leap he did, but not at the Fangs.

Podo slammed his shoulder into the thick side door of the Roundish Widow. The door broke into pieces, and the sound of splintering wood mingled with the sound of splintering bone as Podo's shoulder and ribs cracked. He tumbled to the floor with a cry of pain, but in one motion he rolled over, grabbed the nearest backpack—which happened to be his own—and disappeared into the tavern, cursing Migg Landers all the while. Nia swept Leeli into her arms and rushed through the door after him.

"Go!" Janner screamed at Oskar. He jiggled through the doorway sweeping up the boys' backpacks as he went. Janner grabbed Tink by the arm and rushed through the door, skidding on bits of broken wood.

Claws scraped at his back and legs. He heard the clacking of Fang teeth and the squeak of Fang armor, and felt the heat of Fang breath on his neck. Janner knew Gnag still wanted the children alive, because it would have been an easy thing in that moment for the Fangs to run him and his brother through. But in their scramble to seize the boys, the beasts slammed into the doorway as one and jammed.

Janner crashed into a table and nearly fell. As he ran, he strained to see where the rest of his family had gone, but the tavern was pitch black. All he knew was that he still had Tink's elbow in his grip.

It took the Fangs little time to regroup and enter the tavern in single file, but by then Janner had felt his way through a swinging door and into the common room of the tavern. Two large windows that looked out on Riverside Road faintly illuminated the tables and chairs spaced throughout the room. Janner heard his family somewhere ahead and the Fangs behind.

"Mama!" he cried. "Grandpa!"

"Here!" Nia answered, just as Podo kicked open the front door and the others darted out to the street.

"Come on!" Janner said to Tink.

But the brothers never made it to the door.

From the street came the sound of battle. Podo appeared beyond the doorway, a white-haired terror swinging his sword even as he hugged his wounded side with his other arm. The shadows of the battle stretched long across the room. Janner saw with black dread that Fangs surrounded his grandfather.

He and Tink were stuck. If they ran outside, they'd find themselves in the thick of the fight, and they had no weapons—Oskar had their packs. Behind them, more Fangs poured into the house.

Janner could see the outline of his little brother's face, the glint of his wide, frightened eyes looking to Janner for help. But he didn't know how to help. He was only twelve! How was he supposed to know what a Throne Warden would do? He wanted to ask Podo, or Peet, or Nia—or Esben.

Then came Podo's voice from outside, sputtered between parries and thrusts of his sword: "GET BACK TO THE BURROW! BOYS! MEET AT THE BURR—"

Podo's voice cut short. But another, familiar voice joined it.

"Aha! Thou smelly snakish brutes! Beware the steely shine of the Florid Sword's, er, sword!"

Outside the window, the caped figure leapt into the fight. With one hand, he swung his sword with frightening speed, while the other rested casually on his hip. The cluster of Fangs attacking Podo turned as one and rushed the man in black.

The swinging door behind the boys crashed open and Fangs poured into the shadowy common room. The only thing Janner could think to do was duck. He and Tink scrambled under a table and crawled to the farthest corner of the room. The Fangs sped toward the open front door, crashing through tables and chairs as they ran. Janner and Tink, on hands and knees, held their breath and watched the scaly legs of at least thirty Fangs rush past.

"And now I must needs flee," said the Florid Sword, "for thy numbers art full of bigness! Aha!"

The clash of swords ceased. Janner listened for Podo's voice, for Leeli's scream, for any sign of his family, but he heard nothing except the mutter and moan of tired and wounded Fangs.

"Gone?" said one of the Fangs.

"Yes sir. It was the Florid—"

"Don't even ssay his name."

"Aye sssir. Well, *he* came and we got distracted from the old man—he's a good fighter, 'e is, for a one-legged fella. Took down seven of me Fangs and wounded five others besides. And the fat one, 'e just grabbed a sword and spun in circles so fast we thought 'e might up and float away. Tried to get past 'em to grab the girl but before we could—as I said, sir, we had 'em till the Florid—er, till *he* showed up."

"Lost 'em again, then," said the leader as they moved away. "Khrak won't be happy."

"Khrak's never happy, sir."

Janner and Tink looked at each other in the darkness.

"They got away," Tink whispered.

"I hope so," Janner said.

"But what about us?"

"I don't know."

"What will we do?"

"I don't know."

Long after the last Fang disappeared, the brothers hid under the table and held tight to each other, more alone than they had ever been.

Ronchy McHiggins wasn't a bad man, though he enjoyed his life among the vigilantes and thieves of Dugtown. He enjoyed the stories, the excitement, the way one never knew who might walk through the front door of the tavern with a tale to tell and stolen coins to spend on a plate of sailor's pie.

Ronchy didn't talk much, unlike the other tavern owners who prattled on about problems and rumors and the way this customer jilted him four years ago or that Fang shattered a window just for the laugh of it. Ronchy McHiggins *listened.* He paid attention. That was why Gammon liked him. Gammon knew Ronchy could tell him what was happening in Dugtown, from the construction of more torch towers to the discovery of another Strander tunnel to the movements of the Fangs from one district to another.

So when Ronchy heard word from Glipwood—from a pair of ridgerunners—
that some Annieran heirs, children from the sound of it, were on the run in Glipwood
Forest, he resolved to tell Gammon about it when next he saw him.

Gammon came to Dugtown every few months to check in with Ronchy and who
knew how many other members of his secret force scattered throughout Torrboro and
Dugtown. He looked different every time he came. A master of camouflage, he was,
and a master of deceit. How else could he have survived these many years, gathering
weapons, mustering fellow rebels, and amassing an army in the Ice Prairies that might
someday overthrow the Fangs and banish them from Skree forever? Gammon was a
clever one, all right, or he'd have been found out like all the other fools who dared to
defy Gnag the Nameless and his Fangs of Dang.

Only days before, Gammon had appeared in the Roundish Widow, hobbling like
an old man and filthy as a cave blat. It was such a convincing disguise that Ronchy
had twice batted him with a broom in an attempt to shoo him from the tavern before
he realized who he was whacking.

If only Gammon had come three days later. Then Ronchy would have known
what to do about fat Oskar N. Reteep showing up for the first time in months, wanting to smuggle three children and their guardians to the Ice Prairies. Ronchy knew
immediately these children had to be the rumored Annieran heirs. It was no secret that
Reteep was from Glipwood and believed the tales about the distant isle—the Shining
Isle, it was called in stories.

What was Ronchy to do but help? How was he to know Migg Landers was as rotten as he smelled? If only Gammon had been there, he would've told Ronchy what to
do. Likely, Gammon himself would have smuggled them north.

Now everything was a mess.

The tavern was a mess, and his alleyway door was broken to bits. The children
had been so young, their features so fine, their eyes so hopeful when they looked at
him. And old Reteep, probably dead now or bleeding in a dungeon.

This was what he got for trying to help.

Ronchy still wore his nightgown and cap. He hadn't slept a wink the night before.
He had locked and barred the alley door, trudged upstairs and into bed, and put
Reteep and the rest out of his mind—until he heard the awful scream. The old pirate
called Landers a traitor, then came a crash, then the sound of his beloved tavern being
wrecked. Rather than facing the mess in the dark, Ronchy had lain in bed all night,
dreading what he would find in the morning.

At the first hint of dawn, he came downstairs with a heavy heart, wondering what had become of Reteep, his friends, and the children.

He swept what was left of his back door into a dustpan and tossed the debris into the alley, then pushed through the swinging door and into the common room. He took stock of the windows (none broken, which was a nice surprise), the front door (open but intact, thank the Maker), and the wreck of tables and chairs (seven broken chairs, three broken tables). With a heavy sigh, Ronchy righted the fallen tables and scooted chairs under them. In a few hours his first customers would wander in, and they would want a place to sit. The less they knew about his involvement with last night's events, the better.

Ronchy found them in the back corner of the room. Two boys, asleep in each other's arms. Their faces were filthy, streaked with either tears or sweat, the smaller one's head resting on the older one's chest.

It was such an unexpected thing to discover that Ronchy McHiggins stood over them for a long time, unwilling to disturb such a simple, beautiful thing. The dawn sang through the windows in fat, golden beams, and to his great confusion, tears rose from somewhere deep within him and streamed down his face.

He decided to help them.

33

The Sundering

When Janner woke, he saw before his face the antennae of a bug.

Then the fog in his mind cleared, and he recognized the gaunt face and sweeping moustache of Ronchy McHiggins. The previous night's events came back to him with a panic that caused him to gasp and sit up straight. The movement woke Tink, who yawned and rubbed his eyes.

"Breakfsssst," he mumbled; then he too remembered their situation and opened his eyes as wide as his sleepiness allowed.

"Hush, young fellers," Ronchy said, his croaking voice a strange comfort to Janner. "It's all right. I don't know where your keepers or your sister are, but the Fangs aren't here. For the moment." Ronchy glanced at his front windows. "They may be back soon with questions for me, though, and you can't be here. They might sack the whole place just for the joy of it. Happens all the time."

Janner shook his head, trying to take in all Ronchy was telling him, but sleep still clouded his thinking. "Wait—you betrayed us! Migg Landers—"

"Betrayed *me,* lad. I intended to get you safe to the Ice Prairies, just as I figured Gammon would want me to. Either Migg Landers is one of Gammon's men and he has reasons for wanting you in the hands of the Fangs, or Migg Landers is a thief and a liar. I think Migg is the problem, not Gammon. But then, I'm just an old tavern boss. What do I know?"

"What...where do we go?" Tink asked.

"Not sure yet, but you need to be scarce by the time customers start filing in. Children are a rare thing in this town—Annieran ones even rarer." He winked.

How did he know they were Annieran? Janner thought. And why were children rare in Dugtown?

Then he remembered the burrow. The last thing Podo had said before the Florid Sword appeared was that they should meet at the burrow. He assumed his grandfather meant the burrow on the hill outside of town, the one where they had spent the night. If indeed the others escaped, Podo must have found another Strander tunnel, and the family could be back at the burrow even now, waiting for Janner and Tink to arrive.

Janner stood and pulled Tink up with him.

"I don't mean to trouble you, Mister McHiggins, sir," said Tink, "but do you have—"

"Breakfast? Of course I do. Nobody leaves the Roundish Widow with a rumble in his belly. The rolls should be done by now." Ronchy led the boys into the kitchen, removed a pan of hot, buttered rolls from the oven, and served them with a bowlful of sugarberries mashed into a curious paste, which they ate with wooden spoons. Tink guzzled a cup of water from Ronchy's cistern, burped, then asked nicely for a refill.

"Mister McHiggins, we need to find our family," Janner said finally. "There's a Strander burrow at the edge of town—"

"*Shh!* Keep your voice low, lad, if you're going to talk about such things. Never know when a Strander might have an ear to the wall. They don't take it easy on you if you blab their secrets, and if you know the location of a burrow, then that's a *big* secret. Leave me out of it."

"Sorry, sir," Janner said.

"We just need to get to the east side of Dugtown, up on the hill," Tink said between bites. He had already finished three buttered rolls and the second cup of water and was slurping up the sugarberries.

"The hill on the east side of Dugtown," Ronchy repeated, twirling his moustache between his thumb and forefinger. "Near the river?"

"Yes sir," Janner said.

"Ah. That's a fair walk from here, but it's easy enough to find. Just follow Riverside Road till it wends away from the river…"

The tavern boss croaked out directions, explaining to them how to take a shortcut to avoid a dangerous stretch of Riverside Road.

The more he talked, the higher the sun flew, and without warning, Dugtown awoke. Outside the Roundish Widow, wagons squeaked past, people murmured and grouched, and birds fluttered about in flocks. The great beast of the city stirred into motion, its citizens crawling about on its back like fleas on a dog.

"Now, you lads be careful. This city was a fearful spot long before the Fangs came to Skree. Now that trolls and lizards traipse the streets, things are worse than ever. The Fangs drive us like slaves. They don't pay for their drink or their food or for the damage when they fight. They mock and imprison, and the children—" Ronchy's croaking voice clogged. "They take the children. There are hardly any left in the south side of the city. The Black Carriage comes and takes what it pleases, be it child or mother. How could they kidnap a mother? Even Stranders have mothers and shrink from doing a woman harm, especially a woman with a child."

Janner saw a colored drawing on the wall beside the cupboard. In it, a younger, happier Ronchy McHiggins stood beside a pretty woman who cradled a baby.

"I'm sorry, sir," he said.

Ronchy took a deep breath. He turned and nodded at the boys. "Go. Be wary." Then he dried his hands on his apron and shuffled through the swinging door and into the common room, where he croaked a greeting to his first customers.

Janner and Tink stood alone on the threshold of the door that led to the alley.

The tidy kitchen of the Roundish Widow was a hen's nest of safety, a place where the nearest thing they had to a friend had fed them and filled their flasks with clean water. On the other side of the door stretched a world of Fangs and trolls and scoundrels—a world through which they must pass in order to find their family again.

Janner peeked around the corner and into the alley. To his relief, Migg Landers's body was gone, probably tossed into the river sometime in the night.

"Ready?" he asked, feeling the gravity of the moment.

"Yep." Tink scratched his armpit with one hand and picked sugarberry seeds from his teeth with the other.

Janner led his little brother into the alley and left the Roundish Widow behind.

Looking out from the quiet alley at Riverside Road, all Janner could think of was the thundering white water of the Mighty Blapp. Wagons, horses, trolls, Fangs, merchants, fishermen, boat captains, carriages, cries of surprise and anger and irritation, squeaking wheels, tromping boots, jangling pots and pans, cracking whips—all meshed into a violent, unstoppable rush that scared Janner frozen.

Never had he seen so many people in one place. He had believed the Dragon Day Festival to be a great ruckus—and for the Glipwood Township, it was—but now he saw that Glipwood and its humble festival was nothing but a quaint diversion in a quiet corner of a giant world. This was one street in a city of hundreds of such streets, on a continent of many such cities, in a world of—well, nobody knew how many continents sprawled across Aerwiar.[1] Janner watched the pandemonium with the feeling he was about to leap into the white water of the Mighty Blapp and be swept away to certain death.

"Look at all these people!" Tink said, beaming.

"Yeah. This is going to be harder than I thought," Janner said gravely.

"According to Ronchy's directions, we need to turn left," Tink said. "Left is east. Come on."

And before Janner could stop him, Tink plunged into the river of people.

After several harrowing minutes fighting the current, being bumped, cursed at, elbowed, and tripped, Janner realized the traffic on the river side of the street moved east, the direction they wanted to go.

"Tink!" Janner cried. "Get to the other side of the street! The *other side!*"

Tink ran into the path of a carriage, and the horse reared. Tink darted to the right and out of sight. With great annoyance, the horse and driver pushed on. Janner waited until the carriage passed, then ducked in front of a whiskery fisherman toting a string of redgill over one shoulder.

He stood on his tiptoes in the narrow refuge in the center of the street, where the crowd grumbled past him on either side in different directions. There was no sign of Tink. Janner wanted to call out for him but was wary of drawing too much attention to himself. Then Tink's head appeared above the crowd, under the awning of a boathouse on the far side of the street.

Janner clenched his teeth, waited for a space to open, and dashed into the traffic. He pushed for the far side and nearly fell twice. Before he reached the boathouse, an empty space, a sort of bubble in the crowd, appeared around Janner, and an unbearable odor filled his nostrils. He didn't need to turn around to know a troll was nearby. Janner lowered his head and pushed through to the roadside.

Tink stood on a barrel, staring wide-eyed at the troll as it rumbled past. Dugtowners with purple faces scrambled to escape its smell. The troll thudded along, twirling a club around its finger on a loop of twine. It looked happy as a fed baby, and its chin glistened with slobber.

"Don't do that!" Janner snapped as he yanked Tink from the barrel by his shirt collar.

"Do what?" Tink jerked away from Janner and glared at him.

---

1. The maps bore great blank swaths to the far west of Skree, and nobody knew what lay east of the Killridge Mountains. These unknown areas beyond the edges of the maps were referred to as "the places beyond the edges of the maps."

"We need to stay close. All we did was cross the street, and already I lost you. The only way we'll both get to the burrow is if we stay together."

"Why? We both know where it is," Tink said hotly, straightening to his full height, which was a head shorter than his brother. "I was standing right there when McHiggins gave you directions. Do you think I'm not smart enough to find it alone?"

"It's my job to protect you."

"What if I don't want to be protected?"

"You don't have a choice. I'm a Throne Warden. You're a king. That's the way it is. I have to keep you safe. I have to get you to the Ice Prairies."

"Well, what if I don't *want* to go to the Ice Prairies? What if I want to go home?"

"Are you serious?" Janner rolled his eyes. "We *can't* go home. Besides, Glipwood was never really our home, anyway. Our home is Anniera, and you're the king."

Tink sighed and turned away, mumbling something under his breath.

"What did you say?" Janner demanded.

"Nothing."

"Tink! *What did you say?*"

Tink gave Janner a seething look. "I said, 'I don't want to be king.' And don't call me Tink anymore. My name is Kalmar."

The crowds moved past in a blur, too busy to notice two boys arguing in the shade of a boathouse.

Janner lowered his voice. "Fine, then, *Kalmar.* But it doesn't matter if you want to be king or not. I'm the Throne Warden, and I'm going to get you safe to the burrow. If you don't want to be king, tell it to Mama or Grandpa."

Tink's eyes burned, and a scowl spread across his face, a look Janner had only seen when the two of them wrestled or when they played Ships and Sharks—when Tink was trapped, immobile, unable to move his arms or his legs. It was a look of anger, but even more, it was a look of panic.

Then Tink said something that cut to Janner's heart.

"I don't want this. I don't want any of it. Leave me alone."

And he ran.

34

A Watcher in the Shadows

Janner stood motionless, staring at the empty space where Tink had just been. His skin went clammy, and he realized in a snap that he was alone.

It wasn't just that Tink had run away, Janner realized, though the thought made him so angry he wanted to punch his brother in the nose—it was that Tink had abandoned him.

The river of Dugtowners seemed to grow in speed and size and hostility. The burrow where he desperately hoped the rest of his family waited suddenly seemed impossibly far away, as unreachable a destination as the moon itself.

Why would Tink—Janner refused to think of him as Kalmar—do such a thing? He knew his little brother was uncomfortable with the idea of being king, but Janner was unprepared for this.

Perhaps this was Tink's way of proving himself to his older brother. Janner remembered the many times he had thought the worst of Tink, only to be proven wrong. It was true he had been hard on his younger brother, probably too hard. But this?

Fine, he thought bitterly. *Let him find his own way to the burrow.*

Janner steeled his nerves, rubbed his hands together, put his head down, and joined the mad flow of traffic on Riverside Road.

He tripped, hopped, and ducked, straining to read the street signs over countless heads as he passed. Ronchy said if he took a left at Crempshaw Way, then a right on Tilling Street, he would eventually merge with Riverside again. He said it was the best way to bypass the busiest and most dangerous stretch, where the Fangs were ferried across the Blapp to Torrboro.

Janner looked for Tink, craning his neck in every direction as he bustled along, but saw no trace. It would have been hard to find anyone in such chaos, especially someone as small and quick as Tink. Janner began planning the many things he would scream at his little brother once they were safe in the burrow again.

His thoughts were interrupted by the glimpse of a street sign: CREMPSHAW WAY. A crow perched at the top of the pole. Janner zipped between fishermen, seamstresses, and donkeys harnessed to carts laden with fish meat, until he stood with his hands on his knees, winded, only a few doors past Crempshaw Way.

The door behind him swung open, and out came four Fangs of Dang. They laughed and staggered down the step to the sidewalk where Janner stood. He froze and stared at his feet. The Fangs burped and cackled past, then disappeared into the crowd. Janner darted past a store that sold fishnets, then around the corner to Crempshaw Way. Crempshaw stretched upward from the river and into the heart of Dugtown.

Angry as he was at Tink, Janner hoped to catch up to him here. He told himself he was mainly worried for Tink's safety, but he was just as worried for his own. He tried not to imagine what might happen if he were to lose his way in this maze of streets.

A woman with a kind face carried a basket down the street toward Janner.

"Excuse me, ma'am?" he said timidly. "I'm looking for my brother. Have you seen a little boy, a little shorter than I am…?"

She regarded him sadly, then passed without a word and turned into the rush of Riverside Road. The same was true of everyone who saw him. They looked at him with great sorrow, said nothing, and moved on.

Janner followed Crempshaw past several cross streets, dirt roads lined with plain gray houses much like the one where they had emerged the previous night, until, muttering thanks to Ronchy McHiggins and his good directions, Janner finally saw the word TILLING on a street sign.

The road stretched away in both directions, another gray lane littered with clucking chickens, shards of pottery, and old broken boards. The street boasted no houses, only deserted storefronts with broken windows, the doors long since stolen and used elsewhere. Behind Janner, men and women moved up and down Crempshaw in forlorn silence, but Tilling stood empty as a graveyard. Janner was glad it was still morning, because he wasn't sure he would have the courage to walk such a dead street in the dark of night.

He passed empty building after empty building, looking back with longing at Crempshaw, where at least he wasn't alone. When the dead street curved to the right and concealed Crempshaw completely, he called in a voice barely above a whisper, "Tink?"

There was no echo. The empty windows and doorways seemed to swallow the sound. Broken glass cracked beneath his feet. Rats scurried in the walls of the old buildings. Crows cursed and fussed on perches in the windows of the upper rooms and on the rails of crooked balconies.

"Tink!" he called again, louder.

Janner imagined eyes watching him from the shadows, eyes attached to trolls or Fangs or Stranders waiting for the right moment to burst onto the street and seize him.

So he did what any normal twelve-year-old boy would do: he ran as fast as he could.

He leapt over piles of garbage and weaved between the bricks and rotten barrels that littered the road, aching to reach the far end of Tilling Street where Ronchy had promised it emptied onto Riverside Road again. He no longer cared how much noise he made. If someone or something heard him puff by, they would have to be fast indeed to catch him, frightened as he was.

But the road came to an abrupt end. Janner skidded to a halt before a stone wall as high and flat as the old brick buildings on either side. There was no way out other than the way he'd come.

Why would Ronchy send him this way? He had seemed so kind, so helpful, and the little man had been certain this was the safest, shortest route to the east side of Dugtown.

Janner turned his back to the wall so he could see the street down which he had just run. Nothing moved. That was good. If anything had been lurking in the shadows, it would have attacked by now. In the distance, Janner heard the muted sounds of a busy street. If he could just get over the wall, he could find his way to Riverside Road without having to brave the creepy emptiness of Tilling Street again.

He crept to the alley between the two nearest buildings, but the rear was blocked by another wall. After inspecting a few more alleyways, he discovered that the wall stretched seamlessly behind every building on either side of the street. He was at the very end of what would make an excellent trap.

What worried him most, even more than Ronchy's faulty directions, was that Tink wasn't here either.

Janner sighed. Some Throne Warden *he* was turning out to be. He had to find Tink, and he couldn't do that cowering at the end of Tilling Street.

He took a deep breath and ran back the way he had come, not out of fear for himself this time but because he was desperate to find his little brother.

Halfway back, he heard voices. Without a second thought, Janner ducked through the doorway of the nearest building. The floor was covered with dust and bits of broken glass. The rear of the building was draped in shadows, and against the right wall, a rickety wooden stairway rose past the ceiling. The voices drew nearer. Janner sneaked behind the stairway and peeked through the space between two steps.

Three men appeared in the road. Their long hair was matted and black, and they wore dark clothes and spoke with such thick Dugtowner accents that Janner had difficulty understanding what they said. He heard the word "forks," which sounded more like "farrrks." The men's eyes shifted in a way that reminded him of thwaps in the garden back home. More than once, he was sure one of the scraggly men looked directly at him, but each time the man's eyes moved on, untroubled.

It was so quiet in the decrepit building that Janner could hear his own heart beating. A spider skittered across the step to kill a fly caught in its web, and he heard that too. The dead hush of Tilling Street made every tiny sound conspicuous, from the crunch of dirt beneath Janner's boot to the harsh voices of the men outside. So after only a few moments in his hiding place, Janner became aware of another sound, very near.

Somewhere just behind him, in the deeper shadows, something was breathing.

He closed his eyes and begged the Maker to let it be his imagination. Slowly, very slowly, he turned and saw, in the corner of the hollow beneath the stair, the unmistakable glint of two eyes watching him.

Janner was unable to move. If a gargan rockroach or a toothy cow had appeared before him, he wouldn't have been more afraid. Whoever—or whatever—it was stared at him with such malicious satisfaction that Janner felt like the fly in the spider's web.

The figure lunged.

35

The Hags and the Ragmen

Dirty hands clawed at Janner's neck and face. Hot, rank breath choked him.

An old hag with gray-brown locks of matted hair, bloodshot eyes, and one very long black tooth, reached from the dark.

Janner shrieked. The old woman recoiled and clapped her dirty hands over her ears just long enough for him to slip away.

The men outside saw him burst through the door, his face as white as the moon, screaming so long and loud that beggars and hags emerged from every broken building on the street. When they saw Janner, every ragged soul on Tilling Street lurched or loped or bounded after the screaming boy.

The barren street seemed to stretch forever. Crempshaw must lie directly ahead, but Tilling curved and curved endlessly. Had he really come this far? Janner risked a look behind him. What he saw produced in his legs a speed that rivaled even Tink.

Tilling Street was anything but dead. It crawled with men and women even more broken and forgotten than the buildings where they lived, and they were doing their best to keep Janner from getting away.

Finally, just ahead, he saw a horse and wagon descending the hill toward Riverside Road. Crempshaw!

But between him and the other road gathered more beggars and hags. Janner thought for a moment of lowering his head and barreling through the people just as Podo had shouldered down the door in the alley the night before, but there were too many.

A man in rags limped from a doorway on the left, and Janner did the only thing he could. He ran straight for the man, clenched his jaw, shut his eyes, and slammed into him.

The man flew backward and landed on his back. Janner tumbled over him, found his feet, and sped into the old building. He found the stairs and took them two at a time, trying to ignore the cries just behind him as the throng pursued.

The top of the stairs opened onto a landing with three doorways. Rags, blankets, wads of paper, and hunks of charred wood littered the floor and poured from each bedroom. It was hard to believe anyone would choose such a place to live, but then, these buildings had once housed businesses, offices, workshops, homes. Had it only been since the Fangs arrived that things had gotten so bad? Who were these people?

Janner froze on the landing, unsure which way to go. What had he been thinking, coming upstairs? He felt like the fly in the spider's web again, struggling in vain against the predator at his heels. The stairs had been a mistake. Maybe he had time to go back down and find another way out of the building—

"We hear you, child," came a wrecked voice at the foot of the stair. "And there is no way out. We will have you. We must."

Janner ran into the room to his left, slipping on the junk that covered the floor. In the middle of the right wall was a window, and he climbed out and crouched on the sill. Below lay an alley, and across from Janner stood another building with another window. The hags and beggars would see him any moment. To the right, the alley was blocked by the towering stone wall. His only hope was to leap across to the other window before they thought to look down the alley.

Behind him a voice called, "We hear you, child. Run no more."

Janner steadied himself, trying to imagine flying across the alley to grab the opposite windowsill, but he knew it was impossible without a running start.

"*Caw.*"

He looked up and saw a crow studying him from a gutter that sagged from the roofline, just low enough that he might be able to reach it if he stood. There were plenty of loose bricks for footholds, so if the gutter held, he might be able to get to the roof.

He stretched to his full height, holding with one hand to the inside of the window and reaching with his other to the broken gutter. His legs trembled. If the situation had been different, and he and Tink had discovered this wall on a lazy summer day, they might have wasted hours climbing it. Janner kept that image at the front of his mind as he reached. The wall *could* be climbed. He had to do it. They were coming.

The tips of his fingers brushed the gutter just as a voice said from the top of the stair, "We hear you, child. We *will* have you."

Janner lunged. He caught the gutter with both hands and swung away from the window, his feet scraping at the brick wall for purchase. The toe of his boot found a cleft where a brick had fallen away. He held the gutter with one hand and reached for a seam in the wall, ignoring the pain in his hands and the shouts now coming from the alley below him.

Arms sprouted from the window where he had just been, clawing at the air, and faces frowled at him with all the venom of the Fangs of Dang.

"Come here, child!" they hissed.

Janner pulled himself up a brick at a time, higher and higher, until the roof hung directly over his head and he found a steady hold, far enough away from the window that he could rest for a moment. The alley below was a mass of dirty, angry faces, and the window a clot of the same, as if the building had grown arms and heads. He was surprised to find that he felt pity for these poor souls. What had driven them to this?

He gritted his teeth, found a handhold on the roofline, and dangled. The crowd below gasped and muttered hungrily. It was oddly comforting to know that if he fell, the mob would catch him. They might carry him away and roast him over a fire later, but at the moment that seemed better than splatting on the brick street like a totato.

He swung a leg up, scooted forward, and rolled onto his back, panting.

As much as he would've liked to lie there for hours, he was out of time. The gutter creaked as dirty hands began to climb just as Janner had. He ran across loose shingles to the peak of the roof, vaulted over the wall that had trapped him, and landed on the building on the opposite side.

Immediately, the air changed. He couldn't be sure if it was his imagination, but the air felt cooler and carried more sound. The clamor of the crowd on the other side of the wall was muted and distant. Janner wanted to rest but forced himself to keep going until the horror behind him was behind him for good.

He crept to the edge and looked down. Another alleyway cluttered with debris, but here the buildings were closer—close enough that Janner was sure he could jump across. Before he could talk himself out of it, he trotted to the apex of the roof, turned, and ran for the edge.

When he landed on the other roof, a grin broke across his face. He scrambled to the other side, found another narrow alley, and jumped again.

Janner leapt from rooftop to rooftop, as spry as a squirrel, smiling with triumph with every landing and wishing Tink were there to see it.

As soon as he thought of Tink, though, the smile vanished. If he had been snagged by one of the crazed hags, surely there would have been some disturbance on Tilling Street, but Janner had found it as quiet as a tomb.

So then where was he?

At last Janner stopped running. The sun was high, the air was hot, and fishy smells choked the air. He might be lost, but he knew he was close to the river, and the river would be easy to find—he just had to go downhill and away from the wall between him and Tilling Street.

But first he had to find a way off the rooftop. He hadn't seen any trapdoors or skylights or ladders. The walls of the buildings surrounding him were smoother than those of Tilling Street, so he couldn't climb down that way.

Then he noticed a gutter pipe running down to the alley. It looked sturdy enough for a twelve-year-old, he thought. He just had to swing over and climb down, but now that there were no crazy people at his heels, Janner found it exceedingly difficult to muster the courage to do so. He sat with his legs dangling from the roof, imagining the simple act of leaning over, grabbing the gutter pipe, and scooting off the roof. But he couldn't bring himself to do it.

A ruckus started in the street in front of the building. He crept to the other side of the roof, lay on his belly, and peeked down at the street. It wasn't much different from Tilling Street, in that old two-story brick buildings faced the cobbled lane, but here the windows were intact, the walkways were relatively clean, and ordinary folk strolled and pushed carts and conversed with one another. It seemed safe enough. Then he saw the cause of the commotion.

A Fang stood guard in front of one of the buildings across the street. It sneered at passersby, who lowered their heads and walked on. Another Fang banged on the door.

"Open up!" it growled.

When no one answered, the Fang kicked the door from its hinges, and the two of them slithered inside. The Dugtowners passed by as if nothing out of the ordinary was happening.

Directly below, Janner heard voices.

"What's the fuss about?" asked one man.

"Might be the Florid Sword. Heard he was about last night."

"I heard that too," said a woman's voice. "But I also heard there's some family the Fangs want to find."

"Aye. Migg Landers told me yesterday they were from Anniera or some such nonsense."

"Anniera? Pah!"

"I'm just repeatin' what he said."

"Say, where is old Migg? Ain't seen him today."

"Me neither."

"Well, I hope they find the family sooner than late. Things are bad enough around here without the Florid Sword up to his mischief."

"And the Annierans."

"Pah!"

"I'm only sayin' what I heard."

"Uh-oh. They're coming back out," the woman said.

The two Fangs emerged and moved on to the next building, where the banging commenced again.

Janner scooted back from the edge. He had to get out of Dugtown. He had to get to the burrow. He prayed Tink would be there when he arrived.

The gutter pipe. There was no other way down.

With a sigh, Janner tiptoed back to the edge of the roof near the wall, scooted off, and shimmied down to the street before he could talk himself out of it. He squinted up at the roofline where he had been, impressed with himself.

Then something came between him and the noonday sun. A silhouette of someone's head and shoulders hovered where he had just been. Janner heard a dry chuckle, like the sound of a crackling fire, and in one motion, the silhouette leapt for the gutter, slid down, and landed nearly on top of him.

"We *will* have you, child," said a skeleton of a man. His long, mud-caked fingers wrapped around Janner's arms and held him in an iron grip.

Janner was too frightened to scream, and if he did, it would only bring the Fangs running. Either way, he was caught. Was it better to be in the grip of a mad old beggar or the Fangs of Dang?

Before he had time to wonder, the man whistled, and a rope dropped down from the other side of the wall. In moments the rope was tied around his arms and chest, and Janner was heaved upward. The ragman clambered up the gutter past him, swung up to the roof, and disappeared. Up Janner went, so tired of running that it was a strange relief to finally be caught.

In seconds, he scraped to a stop at the top of the wall, and more of those horrible, dirty hands pulled him over.

Janner landed on his back on the roof of a house with his eyes clamped shut.

The sound of many people breathing, rasping, and whispering was so terrifying that it was several moments before Janner cracked an eyelid. Legs everywhere, like tree trunks in a forest, except the roots of these trees bore ugly yellow toenails as long as toes themselves, curling up and down like monstrous ribbons.

"What...what do you want?" Janner asked.

At the sound of his voice, the crowd gasped and cackled with glee.

"I want what is mine," said a woman.

"Aye, Gorah is next in line," said a man.

"Lucky Gorah," the rest muttered.

Then the hags and ragmen picked Janner up and carried him away.

36

An Odious Arrangement

Janner was carried over their heads, a cork bobbing on the surface of a dirty river. The men and women were mostly silent. Those who made any sound at all wept. His arms were still bound at his sides, and he lay still, lulled by the floating sensation. They took him back to Tilling Street. The hags and ragmen carried him into an old building and set him gently on the floor, to his surprise. The woman, Gorah, stepped forward and poked him in the chest.

"Stay put, boy. We'll find you wherever you may run, just like we find all the others." She lowered her voice. "When darkness comes, I'll get what's mine. You'll see."

She cackled and clapped her hands like a little girl, hopping from one gnarled foot to the other. The others set to wailing and dancing as well. Janner closed his eyes and tried to shut out the sound.

After several minutes, most of the people filed from the room. Gorah and six others remained. They squatted against the wall and rocked to and fro, staring at Janner like hungry dogs.

Janner thought about his family. He felt certain that with Podo in charge, they must have made it safely back to the burrow by now. He had led them through great dangers before. But Tink? There was no telling where Tink could be.

Janner's eyes drooped. Gorah hummed a melody that must have been intended to be a lullaby, and as terrible as it sounded, the song did its work. He slept.

It was dark when he woke.

A single lantern lit the room. Gorah still crouched in the corner, glowering at Janner exactly as she had when he drifted off.

"It's almost time, child," she said, shifting on her feet.

"Time for what, ma'am?"

Gorah laughed so hard that she toppled forward and rolled onto her back, kicking her feet in the air. "'Ma'am!' He called me 'ma'am'!" She laughed until her eyes watered with tears, and Janner realized she was no longer laughing but weeping.

Again, he was mystified by the behavior of these strange people. All he had done was try to be polite, and now she was crying.

"Ma'am?" he said.

"Enough talk." She wiped her face with a rag from the floor. "And if you call me 'ma'am' again, you won't like me half so much as you do now."

One of the ragmen appeared in the doorway with an excited look. "It's time, Gorah."

Gorah walked to Janner, grabbed the end of the rope that bound him, and pulled him to his feet. "Come on, child. The Overseer's waiting."

She led Janner into the street. A crowd, holding torches, stood in the middle of the road. In the center, rising above them like a king on a dais, a round-faced man wearing a black velvet top hat sat atop a carriage so much like the Black Carriage that Janner had to look twice. The man wore fingerless gloves and a tattered suit with tails and purple lapels; in one hand he held the reins, while with the other he waved smugly at the beggars gathered around. When he smiled, his smooth face creased into too many wrinkles, and a wide set of buttery brown teeth gleamed.

When Gorah appeared, leading Janner by the rope, the crowd parted and let them through. The Overseer stood and spread his arms wide.

"A child!" He hopped down from his perch and looked into Janner's eyes. "And a healthy one too! Where did you find him?" He straightened and put his hands on his hips. "If I knew where to find such healthy children, I would trouble you no more, dear citizens!"

"He came to us, Overseer," said Gorah. "Today he appeared on Tilling, a gift from the Maker."

"A gift from the—? Ah. Yes, of course. The Maker." The Overseer gave a dismissive wave of his hand. "And do you have another?"

The crowd parted, and a man appeared, leading a boy with a sack over his head.

"Tink!" Janner cried.

One of the men slapped Janner in the face. "Quiet, you."

Janner was so overcome with relief to see his brother that he hardly felt the sting on his cheek. Then they removed the sack from over the boy's head, and Janner's heart sank. The boy was younger and much skinnier than Tink. Whoever he was, he was terrified.

"Another for you, Overseer," Gorah said.

"Good, good," said the man in the hat, appraising the thin boy. "Mobrik! The ledger!"

He clapped, and the side door of the carriage opened. A ridgerunner skittered out with a thin, leather-bound book in his arms. The little creature was dressed like the Overseer, in a tattered black suit and top hat, and it was plain he was uncomfortable in the human clothes. The Overseer snatched the ledger from him with a show of great impatience.

"Thank you, Mobrik," he droned while he flipped through the pages of the ledger. "Name?"

"Barnswaller," Gorah said meekly.

"Barnswaller...Barnswaller..." The man ran a finger down the page. "Ah. Was his name Jairy Barnswaller?"

Gorah gasped. "Yes! Jairy!"

"Sorry." The Overseer shrugged. "Says he tried to escape and was taken to Throg. Who's next?"

The woman wailed. Her cry cut to Janner's heart. She collapsed to the ground and thrashed about, and he felt tears in his own eyes. The crowd stepped over her and pushed closer to the carriage.

Over the sound of Gorah's grief, a man said, "I'm next. Name's Mykel Bolpin. Her name was Lily. Like the flower."

"'Like the flower,'" the Overseer mocked. He flipped through the pages again. "Will someone quiet the woman, please?" One of the ragmen grabbed Gorah by the wrist and dragged her away. "Thank you. Hard to think around here with all the racket. Now, let's see. Yes! We have a Lily Bolpin. Would you like your daughter, sir?"

The man was too shocked to speak.

"Sir?" the Overseer pressed.

"Y-yes sir. Please, sir." The man clasped his hands together to keep them from shaking.

"Very well, then. I'll take these two. She'll be here at dawn."

The man sank to his knees and looked to the heavens, his eyes shining in his dirty face like jewels in a mud hole.

"Mobrik! Get them," ordered the Overseer.

The ridgerunner took the ledger, then jerked the rope so hard that Janner nearly fell. He'd been staring at Gorah Barnswaller, who wept in the gutter beside the road. The ridgerunner scrambled into the carriage and tugged the rope again. Janner had faced the Black Carriage itself, so getting into the Overseer's carriage was no great feat. He climbed inside, sat on the bench beside Mobrik the ridgerunner, and thanked the Maker there was at least a chance that Tink had made it to the burrow.

The other boy, however, didn't fare so well. He wept and thrashed and fought bravely against his bonds until the Overseer ordered him knocked unconscious. They threw the poor child into the carriage at Janner's feet, as limp as a doll. Through the narrow window, Janner saw Gorah still wailing. He saw the ragged crowd dispersing into the dark of Tilling Street. And he saw the man, Mykel Bolpin, still kneeling in the road with a look of absolute joy on his face.

"S-sir?" said Bolpin to the Overseer.

"What?" The Overseer's voice was flat and cold.

"How old is she now?"

After a moment, the man said, "Mobrik! The ledger!" Mobrik leapt from the carriage again and handed the ledger up to the Overseer. Pages flipped. "She was twelve when she arrived at the factory. That was the year after the Great War. So what's that, eight years ago? Now she's twenty. Twenty years old."

Twenty? In eight years, Lily Bolpin, whoever she was, hadn't been able to escape from the Overseer, whoever he was? Janner felt a dread seep through him. Maybe what Podo always said was true. Maybe there *was* always a way out, like in Ships and Sharks. But what if that way out didn't come for eight years? What if Janner was twenty before he escaped from "the factory"?

"Thank you, sir. Thank you," the man blubbered.

Mobrik reappeared and pulled the door shut behind him. At a snap of the reins, the sad brown horse tugged the carriage away. The last Janner saw of Mykel Bolpin, he sat in the street staring at the heavens, looking less like a beggar and more like a father with every moment.

The ridgerunner squatted in the shadows in the far corner of the carriage, paying Janner no attention. Given his history with ridgerunners, Janner didn't particularly want to talk to the sneaky little creature anyway. After straining again at the ropes and finding them as tight as ever, he leaned against the wall and gazed out the window at Dugtown as it passed by. He saw Crempshaw Way approaching, the hill descending to the river on the left.

When the carriage turned right and the horse strained uphill, away from the river and deeper into Dugtown, Janner spotted the street sign on the corner. What he saw made his cheeks burn and a black rage sizzle in his chest.

The sign said Tilling *Court.* Not Tilling Street.

Moments later, another street sign appeared that said Tilling *Street,* a road that, compared to where he had just been, seemed as safe and pleasant as the lane to the

Igiby cottage. It stretched away east, just as Ronchy McHiggins had said, and in the distance Janner saw where it intersected with Riverside Road.

He had taken a wrong turn. It was as simple as that.

That was why he never saw Tink. Tink was smart enough to read the street signs. *Fool!* he thought.

"Where are you taking me?" he asked the ridgerunner.

The ridgerunner looked at him with surprise. "Why," he said, "to the Fork Factory."

37

Into the Mouth of the Monster

Dugtown was a much bigger city than Janner realized. The clop of hooves and the creak of the carriage settled into an eternal drone, broken only by the occasional crack of the Overseer's whip. Janner leaned his forehead listlessly against the bars of the window and looked out at the torch-lit streets of the city.

The way the Dugtowners hurried by told him curfew fast approached. The Overseer didn't seem to care, even when clusters of Fangs prowled past. They paid little attention to the carriage. The horse plodded on at the same slow pace, even when the bells struck curfew. At once the busy city went to sleep. Now and then a Fang passed the carriage with a grunt of greeting, and the Overseer could be heard saying, "My lord," in answer.

Finally, the carriage squeaked to a stop. The sad brown horse snorted. Janner blinked out of his daze and strained to see ahead through the side window. The ridgerunner stepped past Janner and over the unconscious boy on the carriage floor, opened the door, and leapt to the ground. Janner started to follow him out, but the ridgerunner slammed the door in his face. "You stay," he said.

Mobrik approached a rusty portcullis in the center of an immense brick building. With a great racket, the iron gate slowly rose. The vertical bars of the gate ended in points, which made the building look like a monster opening its mouth to swallow the horse and carriage whole. Above the gate, a big metal sign bore the inscription, in bold, rusty letters, Fork! Factory!

Janner was as unsettled by the overuse of exclamation points as he was by the dreary countenance of the place. With another snap of the whip, the carriage lurched forward into the mouth of the brick monster. Tucked in the shadows just inside the gate stood two children. Their clothes were tattered, their faces blank. They stared at Janner as he passed, then turned away and, taking hold of a fat chain, lowered the portcullis under the watchful eye of Mobrik the ridgerunner.

The carriage rolled through a narrow passageway, then into a large, airy chamber. Mobrik swung open the door and yanked Janner out so hard that he tumbled to the ground. Far above, rafters and planks crisscrossed the ceiling. Chains and ropes dangled down into the light of lanterns on the lower walls. Except for the carriage, the floor of the vast room was bare.

The Overseer, still wearing his top hat, appeared above Janner. He grinned wickedly and pinched Janner's cheek between his thumb and forefinger.

"Welcome, boy!" he said. "A healthy face you have. Mobrik, untie him. I want to see his arms and hands. I believe we have someone to replace that sluggish Knubis girl at the paring station." Mobrik untied Janner. "Yes. Good arms. Good hands. Allow me to greet you properly, child." He dropped to one knee and removed his hat, then ran his fingers through his greasy hair. "I'm the Overseer. You're a tool in my factory, no different from a hammer or a rake. The difference is, unlike a hammer, I have to feed your greedy face to keep you alive. Did you enjoy the ride here?"

"Yes sir," Janner said. Mobrik chuckled.

"What did you say?" asked the Overseer.

"I said. 'Yes sir.'"

The Overseer punched Janner in the stomach. Stars filled his vision, and tears welled up as he struggled for air.

"Tell him," the Overseer said to Mobrik as he stood and donned his hat with great care.

Mobrik stooped over Janner and smiled. "Tools don't speak. They nod, like this." Mobrik nodded his tiny head up and down. "Or they shake, like this." He shook his head from side to side.

The Overseer narrowed his eyes at Janner. "So, child. Did you enjoy your ride?"

Janner considered answering aloud again, just to see the look on the Overseer's face. But he didn't particularly want to be punched again, and with the portcullis shut, he was certain there was nowhere to run, however big this building might be. He sighed and nodded his head.

"Good. A fast learner. The finest tools are fast learners." The Overseer smiled, revealing every one of his yellow and brown teeth. "I'm glad you enjoyed the ride. It was the last look at the city you're ever likely to have. This is your new home. Unless, of course, your parents manage to capture two other children to replace you. I'm a very giving man. I have a quota to meet, and I don't care how I meet it, whether it's you or some other fool at the paring station. Do you understand?"

Janner didn't, but he nodded dumbly. They could call him a tool all day long, but that didn't make it so. *There's always a way out,* Janner thought. And as soon as he found it, he would slip away to the burrow where his family waited. If he could escape by morning, they would only have lost a day. Then they could find another way past the Barrier, and a short walk over the Stony Mountains would bring them to the safety of the Ice Prairies. The thought of a world with no Fangs made Janner smile.

"Why are you smiling?" the Overseer said suspiciously.

Janner started to answer but stopped short. He said nothing but only looked at the Overseer with the same smile playing at his lips. It was fun to see the ridiculous man unsettled. He could punch him in the gut again if he liked. He could call him a tool and send him off to make forks, assuming that was what the Fork Factory produced. But Janner knew he was a Throne Warden, and that gave him a kind of freedom, even though he was, for the moment, captive.

The Overseer laughed.

"Mobrik! Take him to his station. Be sure he has no rest until morning. We'll see if he's smiling then. When you return, we'll see to the other boy."

Janner followed Mobrik, wondering, among many other things, when he would be allowed to eat something. The last time he had eaten was that morning at the Roundish Widow. The faces of the children at the portcullis haunted him. They looked healthy enough, or at least they didn't appear physically wounded in any way, but their hollow, hopeless eyes made him uneasy. They seemed resigned to their fate, as if they had tried and failed so many times to find freedom that they no longer bothered to hope anymore. But surely there was *some* way out, even if it meant fighting. The Overseer wasn't a Fang, after all. He didn't have venomous teeth or unnatural strength or even a weapon as far as Janner could see, other than the whip he applied to the sad brown horse.

The Overseer disappeared through a door in the far wall of the chamber and left the horse harnessed to the carriage. Mobrik led Janner to a set of double doors at the rear of the room.

"Am I allowed to speak to you, or do I still have to wiggle my head?" Janner asked carefully.

Mobrik glanced at him. "Speak if you like. But don't expect an answer—unless you carry a sack of apples I can't see. The Overseer enjoys having me around to boss, but he and I both know the only reason I'm here is for the sweet yellow apples he gets from upriver."

"No apples. Sorry."

"Then no answers."

Mobrik pushed through the double doors and led Janner down a long, dark hallway. At the far end was another set of doors with two square windows that glowed yellow. As they approached, Janner heard an awful racket, and the temperature rose.

Mobrik pushed Janner through the doors and into a world of nightmares.

38

Bright Eyes in a Dark Place

Fire raged.

Flames sputtered from pipes and smokestacks, roared in black ovens, and curled from vats of molten iron. Janner's nose stung with the stench of sweat and smoke. In the center of the enormous room squatted an enormous black furnace. Red-hot pipes rose from it and snaked through the room in a senseless knot. Some of the pipes spewed smoke from ruptured joints, and others dripped black, steamy liquid. Smoke gathered at the ceiling like a storm cloud.

Beside the furnace stood a contraption that shuddered and clanked like nothing Janner had ever known. Glipwood had seen its share of oddities but nothing like this—this was a *machine,* something Janner had only ever read about. It wasn't clear what the machine did besides make an awful racket, but the turn of its gears and the steadiness of its chugging made it clear it was doing something.

In front of the mouth of the furnace were three piles of coal. After Janner's eyes adjusted, he saw figures with shovels trudging the distance between the coal and the furnace. At first he thought they were more ridgerunners. Then he realized they were children.

On the left of the great room were seven aisles divided by long narrow tables. Trenches cut in the center of the tables caught the glowing liquid that poured from spouts hanging from the ceiling. Children tended to the molten steel with pikes and tongs. Janner saw even more children, hundreds of them, gathered around tables and anvils and large stone bowls, hammering, carrying buckets of water to and fro, and stirring the burning liquid with iron poles. Everywhere he looked there was movement.

He considered running back down the long hallway. Maybe if he surprised them with a sudden escape, he could find a way out near the portcullis—for that matter, maybe he could get the two children to open it again. He might even take them with him—but then what? He wouldn't make it far through the streets of Dugtown with two tired children in tow, especially at night when only the Fangs and trolls were about.

"I wouldn't if I were you."

Janner blinked. Mobrik had removed his little top hat and looked at him cock-eyed, a hint of a smile on his lips.

"Kids try it all the time when they first arrive. Truth is, the Overseer *hopes* you'll try to escape. It gives him a chance for some target practice with his whip. Trust me. You're better off at the paring station, boy."

"W-what's the paring station?"

Mobrik the ridgerunner replaced his hat and descended the steps. He stood at the bottom and waited.

"Run if you like. You'll end up here either way. But if you come now, you'll not be bleeding and sore from the boss's whip."

Janner took one last look at the door. With a sigh, he walked down the steps and followed the ridgerunner. As he approached the machinery, the temperature increased. Janner's eyes watered, and he found himself unable to keep from blinking constantly. Mobrik seemed to have no trouble with the heat.

They passed black iron barrels as tall as a house. All around them, flames spurted from pipes and chimneys, and iron wheels clanked. Everywhere Janner looked, he saw children. Some were old enough to pass for young adults, but most were older than Janner. A few glanced at him as he passed, the whites of their eyes the only clean spots in the factory, but most kept their heads down, either shoveling coal, hammering a hot sheet of metal, scraping fragments of debris into a wheeled barrel, or pushing carts piled heavy with lengths of steel—

Swords, Janner thought. He recognized the graceless curve of a Fang blade, though the hilt hadn't yet been attached. He had never wondered where the Fangs got their weapons. Someone had to make them, after all. But children? That explained why the Overseer was allowed to move through the city after curfew and why there were so few children in Dugtown. Whatever children weren't stolen probably lived out their days indoors, under the watchful eyes of their parents. Then Janner remembered the picture on Ronchy McHiggins's wall. They had stolen his child too.

As Janner took the next turn through the maze of the factory, he glanced to his right and saw a set of bright eyes looking straight at him. They were beautiful, round windows of blue sky. Though he could see little of the child's face, covered in soot as it was, a memory tingled in the back of his mind.

."Come on!" Mobrik kicked Janner in the shin. Janner resisted the urge to wrestle the little ridgerunner to the ground and thump him. When Janner looked again, the child with the blue eyes was gone.

Mobrik led him through several more turns before he stopped at a long table. A girl stood in front of the table, holding a pair of giant rusty scissors. On the table before her lay what looked like a Fang sword, but it was shaped wrong.

"She's paring the sword, see?" Mobrik said. "Cutting away the bit of metal that isn't supposed to be there. The machine gets it right most of the time, but now and then there's a bad cut. So it takes tools like this one to fix what isn't right."

Mobrik pointed a thumb at the girl. Her face was covered with streaks of dirt. She wore an apron and had her hair tied in a bun on top of her head. She cut another inch of the metal with every grunt. Her teeth were bared, and though she looked as tired as anyone Janner had ever seen, she was making progress. When they approached, she stopped and straightened without a word. Janner smiled at her. She stared back, expressionless.

"Knubis! The Overseer says you're either to be moved to the coal piles or it's the Black Carriage for you. Do you think you can keep up at the coal piles, girl?"

At the mention of the Black Carriage, the Knubis girl's eyes widened and she redoubled her efforts with the scissors.

"Too late for that, girl. It's the coal piles or the Carriage." Mobrik was enjoying himself.

Janner's insides boiled. His fingers curled into fists, and he took a deep breath, ready to pounce on Mobrik, grab the poor girl, and run for it. Then common sense once again interrupted his anger. Where would he go? He caught the Knubis girl's eyes, and she shook her head.

"Don't," she said, looking at Mobrik, but Janner could tell she was talking to him. She didn't want him to do anything rash.

"What?" Mobrik said.

"Don't...call the Black Carriage. I'll go to the coal piles, and I'll work faster. It's just, my hands..." She held out her hands. They were covered with oozing blisters.

"More gloves coming tomorrow." Mobrik shrugged. "It's a shame you should be abused so. Hard to work if your hands are worn through. The Overseer should take better care of his tools."

"She's not a tool," Janner said, unable to contain himself.

"Don't!" she said, this time looking at Janner.

Janner ignored her, reared his fist back, and let it fly straight at Mobrik's face. The punch never landed.

Figures burst from the shadows and corners and from under the tables. They dropped from chains that hung from the ceiling and rushed at Janner. They shoved him to the floor and punched and kicked and struck him with all manner of blunt weapons. Janner curled into a ball, clenched his teeth, and waited for the torment to stop. Stars swam in his vision, white pain sizzled through his spine and neck. Finally the blows subsided.

Janner lay on his back, staring at the ceiling, the chains above swaying to and fro like the pendulum on a clock. His nose and mouth were bleeding, a tooth was loose, and his ribs hurt with every ragged breath he took.

A face appeared above him. He expected it to be the Overseer again, grinning his yellow-toothed grin beneath the silly top hat, but it was a boy. With the mean look in his eyes, the dirty face, and the smirk on his lips, he looked so much like a Strander that Janner half expected to see a dagger in one hand and a hunk of toothy cow meat in the other. But instead of a dagger, the boy held a length of chain.

"We're always watching, tool," the boy said. "So do as you're told, leave Master Mobrik here alone, and get to the paring. Understand?"

"I'm not a tool," Janner said.

The boy let fly with the chain. It struck the ground beside Janner's head so hard that sparks stung his cheeks.

"You're a tool," the boy said. He gestured to the other boys and girls standing about, all of them looking at Janner with hatred. "We all are. Now get up and get to work."

Mobrik stood behind the children with his arms folded. "The Overseer said this new boy is to work until morning with no rest."

The children smiled.

"Come on, Knubis," Mobrik said to the paring girl, and she followed him to the coal piles.

"Get up, boy. What's your name?"

Janner stood slowly, the bones in his back and shoulders cracking in protest. He wiped his bloody lip with a shirt sleeve. "My name's...Esben."

The boy with the chain stepped forward until he stood nose to nose with Janner.

"Your name is *Tool*. Remember that. My name, in case you're wondering, is Maintenance Manager. That's all our names." He waved his chain at the others as they slunk away into the shadows. "We maintain the machine and the tools that run it. If you work hard enough, you might get to be a Maintenance Manager too. The food's better, the bunks are better, and you get to greet the new tools when they arrive."

Janner stared at the boy with steady eyes, though he could feel one of them swelling shut with every throb. He chose to say nothing. It wouldn't be long before he found a way out of this place, and this tool could go on maintaining his machine for the rest of his life if he wanted.

But right now, he had paring to do.

39

Esben Flavogle, the Factory Tool

All night, Janner stood at the long table and cut metal. Whenever he glanced up, he caught sight of shapes swinging from chains, from rafter to rafter like bugs. The Maintenance Managers were everywhere, supervising the "tools" as they worked.

Sometimes, an actual fork made it to the paring station, which reminded him that he hadn't eaten in hours, nor had he had anything to drink. The hot air of the factory floor sucked the liquid from every pore and left his tongue dry as a dead leaf.

Janner's hands ached. He had done his share of work with rakes and shovels and knew well the feeling of a blister forming beneath the skin. If his hands hadn't been covered in soot, he would've seen the red spots that would soon swell and fill with fluid. He was glad Tink had been spared this fate.

Whenever his eyes drooped, he shook his head and pinched himself to keep awake. As he struggled to close the scissors on a sliver of stubborn metal, he thought of his sweet mother, her strong, easy way of giving him affection and comfort. While he ground the handle of a blade, he thought of Podo's booming voice, of Oskar's flop of hair. When he tossed the reworked pieces into a barrel, he thought of Leeli's curious calm and the magic in her songs. And when he bent forks, he thought of Tink's insatiable appetite. Even as the memories of his family kept him company, they made his heart heavy and lonesome.

It was a miserable night.

At dawn, Mobrik appeared. Janner looked down at the little creature blankly, realizing that in a few short hours, he already looked and acted like the other exhausted children of the factory. He had to escape, and soon, but for now, all he wanted was a bed and something to eat.

"Follow me, child. The Overseer needs to ask you a few questions."

Mobrik led Janner back down the long hallway and into the big, empty room. They crossed to the door in the far wall, and Mobrik knocked. They entered an office with a large desk, where the Overseer sat, still wearing his black top hat. He smiled, yawned, and patted the whip that lay coiled on the desk.

"Forgive me," he said. "I just woke from a delightful night's sleep. My bed is so soft, you see, and large. I trust you found your work enjoyable? The paring station affords much movement and variety, I believe."

Janner was now fully awake. He wanted to leap across the table and knock the silly hat from the Overseer's head. He wanted to haul the man downstairs and make *him* pare the bad blades for an hour. But most of all, he wanted the man to open the portcullis and let him go. Let them *all* go.

"Now," said the Overseer, dipping a quill into a bottle of ink, "I need your full name. In case your parents ever find replacements for you." Janner paused, remembering the punch in the stomach the last time he spoke to the Overseer. "Oh, it's all right," said the man. "You're allowed to tell me your name."

Janner cleared his throat. "My name is Esben…Esben Flavogle."

The Overseer scratched it into his ledger without bothering to ask how it was spelled. "There. Mobrik, show the tool to his bunk."

Below the main factory floor where the furnaces roared lay a dormitory. Bunk beds lined the walls. Janner saw hundreds of children, either snoring in a deep sleep or climbing wearily out of bed to face another day in the factory. No one spoke or laughed or even made eye contact. Mobrik allowed Janner a drink of water from a cistern, then pointed him to an empty bunk and left.

The mattress was lumpy but far more comfortable than the sandy floor of the burrow. Janner realized as he drifted away that he hadn't slept in a proper bed since the day the Fangs had ransacked the Igiby cottage. In Peet's castle he had been quite comfortable on the pile of blankets and animal skins spread on the floor, but it hadn't been a bed. Since then he had slept on the hard ground every night. As he drifted to sleep, he felt the inside of his swollen lip with his tongue and wondered if his tooth would still wiggle in the morning.

When he woke, he smelled food.

But it wasn't the smell that woke him. A bell clanged and clanged and clanged, and it was several moments before Janner was awake enough to realize that a boy beside his bed was making all the racket. The boy had pudgy cheeks and wore a tattered red cap that seemed about to slide off the back of his head.

"All right, all right!" Janner snapped, pushing the bell away from his ear and sitting up.

"Time for breakfast, tool," said the boy, and he marched off to annoy someone else.

The dorm room was busier than it had been that morning when Janner collapsed into bed. Children pulled on boots, washed their faces with water from a trough, and sat at a long wooden table, spooning a watery broth into their mouths. The bell-clanger made his rounds, but otherwise there was very little speaking. These children's spirits had been broken. Who knew how long they had toiled in the factory? Some were old enough to have whiskery fuzz on their chins, and others were barely as old as Leeli. Janner couldn't understand why the Overseer used only children for the labor. Couldn't an adult work longer and faster?

Janner sat at the table, and a boy placed a bowl and spoon before him, along with a cup of water. No one looked at him. No one spoke. The only sound was the chorus of hungry slurps from the twenty or so children at the table.

Janner cleared his throat. "Hello." He waited for an answer. A few of the children glanced at him but kept eating without a word. "My name's Esben. Esben, uh, Flavogle. Just got here."

"We can see that," said the boy directly across from him. The boy raised his bowl to his mouth and sucked up the last drops of soup. "You'll find there's not much to talk about after a while."

"What's your name?"

"Doesn't matter. I'm a tool, just like you."

Janner rolled his eyes. "I'm not a tool."

The boy shrugged and left the table.

Janner turned his attention to his soup. It didn't look very appetizing, but his mouth watered. He picked up his spoon, but fiery pain shot through his hand, and he sucked air through his teeth. Blisters. They cracked and oozed on every finger and all across his palms. Gingerly he picked up the spoon again and ate his soup in silence, surprised to find that it was quite delicious. He was also surprised that when he finished his soup, the serving boy appeared with a fresh bowl and removed his empty one. Janner devoured the second bowl, and then a third, so famished that he forgot the pain in his hands. When he was finished, he got up from the table, not sure what to do or where to go.

"Back to the paring station, tool," said a voice from behind him. Mobrik the ridgerunner stood at his elbow. Janner was strangely glad to see him. "It's my job to make sure the new implements learn the system. You eat soup, then you wash your face, then you head back to the factory floor to do your job. Understand?"

"I guess so."

"Then go," Mobrik said, turning away. Then he stopped and said, "I nearly forgot. These should fit you." He reached into a pocket of his suit coat and tossed a pair of thick leather gloves to Janner.

"Mobrik—wait. Thank you. I need to ask you something."

"Do you have any fruit?" Mobrik asked.

"No."

The ridgerunner walked away.

Janner saw several Maintenance Managers leaning against the wall, watching him, and took a deep breath. He would escape. He just had to wait until they weren't watching him so closely. Maybe later that day, once they saw that he could work fast, they would forget him long enough that he could break away and get out.

"The paring station, then," Janner said to himself. "I hope Tink is faring better than I am."

Another hot, miserable night passed on the factory floor. Another night of blasting heat, roaring flames, creaking wheels, and painful hands.

Janner spent the first several hours thinking of his family, but that proved too saddening. Then he thought about his T.H.A.G.S. and about the books he had recently read. He recalled the characters from the stories, the settings, the themes of the books. But his mind kept slowing to a thoughtless sludge, a world where all that mattered was the hiss of the machines and the cutting of metal. Whenever his table of misshapen blades and forks was close to empty—but never completely empty, to his great frustration—a child appeared with another full wheelbarrow. Whenever Janner attempted conversation with the children, they never answered or met his eyes. He wanted to grab their faces and force them to look at him, to acknowledge his presence, to act as if they were still human.

At last, a pure yellow light crept in through the windows near the ceiling. It diffused the orange-red glow of the furnace fires and torches, changing the heat-choked air of the factory. Dawn.

A Maintenance Manager appeared and said, "Shift's over, tool."

Janner, covered in sweat and soot, dropped the shears to the floor. He staggered past the machines to the dormitory stair, pushed through the double doors, past the crew of sleepy-eyed children on their way to their stations, and collapsed on his bunk without bothering to eat.

He woke to the clanging of the bell beside his ear. It was the same boy with the same satisfied grin on his face. Janner ate two bowls of soup, carefully pulled his gloves over his blistered hands, and trudged out the doors and up the stairs to the paring station.

He couldn't imagine spending another day in the factory. His hands hurt, his back was tired, he hadn't seen the sun in days, he missed his family desperately, and most of all, he could feel his mind *shrinking*. There was nothing to talk about, laugh about, or think about, except the machines. Every child who crossed his path frightened Janner more, because he knew that if he remained in the Fork Factory for long, he too would forget who he was. His eyes would glaze over, he would pass his days in mindless repetition, never thinking, never dreaming, forgetting that a wide, bright world lay outside.

On the third night of Janner's captivity, he made a decision.

He arrived at his station, picked up the heavy shears, and looked around for the Maintenance Managers. He saw one pacing a platform that hung from the ceiling. The boy stopped and leaned over to bark an order at some child on the other side of the nearest machines.

When Janner was sure the Maintenance Manager wasn't looking, he took a deep breath, looked around one last time, and ran for his life.

40

The Coffin

Janner was aware of some movement behind him, probably the Maintenance Manager calling for help, but as long as it stayed behind him, he didn't care. He darted between machines, noting with some satisfaction the looks of surprise on the children's faces as he passed. It was the nearest he had seen any of them come to looking alive.

The factory floor was a maze of metal and fire, and after only a few moments, Janner realized he was lost. He had thought it would be easy to find the stair that led to the double doors that led to freedom, but the machines and the aisles of tables and crates disoriented him. He heard more yelling, from every direction now.

Janner felt an abrupt increase in temperature and rounded a corner to find himself staring at the grim black face of the main furnace. A boy several feet away used a long metal pole with a hook at one end to pull open the hot grate while another child shoveled a serving of coal into its belly; the fire blazed and roared its hungry thanks. The two children looked at Janner with confusion.

But he finally had his bearings. He remembered seeing the furnace and the piles of coal when he and Mobrik had first emerged from the long hallway. Janner spun and saw the double doors and the stairway that led to them not far away. With the heat of the furnace bright on his back, he ran as straight as he could for the stairs, weaving in and out of machinery but aiming always for the doors.

At last, he reached the stairs and risked a look behind him. Five boys, taller and older than Janner, pushed their way toward him, in no great hurry. Two more boys swung from the chains that hung from the ceiling.

Janner had no idea what he was doing. He knew that at the end of this long hallway was the big, empty room where the carriage waited. He knew the Overseer had a whip, and Mobrik said he wasn't afraid to use it. He knew the only certain exit from the building was through a heavy portcullis he couldn't open alone.

But he also knew he couldn't stand another day at the paring station without doing *something*. He wasn't a tool. He was the Throne Warden of Anniera, which meant that though they might capture him, he wouldn't go quietly.

As he ran up the stair, he heard something that startled him so badly he nearly fell.

"Janner Igiby. Don't."

A girl stood at the bottom of the steps. She was filthy, but her eyes were like pearls in the mud, large and luminescent. It was the same child he had seen the day he arrived, the one he thought he recognized.

"How do you know my name?" Janner asked. Every moment the Maintenance Managers came closer, but he couldn't make himself move. "Who are you?"

Her bright eyes filled with tears that streaked her face like white paint on a black canvas. He had to go. If he was fast enough, he might have a few minutes to search for a way out before the Overseer was alerted.

"Janner, you can't get out," the girl said. "Please don't run."

Her voice was sweet and desperate and beautiful, a silver stream in a dark forest. Only such a voice could have stopped him from running. Janner looked at the doors behind him, then at the gang of Maintenance Managers pushing toward him, then at the girl with the bright eyes, and he gave up. Part of him screamed, *Run! Get out!* But something stayed his feet.

The first of the tall boys arrived at the bottom of the stairs, shoved the girl aside, and ascended. Janner didn't take his eyes from her, even when the Maintenance Managers punched him in the gut or twisted his arm behind his back. Her eyes were stars on a stormy night, pinpricks peeking through a break in the clouds.

Janner felt a knee in his back and tumbled down the stairs, head over heels, wondering dimly what it would sound like when his bones snapped. He crashed to the floor, dizzy with pain. Then he found her eyes again.

"Who...are you?" he breathed.

Before the Maintenance Managers dragged him away, she leaned close.

"Sara Cobbler," she said.[1]

Then someone punched Janner, and the stars went out.

When Janner woke, he thought for a moment that he was dead. His eyes were open, but he could see nothing. His body ached, and his hands were so blistered that he couldn't move his fingers. He tongued his swollen lip and tasted blood. He was in bad shape.

---

1. See Book One, page 8.

But where was he? He lay on a hard surface, but his hands and feet weren't bound, which was a relief. He sat up, and his forehead smashed into something hard.

"Ow!" He put a hand to his forehead, forgetting the blisters on his fingers and palms. "Ow!" he said again.

When the pain subsided, he found he was in a box not much wider than his shoulders and not much taller than his chest. He felt himself on the verge of panic. Janner had always been afraid of tight places, even when it was just he and Podo wrestling. Sometimes when Podo held his arms down, this same panic erupted. One moment, Janner would be laughing, and the next he lost all control and thrashed as if in a bad dream. He closed his eyes again and forced himself to breathe slowly.

But he couldn't resist the urge to push on the ceiling, just to see if it would give. He pushed, found it solid and strong, and then he lost his mind.

Janner screamed and scratched at the walls and ceiling of the box, heedless of the pain in his hands or in his fingernails when they tore away. He was trapped in a dark so deep that light itself seemed never to have existed at all. He lost all sense of time. He kicked and scraped until his strength was spent and then lay there sobbing. He cried for ages, until sleep came at last, but he dreamed of a giant nothingness, an empty hole into which he tumbled and disappeared.

When he woke again, he found that the box was not an awful dream but a black reality. He panicked again. He lay panting in the blackness, talking to himself, praying aloud to the Maker, accusing, pleading, screaming things that, while no one could blame poor Janner for saying them, will not be repeated here.

And the Maker's answer was a hollow silence.

Hours and hours passed. Janner wept again, a different weeping than before. These tears were not from fear but from weariness and a vast loneliness. He wanted to feel the touch of Nia's hand on the back of his neck. He wanted to hear Leeli's voice, Tink's laughter. He wanted the musty smell of Podo's breath after he smoked his pipe. He wanted to see Peet the Sock Man's eyes, because the same stuff that made his father swam there. These thoughts floated in his mind like dandelion seeds in a warm wind.

Janner saw himself in his mind's eye, sitting in the field beside the Igiby cottage. The long winter had passed. New, green shoots sighed up from the furrows in the garden. Bright leaves as soft as a baby's feet shone on the trees. Then, as kind as his mother's kiss, the sun broke through and poured light upon his skin.

In the black coffin, his hands cut and bleeding, his face bruised from the fists of the Maintenance Managers, Janner slept. His sleep was sound, untroubled by dreams of Fangs or Gnag the Nameless, or the terrible, wheeling blackness.

The next time he woke, he was aware of his hunger and thirst. Even amidst the terror of his first hours in the box, he had assumed this was a punishment, not a long execution. But now he wondered if they meant to starve him or if they had buried him alive. Maybe he wasn't in the factory at all but in some cemetery somewhere, deep in the ground.

He was too tired to cry anymore, too tired to panic. So he lay there and thought about Sara Cobbler and her beautiful eyes.

"Sara Cobbler," he said aloud, enjoying the sound of her name. Why was it so familiar?

She had known his name, but he had never been to Dugtown. How would she know his name? Then he remembered—Sara Cobbler, the girl who had been taken by the Black Carriage. Janner shook his head in the darkness, trying to remember. He had met a family at the Dragon Day Festival the year before, and they had had a little girl the same age as him. It was only a brief meeting, but Janner had made the mistake of mentioning to Tink that he thought she was pretty. Tink made fun of him for the rest of the day. A few weeks later, Nia told Janner and Tink she had been taken by the Carriage.

But the Black Carriage took children to Fort Lamendron, then to the Castle Throg, like the nursery rhyme said. *"At Castle Throg across the span...you'll weep at how your woes began...the night the Carriage found you."* Why was she here? How many of these children had been taken by the Carriage? How many of their parents assumed they were lost forever, when they were only a few miles away in Dugtown? If they knew their children were here, guarded only by the Overseer, surely they would stop at nothing to tear the walls down and bring them home.

Then he remembered the hags and beggars of Tilling Court. Many of the parents knew exactly where their children were, and it had driven them mad.

Janner wanted more than ever to be in the Ice Prairies, among brave men and women not content to live under the thumb of the Fangs. He ached to live in a world where the Fangs dared not enter. Maybe, when he was older, he would join Gammon's force and be a part of the resistance. He would wield his sword and fight alongside the Skreeans when the time came, and if they could drive the Fangs from Skree, then why not Anniera? And if they could drive them from the Shining Isle and restore his father's kingdom—well, his brother's kingdom—then why not attack Throg itself?

Why not put an end to Gnag and the trolls and the Fangs and every enemy that would beat a twelve-year-old boy and lock him in a coffin?

Janner laughed. It was easy to have daydreams about conquering the world for the good of Aerwiar; it was another thing to do it. He couldn't even make it from Glipwood to Dugtown without nearly dying Maker knows how many times. They had lost Peet, they had lost Nugget, they had been captured by Stranders, chased by Fangs, betrayed, beaten, lost.

And he had no idea what had become of Tink or the others. Janner's stomach curled. How long would they wait at the burrow? How long before they gave up on him and went on to the Ice Prairies? How could they possibly find him?

He forced such thoughts from his mind. He had to get out. That was the only thing to be done.

Janner's mind worked this way for hours before he realized with a smile that he was no longer afraid of the darkness or the coffin. He was afraid of starving to death, but he doubted they would let him die, not after all the trouble the Overseer went through to find children for his factory.

As if in answer to this last thought, a sound came from outside the box—the first thing Janner had heard other than his own voice since he had found himself there.

Footsteps approached. A clicking sound. Then the top of the box swung open and light stung his eyes.

"Out, Esben Flavogle. The Overseer wants to see you."

"Hello, Mobrik," Janner rasped.

Unable to believe he was doing so, Janner sat up and entered the world again.

Janner forced his stiff body out of the box. The room was small and dungeonlike, with stone walls and a squat ceiling. Chains hung from hooks on the wall, and bones lay in piles in the corners. Two coffins lay side by side, open and awaiting their next occupants.

One day there wouldn't be any more occupants, Janner thought. Gammon and his army would sack Dugtown and every other evil place in Skree, and when he did, Janner swore to find this place and tear it down forever. No more children in coffins or in factories or in Black Carriages. No more.

Janner looked at Mobrik with fire in his eyes. The ridgerunner took a step backward and eyed the door, clearly not used to children emerging from the coffin undefeated. Janner Wingfeather had gone in unconscious and had come out more awake than ever.

He considered seizing the ridgerunner and throwing him into the box. He knew he could if he wanted, but it didn't feel right just yet. He had to be careful when and how he took action. No more running blindly through the factory. He would wait, and watch, and plan.

"Let's go," Janner said. "The Overseer's waiting."

41

Four Apples and a Plan

The Overseer sat at his desk, wearing his ridiculous hat and trying his best to look angry.

Janner didn't care. He resolved to play dumb and pretend to be broken. He nodded his head and waited for the man to finish talking about "obeying" and how there was "no chance for escape" and that Janner was "just a tool now." At this last, it was all Janner could do to keep quiet. The Overseer warned him that next time he tried to escape, he would spend *three* days in the box, not just two.

Two days? Janner thought with a shudder. It had felt like a lifetime. He couldn't imagine a third day in the coffin.

As Mobrik led him back across the empty room where the carriage sat, Janner caught a sweet smell. Against the wall near the door sat three baskets of apples, berries, and melons. Mobrik took a deep sniff and giggled.

"Hurry up, tool," said Mobrik. "I've fruit to eat once you're back at work."

"Can't you eat some now?" Janner asked, hoping to distract the ridgerunner, but not yet sure why. He had to be careful from now on, but this might be the last time he would be this close to the exit. "You could take an apple with you. It's a long walk to the paring station and back."

Mobrik paused. "It *is* a long walk."

"And fruit tastes best when it's fresh. 'The longer it sits, the worser it gets,' my mother used to say." Janner forced a laugh. Mobrik stared at the baskets with longing.

"Come on," the ridgerunner said, glancing at the Overseer's door. Their footsteps echoed as they crossed the room to the fruit baskets. Janner caught a glimpse of the portcullis, down the corridor behind the carriage. He wondered if the two children in charge of opening it stayed there or if they only manned it when the Overseer was out and expected to return.

Mobrik ran ahead of Janner to the baskets, the tails of his little coat flying out behind. He ran his little fingers over the fruit, caressing it and testing its firmness. Janner looked back at the Overseer's door. It was still closed.

"The longer it sits, the worser it gets! A true thing for a boy to utter!" Mobrik said, enraptured with the fruit.

Still not sure what he was doing, Janner lifted a head-sized melon from the basket. Mobrik gasped. "Put that back! This is *my* fruit! Mine!"

"Sorry," Janner said. When he replaced the melon, it fell from the basket, hit the floor with a wet *thunk,* and rolled away. Mobrik shrieked and scrambled after it. When the little creature's back was turned, Janner slipped four apples into the pockets of his breeches, thinking as he did that Tink's quick hands could probably have snagged twice that many in half the time.

"Terrible idea!" Mobrik said, replacing the melon with great care. "I should never have let you near my fruit. Never. Come on." He popped a sugarberry into his mouth and shivered with delight. Then he pushed Janner toward the double doors that led to the factory, heedless of the way Janner's pockets bulged.

Janner was sent directly to the paring station. He looked for Sara Cobbler as he wound through the aisles of the factory, but he didn't see her. All the children he passed ignored him intensely, girls and boys with shovels stared at the ground as if it were the most fascinating thing they'd ever seen. Only the Maintenance Managers paid him any attention, and their attentions were of the sniggering, malicious kind. They glared at him from their perches on the walls.

Janner hoped Sara Cobbler hadn't been punished for talking to him. The Maintenance Managers hadn't seemed to notice her in the moments before they knocked him unconscious. The other coffins in the dungeon had been empty, so at least she wasn't there.

He wasn't sure what had happened inside of him at the sight of her glimmering eyes in those moments at the stairs, but he liked it. And the sound of his name on her lips, the tears in her eyes, the bright skin showing through the streaks on her cheeks— all of these produced in Janner an urgency to see her again, to speak to her.

With a sigh, Janner pulled on his gloves, surprised to find that his blisters no longer stung. He worked in a slow, steady rhythm, lost in his thoughts, finding the work almost soothing. It somehow helped him think, helped him dwell on the faces of his family, of Oskar, to think on the things he would have to do to escape.

Before he knew it, the day had passed. He stood before a pile of pared swords and forks, and the boy with the red hat and the bell strolled by, whacking it with a hammer and saying, "Shift's over. Shift's over. Shift's over, tools."

Janner ate two bowls of soup and guzzled cup after cup of water before finding his bunk. When he was sure no one was watching, he slipped the apples from his pockets and stashed them inside his pillow. He lay on his back, grateful he was no longer stuck in the horrible coffin. He stretched his arms as far as they would go, swearing to never again take for granted any room bigger than a closet.

As he drifted off to sleep, he had in his mind the beginnings of a plan.

The next day Janner woke before the bell-clanger arrived.

He had to figure out what to do with the apples. *The longer they sit,* he thought with a roll of his eyes, *the worser they get.* It was obvious he should use them to bribe the ridgerunner, but bribe him to do what? To let him go? Janner didn't think Mobrik would go that far, no matter how much fruit Janner offered. What, then? He could use the fruit to get answers to questions. He wanted to know why the Overseer used children in the factory instead of adults. He wanted to know if the Black Carriage brought all its children to the factory or if it sometimes indeed carried them to Fort Lamendron for transport to Dang. But none of those questions seemed worth a precious apple.

He needed a way out, and as far as he could see, the only way out was through the portcullis. But even if he figured a way to get through the long corridor to the empty floor, he had no way to open the gate. He'd seen the way two children strained to raise it; there was no way he was strong enough or fast enough to do it alone.

But what if he wasn't alone?

Sara Cobbler had helped him once. Maybe she'd do it again.

Janner smiled. He knew what to do. He just had to find Sara.

He scanned the faces around the table carefully. Of the forty or fifty children eating their soup in silence, none was Sara Cobbler. He studied the children serving the soup, the ones who stirred the vats of soup, but none was Sara Cobbler. Throughout his first shift he looked for her, in the faces of those who passed, those who brought him new carts of bad blades, those on the high walkways, and even among the Maintenance Managers. But she was nowhere to be seen. He began to wonder if he had dreamed her up.

When he returned to the dining hall after his shift, he found her at last.

She sat at the table on the opposite side of the room, stirring her bowl mechanically. Her face was still dirty, her hair still matted, but he knew it was her, even before she raised her eyes and rested them on him. *Stars in a storm,* Janner thought again, and he smiled at her across the room. Almost imperceptibly, like the swish of a redgill fin beneath the surface of the river, she smiled back.

Janner's insides swelled. Before he had time to think about it, he walked straight toward her. Her eyes widened, and she went back to her soup, stirring it a little too fast. Janner sat across from her and lowered his voice.

"Thank you," he said. "I remember you—from the Dragon Day Festival last year."

She didn't answer.

A Maintenance Manager passed, and Janner looked down quickly and slurped a spoonful of broth. "I need your help," he said after a moment. "We're going to get out of here—I'll get you back to your parents. But I can't do it alone. Can you help me?"

"I can't," she whispered. "They'll put me in the box again."

"You've been in the...?" Janner's heart ached for her. He wondered how many of the children in the factory had endured that awful place. "Listen. I can get us out of here. Will you help me?"

She shook her head again.

"Sara," Janner said, then he paused while another manager walked by. "I can't stay here. There's something I'm supposed to do. I don't know what it is yet, but my brother and sister and I—"

"I remember them, too," she said, staring at her bowl. "Though it's hard to remember anything before coming here. Her name was Leeli, right? And Tink. Tink was funny."

Janner smiled sadly. "Yes. He still is. But I have to find them. We have to get to the Ice Prairies."

"The Ice Prairies? Why?"

"I can't tell you." He wanted to tell her. He wanted to tell everyone there that his father was the High King of the Shining Isle, though most of these children didn't believe the place was even real. He wanted to tell Sara Cobbler because he thought she would be impressed. "You have to trust me," he said instead. "Please."

She paused. "What do you want me to do?"

Janner grinned. "I knew you were a brave one. I *knew* it."

Sara Cobbler smiled.

Janner was glad she smiled. He knew he would need it to carry him through the next three days and nights in the coffin.

42

A Nefarious Bargain

No sooner had General Khrak arrived at his palace in Torrboro and sat down in his chambers to eat than he was interrupted. He was tired of chasing the Jewels of Anniera, tired of sending disappointing messages to Gnag the Nameless. He didn't understand why Gnag wanted the children, and he didn't care. He just wanted to eat his gruel in peace. He wiped the corner of his mouth with his forearm and said, "What?"

A nervous old woman entered the room and bowed. "My lord, a visitor to see you."

"Who isss it?" he hissed as he toyed with a rat tail that garnished his gruel. "I'm eating."

"My apologies, lord," she said. "A man has arrived in Torrboro from the Ice Prairies. He wants to speak with you. He says his name is Gammon."

Khrak stared at the woman. He loathed her, but she prepared his food with such care, such devotion to his wishes, that he had restrained himself from putting an end to her many times. And now she had interrupted his meal to announce the arrival of what was sure to be an imposter. Gammon would never show his face in Khrak's presence.

But his curiosity was piqued, so he pushed back from the table and left the room, resisting the urge to push the old woman to the floor as he passed.

General Khrak situated himself on his throne and put on his fiercest teeth-baring face before he nodded to the Fang soldier to allow the man claiming to be Gammon to enter. The door swung open, and a man with black hair strode across the hall. He was dressed in furs from head to foot and looked at Khrak with a boldness that surprised him. Khrak was used to the groveling of Fangs like Commander Gnorm or Plube, Fangs who lacked the courage to meet his eye—and wisely so. Khrak had killed enough Fangs for little enough reason that they all shrank from his presence. But this man met his gaze and groveled not.

Khrak was intrigued.

"What do you want?" he asked.

"Are you General Khrak?" said the man.

"I am."

"My name is Gammon."

"Is it?" said the Fang. In a fraction of a second, he could slither down from his throne and sink his fangs into this arrogant fool. And the man must have known that. Yet there he stood, unafraid. Khrak was surprised to find that he respected the man for it. "If it's true that you're Gammon, then you must be a fool indeed to come here where you could so easily be killed. We know about you and your petty gathering in the Ice Prairies. Kimera, is it? Gnag knows all about your plans to ignite a rebellion and drive us from Skree. Do you think it is so easy as that? Do you think Gnag has not made arrangements for the destruction of your little army?"

Gammon spread his hands. "Yes, Khrak. And it is those arrangements I would like to discuss. As you said, you know I've amassed an army. You know I don't want you in Skree. You know I won't rest until you and every one of your scaly brothers is on the other side of the Dark Sea. Or at the bottom of it," Gammon said evenly.

Khrak flitted his forked tongue and waited. He kept his cold black eyes fixed on Gammon until he saw the tiniest flinch in one of his eyes. *Good,* he thought. *The man knows fear after all.*

"After all these years," Gammon continued, "I have finally learned why you came here."

"Oh? And why do you think that isss?" The conversation was far more interesting than Khrak had expected it to be.

"The Jewels of Anniera. Three children. You didn't come here to destroy us. You didn't come here to conquer our land. You came here because Gnag wanted those three blasted kids, and he suspected they fled here. Am I right?"

Khrak leaned back in his throne and toyed with the end of his tail.

"Yesss. That is correct. In the beginning, our Gnag thought little of Skree. It was the jewels that he sought, not your hills and woodlands. He cares not for such thingsss."

"I've learned about the fortress in the Phoobs," Gammon said. "I know what's happening there. And I know we don't have much time."

Khrak wondered how Gammon had learned about the operation in the Phoobs. He had done his best to keep it secret so that when it came time to unveil the plan, he would have the advantage of surprise. But it didn't matter that Gammon knew. It didn't change anything. The more the man talked, the more Khrak wanted to hear him scream for mercy.

"What do you want, then?" Khrak said with a clack of his fangs as he leaned forward. Gammon gulped, and Khrak relished his fear.

"I want," Gammon said with a sigh, "to make a bargain."

Khrak's eyes widened with surprise. He hadn't expected this. "What kind of a bargain?"

"I know where the Jewels of Anniera are. I know where they're headed," said Gammon. "And I know that you haven't caught them yet. How is it, with all your swords and teeth and trolls, you can't capture three little children? I can't imagine Gnag is happy about that, is he?"

Khrak hissed, and the point of his tail fluttered with warning.

"I propose to deliver you the Jewels of Anniera, safe and sound. And if I do, you gather your army and leave my continent. If the Fangs—*any* sort of Fangs—raise a blade against my army, I'll do away with the jewels once and for all. How would Gnag like that? How would he like it if after all these years, the treasure he sought was finally within his reach—and then lost forever?"

The two of them glared at each other. Khrak wondered if Gnag would be angrier that he had lost Skree or that the jewels had been killed. He immediately knew the answer to the question. For nine years the Nameless One had obsessed over finding these cursed jewels. If they were killed, Khrak knew he would be blamed. He was one of Gnag's oldest and most loyal soldiers, but he was no fool. Khrak would be dust on the breeze the moment the jewels were lost.

"I agree."

Gammon's eyes widened. "You what?"

"I agree, fool. If you deliver to me the three Wingfeather children, then we will leave these lands. There is little here that we want, anyway." *Of course,* Khrak thought, *we Fangs will never leave. If Gammon believes that, then he's not as smart as I thought.*

"I have your word? You'll leave, simple as that?" Gammon said.

"Yesss," Khrak said, trying to keep a straight face. *Is it really this easy?*

"Well, fine then. Fine." Gammon nodded. "My scouts have told me where they are. In two weeks, send as many Fangs as you like to the Ice Prairies, and we'll deliver the children. I suggest you bring the whole army. I've heard these children have a way of escaping." Gammon narrowed his eyes. "I have your word?"

"Of course," said Khrak. *The word of a Fang.*

"Because we'll kill them," said Gammon. "I mean it. And there are enough of us to put up a fight, so don't plan any tricks."

"Of course," repeated Khrak. "No tricksss. Will that be all?"

"Yes. That's all. Two weeks." Gammon straightened and left the throne room.

As soon as the door closed behind him, Khrak burst into laughter. He knew humans were weak and cowardly, but he had come to believe that a few at least were of *some* intelligence. Gammon, for instance, was notorious. He had boldly worked against the Fangs for so long that Khrak had even come to respect him. The way he strode into the room only minutes ago had solidified that respect—but now this? Gammon believed the Fangs would pack up and evacuate Skree as easy as that? *Gullible fool!*

As soon as Khrak had the children in his possession, the Fangs would stamp out Gammon's little army with no more trouble than squishing a roach. Gammon was as much a fool as the old woman who prepared his gruel.

"And fools," sneered Khrak to himself, "deserve the iron fist of the Fangs of Dang." He pounded the armrest of the throne. "Woman! Bring my salad!"

43

Three Days in Darkness

Hard as it was to believe, there was something positive about being stuck in the box for three long days: Janner had plenty of time to think back on what he had done to get there and what he would do when he got out. He lay in the coffin and went over it again and again, second-guessing himself, preparing his nerves for the next stage of the plan, wondering if Mobrik suspected anything.

Finding the ridgerunner had been easy enough. He was always zipping here and there, climbing chains, leaping from coal pile to gearbox to table, a sort of Maintenance Manager for the Maintenance Managers. When Mobrik came near during the second shift, Janner had called his name.

"What do you want?" the ridgerunner asked.

"I need a favor," Janner said.

"Do you have any fruit?"

And with great satisfaction, Janner said, "Yes."

"What do you mean?" Mobrik's eyes narrowed. "Where did you get fruit?"

"None of your business. Maybe I had it with me when I got here. Maybe I know things about this factory that you don't. Maybe there's a fruit tree atop the building that drops apples down the gutter and into my pockets."

Mobrik looked at the ceiling, then raised an eyebrow at Janner. "You're being funny. You're trying to be funny."

"Nope," Janner said, and he produced an apple from his pocket.

Mobrik's eyes grew as wide as the apple itself. The little creature snatched it away, then whacked Janner in the head. "That's for trying to be funny with me. I don't know where you got the apple, but you can be sure I'll report this to the Overseer. Now get back to work." He turned to go.

"But I still need a favor," Janner said.

Mobrik stopped. "What?"

"I need a favor."

"Do you have more fruit?" Mobrik asked, this time less sure of himself.

"Yes. I have more fruit, but it's hidden away. If you do the favor, I'll tell you where it is. *Two* more apples."

Mobrik skittered forward and patted Janner's pockets. "Fool. If it's true you have these fruits, I'll tell the Overseer, and we'll search the factory until they're found. Then you'll be thrown into the box again. You don't want that, do you?" The ridgerunner smiled wickedly. "I heard you in there, crying and crying. It was pathetic."

Janner ignored him. "It's true, you might find the apples. But trust me when I say I've hidden them well. It may take you days and days to find them, and by then? The longer they sit…"

Mobrik's face fell. "The worser they get." Just as Janner hoped, the ridgerunner couldn't bear the thought of letting perfectly sweet apples go to rot. "How many did you say? Two?"

"Two sweet, shiny red apples."

Mobrik bit into the apple in his hand. He closed his eyes and chewed in ecstatic silence. "Very well. If I do this favor for you, you will tell me the location of the apples?"

"Once you prove to me that the favor is done, and if you swear by the fruit of the Green Hollows and the Holes in the Mountains that you'll not betray me, I'll tell you where to find the apples."

"The Hollows! The Holes!" Mobrik gasped. "How do you know such things?"

"I just know. You have my word that I'll give you the apples if you'll swear on the Hollows and the Holes that you'll do as I ask."

"I can't help you escape, if that's what you want."

"That's not it. I want you to do something for another of the…tools."

Mobrik cocked his head and thought for a moment. "Fine. What do you want? Hurry, or the apples will worsen!"

Janner had eaten two bowls of broth the night after his conversation with Sara Cobbler, knowing he'd be stuck in the box for three days. After the third shift, when he was easing his tired bones into bed, the ridgerunner appeared again.

"It's done, boy."

"Starting when?"

"Tomorrow, first shift."

"You swear on the Hollows and the Holes?"

Mobrik straightened and adjusted his coat, offended that his honor was in question. "I swear it. On the fruit of the Green Hollows and the Holes in the Mountains."

"Thank you, Mobrik."

"Where are the apples?" he demanded.

"What apples?"

Mobrik looked so shocked he might faint.

"I'm kidding," Janner said. "They're right over there. Under the pillow in that empty bunk."

The ridgerunner darted to the bunk and removed the apples. He held them over his head in triumph, then shoved an apple against each nostril and inhaled deeply.

Janner had smiled as Mobrik skipped away, even though he knew the box awaited him. This would be his last night in a bunk for a long time, if everything went according to plan. He was determined to enjoy it.

That was days ago, as far as Janner could guess. Now, in the darkness of the box, his back ached. He wanted to turn on his side, but there wasn't room. He had thought that his first time in the box would make this time easier. It made the beginning easier because he didn't have to pass through the dreadful experience of discovering he was trapped, but knowing he had to endure three days instead of two was maddening.

Janner's stomach growled again, and he thought about the last apple. He had taken four from the basket, lost one to Mobrik at the beginning, then given him two in exchange for the favor. He hid the last one in his big glove until his second dash through the factory.

He had waited until he found Sara Cobbler at lunch, and she confirmed that Mobrik had indeed kept his word. As soon as Janner returned to the paring station, he steeled himself for another run. He dropped his giant scissors, slipped the apple into his pocket, waited until the Maintenance Managers were looking elsewhere, and bolted.

This time he zipped through the aisles toward the staircase with ease. In fact, he worried for a moment that his escape was going *too* well. He heard none of the cries of alarm this time, no signs of pursuit from the managers. He bounded up the steps, a little frustrated because this time he *wanted* to get caught.

Then he ran into someone. Someone bigger than a child. Someone wearing a ridiculous top hat.

"Another escape attempt, child?" the Overseer said with an evil grin.

Janner shrugged and smiled.

The Overseer pushed Janner to the ground and uncoiled his whip. "You'll not be smiling for long."

The worst part about being stuck in the coffin this time was that he had no way to tend to his wounds. Welts covered his arms, his back, and his thighs. The Overseer had whipped him until Janner begged him to stop. Even the Maintenance Managers looked away, probably because it reminded them of their own beatings from the same whip.

"Pick him up," the Overseer ordered. "Three days in the box."

So Janner lay in the dark, thinking again of his family, of his wounds, of Tink, wherever he was. He thought of the clean snow of the Ice Prairies, the welcome arms of Gammon's people. His stomach growled again, and he decided it was time to eat the apple. It was gone far too soon, but at least it was moist enough to slake his thirst, and it quieted the hunger pangs for a time.

He slept in fits. He descended into a numb trance in which his memories swirled before his eyes like smoke. Every sour thought he'd ever thought, every cruel word he'd ever said to his brother or sister, every selfish action he'd ever taken rose out of the darkness like ghosts and taunted him. He replayed arguments, wishing he'd said some things, wishing he hadn't said others.

He was trapped in a place where all he had was himself, and though he'd never thought of himself as a bad person, every motive, thought, and action that paraded through the blackness told him otherwise. Even his alliance with Sara Cobbler was driven by selfishness. It was true he hoped to help her escape, that he wanted badly for her to be free—but would he be willing to set her free if it meant he had to stay? He was ashamed of the answer. All his justifications—that he was a Throne Warden, that he had to keep Tink safe, that somehow he and his brother and sister might help keep the dream of Anniera alive—all of it was meaningless if he thought himself somehow worthier of being set free than any of the children in the factory, especially pretty Sara Cobbler.

After the third long day, the door to the coffin at last swung open. As before, the light stung Janner's eyes. He groaned and climbed from the coffin stiffly.

"Out, Flavogle. I see you are able to find fruit even in the box," Mobrik said when he saw the browned apple core in the coffin. "He's a sneaky boy, he is. Come on. The Overseer wants to speak to you."

Janner, though he was weary to the bone, though his body was bruised from the whip, though he was hungry and thirsty and covered with filth, grinned. He couldn't wait to visit the Overseer.

44

Mountains and Shackles

Janner climbed the steps from the dungeon slowly, willing his stiff legs to work. He would need them very soon.

Just like last time, Mobrik led him into the big, empty room where the carriage sat. No sunlight shone through the high windows, which meant it was nighttime. *Perfect.* As long as Mobrik hadn't changed the schedule, things were lining up exactly as Janner had hoped they would.

In the center of the room, the sad brown horse was harnessed to the carriage, just as before, except that it faced the portcullis, as if the Overseer were preparing to leave, perhaps on one of his trips to Tilling Court to pick up more kidnapped children.

Janner's mind buzzed, but he was too tired, too stiff to sort out whether or not this unexpected change would affect his escape. Before he could worry about it anymore, Mobrik pushed Janner through the door to the Overseer's office.

The Overseer sat at his desk, a ledger open before him. The top hat, to Janner's surprise, wasn't on his head but on a hook beside the door. The whip dangled from a hook beside the hat.

"Eyes on *me,* tool."

Janner nodded, trying to appear more exhausted than he really was. He wanted the Overseer and Mobrik to believe he was finally beaten.

"Now. It has come to my attention that you are a…resourceful tool. Mobrik here informed me that you were able to locate three apples."

"Four, sir," said Mobrik, holding up the apple core from the coffin.

Janner's heart pounded. He felt certain that somehow they had found him out. He bowed his head and closed his eyes, praying Sara Cobbler hadn't been punished.

"Four?" said the Overseer. "So. You managed to carry food into the box with you. As I said, *resourceful.* Would you agree, Mobrik?"

"Yes sir."

"Now, tool. It's obvious you managed to outwit Mobrik here. You took the apples from his fruit basket when he wasn't looking and saved them for later snacks. Mobrik told me he caught you trying to eat them in your bunk."

"That's right, sir," the ridgerunner said with a nervous glance at Janner. "Caught the tool crunching away in his bed. I snatched the apples and ate 'em myself. Couldn't let them go rotten, sir. You know what they say. The longer they sit, the worser they get."

The Overseer raised an eyebrow, and hope flickered in Janner's heart. The ridgerunner had lied about the apples. Maybe that meant he had kept Sara's transfer a secret after all. Maybe the ridgerunner had indeed honored his oath.

"Yes, we know you're very passionate about fruit, Mobrik. Thank you. Now shut your mouth." The Overseer turned his attention to Janner again. "So I propose to you, tool, that you accept a probationary promotion to the rank of Apprentice Maintenance Manager. I keep my eyes open for the resourceful boys and girls. You would no longer be forced to pare the blades. You would be given certain…*freedoms*. A new bunk, for instance. Nothing so hard and lumpy as the one you're in. And in time you would work shorter hours—as long as you performed your function well."

Janner tried to look grateful.

"Best of all, you'll get bread with your broth. How would that sound?"

Janner nodded again, suddenly unsure of himself. The thought of a softer bed, bread with his meal, and most of all, never having to lift the metal shears again, made him hesitate. Was he acting too soon? He had only been in the factory for a week, and already he was being promoted. If he stayed longer, maybe he would discover other opportunities to escape, opportunities that weren't so risky. After all, if his current plan didn't work, he would be whipped and thrown in the box again. He gulped. Four days in the box with no food or water, no light, no room to move, and this time without even an apple to sustain him—it would be too much to bear.

"Very well," the Overseer said. "Finish your current shift at the paring station, and tomorrow we'll assign you a Managerial Trainer. What about Gimbleton, Mobrik?"

"Eh, sir?" said Mobrik, who had been nibbling at the last bits of apple on the core.

"I said, do you think Gimbleton would be a good trainer for our tool here?"

"Aye sir. Gimbleton's resourceful too. And mean. The tool has already met him. Remember the boy you met the first day here? The one with the chain?"

Janner remembered, and the thought of working with that rotten boy made him sick. He didn't want to learn anything from Gimbleton or Mobrik or the Overseer. He wanted to find his family.

The Overseer stood and closed his ledger. "Escort the tool to his station, Mobrik, then come back quickly. We're off to Tilling Court again." The Overseer removed his hat and whip from the wall. "Word has come that the bereaved have collected more tools for exchange. And Mobrik?"

"Sir?"

"Do keep an eye on your fruit this time. The tool here is a sneaky one."

Mobrik bowed and pushed Janner out of the office behind the Overseer.

"I'd like you to drive tonight, Mobrik. I'll be in the carriage," the Overseer said as he crossed the large room with his hat and whip in hand. Mobrik prodded Janner toward the double doors that led to the factory.

The moment had come. Janner had to decide. Either keep quiet, obey the Overseer, and learn to become a Maintenance Manager, or run like mad and pray that young Sara Cobbler was as brave as her eyes were beautiful. But he hadn't counted on the Overseer leaving. He was supposed to stay at his desk in the office, like last time. Janner's heart thudded like a galloping horse. If anything went wrong, it would be the coffin again, and not just for him but for Sara Cobbler too.

He couldn't do it. Even if he was willing to endure the box again, he couldn't bear the thought of Sara in the coffin, all because of his foolish, hasty plan to escape.

As he approached the double doors, he clenched his fists and his jaw with frustration. He hated the thought, but maybe it would be best to bide his time as a Maintenance Manager, learn the ways of the factory better in order to find its weak spots. Then he would find a way out that didn't put Sara at risk. Of course, he would have to treat the children with as much cruelty as the other managers or they would demote him to the paring station again.

Janner looked at his hands. The blisters had healed and left knotty, leathery calluses on his palms and fingers. They reminded him of Podo's hands, and Janner stopped in his tracks.

At the thought of his grandfather, some hidden, reckless strength that ran in Janner's blood came alive and crackled like lightning. Energy flamed in his joints and straightened his bones. If Mobrik had been watching Janner instead of the floor, he would have seen the boy grow two inches before his eyes.

In his mind's eye, Janner sensed a swirl of color and heat that spun like a water mill for a moment and then settled into an image. He saw his sister, as real as the double doors in front of him. Leeli sat in a bright place, surrounded by snowy mountains, holding her whistleharp to her lips. Janner saw blurry figures in the background but couldn't be sure who they were. Then one of the figures limped past, unmistakably Podo wrapped in furs.

But where was Tink? The image swirled again and made him so dizzy that he staggered.

As if from far away, he heard Mobrik say, "What's wrong, tool? Too long in the box this time?"

The image settled again, this time on Tink's face. He looked afraid; his eyes were bruised and swollen. *Where is he?* Janner thought. As if in answer, the image widened and he saw that his brother was in a cage. Shackles bound his ankles and wrists, and in the hazy edges of the image, Janner saw several figures, so dirty and muddy that they could only be Stranders. The nearest of them bent over the cage and spoke to Tink. Janner couldn't hear the voice, but he knew even before the Strander in the image turned that it was Claxton Weaver. The image swirled again and was gone as fast as it had come.

Janner blinked and shook his head, trying to make sense of what he had just seen. He felt a rush of emotion: exhilaration at the sight of his sister on the icy peak and fear for Tink in the cage. But was this something happening now? Was this just a dream or another vision like the one Leeli had caused at the cliffs, when the sea dragons had spoken?

It didn't matter. All uncertainty was gone. Janner felt as though he could burst through the portcullis with his bare hands and run all the way to the burrow as fast as a horse.

"Tool!" Mobrik yelled.

"What? Sorry," Janner stammered, pretending to still be dizzy.

"What's the matter?" called the Overseer. Janner turned to see him leaning out the carriage door, hat in hand.

"The tool stopped walking, sir. Nearly fell over," said the ridgerunner over his shoulder.

"Do you need the sting of the whip to wake you, tool?" the Overseer called.

Janner shook his head.

"Then hurry up. The hour grows late, Mobrik." The Overseer disappeared into the carriage again.

Janner pushed through the double doors and into the long dark corridor to the factory floor. Mobrik prodded Janner on the back again and again, eager to turn him over to the Maintenance Managers and return to the carriage where the Overseer waited.

But halfway down the dark corridor, Janner stopped. If there had been more light, Mobrik would've seen that Janner's eyes were as fiery as the windows in the near distance.

He would've seen that his fists were clenched and his jaw was set. In fact, the little ridgerunner would probably have run.

Janner grabbed Mobrik by the shirt collar. He lifted the little creature and pinned him against the wall, clamping a hand over his mouth before he had time to scream for help. Janner leaned close.

"I don't intend to stay here another moment, ridgerunner. There's much to do and far to go. Now, I'm glad you kept your oath by the Holes and the Hollows, and I'm offering you another chance to do your race proud."

Mobrik's eyes widened.

Good, Janner thought. *He has reason to be afraid.*

Strength like a cool wind flowed through him, as if he were more than a twelve-year-old boy or was being made into more than one with every surge of the royal blood in his veins.

"If you swear to keep quiet and give me time to escape, then we'll leave it at that. I think you'd rather the Overseer didn't make you wear that ridiculous suit or order you about like he does. I think you wish you were still in the Killridge Mountains, trying with your kinsmen to outwit the Hollowsfolk of their fruit. Am I right? Then you remember what it was like before Gnag and his Fangs upset everything. If I can get out of here, there's a chance that—that things can go back to the way they were. You and your people could go home. Do you understand?"

Janner hardly understood himself, but Mobrik nodded.

"So are you going to keep quiet? I just need ten minutes. Can you give me that?"

Mobrik nodded again.

"Good. Now I'm going to let you go. Stay here in the corridor for ten minutes, and the Overseer won't know you helped me. Tell him—tell him I punched you and left you unconscious or something." Mobrik nodded again. Janner released Mobrik's mouth, though he kept his fist balled and ready to strike should the little man try to raise an alarm.

Instead, Mobrik asked, "Who *are* you?"

Janner took a deep breath. "My name is Janner Wingfeather, Throne Warden of Anniera."

Mobrik gasped. "You're one of the jewels!"

"That's right. Now swear it, by the Holes and the Hollows."

"Certainly, child. I have no love for Gnag or the Overseer. Go, and do whatever it is that's so important." Janner studied the little man's shadowy face. He would have to trust him.

"All right. Ten minutes, then sound whatever alarm you wish. I'll be long gone."
Janner released him.

So suddenly that it took Janner a moment to understand what was happening, the ridgerunner dashed toward the doors that led to the carriage, screaming at the top of his lungs.

45

The Fate of Sara Cobbler

No!" Janner cried. He ran after Mobrik as fast as his aching legs would carry him, but few men could outrun a ridgerunner. Just as Mobrik slammed into the swinging double doors, Janner gathered all his strength and dove after him. His fingers snagged just enough of Mobrik's boot to trip him, and the two of them struggled in the doorway. Janner dragged him back into the dark corridor, noticing as he did that the door of the carriage swung open.

To catch a ridgerunner is nigh impossible. However, subduing one once caught, while not an enjoyable experience, is easy enough. Much as he hated to do it, Janner closed his eyes, reared back his fist, and socked Mobrik in the face with all his might.

Janner had fought with Tink many times, but they had an unspoken rule that punching or slapping the face was unacceptable. This was the first time Janner's fist had ever been employed in this way. He felt a dull ache in his knuckles, and the ridgerunner went limp. The Overseer's footsteps approached the door.

Janner dragged Mobrik to the wall and looked around frantically, wondering what to do. The Overseer wasn't a big man, but he was much bigger than Janner, and he had the whip. Mobrik had no weapon; Janner had no weapon. His only advantage was his speed.

That was it, then. As soon as the Overseer opened the door, Janner would run for it.

He backed away from the doors, dropped into a sprinting position, and waited.

The Overseer stopped on the other side of the door. "Mobrik?" he called. "Are you there?"

Janner waited. Through the dirty window he could see the top hat tilting as the man listened.

The Overseer shifted and took a step nearer the door. "Mobrik?"

Janner could stand it no longer. He ran with every ounce of strength he could gather. He closed his eyes, bared his teeth, and rammed his shoulder into the swinging door. It hit the Overseer in the face, knocking him backward. He landed hard on his back.

Janner's feet barely touched the ground as he ran. Out of the corner of his eye, he saw pain and confusion on the Overseer's face, and without thinking or knowing why, Janner swept up the top hat from where it had fallen.

"Sara!" Janner screamed. "Open the portcullis! Now!" Janner ran straight for the gate, praying with every step that Sara was one of the two children in the cleft and that she would find the courage to follow through with the plan.

"TOOL!" howled the Overseer.

Janner looked back to see the Overseer pull himself to his feet and limp to where his whip lay.

"Sara!" he screamed again.

The portcullis wasn't moving. What if Sara wasn't on this shift or couldn't get the other child to help her?

"Sara, please!" he wheezed, almost to himself. His burst of strength was ebbing. He had spent three days in a box with nothing but an apple to eat, and he was beginning to feel it.

"TOOL!" the Overseer raged again. "There's no escaping the factory!"

Then Janner saw a crack between the cobbled street and the teeth of the portcullis. It was rising.

As he passed the horse and carriage, an idea struck. He bounded from the front wheel of the carriage to the driver's seat, grabbed the reins, and snapped them.

"Up! Up, boy!" he cried, and the sad horse lowered its head and heaved. Janner looked back to see the Overseer lurching nearer, cracking the whip wildly. But he was hurt. His back was hunched, and one leg dragged behind him.

The Overseer screamed again and again, but Janner had stopped listening. If Sara opened the door in time—it was most of the way open already—he would reach down and take her hand. He would swing her up to the carriage seat, and they would gallop through the empty streets of Dugtown until they were sure they had outrun their pursuers.

The horse moved at a trot. Janner ducked his head as the carriage passed into the entryway. Through the open portcullis, he could see the dark streets of Dugtown.

He stopped the horse at the gate and peered into the darkness where Sara stood. She and a young boy held the chain that kept the portcullis open. Her eyes were wide with fear.

"Sara, come on. There's no time."

She shook her head.

"Sara! The Overseer's coming. We need to go." Janner reached for her, just as he had planned.

But Sara shook her head again. "There's nowhere for me to go, Janner. I'll die out there."

"No you won't! I'll take you to your parents. Don't you want to see your parents again?"

"The Fangs will find us. They'll put me in the Black Carriage again. I can't bear it. I can't. At least here, there's food and water and a bed to sleep in."

"Sara, please. You have to come with me. The Overseer—he knows you helped me. He heard me call your name."

The Overseer's enraged voice echoed from behind them. The boy beside Sara started to cry.

"Hush," she said. "It'll be all right. Janner, go."

Janner was determined not to leave her. He didn't want to leave any of the children in the factory. He wanted to tie the Overseer's arms, lock him in his office, and swing wide the doors of the factory and set the children free. But where would they go? Maybe Sara was right. They would pour into the dark streets of Dugtown and try to find their parents, but many of these children weren't from Dugtown at all. Like Sara, they had been snatched by the Black Carriage and taken here instead of Dang. There seemed to be no safe place in all the world for children—no safe place but the Ice Prairies.

"Sara, listen," Janner pleaded. "If you stay, the Overseer will throw you in the box again. He might send you off in the Black Carriage anyway. At least with me you have a chance. Please."

Sara took a deep breath. Janner held out his hand again. She nodded and with a trembling hand, reached for the mechanism that secured the portcullis.

"Tools," came the Overseer's wicked voice. He stood at the rear of the carriage, leaning against the wheel for support. He cracked his whip and sneered at Janner.

Sara screamed, and the boy with her let go of the chain and clamped his hands over his eyes. He pushed himself into the corner and curled into a ball. The portcullis lurched down a notch.

"Janner, go! I can't hold it!" Sara shrieked, not looking at Janner but at the Overseer, inching his way between the carriage and the brick wall.

Janner could stop him. He had done it once, and now the crazed man was hurt. He would have to be quick, but he could do it.

Just before he sprang to the ground to confront the Overseer, Mobrik appeared. He moved in a blur, past the carriage and into the cleft where Sara stood. The ridgerunner pulled her hair and clawed at her hands, trying to force her to release the chain that held the portcullis. The gate lurched down another notch. Any more and the carriage wouldn't fit.

"Go!" Sara screamed again.

Already burning with guilt, already aching from the sadness he knew he would feel, Janner snapped the reins. The carriage pulled forward, bouncing as it rolled over the Overseer's foot and dragged him to the ground. Mobrik finally overcame Sara Cobbler, and the portcullis came down. The rear of the carriage cleared the falling gate by inches.

Janner turned, tears stinging his eyes, and caught a final glimpse of the FORK! FACTORY! sign. Below it, through the bars of the gate, he saw the Overseer rolling on the ground, screaming. He saw Mobrik's face, his lip curled with hatred as he watched Janner escape.

And he heard Sara Cobbler crying.

For several minutes, Janner knew nothing but that sound. It filled his head and became not just Sara's voice, but the voices of all the children in Skree, all the parents in Skree whose lives were torn and trashed like old paper.

46

The Strander Burrow

The carriage careened through the streets of Dugtown, and soon Janner realized he was crying and so tired that he felt he could fall asleep on the bouncing, swaying bench of the driver's seat. He closed his eyes and let the horse run.

He wasn't sure how much time had passed when the horse finally stopped. Janner opened his eyes to find that the carriage had stopped in the middle of an intersection of two streets: Green Blossom Avenue and Vineyard Avenue. It looked much the same as the other streets he had seen—tall buildings with dark windows slept in the glare of the torch towers, and trash littered the gutters. Nothing moved.

"Oy there! Overseer!" came a voice from above.

Janner froze. He squinted up at the torch tower nearest him. A Fang crouched at the edge of the platform, silhouetted by the fire. Janner's mind went blank with terror.

"Where are ye off to tonight, eh?" the Fang called.

The top hat. It sat on the seat beside Janner. As casually as he could, he placed it on his head.

"Er, Tilling Court, sir," he said gruffly.

"More children to exchange, then. Good. The boss will be glad about that."

"Yes. Er, yes, he will."

"Well, then," the Fang said, "get on with it."

Janner nodded and pulled away as quickly as he dared. He turned the carriage onto Green Blossom Avenue. If he remembered correctly, Green Blossom intersected with Riverside Road, and then he just had to turn left and follow it out of Dugtown.

A few minutes after he turned onto the wide road, a regiment of Fangs marched by. Janner fought every urge in his body to leap from the carriage and flee. Instead he lowered the hat and drove on without looking at the Fangs. They marched by without a glance.

Several minutes later, Janner reached the corner where the Florid Sword had dealt with the Fangs. Two doors down hung the shingle of the Roundish Widow. Janner gulped as he drove the carriage past, hoping Ronchy McHiggins was safe and sound, fast asleep in his lonesome bedroom. He looked sadly down the alleyway beyond the tavern. It was there that he had last been with his family and Oskar. It was there that things had gone so horribly wrong, thanks to Migg Landers.

Then he remembered with a start that the Overseer and Mobrik would surely raise an alarm. They would get word to the Fangs that he had escaped—and Mobrik would tell them who he was. They wouldn't just be looking for some boy but for one of the Jewels of Anniera.

The carriage rolled past boathouses, past the place where he had last seen Tink, past Crempshaw, the shortcut that had sent Janner to Tilling Court. As he rolled by, the torch towers hissed and crackled above, but none of the Fangs on watch said a word, though Janner sensed their eyes on him. To his right, blacker than the night sky, lay the Mighty Blapp. Janner was aware of it only as a stretch of darkness with a fishy odor, and now and then he heard a splash of water or the thunk of a boat against a dock.

At the edge of Dugtown, the buildings grew sparser and the roads rougher. Missing cobbles jarred the carriage again and again, until Janner found himself bouncing down a muddy road pocked with potholes.

He reined up the horse and looked back at the town. He had been traveling gradually uphill for some time, and the river now lapped at the bottom of a steep bank that dropped away to the right. He had passed the last of the torch towers and felt much safer in the darkness on the edge of town.

Judging from the view of the city below him, the house with the Strander burrow should be close. For the first time since his escape, Janner believed he might actually see his family again. He tried not to think about the image he had seen of Leeli in the snowy mountains. If it was true, it meant his family had left him behind. They had abandoned him. It had been days—he wasn't sure how many—since their separation at the Roundish Widow, and the rational part of him knew they couldn't wait forever. Podo had Leeli to think about, not to mention Nia and Oskar.

But how could they just leave? No, they would still be there, waiting.

He imagined his mother's warm embrace and the look on Leeli's face when he appeared in the burrow. Podo would clap him on the back and roar his approval that Janner had found a way back.

But what about Tink?

The image of Tink in the cage killed all thoughts of joy and happy reunion. If the vision of Tink in the cage was true, there would be no time to rejoice.

Janner forced such thoughts away and dismounted the carriage. There was nothing to do but find the burrow and pray his family was still there.

He unbuckled the horse's harness, then swatted his rump and watched him gallop away.

Then Janner ran too. He hopped over potholes as he trotted up the hill, keeping a close eye on the buildings to his left. He worried he wouldn't remember what the old house looked like, but then he saw it.

He stopped in front of the house, wondering where the old snoring man might be, and listened. He heard the great silence of the river behind him. Goats and chickens fussed in their sleep nearby. Frogs chirped. And a bell rang.

Janner's skin went cold. He looked down the slope at Dugtown and saw movement. The bell clanged and clanged, then more bells joined it. The sound rolled up the hill like an invisible wave. Suddenly the fires on the torch towers flared, first one, then another and another, until all of them burned twice as bright as before. Even from this distance, Janner felt exposed. Then, like a long, many-eyed serpent, a host of Fangs with torches moved through the streets and coalesced on Riverside Road.

He had seen Fangs assembled in this way the night they coursed into Glipwood from Fort Lamendron. They were on the move and coming straight for him. Already he could hear the *thud-thud-thud* of the march.

Janner ducked into the darkened house.

The Fangs were already near enough that he could hear the pace-keepers bellowing a chant and beating a drum. It was hard to believe he was the cause of all this trouble. *Do they really need a whole army of Fangs to find one boy?* he thought.

His foot bumped the iron ring of the trapdoor that led to the cellar. He flung it open, climbed down, and pulled the door shut. He groped his way in the darkness to the wall where Podo had triggered the mechanism that opened the secret door. He felt along the cracks in the wall just as Podo had, cringing at the thought of the insects he might disturb.

Please, Janner prayed, *let them still be here.* If the Fangs were going to catch him at last, then he didn't want to be alone. He grew more and more frantic as the mechanism eluded him, on the verge of tears, begging the Maker to let his loved ones be in the burrow. Finally, he felt a tiny metal wire with a loop in the end. He stuck his finger in the loop and tugged. He heard a click, then the creak of the trapdoor swinging open somewhere behind him.

He dropped to his hands and knees and crawled to the hole in the floor. There was no glow of lamplight, no sound of breathing. A black, empty silence awaited him in the burrow. Janner's heart sank. *Maybe they just snuffed the candle, or maybe they're hiding in the tunnel,* he thought, knowing it was a fool's hope.

With a heavy sigh, Janner swung his feet into the hole and climbed down. He pulled the second trapdoor shut and descended into darkness as thick as that of the Overseer's coffin. After a moment of searching, he found the lantern beside the ladder and the box of matches with it.

When yellow light from the strike of the match filled the chamber, Janner was so shocked by what he saw that he wouldn't have been surprised if his heart leapt up his throat, out of his mouth, and landed with a splat on the dirt floor.

Someone sat against the opposite wall, staring at him.

She was dressed in rags, her skin leathery and caked with grime, and her eyes were bottomless pits set in the wrinkled landscape of her face. She looked familiar, which told Janner she must be one of the hags of Tilling Court.

He dropped the match and everything went black.

She laughed. It was a dry, papery laugh, a dead crackle.

"Child," she whispered.

Janner was too terrified to move. He imagined her crawling toward him in jerking movements, those wide, black, spidery eyes able to see him in the dark somehow. Fangs bumped and growled in the house above. He wondered which was worse: capture by the Fangs or the wet stink of the hag in the cellar.

"Child," she whispered again, louder.

Janner closed his eyes and tried to shut out the world. When he heard the woman grunt and drag herself across the floor toward him, his breaths came in short, desperate gasps. His head seemed to thicken; bright points of light danced across his eyelids.

Her hand touched his foot, and Janner tried to scream, but his voice made no sound. The stars burst into fiery colors, and he had the sensation of falling slowly upward and into the dreadful, silent well of space.

47

A Change of Heart

The next thing Janner knew, he was coughing. Dirt filled his mouth. He sputtered and spit, aching for a cup of water to wash the grainy sand from his teeth and tongue. When he opened his eyes, he was surprised to find there was light. Then he remembered the hag, the Fangs, the hand on his foot—

He sat up.

The woman sat against the wall, the lantern at her side.

"Child, ye forgot to cover your tracks." He didn't know what she was talking about, so she pointed. "The string, child. Always pull the string."

Janner looked up at the ladder and saw a string dangling near the wall. He remembered Podo had pulled it to release dirt from the ceiling to hide the trapdoor.

"Sorry, uh, I forgot. The Fangs," he said, "they're gone?"

"Oh, they're always nearby, slitherin' about their murderous work." She paused. "You don't remember me, do ye?"

He shook his head. Her face was familiar, but her accent was much thicker than Gorah the hag's. She was so dirty she may as well have been wearing a mask.

"I knew yer grandpa, remember?"

"Nurgabog?"

"Aye." She sighed.

"But—what are you doing here? What happened?"

"Easy up on the questions, lad. First things first. Ye want to know where your family is, don't ye?"

"You know where they are?"

Nurgabog shook her head. "First things first, lad."

She coughed, and Janner saw that her breathing was shallow and watery.

"What's wrong?" he asked.

"Claxton. He's mad as a blat." Her chin quivered. "Hurt his own mother, he did." She waved her hand in the air. "No matter. Right now I need water, and I need ye to help me change the dressing on me wounds."

She held the lantern up so that he could see her side. Blood soaked her ragged dress.

"Claxton did this?" Janner asked quietly.

"Aye. Now scurry up the ladder and find a cup or a bucket. Creep down to the river and bring back some water. All the supplies here are gone—gone with your family."

"Please, tell me where they are," Janner said.

"If ye don't get me any water, I might faint and never wake up. It's been days, lad. Go. Shouldn't be hard to find a vessel in all that junk. And be mindful of the Fangs. I've heard naught of 'em since you took yer little nap." She laughed again, that weak, crackly laugh that set her coughing so badly she toppled over and lay on her side in the dirt.

Janner didn't wait to be told again. He scrambled up the ladder. At the top he listened for movement and heard none. When he pushed the trapdoor, it didn't open. He pushed again but was afraid to break the latch.

"Er, Nurgabog?"

"It's behind…the ladder," she moaned.

He found another looped wire behind the top rung of the ladder, tugged it, and the door clicked open, spilling dirt into the shaft.

When he emerged from the house, Janner found dawn fast approaching. No Fangs marched past, and no old man snored on the stoop.

In the rosy gold light of the sky just before the sunrise, Janner searched the debris around the house until he found a large clay pot. There was no sign of Fangs, so he sprinted across the road and skidded down the bank to the water's edge. The surface was glassy, undisturbed except by occasional rings where water bugs alighted. Suddenly a fish broke the surface with a great splash and hung in the air for a moment before pointing its needle-sharp snout back into the water and sinking away.

"A daggerfish!" Janner said with wonder. Then, more seriously, "A daggerfish." He filled the pot and scrambled away from the water line.

Nurgabog was unconscious when Janner returned. He nudged her and helped her to a sitting position. She smelled awful and looked even worse, but Janner felt a surprising affection for her. She had known and even loved Podo in his younger days, which made her less like a hag or a Strander and more like a long-lost grandmother.

"Much better," she said after she had a long drink. "Now tear off a bit of that shirt you're wearin' and clean it good."

Janner hated to ruin his only shirt, but he did as he was told and set about changing Nurgabog's bandage. The wound in her side reminded Janner of Podo's the night he almost died in the weapons chamber at Anklejelly Manor. If only he had the flask of water from the First Well. Old Nurgabog certainly needed it more than the gargan rockroach.

"Better," she said when they were finished. Her eyes were clearer. "I didn't want ye runnin' off without takin' care of old Nurgabog first. Can't trust a soul on the Strand."

"You can trust me," Janner said.

Nurgabog studied his eyes for a moment and smiled. "Aye. I believe I can."

"Where's my family? Where's Tink?"

"Tink?"

"Kalmar, I mean. Where are they?"

"Well, lad," Nurgabog said carefully. "You're not gonna like the answer. And mind you, all I'm about to tell ye came from several Stranders from several clans. Word gets about, you know."

Janner nodded.

"Yer family left three days ago. Your mother was afflicted with a fierce grief over you and yer brother. They never heard her say a word, but she cried aplenty. Cried like the sun had set forever, they told me. But Podo kept tellin' her that you boys would be fine. Said ye knew how to take care of yourselves, and Maker forbid, if ye didn't, there was nothing he could do about it. They had the girl, see."

"Leeli," Janner said. His heart grew heavier with every word Nurgabog spoke.

"Aye. And he said that with you boys missing and like as not caught by the Fangs, it was their job now to keep her safe. They waited as long as they dared, then they set off to the Ice Prairies with many a prayer and a tear for you lads."

Janner hung his head.

"Podo was right when he said there was nothing else for 'em to do," she told him. "He would've come for you, lad. Believe that. But he didn't know where you were, and even if he did, he couldn't storm Fort Lamendron or the Palace Torr with a little girl, an old bookseller, and a bereaved mother to tend to. Maybe in his younger days—ah, lad! You should've seen him in his younger days." Nurgabog wore a toothless smile and a faraway look in her eye.

"They left me," Janner said, pushing down the lump developing in his throat.

Nurgabog nodded. "Aye. They did. I'm sorry, boy."

"Wait." Janner lifted his head. "What about Tink? What about Kalmar? You didn't mention him. He's with them, right?"

Nurgabog sighed and shook her head.

"Then where is he?"

"He made a choice, lad."

"What is that supposed to mean?"

"He followed the road here, same as you." She paused. "But he kept walkin'."

"That doesn't make sense," Janner said.

"Never even stopped to see if they were still here," she continued. "And the worst part of it? They *were*. Yer whole family, sitting down here in the dirt and the dark, sendin' up prayers to the great silent Maker that you'd both show up safe and whole. And Kalmar Wingfeather marched right past with nary a look back, four days ago."

Janner felt a sob in his throat. "Why? Why would he do that?"

"Because whatever it is inside a man that calls him to the edge of things, calls him to the shadows and away from the light, must have been mighty loud in his ears. Yer brother is a Strander now, lad. That's what he wanted. He showed up in the East Bend with a fire in his eye, swinging Claxton's pone about like he owned the place."

It was hard for Janner to hear anything Nurgabog said after those words. It felt as if his insides were boiling. Rage, then disbelief, then confusion, then sorrow, then guilt—Janner's tears soaked the ground of the Strander burrow.

Why would Tink do such a thing? The Stranders were vile, thieving, murderous villains—like Fangs without scales. Why would he choose to join with such people? The High King of Anniera. Janner was glad his father wasn't alive to see his son betray the kingdom so. He knew Tink was afraid, that he didn't want to be the king. But this? A Strander?

Fine, Janner thought, wiping the tears from his eyes. *Let the Stranders have him.*

He stood and looked down at Nurgabog coldly. "How do I get to the Ice Prairies?"

"Eh?"

"I have a long way to go," he said.

Nurgabog stared at him with a sad look in her eyes. "So you're leavin' him behind?"

"You said he made a choice," Janner spat. "I'm not risking my life to try to convince him to do something he should *want* to do. I'm tired of chasing him, tired of his jokes and his selfishness. I'm tired of him. If he wants to be a Strander, I can't stop him. He would have made a lousy king anyway."

Nurgabog said nothing.

"Well?" Janner demanded.

"North of here," she said after a moment. "After about a day's walk, you'll come to the Barrier. Go east till ye find an old dead glipwood tree. Thirty paces past it, you'll find a breach in the wall. The dead tree is a snickbuzzard's roost, so be wary. Move quick, or they're likely to make food out of you. It's easy enough to slip through when the Fangs are lookin' elsewhere, especially now that the patrols are so few."

"Why are the patrols fewer?" Janner asked as he crossed the room to the ladder.

"Don't know. But the Fangs seem less and less worried about Skreeans slippin' through to the Ice Prairies, which makes me a fair bit worried about what old Gnag the Nameless is doing that we don't know about."

"Thanks for your help," Janner said. "What will you do?"

"Old Nurgabog will be fine, lad." She smiled again. "Thank ye for the thought, though." She paused, looking at Janner like she wanted to say more.

"What?"

"I've a mighty argument kickin' around in me head, lad."

He waited.

"I don't know much about Anniera. Not even sure there is such a place. I don't pay much mind to what's happenin' in the great world that don't affect me. I let things pass as they will," she said. "But yer Podo did somethin' for me that nobody else ever did. I care about 'im, see. Which is to say that I care about what *he* cares about. I know he cares about you and your brother, so now I've got to wonder if he'd want you gettin' safe to the Ice Prairies alone or you doin' what's right—and maybe neither you nor your brother makin' it."

"I don't understand," Janner said.

"Don't ye want to know what happened to me? It's not every day I get stabbed by me own son."

Janner was ashamed he hadn't bothered to ask about Nurgabog's wound. "I'm sorry," he said. "What happened?"

"Your brother may have quick hands, quicker than any Strander I ever saw, but old Claxton's got talents too. Didn't take him long to find out Kalmar Wingfeather was back on the Strand. Quick hands don't make a boy invincible, do they?"

Janner's anger at Tink cooled a little, and he felt a prick of fear. "What happened?"

"It's the Black Carriage, lad."

"What about the Black Carriage?"

"The Fangs swing through once a week, thanks to an agreement Claxton made with 'em. He wanted the Stranders of the East Bend to rule more than just our little section of the river, see. Wasn't content with the way things have always been. Ye may not know it, but the Fangs are under heavy orders to collect more and more children, and children are gettin' harder and harder to come by. The Fangs allow those of us in the East Bend to carry daggers and leave us be—as long as we give 'em a few fresh children each week for the Black Carriage."

"What does this have to do with Kalmar?"

"Claxton's got 'im in a cage, waitin' for the Black Carriage right now. Kalmar thought he'd be welcome in the East Bend like a long lost son. But like I said, ye can't trust a soul on the Strand. No sooner had your brother strutted into the East Bend than Claxton beat him near to death and took back his pone."

"No," Janner said.

"Aye. It's true. And old Nurgabog tried to stop it all. Didn't want to let me old sweetheart's grandbaby get carted off. But Claxton is mad as a blat, like I said. Stabbed me in the gut and kicked me into the river. His own mother." Nurgabog covered her face with her hands.

Janner knew the Stranders were an evil bunch, but this was worse than he had imagined. And Tink wanted to join them. It made Janner sick.

"I survived, of course," Nurgabog said with a sniff. "Got word Podo was holed up in this burrow, so I came as fast as I could. Too late, you see. They were gone by the time I got here. And yer brother will be gone after tonight, when the Black Carriage rolls in."

Janner didn't know what to do.

"So," Nurgabog said, "you see my dilemma. If I kept quiet, ye'd scoot off past the Barrier and have at least a chance to find your family again. But now that I've told ye Kalmar's in a cage, you're gonna do what any good brother would. You'll try to save 'im. And you'll be caught, and you'll both be carried away." She sighed. "And now I've doomed not one but two boys to the Deeps of Throg. Of course, ye could forget what I told ye, run to the Ice Prairies, and leave Kalmar to whatever fate the Maker has for 'im, as you said you would."

Janner stood at the foot of the ladder with his head bowed low. He couldn't leave his brother.

"Thank you, Nurgabog," he said. "I'm glad you told me everything."

"So you're goin' to try and save 'im, then?"

"Yes ma'am. I have to. I'm a Throne Warden."

"Then you'll need these."

She triggered another hidden latch in the wall, and a small, square door swung open. Janner gasped. Inside were two leather backpacks, the ones Nia had made for him and Tink, complete with swords and bows.

"I reckon Podo left 'em for ye. Proof the old man believed you'd make yer way here sooner or later. The dried diggle meat is gone. I ate it. My apologies." She gave him a gummy smile.

In his pack, Janner found a folded parchment with his name on it in his mother's handwriting. He slid to the floor and opened the letter, heedless of the sad way Nurgabog watched him.

My dear Janner, it began.

I have in my life been forced to make many difficult decisions. The decision to marry your father, though it meant leaving the Green Hollows and most of my family. The decision to leave your father as the castle burned. The decision to keep his memory hidden from you and your siblings. And now it seems I am forced to make the hardest decision of all.

We can't stay here forever. The Fangs prowl, and the Stranders are an ignoble brood. Their lips flap like flags in a storm, spreading news of our flight from here to the edges of the maps. It is only a matter of time before the Fangs discover this burrow. We must, though it is more painful than I can bear, leave you.

Your grandfather assures me that you and your brother are more capable than many men he has fought beside and that you will find your way. My tears have wet the ground, and I have fought him, but I have lost that fight. Your sister must be safe. We must move on. My hand trembles as I write this, so great is my fear for you. Keep your brother safe. Keep yourself safe. And find your way. Know that a fire of welcome burns for you in the Ice Prairies. Maker help you.

Love,
Your mother

Janner sniffed and wiped his eyes. At the bottom of the page, written in a much less refined hand, was a note from Podo.

Lad,

Stay away from the roads. You and your brother need to find a breach in the Barrier, then push through the mountains. I've word from an old Strander that the Stony Mountains look tamer to the west but that its a lie of the land. The only way through is east, into the crags. Find the trail that winds over the right shoulder of the highest peak. Its called Mog-Balgrik, which Oskar tells me means "the Witch's Nose."

Once you're past Mog-Balgrik, the land slopes away into the Ice Prairies. After that your guess is as good as mine. Keep clear of bomnubbles and snick-buzzards and cliffs. The good thing is, you'll see no Fangs. Keep your little brother safe. He needs you.

Podo

Beneath Podo's signature was a line written in a careful, flowing script:

Janner, I have your book. I'll keep it safe until you arrive. In the words of Bronwyn Silverfoot, "I hope you don't mind."

Oskar N. Reteep,
Appreciator of the Strange, the Neat, and/or the Yummy

Janner tossed the packs over his shoulder and hugged Nurgabog (careful not to breathe through his nose while he did so). She pinched his cheek and told him where to find the lever to open the cages, then Janner clambered up the ladder to rescue the High King of Anniera.

48

The Cages

As soon as Janner left the house, he spotted Fangs.

A company of them marched west, down the hill to Dugtown, and in the distance more approached from the eastern reaches of the Strand. Janner slipped back into the house and peeked out the window. The wind shifted, and Janner caught the smell of fire mingled with the reek of the river and the Fangs. Then he saw that houses all along the Blapp were burning. That probably meant they would soon torch the house where he was hiding.

His first thought was for Nurgabog. But even if the house burned to the ground, the burrow would remain hidden beneath the ashes. He didn't doubt she could find a way out through one of the hidden passageways. But how would he get all the way to the East Bend of the Strand in broad daylight? It would have been difficult even without the Fangs seeking, of all the souls in Aerwiar, Janner himself.

He took a deep breath. There was nothing to do but run and avoid the road.

Janner jumped the fence behind the house, squelched through the mud of what used to be a pigpen, and sprinted across the clumpy back field to a stand of trees that had overgrown a fence line. As he ran, the two backpacks bounced and rattled and reminded him of Tink with every bump. At the trees, Janner caught his breath and looked for his next point of cover. He spied a tangle of brush and thorn on the opposite side of another pasture, and ran.

In this way Janner pushed eastward, bursting from sagging barns, across fields, to shallow, weedy streams, up gradual hills, and so on, until he was covered with burrs and cut by thorns.

He didn't allow himself to think of Sara Cobbler, or Nurgabog, or even himself. He thought of nothing but the vision of Tink in the cage. In the vision he was frightened, cold, alone, and helpless. Janner still wanted to grab him by the shoulders and shake some sense into him, but there would be time for that after he was safe.

It wasn't long before Janner spotted signs of a Strander clan. Smoke rose from a small fire at the opposite end of the field. Figures moved about. Laughter drifted across to where Janner squatted in the brush. After several minutes he crawled through the tall grass until he was sure he was far enough away to stand unnoticed; then he moved on, hoping the rest of the clans would be as easy to avoid.

A few hours after the sun began its descent into the west, Janner stopped to rest. The water skin was empty. Leaning against the ivy-covered stones of an old dry well, he ate the last seven salted nuts in his pouch. After rummaging through both packs, he was finally convinced he had eaten all the food and drunk all the water. He looked into the well, as if clean water might seep up from the mud as he watched.

Janner hadn't had a proper meal since the bowls of broth five days earlier, if the broth could be considered a proper meal. Then he remembered the apple in the coffin. It had perhaps been the finest apple he had ever eaten. In spite of the heat and the worry and the hunger that plagued him, Janner smiled at the thought of the Overseer and Mobrik, mad as fire that perhaps for the first time a boy had escaped the Fork Factory. But his smile vanished when he remembered Sara Cobbler's pretty eyes shining through the soot on her face.

Janner stood and sighed. There was no time to sit around thinking about food and friends he had left behind. Not when Tink was in danger.

When Podo had led them from the Strander camp of the East Bend to Dugtown, the journey had taken a full day. But they had moved at a slug's pace compared to Janner now. Even though he had to sneak past five more Strander camps, he was still making good time. He didn't think it would be long before he reached the East Bend—though he had no idea what he would do when he got there. That he had managed to slip past the Stranders so easily gave him hope. There were advantages to being small and alone.

But there were disadvantages too.

When the north wind rushed over him, carrying with it the blood-chilling howl of a horned hound, for example, Janner ached for the strong, sure hand of his grandfather. When his stomach complained of its hunger, Janner longed for the comfort of the Igiby cottage thick with the aroma of his mother's stew. When a gulpswallow fluttered overhead and perched on a birch limb to sing its song, Janner thought of Leeli and the music that hovered around her like spring pollen in a sunbeam.

He didn't want to be small and alone for one second longer than he had to be.

When the sun set and the colors of the world deepened, Janner came to a rise in the land that overlooked the great river. He sat on a mossy boulder with his knees tucked under his chin and felt the day breathe its last. The river narrowed here, its glassy surface carved with eddies and a quiet unrest from the hidden and quickening currents that played beneath. Beyond the Blapp, the tree-spiked land sloped away to the south. Somewhere in that direction lay the road that led east to Glipwood and west to Torrboro. Along the nearer bank, Janner could see the muddy road he and his family had traveled when they first left the East Bend. To the east, Glipwood Forest gathered, wild and ancient, a thirsty shadow that opened its mouth to swallow the Mighty Blapp.

He was close. The Strander camp lay where the river and the road and the forest converged. Janner looked again at the sky in the west. The gold was gone. The dark blue sky reached from the east to snuff it out so that the stars might waken.

Somewhere nearby, if Nurgabog was right, Tink sat in a cage. Somewhere to the north, the Black Carriage came nearer and nearer, and cruel crows whirled above it. Janner imagined it as a deeper darkness creeping south along the edge of the forest.

He had to get Tink free before the Carriage arrived. By the time he reached the fringes of the settlement, the night would be complete. In the cover of darkness he would once again be glad to be small and alone.

It was time to go.

Janner crawled so quietly, with such careful placement of each hand and each knee on stone and grass, with such slow and deliberate breathing, that when he came face to face with the rabbit in the brush, it didn't flee. It considered him for a moment, whiskers twitching, then loped away as if the boy were one of its litter.

A stone's throw to his right blazed the fire where the Stranders gathered. They laughed and spat and bickered over slabs of toothy cow meat pulled sizzling from the spit. Janner's empty belly clamored for attention, but he ignored it, focusing instead on the cages that held Tink.

The ramshackle buildings and piles of firewood provided good cover from the light of the fire. Once he had descended the hill and sneaked through clusters of brush and thorn, he caught sight of the campfire's glow and heard the noisy brutes around it. He dropped the backpacks and pushed them deep into the weeds. He'd be quieter without them, and he and Tink could pick them up on the way back out.

He had inched his way into the shadows behind a shack, which was when he saw the cages. They sat on a platform beyond a stand of tall grass cut through with footpaths. It wasn't much cover, but it was enough for someone small and alone.

That was where Janner encountered the rabbit.

He paused and listened for any sign of a clan member not at the fire for some reason. But Janner was alone—other than Tink and whatever other children Claxton had in the cages. Janner slipped across a footpath and froze in the grass, then crossed another footpath and froze again. The cages—four of them—were only a few steps away.

Janner crawled to the foot of the platform. He felt in the dark along the leg of the platform and found the release lever, just where Nurgabog said it would be. He eased the lever downward until he heard a *click*. Janner held his breath, praying to the Maker the Stranders didn't hear it.

Finally, Janner stood and peered inside, already pressing a finger to his lips to silence whomever he might see.

The first cage was empty. Doubt flashed in Janner's mind. Nurgabog had sent him on this fool's rescue mission so he would be caught like a thwap in a snare. Janner looked in the next cage and found it empty as well. Cheeks burning with embarrassment and anger, he looked in the third cage and saw two eyes staring back at him.

"Tink!" he whispered, louder than he intended.

The figure in the shadows leaned closer.

"Tink?" Janner repeated softly.

"I ain't Tink," said a girl's voice. "I'm Maraly. Don't know no Tink."

"Kalmar, I mean," Janner said. "Is he here?"

"Kalmar Wingfeather? Ah, I remember you. You're his brother, ain't ye?"

Janner nodded. "Where is he? Where is Kalmar? I have to get him out before the Black Carriage comes."

Maraly shook her head and settled back in the rear of the cage. "He ain't here."

"What? Where is he?" Janner said, pressing his face against the bars.

"You're too late. The Black Carriage came early this time. Showed up last night a few hours before dawn. Whole bunch of Fangs come with it, lookin' for a boy on the run from Dugtown. I figure that would be you, eh?"

Janner felt the blood drain from his face.

"Claxton gave 'em Kalmar and the other kids he'd collected. The Fangs threw 'em in the Carriage and carried 'em away screaming, just like always."

"But—but—what about you? Why didn't you get carried off too?"

Maraly snorted. "I ain't in here for the Carriage. Even Claxton ain't so wicked he'd send off his own daughter. I'm in here for punishment."

Janner was too stunned to speak.

"Punishment," said Maraly, "for trying to help Kalmar get away. Didn't do much good, I'm afraid. Sorry. He's on his way to Dang by now."

Tink was gone.

Janner couldn't think. He stood at the cage staring at nothing, seeing in his mind's eye the image of poor Tink sitting in the cage, but now it wasn't a cage. He was in the dank belly of the Black Carriage, where death was a good dream.

"What do I do?" Janner heard himself say aloud.

"The first thing I'd do if I was you," said Maraly with a chuckle, "is run. They've seen you."

Janner snapped out of his grief to see Claxton Weaver at the fire, staring directly at him, a dagger bright in his fist.

"Come on!"

Janner flung open the cage door and yanked Maraly out. Her eyes were wide and fierce, and Janner thought for a moment she was going to pounce on him. Instead, she looked at Claxton, then at Janner, then at Claxton again.

"Maraly!" Claxton called with an edge of warning in his voice.

Then she spat in his direction, shrugged, and said to Janner, "Follow me."

She disappeared so completely into the brush beyond the cages that Janner wasn't sure at first which direction she had gone. Then he heard her voice not far away: "Hurry up!"

Janner dashed into the darkness, trying to ignore the howls of rage in the Strander camp. The whole clan, with Claxton at the fore, poured after the two children like a swarm of wasps. Maraly ran north, cutting left and right around bushes and small trees without a single look behind her. Janner huffed and puffed after her, barely able to keep up.

"Maraly, wait!" he gasped, "The packs! I have to get the packs!"

She didn't seem to hear him at first, but then she zipped away to the left and dove into a thorn bush. Janner clamped his eyes shut and followed, heedless of the sting where the briars cut his face and arms.

"Be still," she whispered, and Janner was still.

Claxton roared past, cursing his daughter Maraly with words Janner had never heard even from Podo. The rest of the clan followed, a parade of daggers and mud and anger, blind to the two children bleeding in the dark.

When the Stranders were gone, Maraly said, "So where are these packs, then?"

They winced their way out of the thorn bush and hurried past the empty camp to the place where Janner had stashed the two packs. He gave her Tink's, shouldered his own, and they were off.

Maraly knew every nook and hollow in the East Bend, and more than once Janner wondered how he would've found his way without her. She led him clear of the many Stranders traipsing through the night, growling Maraly's name and describing the terrible things they would do to her when she was caught. She showed no concern, however. She slipped from tree to tree without a word, checking now and then to be sure Janner was close behind.

As the trees thickened, the sounds of the Stranders faded into the distance, and Janner began to worry more about the toothy cows they might encounter. But he reminded himself that Maraly had lived there for many years; if there were toothy cows, she would know.

They traveled north for hours. Neither child spoke.

At last, when the air changed at the first hint of dawn, Maraly stopped. She sprang into the branches of a glipwood tree and shimmied to its swaying heights. Janner craned his neck to see her silhouette against the silver stars. He wasn't sure if he should follow, but she said, "Come on." So he climbed.

She settled into the crook of two limbs and closed her eyes.

"Maraly?" he said.

She didn't answer.

Janner made himself comfortable and lay back with his pack hugged to his chest. The sway of the tree brought to mind fine memories of Peet's tree house, and he slept. His dreams were of his brother.

In them, Tink was screaming.

49

The Fortress of the Phoobs

Peet the Sock Man woke feeling sick.

His arms were chained to his sides, as they had been since his capture after the rockroach gully. For days, his mind had turned from madness to grief, and finally to a grim understanding of exactly who and where he was. He was aware of a creaking, a salty smell, and the sound of weeping.

He blinked and looked around. He sat in the dank hold of a ship, and filthy water sloshed about his feet. All around him were people in chains. They weren't wrapped from head to foot like Peet, but their wrists and ankles were shackled to the walls of the hold. Most of the prisoners were children. Light slipped through the slats in the ceiling and fell on them like prison bars. Peet strained against his chains for the thousandth time, but the Fangs had done their work well. He couldn't move an inch.

In these moments when his mind was clear, he knew who he was. He knew he was the Throne Warden of Anniera. He knew he had been separated from his charges, his nephews and niece, the hope of the Shining Isle. His mind thrummed with words and stories and thoughts he ached to chase to their end with a pen and parchment. It had been a long time since he had held a quill. The talons where his hands used to be were good for nothing but battle.

He looked among the children for Janner, Tink, and Leeli and was relieved not to find them. But what he saw made him angry: so many children torn from their families, forced into the Black Carriage, then chained and thrown into the belly of a Fang ship.

His heart sank. He knew this wasn't even the worst of it. The ship would be rocked by storms in the weeks it took to cross the Dark Sea of Darkness. The children who survived the journey would be dragged out of the ship's hold and into the harsh desert light of the Woes of Shreve. For days they would travel in the deadly heat of the Woes to the foot of the Killridge Mountains. And even that, Peet thought sadly, would not be the worst of it. The worst would come after they had been hauled to the icy

steeps of Throg, Gnag's fortress. There, Gnag the Nameless would send them deep
into the dungeons where he would do his evil work on them.

Peet's mind grew cloudy, and that familiar madness slowed his thoughts. He knew
the Deeps of Throg. He had been there and would not—*could* not—go back. It was
too terrible a thought. But the ship was taking him there, and he could not stop it.
The chains held fast, and the wind blew steady. There was nothing he could do.

At that thought, Peet's breath began to come in short gasps. He heard himself sob,
and many of the children looked at him with big, empty eyes. The madness crept in
further, and this time he knew it wouldn't abate. He would lose himself, and a part of
him was glad. He didn't want to remember who he was. He didn't want to remember
that he had failed his family again or that he was bound for the blackest place in all
the world for a second time.

Then the bow of the ship thudded into something.

He heard shouts from above, then many footsteps on deck. For a long time the prisoners stared at the ceiling. Peet knew they hadn't arrived at Dang. They had left Fort
Lamendron but a day ago, and he didn't know why they would be stopping already,
except perhaps to gather supplies. But wouldn't they have done that in Lamendron?

Then the door in the ceiling swung open, and a wolf leapt into the hold.

Peet shrieked, not out of fear for himself but for the children in chains. He had
encountered many wolves over the years and knew what they could do. His every
instinct demanded he protect the children from this beast. He prepared himself for
the screams, and screams he heard—but not screams of pain. Peet forced his eyes
open and saw a terrible thing.

The wolf stood on two legs.

The wolf wore armor and held a ring of keys in one claw.

The wolf stared at him with red, evil eyes and smiled a vicious smile.

It waded through the water to Peet and put its snout in his face. It sniffed him,
growled, and narrowed its eyes. Then it spoke.

"You're the one they're all so afraid of, then." Its voice was deep, its manner mea-
sured and calm—not like the Fangs, who crackled and cackled and carried on like
unruly children. Peet looked into its eyes and saw something that worried him: intelligence. "You won't be so fearsome after we're finished with you, birdman. Welcome
to the Phoob Islands."

The wolf turned away and set to work loosing the children and herding them up
the ladder to the deck.

The Phoob Islands? Peet thought. Then he remembered. *"It's the Phoob Islands for you,"* Khrak had said in Fort Lamendron. The Phoobs were in the north, between Fingap Falls and the Ice Prairies, a scattering of small islands, some of which boasted port cities crawling with pirates and sailors and traders—or so he had heard. He had never been there, but he had seen the islands from the cliffs. They were brown stony bumps on the back of the sea, like a flock of giant turtles resting off the coast.

Peet couldn't understand why they were here and not on the way to Dang, but he understood all too well where the walking wolf had come from, and it filled him with dread.

The wolf dragged Peet out of the hold and with one hand threw him overboard. He sank fast in the frigid water. He didn't think they'd let him drown, but even so he was thrashing with panic when the wolf finally drew him out by the chain like a fisherman hauling in his catch. Peet lay shivering on a rock and stared at a cold blue sky. Above and to his left, sad-eyed children in shackles walked the gangplank from ship to pier under the watchful eye of the walking wolf.

The creature stood with one foot propped on a crate and stared at Peet as he waved the children on. When the last child crossed over, the wolf lifted Peet to the pier and stood him where he could look out at the Dark Sea.

"Gnag no longer needs to send them to Dang, you see. He has moved his operation here and has made many…improvements." The wolf took a deep breath and smiled. "Ah, the cold air. Do you feel it? It's good for a Grey Fang."

The wolf spun Peet around. High above towered the cliffs at the edge of Skree. At the verge of the cliffs, he saw instead of trees the shine of snow and ice. At the foot of the cliffs a narrow road led to a ferry crossing. The ferry itself was moving across the channel to the island. Peet couldn't make out what was on the ferry, but he saw movement and perhaps a few horses. At the end of the pier where he stood began a path that led to a fortress carved into the brown stone of the island. The walls were thick and covered with lichen, worn from a thousand years of weather and battle. Along the top of every wall, on every turret and along every road were more of the walking wolves—Grey Fangs.

Thousands of them.

"In fact," said the Grey Fang, "we love the cold air so much that we're planning a visit to the Ice Prairies. Perhaps you've been there? They say it's beautiful and that many Skreeans over the years have made the journey. Don't you have some family in the Ice Prairies, Wingfeather? We'll be sure to greet them for you when we arrive."

Peet could scarcely believe it, but it sounded like Podo had led the children and Nia to the Ice Prairies. They'd survived.

But they weren't safe. They had no idea the Grey Fangs existed. Peet struggled and tried to speak through the chain stretched across his mouth.

The Grey Fang didn't laugh or taunt the Sock Man. It just watched him with those intelligent, evil eyes and smiled.

50

The Witch's Nose

When Janner woke the next morning, the first thing he saw was a fazzle dove. It perched on a branch just beyond his feet, eying him with great irritation. Maraly was nowhere to be seen, but Janner wasn't surprised. She was a Strander, which meant she couldn't be trusted or relied upon. As he had drifted off the night before, he decided that if he was alone when he woke up, he would push on to the Barrier and not give her a second thought. He had survived the Fork Factory, Miller's Bridge, and countless Fangs. He knew the journey to the Ice Prairies would be difficult, but he believed he was capable of making it alone.

The fazzle dove *hoodle-oodle-oodled* and flapped away. Janner stretched and sat up. The air was chilly enough that he could see his breath lifting through the yellow leaves of the glipwood tree. Then a fine smell drifted into his nose. He looked down through the branches and saw Maraly poking at a small fire near the trunk of the tree.

"Hey," he said.

"Hey," she answered.

He climbed down. She sat on her haunches, picking her teeth with a small bone. All around the fire lay gray and white fazzle dove feathers. Maraly pointed at a flat stone beside the fire where the remainder of the bird lay.

"Thanks," Janner said, and he meant it. The meat was hot and juicy, but there was too little of it. "Is there any more?" he asked when he had picked the little bones clean.

"You can catch one of your own if ye like. Might take ye awhile, though."

"Oh." He hadn't eaten that well in days, and it only made him hungrier. "Is there any water?"

Maraly stood and wiped her greasy fingers on the front of her shirt. "Aye. There's a creek about an hour north. Up near the Barrier. I see that's where you're headed," she added when Janner's face lit up.

"Yeah. Do you know a way through?"

Maraly snorted. "Gettin' through's easy enough. Especially now that the Fangs are scarce. It's *after* the Barrier that's the hard part. Where do ye aim to go, anyway?"

Janner hesitated. He wasn't sure he wanted to tell the daughter of Claxton Weaver about his plans, even if she *had* tried to save Tink. But what difference would it make? He didn't think she would be going back to her Strander camp anytime soon, not after the way Claxton growled and cursed at her during the pursuit.

"I can't say," he told her.

She raised an eyebrow. "Ye can't say."

"Well—I don't know if I can trust you."

She snorted again. "Don't tell me, then. I reckon this is where we part ways." She kicked dirt over the fire and strode into the woods before Janner had time to stop her.

"Go on, then," he said under his breath when she had disappeared into the forest. "I don't need you."

Janner made sure the fire was out, then shouldered the two packs, took a look around, and realized he didn't know which way was north. The sky was overcast, and as hard as he tried, he could see no clear shadow. He tried to remember which way they had come, but every direction looked the same.

Something moved in the woods not far away.

"Maraly?" Janner said timidly.

He heard the noise again, a snap of twigs.

"Is that you?" he said.

A quill diggle hissed and burst from behind a nearby tree. It skittered toward him and turned to sling its quills.

Janner fumbled for his sword, but the second pack over his shoulder bumped the hilt out of reach. The quills vibrated and the diggle made a clicking sound with its mouth, a sign it was about to strike. Janner forgot his sword and ducked behind the tree just as the quills flew. Hundreds of them stuck into the trunk, and four of them sank into his calf.

"Ow!"

The diggle chattered on the other side of the trunk, then dashed around the tree and turned to strike again. Janner ran back to his pack, drew his sword, and spun around.

But the diggle was already dead.

Maraly leaned against the tree, still picking her teeth with the bird bone, holding the dead diggle by the leg. Her dagger protruded from its throat.

"I would've killed it," Janner sputtered.

"Sure ye would've."

"Just caught me by surprise is all."

"Sure it did." She pointed at his leg. "Better get those out quick, or you'll be sick as a dead dog."

"Oh." Suddenly nauseous, Janner staggered backward, tripped, and landed on his rump.

Maraly removed the quills, which hurt much worse than Janner thought it would, and put a poultice of spit and ashes over the wounds. She pulled him to his feet.

"So where are ye headed then?"

"The Ice Prairies." His cheeks burned.

"All right."

And they were off.

They traveled north for an hour. Twice Maraly calmly told Janner to get into the nearest tree just as a toothy cow charged past. Janner never heard them coming, and he thought each time how glad he was that Maraly was with him. He would never have made it this far alone.

When they reached the stream, they dropped to all fours and drank deep from the clear water. After they filled the water skins, Maraly cleaned and inspected Janner's diggle wounds.

"You'll be fine," she said. "Now listen. The Barrier is just over the next rise. Don't know the last time I seen a Fang patrol this far east, but keep watch anyhow. There ain't no breach, but there's enough trees that we can climb right over. Once we're past the wall, the goin' ought to be easy enough. Until we get to the mountains, that is. Do ye have a map or somethin'?"

Janner showed her the instructions on the letter, and she nodded.

Just over the next rise, he got his first glimpse of the Barrier.

He wasn't sure what he'd expected, but he was far from impressed. He was only twelve, and he felt he could've done a better job than the Fangs had done. The logs that made up the Barrier were roughly hewn, and some still had branches sticking out at odd angles. They were of uneven lengths, different sizes and kinds of trees. It looked as if the Fangs had built the wall in a day, with blindfolds on.

And yet, it *was* a wall. It stood between them and the foothills of the Stony Mountains and indeed made it much more difficult to travel that way, so it accomplished exactly what the Fangs intended.

If the wall hadn't been so rickety and tall, it might have been easy to climb up one side and down the other. But as Maraly had said, the Barrier wound through Glipwood Forest, so they took to the trees. They climbed an oak, scooted along a fat limb

Snickbuzzard

Common in the Stony Mountains, the snickbuzzard is a creature of great confusion to those who study and classify species. The large bird has feathers, fine fur on its batlike wings, and most confusing of all, a bellybutton. Avoid snickbuzzards at every opportunity.

From Pembrick's *Creaturepedia*

that hung over the wall, then down another tree. As simple as that, they were on the other side.

There wasn't a Fang in sight.

Janner and Maraly sat with their backs against the Barrier and rested.

"Have you been to this side before?" he asked.

"Nope. This is new territory for me."

"You don't have to come with me, you know."

Maraly nodded. "I know I don't. But what else am I gonna do?"

"You can't go back?"

"I could."

"But you don't want to."

"Nope."

They sat in silence.

"Sorry about Kalmar," Maraly said.

Janner said nothing. He had been trying not to think about his brother. He was angry at himself for failing him. He had failed everyone. If he and Maraly made it safely to the Ice Prairies, how would he face his mother? Podo? Leeli? How would he explain to them that he had lost Tink to the Carriage?

Then his anger turned toward Tink—Tink, who had run straight past the Strander burrow and to the scoundrels of the East Bend. Straight to Claxton Weaver!

"Let's go," Janner growled, and he stormed away from Maraly.

They walked in silence all morning and into the afternoon. The hills steepened and trees grew sparser. A north wind snaked over the land and howled at the children, as if warning them they were unwelcome. The air grew colder with every step, and Janner began to worry about keeping warm. The gray sky hinted at the coming winter, not to mention the cold north. They would have to find skins or thicker clothing if they were to survive. Maraly didn't seem concerned, however, which gave Janner hope that perhaps she knew something he didn't about finding warm clothing. She seemed to know a lot of things Janner didn't.

Her dagger provided their food. Whenever a flabbit or thwap or diggle ran across their path, she flung her blade faster than Janner could blink. Each time, they stopped so she could clean the meat and store it in a satchel until they stopped for the night.

Once, she grabbed Janner by the elbow to stop him. She held a finger to her lips and pointed at a slight depression in the ground, no bigger than a wagon wheel. She crept to the edge of the circle, slid her fingers beneath a sort of lid, and flung it open. With a great croaking and belching, an enormous bumpy digtoad leapt from its nest and slopped away into the woods. Maraly fell onto her back, howling with laughter at the look of surprise on Janner's face.

Toward the end of the day, Janner and Maraly climbed a slope that seemed to go on forever. The hill was barren but for one leafless elm at the top. Maraly pointed at the tree.

"It's a snickbuzzard," she said.

Janner wasn't sure he believed her at first. Nothing in the tree moved. Then a black shape at the top spread its wings and adjusted its position.

"Is it dangerous?" Janner said.

"Yeah," she said, "but there's just one." And she charged it.

Janner watched helplessly as the snickbuzzard swooped down at the girl. She screamed as she ran. When the bird dove, she dropped into a roll and the snickbuzzard's talons just missed her. Maraly spun around and flung her dagger. The bird squawked, tumbled to the earth, and lay still.

Maraly brushed herself off, dragged the snickbuzzard to the tree, and gathered branches for a fire. Janner shook his head and climbed the hill, wondering what other surprises Maraly Weaver had for him.

When Janner topped the rise, he froze.

Before him stretched the magnificent crags of the Stony Mountains. The snowy peaks jutted into the sky like shards of glass. Clouds gathered and poured through the passes like a slow-moving waterfall.

Janner had never seen anything so big. He felt small and weak and a little dizzy.

To the west, the mountains were smaller, and soft hills rolled at their roots. In the east, where Podo's note had told him to go, the way looked impassable. He saw nothing between him and those peaks but cracks and fissures and jagged cliffs. At the center of the eastern range rose the Witch's Nose, Mog-Balgrik. It towered above the other peaks, and truly looked like the hooked nose of a witch from a children's scarytale.

"Once you're past Mog-Balgrik, the land slopes away into the Ice Prairies. After that, your guess is as good as mine," read Podo's note.

Janner squinted at the pass to the left of the Witch's Nose. "Maker help us," he said. "That's where we're going."

"What?" said Maraly from behind him. She had removed the head of the snickbuzzard and was busy plucking its feathers beside a crackling fire.

"Look," Janner said.

She stood and looked north for the first time. "Oh," she whispered.

A gust of icy wind blasted the hilltop where they stood.

51

The Song of the Ancient Stones

The Grey Fangs that lined the corridor watched Peet in silence. Some held torches, and all held weapons. Blades and eyes shone in the dim light. A Grey Fang carried him down several flights of stairs and turned left and right so many times that Peet lost all sense of direction. He only knew he was deep in the earth, where water seeped through stone. The place looked and felt so much like the Deeps of Throg that he wondered if he had dreamed his way across the Dark Sea after all. But the Grey Fangs were no dream. Neither were the children.

On either side of the passageway stood many iron doors, beyond which children wept in the darkness. Peet's heart broke for them even as he marveled that there were so many. For years, the Black Carriage had done its slow work, stealing a few children every night.

Gnag had been busy.

At the end of the corridor stood a thick door. When they approached, the door swung open to reveal an enormous room. Fires blazed in the corners, and torches lined the walls.

On the far side of the room was the mouth of a tunnel much taller and wider than the corridor through which Peet had come. As he watched, an orange glow flickered from its depths. The Grey Fangs saw it too and waited in silence as the glow intensified. Something was coming. In moments, four black steeds emerged, harnessed to the Black Carriage. A figure in a flowing black robe sat atop the carriage with a torch in one hand. Crows followed the carriage even here; they cawed and flapped around the driver, and one perched on its shoulder.

"You'll want to watch this," said the Fang as it lowered Peet to the ground.

The driver halted the carriage and released the children in the six casketlike cages. They crawled out and huddled together. Even from this distance Peet could see they were trembling.

Two Grey Fangs chained the children hand and foot and led them to a dais in the center of the chamber. On the dais was an iron structure about the size of a house. A door swung open, and out walked a tall, robed figure. The figure held out a hand and spoke a few words to a little girl. The girl answered, and a Grey Fang beside the dais scribbled something in a book. She nodded and took the figure's hand, and they stepped together through the door.

"It's good to do it as soon as they arrive," said the Grey Fang to Artham. "The fear and fatigue makes it easier to reason with them. The ones who have been here awhile, they get ideas in their heads that cause us all manner of trouble. We break them eventually. Of course, you know what I'm talking about, don't you?"

Artham tried to ignore the beast.

Another Grey Fang appeared at the opposite side of the chamber with a wolf on a leash. The Fang talked to it and stroked its fur. The wolf walked beside the Fang like a pup with its owner all the way to the dais.

Artham felt the madness lurking at the corners of his mind. He remembered a similar chamber and a similar iron box. He remembered wet stone and screams and blazing fires, and a horrid music that had driven him mad. He shook his head and shut his eyes, willing himself to remain present and aware. But when the Grey Fang opened the iron door to the box and led the wolf inside with the girl, Artham felt himself slipping away.

The iron door closed. Artham heard a guttural melody from within, a sound that filled his mind with wormy terror. He shook with such violence that the chains rattled. A moment later a red light filled the iron box and shot through the seams in the door.

Then the light went out.

One of the Grey Fangs opened the door of the iron box and stood back from the dais. Fog poured forth and spread across the floor of the big room, collecting around the ankles of the other children as they watched. Soon the robed figure emerged, leading the little girl who was no longer just a little girl. She had a snout, long teeth, and gray fur.

"Behold," said the robed figure in a thin voice, "a new creature! Her name is Scavra!"

The little Fang flexed her claws, arched her back, and howled.

"Sing the song of the ancient stones," said the Grey Fang into Artham's ear, "and the blood of the beast imbues your bones."

Artham closed his eyes again.

"Of course, you've heard that many times before, haven't you? They tell me you started to sing the tune but never finished. What was it, a hawk? An eagle? Think, you might have been soaring around the peaks of the mountains. Instead you're little more than a rat with socks on his arms. Pitiful."

The newborn Grey Fang was helped on wobbly legs down from the dais and carried away. Then a boy was forced up the steps to the iron box as another Grey Fang appeared with another wolf. The boy fought and screamed, but the figure in the robe again spoke a few words, and he stopped struggling and responded. The Fang beside the dais wrote something in the book. The boy nodded, took the figure's hand, entered the box, and the door closed.

After a longer wait this time, the melody was sung. Then came the red light, the door opened, and the robed figure emerged with a young Grey Fang, prone in her arms.

"His name is Ghrool," said the robed figure.

Peet shrieked his birdlike shriek, then fainted.

When Peet awoke, he found himself swaying again, wondering what his own name might be. He sat up and was surprised to find that his arms and legs were free; the chains that had bound him for so long were gone. Then, like a bubble floating to the surface of a pond, his memory returned.

Artham was not in another ship but in a cage. It dangled from the ceiling of the cavern, swaying to and fro. The bars were as thick as Artham's wrists, the lock even thicker. He tried in vain to squeeze between the bars, but he was neither skinny enough nor strong enough to escape. He sat down in a huff and surveyed the room below.

The Black Carriage was gone. A long line of men, women, and a few children descended the steps from the corridor and waited their turn to climb the dais and enter the iron chamber, where they gave themselves over to the wolf.

Artham was forced to watch with horror as one after another of the prisoners nodded at the Grey Fangs, took the robed figure's hand, and entered without a struggle. Some of the prisoners actually *smiled*. Artham narrowed his eyes and saw eager expressions and idle chatter among those in the line, especially when a prisoner emerged with gray fur and pointed ears. The people gestured and shook their heads with wonder.

It was always the same: a wolf and a prisoner entered the box, red light flashed while the ugly music played, and a new Grey Fang either stumbled out or was carried. Each time, the robed figure announced the creature's new name to the onlookers. Try as he might, Artham was unable to see more of the figure than the black robe. Its movement was lithe and even ghostly. Whatever the figure was—some creation of Gnag the Nameless or a human—it had great power.

As Artham watched, one of the female volunteers changed her mind and fled down the steps, but one of the Grey Fangs—and even a few of the other prisoners in line—seized her. The poor woman shook her head and thrashed, but when the robed figure extended its hand and spoke in a voice too quiet for Artham to hear, the woman calmed at once. She nodded, smoothed her tattered dress, and took the box keeper's hand. Minutes later, she was half animal.

Artham wondered where they found all the wolves. He wondered where the new Grey Fangs were taken and how Gnag had convinced this many Skreeans to volunteer for this awful transformation.

He looked down at his talons. He missed his hands. He missed the feel of a sword hilt, the feel of another's skin beneath his fingers. All he had left were these claws—black, shiny, inhuman things at the ends of his arms to remind him of his weakness. To remind him that they had broken him and that he had fled. He wondered if it would have been better if he had just sung the song of the ancient stones so long ago. Instead he had endured year after year of torture and loneliness, year after year of listening to that foul melody accompanied by screams in the Deeps of Throg.

"Birdman," said a voice.

Artham turned to find a small window in the nearest wall. A Grey Fang leaned out, licking one of his paws with a long black tongue.

"Do you like your quarters? You make a fine pet. She said she likes to see you up here."

She? Artham wondered.

"She asked me to give you a message."

"Shoo's he? I mean—who's she?" Artham asked.

"The Stone Keeper. Down there."

The figure in the black robe was watching him. He shuddered.

"She says if you'll let her finish what Gnag started—let her turn you into a snick-buzzard or a falcon, wherever you got those talons—she'll set these children free. Said that if someone as strong as you was a part of Gnag's army, he wouldn't need any more soldiers. I think she's a fool, but what do I know? I'm just a Fang. She's been here since the beginning."

"Who is she?"

"Don't know. She's the Stone Keeper. That's all."

"And she'll let these children free if I sing the song?"

"Aye. That's what she says. Though I don't know why she'd want to. She's doing the children a great favor. Making them more than what they are. Giving them power and purpose. That's why they line up like they do—so sick of their lives they'll do anything for a chance to *cause* fear instead of feel it. None of 'em *have* to sing, you know."

"I don't believe her. Don't believe she's truthing the tell. She'd never let them free-fee-fee."

The Fang wrinkled his nose at Artham, then shrugged. "Fine, then. Here's your dinner."

The Fang hooked the cage with a long pole and drew it close enough to toss in several hunks of raw meat and a flask of water. When the Fang released the cage, Artham swung like a pendulum far above those waiting to enter the box. Some of them looked up, curious about what had captured the attention of the Stone Keeper. The woman in the black robe watched Artham's cage for several moments, then turned and welcomed the next person in line, a burly fellow rubbing his hands with excitement.

Artham hugged his knees to his chest and rested his forehead on his red arms. If the Stone Keeper, whoever she was, kept her word, all he had to do was sing the song and give himself over to the madness once and for all. He would forget what he had done. He would forget that he had failed his brother. He would lose himself, but at least the children would be free of this place. Then he remembered the jewels, and he knew he couldn't. Much as he would like to give up his fight and let Gnag do with him whatever he would, he couldn't abandon Janner, Tink, and Leeli. He couldn't abandon Anniera.

When the last in the line of volunteers was transformed and taken away, another door opened and the children from the dungeon were led to the dais. Artham pressed his face against the bars and watched with agony as a Grey Fang unchained them one at a time and dragged them to the Stone Keeper.

I can stop this, he thought.

Then he curled up on the floor of the cage and cried because he didn't know what to do. When he clamped his hands to his ears to block out the howls from below, the talons were cold against his skin.

52

The Bomnubble and
the Lake of Gold

Janner and Maraly walked for two days over a ragged landscape. The grass was no longer green but brown and scraggly. The boulders were giant brown eggs, rounded and smooth from ages of wind and rain, some of them big as houses, and bigger the farther they walked. At times the boulders so covered the foothills that the children were forced to weave between them or climb them and leap from rock to rock. But for most of their journey, they tramped up long, barren slopes of yellow grass with the Stony Mountains looming white and sharp in the distance.

They spoke little, but the silence wasn't unpleasant. Janner was glad to have a companion, Strander or no. Maraly seemed happier the farther they got from the East Bend and her father.

The wind cut through Janner's shirt and breeches, and he worried more and more about how they would survive the snow and ice. He was uncomfortably cold, but since Maraly didn't complain, neither did he. The only animals they saw were squirrely creatures Maraly called browndogs. They chittered and vanished into holes in the earth whenever the two children passed. Maraly's skill with her dagger was put to the test, but she was able to catch and clean three as they went. Her bag filled with meat, and since the weather had turned so wintry, there were no flies.

In the middle of the second long day, they reached the foot of the mountains. The steepening hills fell away to cliffs, as if they had been cut in two and the north side removed. Janner and Maraly scrambled down the pebbled slopes and several times had to retrace their steps and find another way around. All the time, the wind grew fiercer.

"You gettin' cold yet?" Maraly said over her shoulder.

"I've *been* cold."

"Aye." She sprang from one boulder to the next.

"What are we going to do?" Janner asked after they slid to the ground again.

"Don't know. Was hopin' you'd have an idea."

"Well, we can't go back. It's too far and too dangerous. We have food, and there's plenty of water. We just don't have anything to keep us warm."

"There's them bomnubbles," she said.

Janner waited for her to say more, but she didn't.

"I know what a bomnubble is," he said. "What does that have to do with anything?"

"We could get one. I ain't never seen one, but I've heard me Granny Nurgabog talk about 'em. Said they're big as a tree and furry as the hair on her toes."

"We can't kill a bomnubble," Janner said. "Even the rangers could barely kill them in the old days. Rangers tried to get rid of them to make travel in the Stony Mountains safer, but they lost too many men, so they gave up. They claimed bomnubbles were too scarce to be much threat anyway."

"What makes ye think you know so much about bomnubbles?" Maraly asked, rolling her eyes.

"Books."

"What?"

"Books. I read about them in one called Pembrick's *Creaturepedia*."

"Books, eh?" She stopped in her tracks. "*Shh!*" She flung her dagger at a brown-dog at the foot of a nearby rock. She missed, cursed under her breath, and retrieved the weapon. "Well, did your precious book tell ye how to find one?"

"A bomnubble?"

"Aye."

"No, not that I remember. It said they live in caves in the Stony Mountains, that's all."

"Well, Granny Nurgabog told *me* how to find one."

"Maraly, it's too dangerous. We can't—"

"*Shh!*" she said again, but this time she didn't throw the dagger. She squinted one eye and pointed at the nearest slope. At the foot of the mountain lay a cluster of what looked like dark green bushes—by now Janner knew they were actually trees, dwarfed by the distance and the enormity of the mountain. Above the trees, the mountain face was covered with what looked like pebbles but were actually boulders that had slid down the slope.

"See the snow?" Maraly asked.

Janner saw the snow, just above the line of trees, swathed across the stones like strokes of white paint.

"Look there, to the left," she said.

At first Janner saw nothing but more snow. Then it shifted. A speck of grayish white moved down from the snowfield to the tree line. Even from this distance, Janner's stomach tingled with fear. He knew the bomnubble couldn't see them (Pembrick's *Creaturepedia* said the monsters had poor vision), but he still felt vulnerable. If the bomnubble decided to have them for its dinner, there would be little they could do; the creature knew these mountains far better than the children did.

"We need to get out of here," Janner said.

Maraly sniggered and drew her dagger. "Nurgabog told me their caves are usually in little forests like that one. I've been watchin' for it ever since I spotted the trees. Sure enough, old Nurgie was right. Let's go."

"Maraly, wait!" Janner hissed, but she ignored him.

Janner watched her go, feeling a familiar anger. She didn't think about consequences. She didn't care what Janner said. She was reckless and foolish. She was, Janner thought, a girl version of Tink. And as with Tink, Janner found he couldn't resist the urge to follow.

They sneaked from rock to rock until they reached a dried streambed that provided cover for several hundred yards. Maraly crept along in silence, and every time Janner's foot slipped and sent a pebble clattering away, she glared at him with great annoyance. Soon the stand of trees was an arrow shot away, close enough that it blocked the view of the snowfields above it, where they had seen the beast.

Maraly sat on her haunches in the creek bed and drew her dagger. "Well, are you gonna draw yer sword or what?"

"Maraly, this is foolishness!" Janner whispered. "You have to listen to me. This isn't as easy as killing a browndog. Have you ever seen a bomnubble up close?"

"Nope. You?" She grinned.

"Well, no, but I've seen pictures. They're twice as tall as a man and mean as fire."

"Aw, they can't be *that* hard to kill. Besides, we need somethin' to keep warm, don't we?"

Janner had to admit they did.

From just over the rim of the creek bed came a grunt. Janner and Maraly froze. The bomnubble snorted and smacked, so near that both children were afraid to breathe. After several moments, the creature moved away. Maraly grinned and peeked over the bank, despite Janner's frantic gestures to stay hidden.

When Maraly's head wasn't bitten off, Janner gulped and took his first look at a real bomnubble in the wilds of the Stony Mountains.

Only a stone's throw away, in a little clearing among the trees, stood the beast, its back to the children. It was even taller than Janner had imagined and covered in fine white fur, so long that it swayed in the wind. Its legs were short and stout, but its arms were enormous and thick as a tree. Its back and shoulders rippled with muscle, visible even through its fur. The bomnubble was eating something and seemed to be enjoying itself.

Just beyond the beast, on the higher side of the clearing, was the mouth of a cave.

Maraly's face was ashen. Janner wasn't used to seeing her afraid, and he felt a little sorry for her. But to his surprise, she took a deep breath, winked at him, and mouthed the word, "Ready?"

A howl echoed through the clearing.

The bomnubble stood to its full height and turned enough that Janner could see its fearsome face. Its eyes were hidden in locks of white fur, its nose small and black, but its mouth was huge and bright with blood from its meal. Two teeth as long as Janner's forearm curved up from its lower jaw.

They heard another howl, and the bomnubble bounded to the mouth of its cave and threw the carcass inside. Then the beast climbed up the side of the mountain and out of sight.

"Blast!" Maraly said. She plopped down on the ground with her arms folded, pouting like a two-year-old. "We would've had it!"

Janner stood, looking into the dark mouth of the cave. "Maraly, did you see what it was eating?"

"Nope," she said grumpily.

"It was a wolf."

"So what?"

"I have an idea."

He hopped out of the creek bed and bolted into the clearing, reveling, for once, in the fact that he was the one rushing ahead.

"Wait!" Maraly said, and Janner smiled.

He skidded to a halt at the entrance of the cave and listened. Maraly caught up with him a moment later, and they both leaned over and looked inside. The smell issuing from the blackness was overpowering. Janner felt himself on the verge of throwing up, but he forced himself into the cave.

On the floor lay the mangled carcass of the wolf. Its fur hung from it in tatters.

"Ahh," Maraly said. "Now you're thinkin' like a Strander."

Janner grimaced and pulled the wolf's skin from its bones. Deeper in the cave they found the remains of animals Janner had never read about, some with the remnants of scaly skin, some with bony exoskeletons, and some, to his relief, with thick coats of fur. Most of them had decomposed beyond any usefulness, but several were fresh kills, and the children emerged from the cave minutes later with armfuls of smelly—but wonderfully warm—pelts.

They sprinted back to the creek bed and hid just as the bomnubble leapt into the clearing again, dragging another big wolf behind it like a toy. It grunted its way into the cave and stayed there until the children were far away.

That night on the slope of the mountain, Maraly cooked a fine meal of diggle and browndog meat. When clouds hid the bright stars and snow fell, the children slept in a mound of furs. Maraly admitted it had been far easier to scavenge the skins than to fight the bomnubble, and Janner fell asleep with a proud smile on his face.

They spent most of the next morning making the pelts into something each of them could wear. Maraly poked holes in the skins with her dagger, and Janner sewed them together with twine from his pack. By the time the sun began its descent, Maraly and Janner were draped and hooded in furs. They looked like fierce little bomnubbles themselves and felt capable of living happily in the Stony Mountains for years if need be.

Later that afternoon they discovered a lake so round and blue it looked like a jewel cut from the sky. It rested between the shoulders of two white-capped peaks that blocked the constant wind and left the surface of the water smooth as glass. Maraly and Janner knelt at the water's edge in silence. There was some great peace in the place they didn't wish to disturb. They dropped their packs, filled the water skins, then sat on a stone a short distance from the shore.

Before them, between the V of the slopes that cradled the lake, rose Mog-Balgrik. The Witch's Nose stabbed at the sky and carved the clouds in two. The ridge to the left of the nose bore a depression that looked like a shadowed eye socket, and to the right of the nose lay a cut in the mountain that formed a mouth curved in a jagged frown.

Podo's note said they were to find a trail that wound around the right shoulder of the peak—right over that jagged mouth. Janner shivered. It was too easy to imagine the great sleeping witch eating them as they passed.

"So that's where we're goin', eh?" said Maraly as she removed her hood.

"Yeah. Somehow we have to get over that mountain. There's supposed to be a trail. I guess if we keep going that way, we'll cross it eventually."

"Aye." Maraly sighed. "Want to camp here tonight?"

The hollow seemed safe enough. It was the first peaceful spot they had found in the Stony Mountains, and he hated to leave. They gathered enough sticks and scrub for a fire and settled in to cook a meal.

The setting sun broke through the clouds and shot a golden beam at Mog-Balgrik. The light transformed the hideous semblance of a face and showed the peak for the ancient beauty that it was.

"Look!" Maraly said.

Janner pulled his gaze from the bright mountain and saw what appeared to be a cloud of yellow flower petals floating down from the slopes to the lake. Then they heard the flutter of wings and the twitter of birdsong. Thousands of yellow birds alighted on the surface of the lake, so many that it looked like the water itself had turned to gold. They sang and groomed their wings in the twilight and were visible long after night fell.

"Hmph," was all Maraly said, but Janner noticed that she wiped her eyes.

The children fell asleep to the pleasant play of the birds on the water. Janner woke more than once that night to see the starlit creatures still floating on the lake, and he went back to sleep with wonder in his heart.

In the morning, the lake was glassy and still, and the yellow birds had flown. The Witch's Nose was grim as ever. Janner crawled out of his blanket of furs and walked a little way along the shore. He drank deep at the edge of the lake before he saw the man with the sword. He stood just a few feet away, leaning against a boulder. His hair was black, and he wore a heavy, fur-lined coat that hung to his ankles.

"The Fangs are coming," he said.

After so many days alone with Maraly, the man's presence startled Janner so badly that he staggered backward, tripped over a stone, and nearly fell. Janner couldn't tell from the man's smile if he was a friend or an enemy. Could he be one of the rebels? one of Gammon's men?

Maraly still slept under a pile of furs at the camp, a stone's throw away. Janner glanced at his pack, where his sword lay.

"Don't do that, boy. I'm fast. Faster than a bomnubble."

The man lifted his coat and tossed something big, white, and furry. It thudded to the ground and rolled to Janner's feet. The grisly head of a bomnubble stared at him with dead eyes.

"It was on your trail," the man said. "Caught your scent after you and your friend ran off with the pelts."

Bomnubble

The bomnubble (hairy) is one of the most dangerous beasts in the Stony Mountains. Its diet consists of wolf, snickbuzzard, chorkney, and human, though it is known to have eaten root, branch, snow, and rock when the mood strikes. The Bomnubble Problem, as it was called by rangers before the war, made tourism in the Stony Mountains and Ice Prairies difficult and most inadvisable.

From Pembrick's *Creaturepedia*

Janner's face flushed.

"Don't feel bad, boy. It was a fine idea, and mighty brave of you two to enter a bomnubble den. But you're lucky there wasn't another asleep in the back of the cave."

"Who are you?" Janner asked.

"Someone who's been watching you."

Janner said nothing, but the sea dragon's warning rang in his mind: *He is near you. Beware.*

"You're making good progress, if it's to the Ice Prairies you mean to go. That *is* where you mean to go, isn't it?" the man asked with another of his mysterious, too-friendly smiles.

"Maybe," Janner said, and he felt like a fool when the man doubled over with laughter.

"Well, *maybe* you'd like to fall in with me. That's where I'm headed too, and I've made the trip a number of times. Besides, these mountains are crawling with Fangs you probably don't want to meet."

"Fangs? You're lying. They can't survive the cold," Janner said.

"That used to be the case," the man said, growing serious. "Not anymore. These Fangs do just fine in the cold. Too fine. So fine, in fact, that all I've worked for is in danger. My army, my weapons, my hopes to defeat the Fangs and banish them from my land—all of it will be lost unless I can find a way to stop the Fangs."

"Gammon?" Janner asked.

"Aye," said the man. "And your name is Janner Wingfeather. I'm here to help you get to Kimera. The rest of your family is waiting."

"What? How do you know?"

"Got word from one of my men that a peglegged pirate, a little girl, her mother, and a round old man with spectacles arrived in Kimera a few days ago. They said their two boys were missing, so I've been looking for you. Why don't you and your brother there come with me? Ordinarily I wouldn't be in such a rush, but I have an appointment to make."

Janner's shoulders slumped. "It's not my brother. That's Maraly—she's a Strander. My brother was taken by the Black Carriage."

Gammon's eyes flickered with—something. Janner assumed it was disappointment and hung his head.

"I'm sorry to hear that, Janner," said Gammon quietly. "Then Gnag the Nameless has caught his prey. Maker only knows what he will do with him."

"Gnag doesn't know who he is," Janner said. "They think he's just another boy from the Strand."

Gammon thought for a moment. "Well, there may not be much hope for your brother, but if the Fangs don't realize who they've caught, there may be some hope for the rest of us." Gammon stepped forward and held out his hand. "You've had a hard journey, lad. Why don't we move on? If we hurry, we'll be safe in Kimera by sundown, and you can rest in the company of those who love you."

Janner felt a rush of relief, and all his suspicions about this man in black vanished. He nodded at Gammon and shook his hand.

53

A Grimace of Snickbuzzards

When Maraly woke to find a man in her company, she shrieked, leapt to her feet, and would have flung her dagger at him if he hadn't sprung forward and seized her wrist. Only after Janner assured her that he was a friend did her snarling cease and Gammon release her.

"You're strong for a girl," said Gammon.

"Girl or boy makes no difference to a Strander," she said gruffly as she snapped her dagger into its sheath. But it was clear the compliment made her proud.

"We could use more like you in Kimera. Strong and quick and willing to fight when the time comes. That's why all of Skree is in this mess, after all."

"Because no one fought when the Fangs came?" Janner asked.

"Aye. My countrymen scattered like hens in a coop." He winked at Janner. "But in a few days' time, we'll see another kind of scattering. I've a plan that just might save us all."

"What plan?" Janner asked.

Gammon paused, and Janner again thought he saw a shadow pass over his face.

"I can't exactly say. Nine years of slipping in and out of lower Skree, dodging Fangs and trolls at every turn, makes a man keep his secrets in his own head. Migg Landers is a fine example of that. He was loyal to me for years, but men have a way of wearing down. Betrayed you, Ronchy, and me too. Got himself a Fang bite for his trouble. Don't look so surprised. I know all about what happens in Dugtown, boy. Hardly a troll burps that I don't find out about it from one of my men. Whatever plan I have, I aim to keep it to myself. But you can trust me—this goes for you too, lass," he said with a nod to Maraly, whose distrust was plain on her face. "You won't find another fella more eager to get these Fangs out of Skree, nor a man more loyal to his land."

Janner was convinced, and even had he not been, he still would have fallen in with Gammon just to make it safely through the mountains to his family.

"I can see from the way you two are eying each other that you need to have a talk,"

Gammon said. "I'll move on to the north side of the lake and wait for you there. But don't take too long. The far slope of the Witch's Nose is a bad place to be after dark."

Gammon strode away until the furs on his back gave him the look of a bear moving along the water line.

"Are you worried?" Janner asked. He trusted Gammon, but he cared a great deal what Maraly thought. She was shrewd and had far more experience around crooked men.

"Aye. I'm worried," she said as she kicked dirt over the embers. "Question is, which is more dangerous, the mountains or the man?"

Janner looked across the lake at Gammon, visible as a small brown patch amidst the rocks. Beyond, in the distance, towered white-toothed Mog-Balgrik. The mountain looked much more dangerous than the man.

"I just want to get to the Ice Prairies," Janner said. "Let's go with him, all right?"

Maraly sighed. "Aye. But I'll have me dagger handy."

"Good," Gammon said when they approached a few minutes later, their packs on their backs, furs draped over every inch of their bodies.

The three of them left the lake and walked into the bitter wind. All that remained of their camp was the bomnubble's head, upon which a little yellow bird perched and sang.

The day was clear and cold.

Janner's heart fluttered with the thought that he might see his mother as soon as that evening, that he might embrace Leeli and feel Podo's whiskers against his cheek. But between him and his family lay what seemed an eternal expanse of stone and snow and wind.

After they pushed through the pass, the ground fell away to reveal a magnificent hollow in the earth. They stood for a few minutes, agape at the airy nothingness before them. Far, far below, a greenish river snaked through the canyon, as narrow as a thread from this height. The walls of the canyon were so steep and smooth that not even snow found purchase. To the left and right, the Stony Mountains parted so that Janner felt he was looking out at the edge of the universe. On the far side of the canyon the mountains continued, and Mog-Balgrik was their champion. Though the sky was unbearably blue and free of a single wisp of cloud, the peak of the Witch's Nose pinned a swath of ghostly mist to the heavens.

"I stop here every time," said Gammon. The wind whipped locks of black hair across his face, and he held one gloved hand up to shield his eyes from the light. Janner had the feeling he had seen this man before, but he couldn't place where. Something about his jaw line or the tone of his voice tickled at Janner's memory. "Grand, isn't it?"

Janner and Maraly were speechless.

Gammon pointed at Mog-Balgrik and grinned. "That's where we're headed. I know it looks like we'll never arrive, but the going is easy until we get to her foot. Then it's up around her shoulder and down into the Ice Prairies."

Janner smiled, but Maraly did not.

"You all right?" he asked her, then immediately regretted it. Of course she wasn't all right. With every step, Janner was closer to those who loved him, but Maraly was farther from her only family. The fact that they wanted her dead only made it worse.

Maraly shrugged. "Well, are we goin' or not?" she said, then spat. The wind took it, and the three of them watched the little ball of spittle float down into the canyon.

Gammon led the children along a trail that was barely visible but simple enough to follow, and the company walked eastward around the canyon rim to the north side. Always the drop was to their left, and Janner thought many times of the cliffs at Glipwood and the Glipper Trail just behind the Igiby cottage.

If someone had told Janner earlier that summer that he would have seen the things he had seen, he would have scoffed. He had braved Fingap Falls, felled Fangs (though not very many) with his bow and arrows, survived the Fork Factory, torn through the empty streets of Dugtown by the light of the torch towers, and now he was deep in the Stony Mountains, covered in wolf skins. Mog-Balgrik was a terrible sight but no more so than many of the things his young eyes had seen. More than ever, though, he ached not for faraway lands or wild adventure but for a fire in the hearth and the sound of laughter—or a bed! *Even just a bed would be fine,* Janner thought. Something to lay his head on besides a smelly wolf skin and the cold ground.

The sun sailed across the clear sky and slipped behind a mountain.

At last the canyon was behind them, and they zigzagged up the face of the Witch's Nose. Even Gammon was winded, and he stopped every few minutes to allow the children to catch up and find their breath. The trail was littered with shale and pebbles, and the higher they climbed, the more snow was piled above and below.

"We have to...hurry," Gammon said between breaths. "It's not far now." He pointed to a cluster of boulders above and to the right. "We just have to make it to there; then we circle the mountain and…well, you'll see. I think you'll enjoy the last bit of our journey. Quick now! The sun descends!"

There it is again, Janner thought. *That tickle of recognition.* He knew he had seen Gammon before—but where?

Gammon sprang up the face of the mountain toward the boulders. Pebbles clicked and tumbled into snowdrifts below. Janner took a deep breath and followed, Maraly close at his heels. The air was thin, the wind biting, and the first stars shimmered in the air above the great peak.

At last they reached the boulders. A well-used trail wound between them, and Janner found Gammon resting inside. The rocks provided a buffer from the wind, and after so much time in the great openness of the range, the cleft was a nest of safety.

"It's dark, lad. The snickbuzzards will be wheeling."

Janner's face fell. Maraly drew her dagger and clenched her jaw. Gammon nodded at her with admiration. Janner fumbled to find his sword and with a great commotion managed to draw it from the skins draped over his backpack.

"What do we do?" he asked, hating how frightened he sounded.

"The dusk isn't gone just yet, so we might get lucky and only see a few birds. Listen close." Gammon bent over and looked the children in the eye. "Keep as close to me as you can, clear around the mountain. It's not a short distance, but it's not too far to run without a rest. Can you keep up?"

"Yes sir," said Janner. Maraly nodded and spat again.

"Once we're on the east side of the mountain, we're all but home. We just have to mount the boggan and slide to safety. But as I said, the buzzards will be wheeling. If I were alone, I'd sleep here for the night and press on in the morning. But time is precious, and with you two warriors on guard, I think we'll make it without a scratch. All clear?"

"Er," said Janner, "what's a boggan?"

Gammon laughed. "Don't worry about that. You'll see soon enough. Get behind me and have your blades drawn. When the snickbuzzards swoop, hack away."

"Hack away," Janner said with a gulp.

"Hack away," Gammon repeated, clapping Janner on the shoulder. "You ready, little lady?"

Maraly narrowed her eyes. "Aye, I'm ready. Killed more snickbuzzards than you, old man. Eaten more too, I'd bet."

Gammon straightened with a chuckle. "That you have, lass. I'm certain of it." He led them through the corridor between the boulders and halted at the exit. "You two ready to run? If we're lucky, they'll have soup on the stove for us. There's always a grand welcome for Skreeans in Kimera."

"Ready," Janner and Maraly said.

"Now!" Gammon cried, and they burst from their cover.

They ran through the snow across the face of the mountain for so long that Janner's chest burned like he had swallowed hot coals. His throat narrowed, and he wheezed like an old man. Maraly passed him just like Tink would have done, and Janner cursed his slow, lanky legs as his two companions raced ahead.

All that remained of the daylight was a smudge of pale yellow at their backs. Before them, beyond the mountain, stars shone like diamonds, and it was a long time before Janner realized the sky wasn't obstructed by more mountains. As they rounded Mog-Balgrik, the moon came into view, yellow as a wolf's eye and casting a rich light over the vast sweep of the Ice Prairies.

Janner's vision blurred and his legs trembled. He couldn't run much longer. He would have to stop for air, and if the snickbuzzards came for him, so be it. Moments before his will was snuffed, he crashed into Maraly and they tumbled into the snow. They came up sputtering, covered with snow and slush.

"Get up!" Gammon cried. "They're coming!"

Janner pushed himself to his feet and pulled Maraly with him. Gammon struggled with an object buried in snow, casting nervous glances at the sky. Janner craned his neck and saw, silhouetted against the blue-black sky, blotting out star after star, a descending cloud of snickbuzzards.

The three of them stood on the great mountain at the height of the world, knee-deep in snow, blades aglow in the moonlight, and waited for the birds to strike. Janner had one thought as the first snickbuzzard swooped within reach of his blade: *What in Aerwiar is a boggan?*

54

The Ice Prairies

*T*hunk!

The bird split cleanly in two and *poofed* into the drift beside Janner in a spray of snow and feather. Maraly hissed and flung her dagger at the next snickbuzzard when it was still fifteen feet above them. The bird squawked and tumbled to her feet. She snatched her dagger from its breast and braced herself for the next attack.

Janner saw buzzard after buzzard wheeling in the sky, black swaths against midnight blue. Except for the sound they made when the children struck, the birds were eerily silent as they circled.

When the next snickbuzzard dove at Janner, he swung too late. He killed the bird, but its talons found his shoulder and tore through his covering of skins like a knife through paper. He pushed the pain away and readied himself for the next attack, trying not to pay attention to the way his left arm trembled.

Maraly killed another bird and screamed, "Hurry it up, Gammon!"

"Got it!" he cried before she finished her sentence. "Get on! Quick!"

Janner tore his eyes from the sky to find Gammon kneeling at the front of a sort of sled. It was long and flat with no sides, but ropes ran from the rear of the boggan, looping through pulleys and into holes in the curved nose to form what must have been some kind of steering mechanism. Gammon held the ends of the two ropes in one hand and waved the children on with the other.

Janner halved another snickbuzzard and leapt after Maraly onto the boggan. Maraly knelt behind Gammon, and Janner took the rear.

"Janner! Pull the anchor!"

"What? Where?"

"Hurry!"

Maraly hissed again, and Janner knew without looking that she had flung her dagger. A dead snickbuzzard crashed into Janner and sent him sprawling. From beneath the smelly pile of feathers, he saw Gammon leap to the rear of the boggan and pull a stick from a hole in the deck. Immediately, the boggan slid forward.

Janner heaved the dead bird off himself and raised his sword as another bird
swooped. A heartbeat later the boggan was carrying Gammon and the children down
the slope so fast that snickbuzzards no longer swooped at them but glided right
beside the sled. Janner saw by the light of the moon their black eyes set in fleshy sock-
ets; the hard, curved beaks; the featherless necks; the batlike wings. A string of the
birds flapped behind the boggan like feathery smoke so that whenever Janner or
Maraly killed one, another took its place. Every moment the boggan picked up speed
and the snickbuzzards became less interested in their quarry, until finally the birds
were gone.

Janner and Maraly whooped in spite of their exhaustion. They hugged and
laughed along with Gammon as the boggan zoomed down the long slope.

"Well done, little warriors!" he cried.

Janner and Maraly sheathed their blades and looked out at the Ice Prairies for the
first time. Mog-Balgrik's western slope was formidable, a steep sentinel warning travelers weak of spirit to keep their distance, but if the traveler braved her icy face, the
reward was sweet. A long, smooth descent to the frozen desert of the Ice Prairies lay
at her back, and to those like Gammon who knew where to find them, boggans hid
in the snow to bear them home.

Janner's eyes watered, and the wind of their passage deafened him, but he smiled
so wide that the muscles in his cheeks throbbed. The moon cooled to white as it
climbed, and it lit the ice fields so that Janner could see as clearly as if it were day. For
hours the three of them glided down from the mountains, faster than the fastest horse,
with a plume of snow arcing behind them like a spray of water. Moonlight caught the
flying snow, flashing prisms of color on the prairie surface as they passed. White mice
and snow foxes, burrowed beneath the snow for the night, twitched their ears when
the boggan zoomed by, thinking that perhaps the Maker had bent low to the earth
and whispered, "Shh."

Janner slept for a while, and when he woke, the moon looked straight down at
him. When he didn't see Maraly, he gasped and sat up, thinking she had fallen off
sometime in the night. Then he heard murmurs from the front of the sled. She knelt
next to Gammon and held the ropes as he instructed her in a quiet voice.

"Don't pull too hard, now," he said. "That's it. See the bank up ahead? Swing us
wide around the left side. Good."

"Are we close?" Janner asked with a wince. His wounded arm was stiff and stung
when he moved. Gammon and Maraly turned, and Janner was surprised to see her
smiling.

"Yes," Gammon said. "Very close, in fact. See that rise in the distance? Over to the right, just below Tirium?"

"What's Tirium?" Janner asked. He could only see moonlit prairie stretching away forever.

"It's a constellation, just above the horizon. It makes a triangle—see it?"

Janner did. Three bright stars, a perfect triangle tilted and slipping into the horizon, and just below them a gentle slope in the snow.

"I see it. Is that Kimera?" asked Maraly. Her voice had lost some of its edge. She sounded more like an ordinary girl than a dagger-throwing Strander.

"That's Kimera," Gammon said.

Janner could hardly contain himself. He was hungry and cold and tired, and he missed his family so much that he felt like he might cry.

At last Gammon took the ropes and pulled back on them like he was reining up a horse. Something at the back of the boggan shifted, and the sled slowed gently to a stop, just at the foot of the rise Gammon had pointed out.

"Here we are," he said with a smile. "Kimera."

Janner leapt from the boggan into ankle-deep snow. He expected to see a village, smoke rising from chimneys, yellow lamplight pouring from windows, but he saw nothing but snow. Everywhere he turned was snow, from horizon to horizon. Not even the mountains were visible anymore. Was this a trick? Was that the shadow that had passed across Gammon's face, that there was no Kimera after all? What if it had been a lie that Podo, Nia, Leeli, and Oskar had found Kimera? Janner couldn't believe he had allowed himself to believe anything good might happen to him, that anyone might be worthy of his trust. He felt hot tears rise in his chest. He was certain he would never see his family again and that Gammon had planned to turn him over to the Fangs all along.

"Janner?" said a voice.

Janner froze.

"Son?"

He turned slowly around.

A wide trapdoor rose from the bed of snow. Yellow light streamed out of the hole, and a figure ascended a long, curved stairway. It was Nia. She wore a green, long-sleeved gown, her wrists and collar adorned with fine white fur, and a gold necklace hung at her neck. After so many hours beneath the cold white stars, sailing on a blanket of blue-white snow, the yellow and gold that surrounded his mother was the most magical color Janner had ever seen. And his mother! She was clean. Her hair was braided into fine, intricate loops that cascaded around her shoulders like a gilded waterfall. She *was* a queen. If ever Janner had doubted it, now he knew.

"Mama?" Janner breathed.

Nia's breath caught in her throat, and a hand went to her mouth.

A moment later the two of them rushed forward—a boy wrapped in animal skins, wounded and sore, skinny as a tree branch, and the Queen of Anniera, wrapped in gold and light. They embraced, and Janner all but melted with joy.

55

The Surrender of Artham Wingfeather

For days Artham drifted in and out of sanity. He lay on his back in the cage with a shine of drool slipping toward his ear from the corner of his mouth. He stared at the stone ceiling and gibbered words that had no meaning. But at times he sat bolt upright as if he had just awoken from a nightmare, and he knew himself and where he was.

All the while he ached to abandon himself, to agree to the Stone Keeper's offer and allow her to turn him into a winged beast. It would be so easy to sing the song and know no more. He had much he wanted to forget. He had broken his deepest oath, and even in his sanest moments he was unable to think on that fact without trembling.

I left him!

His mind had screamed these words so many times over the years that they were burned into his core. No matter how he tried, he could not escape that one fact, that one decision that had haunted him all these years. No matter how he ran, no matter how he fought to protect the jewels, Peet's deepest heart was rotten and dying from those three brutal words.

All he had to do was give up and it would all be over. He could wave at the Grey Fang in the window, and the Stone Keeper would take his hand and trade his sorrow for the mindless nothing of the iron box. The red light would flash, and all that was left of Artham Wingfeather would disappear.

For days the Grey Fangs delivered more of the frightened children to the Stone Keeper, and she calmed them and welcomed them and killed them.

That's right, thought Artham, *killed them.* She took away their lives. Still, he felt a stab of guilt for the Fangs he had slain—had they been children like these?

No, these Fangs were no more men than an ax handle was a tree. It was *Gnag* who had done the killing. He had killed the living thing and made something different from it, given it a half-life. That was why the Fangs turned to dust and blew away when they died.

Artham was so tired and lonely and full of regret that all he wanted in the world was to turn to dust and blow away.

On the fifth day in the cage, he gave up.

He could no longer bear the ghostly gaze of the Stone Keeper, or the sickening excitement of the Skreean volunteers as they entered the box, or most of all the tears of the children. So many children, pulled from the Black Carriage or marched in from the dungeon, helpless in a place no child should ever see. He doubted the Fangs would keep their word and set the children free. He hoped they would.

But worse than the horror of the world he lived in was the world *within* him. He could not stop remembering. He hung in a birdcage above this dungeon so much like the one from which he had escaped, and the voices in his head and the bitter remembrance of all that had happened in the Deeps of Throg gnawed at his spirit. It was a greater torture than even what he had endured from Gnag.

When the Grey Fang with the meat pulled the cage close, Artham said, "I'm finished."

"What's that?" said the Fang.

"If it's true the Stone Keeper will free the children, then she can have me. Do with me what she will."

The Fang stared at Artham, nodded, then disappeared from the window.

Artham sat in the cage with his head hung low, twirling a lock of his white hair around one of his talons. A few minutes later the cage lurched, then lowered a click at a time to the dungeon floor. A door on the far wall opened, and a host of Grey Fangs poured from it. They surrounded the cage with swords drawn.

Artham stared at the floor. The voices roared in his mind. He heard the old, familiar one screaming, *I left him,* but now there were more.

Coward, they said. *Weakling.*

Artham sat with his eyes closed and shut himself off to everything.

"It's almost over," he mumbled again and again. "It's almost over."

The Fangs stepped aside. The Stone Keeper entered the room. She approached the cage, a tall, slender, hooded figure in a flowing black robe. Artham opened one eye, then the other, and peered up at her. Her face was invisible in the cowl, but he sensed none of the hatred or evil he expected.

"It's almost over," he said again.

"Yes," she said, in a voice so beautiful that Artham stopped trembling. "Everything will be fine, Artham Wingfeather. You have nothing to fear."

She bent close to the cage and removed her hood.

Her face was pale, her hair black as raven feathers. Her eyes were dark jewels in a field of snow. She was beautiful, but it was a terrible beauty. Artham was afraid to look away; neither did he want to. At once he understood why the children calmed when she spoke to them. He felt that he would do whatever she asked, no matter how wrong it might be.

"Poor Artham. How long have you been running? Nine years? And now," she said, her voice as quiet as a purr, "you can rest. The Black Carriage is coming with more of the broken, more who are tired like you. But I will set them free if you will sing the song. Is that what you want?"

Artham nodded.

"All right. But first, they're going to watch you. I'll let them see the magnificent thing you've become when you step back through the door. And then I'll let them choose. If they want to go free, I'll set them free. I'll turn them out into the wilds of Skree, powerless and alone, as you wish—or they can give themselves to Gnag's service. I can make them strong and give them an army of comrades." She straightened and raised her voice to the Fangs. "Can I not?"

They howled and barked and snapped their teeth.

From deep in the tunnel came the rattle and squeak of the Black Carriage. Artham saw the lantern swaying to and fro, larger and brighter every second. The four black horses appeared, and the crows, the robed driver, then the thing itself—a graveyard on wheels.

The Stone Keeper replaced her hood and stood on the dais.

The driver opened the coffins, and the children climbed out, blinking and frail.

"Line them up!" said the Stone Keeper.

The Grey Fangs stood the children in a line at the foot of the dais. All of them trembled and cowered at the sight of the walking wolves.

All but one.

One of the children didn't tremble. He only stared at the ground.

He was skinny as a rake, with sandy brown hair. The look on his bruised and swollen face was not one of fear but shame. He merely glanced at the Fangs, the children, and the iron box, and sighed. Then he hung his head and closed his eyes— much as Artham had done when he gave up all hope.

As soon as Artham laid eyes on the boy, he leapt to his feet. His head smashed into the top of the cage, but he didn't care. He squawked and flapped and screamed, trying with all that was in him to cry the name, "Tink!"

Before Artham could catch Tink's eye, the Grey Fangs closed in and blocked his view.

56

Two Kinds of Shame

Seconds after Nia wrapped her arms around Janner, guilt bubbled in his stomach and weakened his knees. He dreaded the question he knew would come. He dreaded it so much that he felt the world around him buck like a pony, and his head spun. As if from a great distance he heard Nia's sniffles, the tiny, warm sound of her kisses on his forehead, the rustle of her clothes against his furs, and, at last, the words that caused him to black out completely: "Janner, where's Tink? Where's your brother?"

While he slept, Janner dreamed of the Black Carriage and of the Overseer and at last of the box where he had spent so many days alone with his thoughts. In the dream, he lay in the deep dark of the box for days before he realized some wicked thing was inside with him, watching him in the blackness. Again he heard the sea dragon's voice in his head. *"He is near you. Beware."*

Janner woke in a panic. He thrashed, sending the blankets piled on him to the floor in a heap, and sat up in a cold sweat. It took him a moment to understand where he was, and then it came to him in a flash—Kimera. He had made it! His joy was tainted by shame about Tink, but the realization that he had traveled such a terrible distance and reached his destination brought a smile to his face.

He lay in a bed of soft white fur. The covers were fur, too, but nothing like the smelly, stiff wolf skins he and Maraly had scavenged. These were soft as feathers and warm. Someone had replaced his clothes with a nightgown made of a downy fabric. The floor was cobbled stone, but the walls were glassy and white, and it wasn't until he touched them that Janner realized they were made of ice. His finger stuck to the wall, and when he pulled it away, a little wisp of steam evaporated as his fingerprint disappeared.

Someone knocked on the door.

"Come in," he said, and the wooden door swung open to reveal a girl on a crutch. She wore a simple white dress, and her hair was pulled back in a long braid.

"Leeli!" Janner cried, and he swept her up in a tight hug.

"It's a good thing you fainted," she giggled. "They had to sew up your shoulder."

He had forgotten about his snickbuzzard wound. Janner pulled back the collar of his nightgown and was surprised to see a bandage wrapped around his upper arm.

"It doesn't hurt," he said, moving his shoulder in circles.

"They put garp oil on it," she said. "It's a kind of fish—which is what we eat around here, mostly. It doesn't speed up the healing, but it takes the pain away for a while."

"How long have you been here?" Janner asked as he sat at the foot of the bed.

"We got here ten days ago." Leeli looked at the floor. "I'm sorry we left you. I didn't want to. None of us did. But the Fangs—"

"Hush," Janner said. "It's all right. I had a lot of time to think about it, and I understand. It was the only thing that could be done to keep you safe. Where's Maraly—the Strander girl?"

"She's with Gammon. I don't think she wanted to get cleaned up, but Mama made her. You know how she is."

"What about Grandpa and Oskar?"

Leeli rolled her eyes. "They got tired of waiting for you to wake up, so they're in the tavern playing cards. That's where Grandpa's spent most of his time."

"There's a tavern? Underground?"

"Sort of. We're not actually underground. We're under snow. Deep snow. After a while, it seems like an ordinary town, with streets and houses and places to play. What's wrong?"

Janner hung his head, thinking of his little brother and how much he would have loved Kimera. Janner couldn't bear to say his name.

"It's not your fault," said Leeli. She limped across the room and sat beside Janner on the bed. "Nobody thinks it's your fault."

"But I'm a Throne Warden!" Janner snapped. "My one job in the world is to protect him, and I couldn't do it!"

Leeli was silent.

Janner felt a sob rising in his throat. He had spent days and days on the run. He had thought about Tink many times, but always, at the front of his mind, was his quest to reach the Ice Prairies. He had dreamed of his mother's embrace. He had dreamed of rest and food and safety. Lurking underneath it all was the stark, awful image of Tink in the Black Carriage, eyes wide and full of terror. All that time, Janner had been able to push the guilt away because he wasn't sure he was much better off.

But now that he was in a soft bed in a warm room with his family so near, it felt unfair. He didn't deserve such comfort when his brother was—wherever he was. Janner wanted to tear off the soft nightgown, wrap himself in wolf skins again, and trudge back through the Stony Mountains to Dugtown. He would march right up to the nearest Fang and turn himself over. The Black Carriage seemed a better fate than this unbearable guilt.

"Aha!" said a raspy voice.

Podo burst into the room. He looked like Podo always looked, with his bushy white eyebrows and his wild white hair, but one of his arms hung in a sling. Janner remembered that on the night they were separated, when Podo had broken down the door to Ronchy McHiggins's tavern, he had heard the crunch of bones. But if Podo's wound hurt, it didn't show. He rushed forward and tackled Janner onto the bed. He smelled of pipe smoke and ale. He poked Janner's ribs with his gnarled old fingers and laughed, but Janner only lay on his back, motionless.

Podo's mirth vanished. He plopped down on the bed beside Leeli with a heavy sigh and placed a hand on Janner's leg. Nia and Oskar appeared in the doorway and took in the situation at once. Oskar's cheeks were rosy, his swath of hair was neatly pressed to the top of his head, and his folded hands rested atop his belly. Nia wore a different gown, but she looked no less regal.

Without a word they crossed the room and sat on the bed so that Janner found himself enclosed by his family. He was in a nest, the walls made of those who loved him. They were silent. Janner stared at the ceiling.

"We love you," Nia said at last, placing a hand on Janner's face.

The sob rose in his throat and spilled out.

"I lost him," he wailed. "I tried to find him, but he was gone. I'm sorry. I'm sorry." Tears streamed down his face. He cried so hard he could barely breathe. Over and over again he said, "I'm sorry, I'm sorry." And over and over again, Nia said, "We love you, we love you."

When Janner's tears finally ebbed, Podo gathered him in his big arms and held him close. Janner's eyes closed. He felt his mother's hand in his hair, Leeli's head resting on his arm, and Oskar's hand on his foot.

Then the silence broke. Leeli prayed aloud to the Maker for protection for Kalmar Wingfeather. When she finished, Janner's well was dry. He had no more tears to cry, and his best hope was that the Maker indeed heard the name Kalmar Wingfeather and would stoop to Aerwiar to help him.

Leeli raised her whistleharp to her lips and played. It was a new melody, something she was improvising, much as she had when she played Nugget's song over the waters of the Dark Sea. Janner's eyes were closed, but within seconds the blackness swirled and took shape, and he could see things far, far away.

"Keep playing!" Janner said, leaping to the floor. The adults watched him with concern, but he didn't care. Leeli looked confused, but she kept playing. Janner turned slowly with his hand outstretched, willing the images in his mind to solidify. He didn't know it, but when he stopped turning, he faced south and east, and if he had been a bird flying that direction, he could have soared over the Ice Prairies, across the waters of a narrow strait, and to a rocky island where Peet the Sock Man struggled in a cage.

But Janner saw none of that. He saw only blurry images and darkness.

But then he realized the darkness was what he was supposed to see, and that the blurry images weren't blurry at all. They were beams of light slipping through cracks. His head swirled with Leeli's melody, and finally he saw what he was looking for: two specks of light, deep in the shadows, and the outline of a dirty, swollen face.

A red light exploded in the darkness, and Tink's face filled Janner's vision. His lips moved. His eyes were hollow and profoundly sad. When the light was brightest, Tink's eyes fell wearily shut, and he vanished.

Janner's heart pounded so hard that he put a hand to his chest. "I saw him!" he cried. "He's alive!"

"Silence him," said the Stone Keeper, waving a hand toward Artham. "He's frightening the children."

"Quiet, birdman," growled one of the Grey Fangs, "or we'll run you through."

Artham knew they wouldn't, not after all the trouble they'd gone through to bring him there, so he screeched even louder.

"I said silence him!" the Stone Keeper commanded.

Two of the Fangs took hold of his talons and jerked his arms through the cage. His face slammed into the bars and they pinned him there. One of the Fangs put his paw over Artham's face, which didn't stop the screeching, but muffled it. Try as he might to see Tink, it was no use; Fangs surrounded the cage.

Artham realized that neither the Stone Keeper nor the Fangs understood the High King of Anniera was in their grasp. They thought he was just another boy. Artham stopped struggling. Perhaps it was better if they didn't know who Tink was. But if they knew—if they knew, then maybe they wouldn't send him into the box.

"Which is it, then? First you say you'll comply, and now you struggle," said the

Stone Keeper to Artham. "You value yourself more than these children? Fine. We'll make *you* watch. Bring a wolf!"

Through the cluster of Fangs, Artham caught a glimpse of the Stone Keeper extending her hand.

"You, little boy," she said in a soothing voice. "Come nearer."

He heard each footstep as Tink climbed the stairs.

"Tmmmmk!" Artham sobbed into the Fang's paw. "Tmmmmmk!" The Fang punched Artham in the face so hard that his vision blurred.

"Don't pay any attention to them, child," he heard the Stone Keeper say. "Keep your eyes on me."

"All right," Tink said.

"What's your name, child?" asked the Stone Keeper.

Artham froze. He wondered what the woman would do when Tink told her his name. Would she recognize him?

"Uh, Weaver," Tink said in a small voice.

"Where are you from, Weaver?" asked the woman. Tink was silent. Artham heard the *skritch* of the Fang beside the dais writing Tink's answers in the book. "It's all right. It's been a terrible journey, hasn't it, boy? But the journey is over. You will soon have a new home, and a new name, and great strength. Would that please you?"

"Yeah," Tink answered quietly.

"No," Artham slurred through the Fang's paw. *No!* his inner voice screamed.

"Come inside with me and fear no more," said the Stone Keeper.

Tink sighed. "Yes ma'am."

Artham heard the iron door squeak open. He heard Tink walk inside. He heard the door close behind him.

And then he heard the first notes of the dreadful song of the ancient stones.

57

Bumblebees and Old Bones

Leeli lowered the whistleharp from her lips, and the image in Janner's mind disappeared.

"What do you see when Leeli plays?" asked Nia, leaning forward.

"Pictures," Janner said with a shrug. "But it's not every time she plays, and all three times it's been a different song."

"Three times?" Leeli said. "I only remember it happening with the sea dragons."

"It happened again when you were in the mountains," Janner said, smiling at the surprise on Leeli's face. "I saw you all. I didn't understand what I was seeing, and I didn't want to believe it, but I saw you in the snow, high in the mountains. At the same time I saw Tink in the Strander cage."

"In the Strander cage?" Podo growled. "Was it them who turned him over to the blasted Carriage?"

"Yes sir," Janner said quietly, and Podo's chest rumbled. "Mama, why does Leeli's song do that? Is it magic?"

Nia smiled. "What's magic, anyway? If you asked a kitten, 'How does a bumble-bee fly?' the answer would probably be 'Magic.' Aerwiar is full of wonders, and some call it magic. This is a gift from the Maker—it isn't something Leeli created or meant to do, nor did you mean to see these images. You didn't seek to bend the ways of the world to your will. You stumbled on this thing, the way a kitten happens upon a flower where a bumblebee has lit. This is like the water from the First Well. The music Leeli makes has great power, but it is clear the Maker put the power there when He knit the world. If it seems as though we have uncovered some secret, it is only because the wars of the ages concealed what was once as common as grass."

"Aye," said Oskar. "I've learned much from your First Book, lad. Much about Aerwiar and the cause of its breaking. Anyara—Anniera—was such a bright city, my boy. Justice and gladness were the jewels in its crown." He removed his spectacles and wiped the corner of his eye. "But Ouster Will laid waste to it all. He saw the gifts the Maker gave, corrupted them, and bent them to his own will. But that was much later," he said as he replaced his spectacles. "When the city was bright, the children sang music that made flowers change color overnight. Other children wrote poetry that it was said raised the great stone arches of the city gates. Still others painted pictures that, when the right child sang the right song or read the right tale, *moved*."

"The pictures moved?" Leeli asked breathlessly.

"That's what it said," Oskar told them in a whisper, "and I believe it." He looked from Janner to Leeli with shining eyes. "All my life I've wanted to believe the stories are true. I've never been able to quiet the pleasurable ache between my heart and my stomach that I felt as a boy when I read these tales. And now that I am wrapped up in the Wingfeather saga, that ache has grown so that I can hardly bear it. Here I sit in the presence of queens and heroes and *magic*. Yes, magic. It is only when we have grown too old that we fail to see that the Maker's world is swollen with magic—it hides in plain sight in music and water and even bumblebees."

"I have seen many things, child," said Nia, and a faraway look came into her eyes. "Wonderful things. The old stories might call it magic, but I call it beauty. I might even call it love." She blinked and came back to herself. "That you can see these things when she plays is a gift. Never try to become its master, but serve it. Allow it to be what the Maker meant it to be."

Janner's mind spun with a thousand questions. Why did Leeli's song only work some of the time? Why did Oskar say it was only children whose songs and poems and paintings had power? Was Tink in the Black Carriage? What were they going to do?

"Are we gonna sit here and blather about kittens all day?" Podo asked impatiently. "We came here to fetch Janner for dinner, if ye recall."

"Yes, yes," said Oskar, rubbing his chubby hands together. "Might we continue this discussion over cider and garp chowder? I have much to tell you about your First Book, Janner! On page twenty-seven your mother and I translated some old whistle-harp music—a song called 'Yurgen's Tune,' as far as we could tell. Imagine our surprise when Leeli played it and it was very like an old nursery melody your mother used to sing to you. Think of it!" Oskar jiggled with excitement. "And of course we need to learn about what happened to you, and we may have planning to do. 'Learn and plan over food if you can,' said the great R. T. Crunk. I'm inclined to agree."

Everyone laughed, but Janner's stomach growled at the mention of food, which made them all think of Tink again. They filed from the room in silence.

Kimera was a maze of round tunnels. Because many of the walls were made of ice and hard-packed snow, light from lanterns that lined the walkways fragmented and scattered, giving the impression that the city was high in the sky, cut from cloud and sunlight, and not deep in the ground. Janner was cold, but not as cold as he might've thought. There was no wind. He realized that for days he had slept outside and walked outside, contending with an eternal, biting wind that cut through every layer of wolf skin he wore. Kimera was warm by comparison.

A delicious smell wafted through the bright tunnel and grew stronger with every step. They passed several wooden doors, set into the hard ice just as they would have set in a wooden frame.

"Oy," said Podo as he led the company past two men with buckets of water. They wore leggings but no shirts. Their chests were hairy and broad as a bomnubble's, bigger even than Podo's. Their hair was long, but their beards were longer, and though their faces were hard and cold, they broke into fine, handsome smiles at Podo's greeting.

"Oy back at you, old man," said one of the men as he splashed an entire bucket of water at the wall. The water crackled and turned to ice before it reached the floor. The other man dipped a rag into his bucket and rubbed the wall smooth.

"They get fresh water from a wellhouse, deep underground. Gets warmer the deeper you go. Ain't that surprising?" Podo said. As they walked he explained how the Kimerans repaired the ice walls and how they got food either by hunting or fishing.

"Fishing? Are we near the Dark Sea?" Janner asked.

"Yes and no," he said. "These garp are from a river they say runs beneath the ice near the city. That's where they get most of their food. As for the sea, if we walked across the surface it would take days, but that's only because the ice stretches for miles over the water.

"The Kimerans are smarter than that, though. Epochs ago they cut tunnels that led to the Dark Sea, great caverns in the ice where waves lap at a frozen shore. In fact, there used to be a Kimeran port before the war. Sailors could steer their ships right into an icy corridor just wide enough for the oars, then row for miles through a white canyon." Podo's voice changed, and Janner didn't need to ask if the old pirate had been there himself. "At the end of the canyon is the mouth of a tunnel, and the maddest captains would wait until low tide and sail right in. Miles the tunnel went, right to the port at Kimera, where there was always good trade and garp chowder to warm the bones."

"Speaking of chowder," said Oskar, and they rounded a bend in the iceway and stopped at a set of giant wooden doors.

Podo pushed them open, and Janner's senses were assaulted. Hundreds of people

sat at long candlelit tables, laughing, shouting, singing, and chattering. The domed
ceiling was smooth as glass, and just transparent enough that Janner could see the
orange glow of the setting sun at the western edge. The sunlight gave all the Kimerans a happy radiance that deepened even as Janner watched. The stone walls glistened
with water that melted from the icy dome and trickled into a gutter that lined the
perimeter of the floor and sent the runoff away through a culvert.

The air was thick with the rich scent of garp chowder, but he also smelled hot
bread and the glad aroma of a fire. On the opposite side of the room sat the largest
fireplace he had ever seen. The opening was as tall as a man and wide as a barn door,
and whole trees crackled in a fire so warm that Janner felt it on his face from the opposite side of the room. It was made of sea-smoothed stones, gray and black and layered
with patterned shades. The chimney soared upward into the ice. Above the fireplace
was an enormous mantel on which lay an arrangement of the bones of a large creature
Janner couldn't identify.

"What's that?" he asked. "The bones, I mean."

"A sea dragon," said Oskar.

"It's too small," Janner said. "The dragons are enormous."

"That's because," Oskar said sadly, "it was one of their young. Not more than a
few years old. Many years ago, baby sea dragons fetched a high price. They were nearly
impossible to catch, but their hides were worth more than many jewels. The meat of
a young sea dragon was one of the finest delicacies in all of Skree. Only the wealthiest
could afford it."

"That's terrible," said Leeli.

"It was, dear," said Nia. "The kings of Anniera, it is said, once had an alliance with
the sea dragons. For epochs Annierans tried to renew the old alliance, but they didn't
know how to communicate with the beasts. Still, our people always believed that of
all the Maker's creatures, the sea dragons were sacred." Her voice darkened. "But to
the dragon hunters there was nothing sacred but riches. Wicked men will do anything
for money. Annierans despised the dragon hunters and were right to do so."

Janner shivered. The dragons were creatures of such terrible beauty. He couldn't
imagine killing one, let alone one of their young.

"This is the oldest part of the city," said a familiar voice from just inside the
room. Dressed in black, Gammon leaned against the wall with his arms folded, smiling at Janner. "It's the one room in all the city where we can burn the driftwood as
hot as we like and not worry about the walls melting." He pointed at the ceiling. "We

pump water from the well to a fountain that pours onto the glass dome night and day. The air outside is so cold that it stays thick and clear no matter how warm it gets down here."

"Gammon," Podo said in greeting, "you've done a great work here. I can't tell ye how fine it is to live in a city with no Fangs. Skree is lucky to have such a one as yourself."

Janner wasn't used to Podo speaking to another man in such a way. The old pirate actually liked him. Janner was glad, because he liked Gammon too. In the Stony Mountains he had placed his trust in the man, and he was relieved to see that Podo would have approved.

"Thank you, Podo. I'm glad you're here. Make yourself at home. Kimera is a free city, as free as Skree before the war, and as free as Skree will one day be again. Janner, you're probably wondering about Maraly. That's her at the table by the wall."

Janner was shocked to see a girl in a red dress. Her hair was still boyish and short but clean and adorned with a string of pearls. If Gammon hadn't pointed her out, he never would have recognized her. Beneath all the dirt and meanness, Maraly was quite pretty. Then she leaned over, snorted, and spat on the floor beside the table. She wiped her mouth with her sleeve and shoveled a lumpy spoonful of chowder into her mouth. A glop of it landed in her lap and she scooped it up with her fingers and licked them clean, then absentmindedly wiped her fingers on the front of her dress as she scooped up another spoonful. Janner smiled.

Nia raised one eyebrow. "I see we have some work to do with that one."

The Igiby family joined Maraly at the table, and three Kimeran women appeared with steaming bowls of garp chowder and mugs of cider.

It was the finest meal Janner had ever eaten. If he hadn't been sitting next to his mother, he would have gobbled the food just like Maraly, but he forced himself to keep his back straight and take modest bites. Several times during the meal, various men, women, and children stopped at the table to welcome Janner and Maraly. They were kind and respectful, especially to Nia, who was most clearly some kind of royalty.

Maraly said little and ate as noisily as Podo for the duration of the meal. When she finished off her cider, she belched and patted her stomach. Podo would have laughed had Nia not fixed him with a hot glare. Janner could tell she was trying very hard not to let her disapproval show.

"So tell us the story, lad," said Podo. "What happened?"

All eyes turned to Janner.

He knew this was coming. He had always loved Podo's stories and dreamed of the day he would have his own, but now that he had a story to tell, he found the telling was difficult. So much had happened. How could he tell it all? He was afraid to relive parts of it and was ashamed of others. Podo nodded at him.

"I know it's hard, lad, but it's yours. Ye'll find healing in it, like it or not. Start at the beginning—at Ronchy's place. What happened after I broke down the door?"

Janner took a deep breath and began.

He told them all of it. He told them about his anger at Tink. About the horrors of Tilling Court, about the awful darkness of the Overseer's box and the peace he found there. He told them about Sara Cobbler and Nurgabog and Maraly.

They listened with wide eyes. They asked him questions now and then, and more than once Nia's eyes brimmed with tears. But what Podo had said was true—telling the story hurt and helped all at once. Already he could see ways the story had changed him and would go on changing him.

"I fell asleep on the boggan," he continued, "and when I woke up, here I was."

Oskar leaned back in his chair and dabbed his brow with a napkin.

"Now *that's* a tale," Podo said.

Nia put an arm around Janner and squeezed.

"But we need to do something about Tink," said Leeli. "If Janner saw him in the song, that means he's alive, doesn't it? And if he's alive, then we have to find him."

"How?" Janner asked. "All I could see was that he was in a box. That could mean he's in the Black Carriage or a dungeon or—or a ship, even. It would be no easier to find him than it would have been for you to find me when I was in Dugtown."

"Ain't no hope for Kalmar," said Maraly. It was the first she'd spoken since Janner's tale began.

"Don't say that," Nia snapped.

Maraly narrowed her eyes at Nia, and the Strander returned. "It's true. Nobody who gets taken by the Carriage ever comes back. Me pa sent I don't know how many kids—some of 'em were from our own clan!—to the cages, and they never come back. Friends of mine too. Boys who could fight a lot better than Kalmar ever could and who knew the forest better than me. They promised they'd find a way back, and they never have. Not *once*. What makes ye think Kalmar's any different?"

Many of the Kimerans seated nearby looked up from their chowder when Maraly's voice rose. Gammon excused himself from his table on the opposite side of the room and strode over to them.

"Easy, lass," he said to Maraly, who smiled at him. He spread his hands and looked at the Igibys. "For years we've eaten our meals in peace, and no sooner do you good people arrive than we have a scuffle."

Maraly's smile vanished, and she scowled at Nia. "*She's* scufflin'."

"Me apologies, Gammon," said Podo. "You know how womenfolk can be"—Nia's jaw dropped at this—"always bickerin' amongst themselves. We'll keep it down. Won't we, daughter?" Podo looked sternly at Nia, who returned a smoldering gaze.

"Good," Gammon said. "What was the source of the spat? Perhaps I can help."

"We were discussing how we should go about finding Kalmar," Oskar said.

"Oh? I thought he had been taken by the Black Carriage."

"He has," Janner said.

"Then I'm afraid there's no getting him back," Gammon said gravely.

"That's what I told 'em," said Maraly without looking up.

Nia threw her napkin on the table and left the room.

"Listen, sir," Podo said. "We're guests here. I know we owe you much for gettin' Janner here safely. But ye have to understand somethin'."

"What's that?" Gammon asked.

"Kalmar is her boy. We have reason to think he might yet be breathin', and as long as that's true, we don't aim to forget him or to give up. We'll keep the candle burnin', just as we did with Janner here."

"I hear what you're saying, Podo, but there's something *you* need to understand too. Nobody gets out of the Carriage. There's too many Fangs."

Podo scoffed. "We both know the Fangs ain't as much trouble as a snake in the grass if you know how to use a blade. Dust and bones is all they are."

"Not anymore," Gammon said.

"What do ye mean?"

"I mean they're stronger. Faster. More dangerous than they used to be, and now that they come from the Phoobs they can get here quicker—"

"The Phoob Islands? What about 'em?"

"Nothing."

Podo glared at him and waited for an answer.

Gammon sighed and glanced around to be sure none of the Kimerans were listening, then leaned in close. He opened his mouth to speak, then shook his head. "I can't tell you. Too many ears."

Podo rolled his eyes. "What, ye can't trust your own?"

"No. I can't. Remember Migg Landers?" Gammon asked. Podo growled. "He was one of my own, and I couldn't trust him, could I? I have a plan, but I don't mean to tell it to a soul until the time is right. In the meantime, you and your family just stay put. Kimera welcomes you. Enjoy the rest." He rose from the table. "One more thing. I know you loved your grandson, and I know he was important in Anniera. But if he's been taken by the Carriage, it's best you put your hopes to rest. Even if he's still alive, the Kalmar you knew is gone by now. I'm truly sorry."

Janner didn't understand what he meant, but Gammon's eyes were sincere and sad. Podo studied the other man's face for a moment, then nodded stiffly, and Gammon left.

The company sat at the table in silence. The roar of the great fire, the laughter and conversation from the nearby tables, the clatter of spoon on bowl—all mocked the terrible thing Gammon had said. Tink was gone. Janner felt foolish for allowing himself to hope that his brother might be saved. He hung his head.

"I know somethin' about the Phoobs," Maraly said.

"What might that be, dear?" said Oskar.

"What do you know?" Leeli asked, sounding like her mother.

"I heard me pa say the Black Carriage sometimes went there instead of Lamendron. Said the Fangs had some new plan. Might be that Kalmar is there. I still say nobody could ever escape the Carriage, but—" She paused and cocked her head sideways.

"But what?" Leeli said.

"Nobody's ever escaped before, but then, nobody's ever had help." She shrugged. "Maybe we could go get 'im. Wouldn't mind finishin' that tackleball game we started at the East Bend."

Podo smiled. And like a cloud slipping aside to allow sunlight through, the shadow of Gammon's words drifted away, and hope returned.

"Let's find Nia," Podo said. "I don't know what we'll do or how we'll do it, but we're gonna get me boy back, with or without Gammon's help."

58

Gammon's Bargain

The first time she tried it, they were in Podo's room. Maraly, Oskar, and the Igibys sat in a circle on a rug in the center of the floor. Leeli raised her whistleharp to her lips and played a reel called "Shovel the Hay, It's Donkey Food." Janner clamped his eyes shut and thought about Tink. In the darkness of his vision, he saw geometric shapes drift and blossom, but nothing special happened. When Leeli had played the song through a third time, he gave up.

"Nothing," he said.

"Maybe I'm not playing well enough," Leeli said.

"No, you're playing it just fine," Nia said. "Perfectly."

"Maybe it has to be a certain song," Oskar suggested. "What about the one from the First Book?"

"Or the one you played for Nugget. Do you remember that one?" Janner asked.

"I remember it exactly," Leeli said.

"Try it, dear," Nia said.

Once again she played, and though it brought back to Janner's mind all the memories of that day on the cliffs when he had first heard the sea dragons in his head, he saw nothing.

He opened his eyes to find them all looking at him. "Sorry," he said, and they bowed their heads with disappointment.

"Maybe we should leave you two alone," Nia said.

They filed out of the room, leaving Leeli and Janner facing each other on the rug. Leeli played song after song, and Janner thought so hard that his head hurt. But nothing happened. They found the others in Oskar's room, and they leapt to their feet when Janner and Leeli entered.

"It's not working," Janner said. "I'm sorry."

"We've been talkin', lad," said Podo, "and it makes no difference either way. We're gonna go get 'im. All of us."

"All of us?"

"Aye. Seems to me that every time this family splits up, bad things happen. We'll head south again, then figure out what to do next. Maybe we'll head to the Phoob Islands." Podo cleared his throat and glanced away. "I remember there's a fort there. That must be where, the Fang outpost is—though it doesn't make much sense. Last time I was there, it was white with snow and sea foam. Not a likely place where the lizard men would be able to survive, but Gammon said these were different, that Gnag's enlisted another breed of Fang that can kick the cold. Point is, we can't sit here and do nothin'. Let's go get yer brother."

"Yes sir," Janner said, then he ran to Podo and hugged him tight.

"When do we leave?" Leeli asked.

"First thing in the morning," Nia said. "We need to arrange with Gammon for the use of a few boggans and a team of chorkneys."

"Chorkneys?" Janner said.

Leeli's eyes glowed. "I have to show you! They're beautiful, with the softest feathers. The keepers let me feed them sometimes."

"There'll be time for that in the morning," Nia said. "You children should go to bed. I'll stock the packs and make ready so we can get an early start in the morning."

Janner told Maraly and Leeli good night and went to his room, where he lay under his covers and stared at the icy ceiling. The frustration about the song was gone. The regret that he would be so soon in leaving the comforts of Kimera was gone. His heart sang with the hope that there was even the faintest chance he would see his little brother again.

At last, he slept.

A knock at the door woke him. Janner sat up and rubbed his eyes, remembering at once that the journey awaited. He threw on his clothes, grabbed the fur coat from the hook, and flung open the door. His smile vanished.

A Kimeran stood before him, his long beard caked with ice. He was out of breath, and he wore a burly gray fur coat that hung to the floor.

"What is it?" Janner asked.

"Sorry," the man said, and he lunged forward and tied Janner's arms behind his back before the boy knew what was happening.

He pushed Janner ahead of him, past Leeli's empty room, then Nia's room, then Podo's. They were all empty. Podo's door hung crooked, and his bed had been toppled in a struggle.

"What's happening? Where's my family? Where's Gammon?" Janner asked, but the man said nothing.

They passed the big doors to the dining hall and snaked through the iceways of Kimera, past storefronts cut into the ice, past kitchens and dwellings where children played. Whenever they met Kimerans, they looked confused and backed against the wall so Janner and his captor could pass. Finally, they rounded a corner, and Janner saw him, flanked by a small company of armed Kimerans.

"Gammon!" he cried. "What's happening? Where is my family?"

"It's all right, lad. It'll be fine. I just can't let you leave." He turned to the man behind Janner. "Thank you, Errol. It's safe to go inside."

"Yes sir," said Errol, and there was worry in his voice.

He led Janner into a small chamber. Oskar, Podo, Nia, Leeli, and Maraly sat gagged and lashed to a long bench in the center of the room. Janner noticed Maraly no longer wore a dress but breeches and a coat, just like Janner. The walls were made of stone instead of ice, and a torch sputtered on the wall. When Podo saw Janner, the old man grunted and struggled at his bonds, and Errol tensed.

"It took four of us to bind him, lad," said the Kimeran.

"Nearly killed one of us, even with the bad shoulder," said another warrior just outside the door. "He's a strong one, your grandfather."

"Why are you—" Janner began, but the man tied a rag around his mouth, and in moments he found himself strapped to the bench beside the others.

"That will be all, Errol," said Gammon. "Be sure Elmer and Olsin are well tended to. They took quite a beating." He lowered his voice. "Then make ready, as we planned."

"You're certain?" asked Errol quietly.

"Yes. More than ever. Thank you, friend. Be ready."

"Yes sir," said Errol, and the men clasped hands.

"I didn't want it to come to this," Gammon said to the Igibys. "I told you to stay and rest. I told you to make yourselves at home. I told you to give up on Kalmar. But you wouldn't listen, and there you sit. My men have learned that it's good to listen to me. Haven't you, men?"

"Aye sir," they said from the hallway.

"You must understand that I would do anything to protect Skree. I can't just let you go, not when the Fangs are expecting me to deliver you. If I thought there was any other way but to hand you over, I'd set you free. But it's you Gnag wants, not Skree. All I have to do is give you to him and he's agreed to leave these lands. Call me evil if you like, but the greater evil is the suffering you brought to my country. Do you need me to convince you?" Gammon placed a foot on the bench where they sat. "Olfin, Urland, come here!"

Two of the big men from the hallway stepped inside the chamber.

"Olfin lost his parents to the Fang invasion. Burned his home, killed all his livestock. Urland has a similar story. Don't you, Urland?"

"Aye sir. My whole village was razed. I'll be right glad when you turn this lot over to the Fangs, sir."

Gammon spread his hands and smiled. Sent word by crow as soon as we arrived that the Jewels of Anniera were caught at last."

Podo, Janner, and Maraly all growled and struggled. Janner was tired of betrayal. He was beginning to believe that no one in all of Aerwiar was trustworthy. The older he got, the more the world proved itself a crooked place.

Beware, said the sea dragon, and now Janner knew. It was Gammon all along; Gammon who wanted to use the young ones for his own ends. And Janner had been too foolish to see it. He had followed the man right into Kimera.

"I had a farm," said Gammon. Janner grew still. He tried to imagine Gammon without his black clothes and commanding presence. He pictured him with a hoe and a straw hat, but it was so ridiculous that he snorted.

Gammon shot a look at Janner. "Funny, is it?" he said, and Janner feared the man would strike him. But Gammon chuckled. "I suppose it is. I must tell you; I'm a much better soldier than I was a farmer. I could hardly grow a totato bigger than a grape. But my wife, Yona, could turn even the smallest totatoes into a fine meal. When the Fangs came, my poor Yona was killed. They left me my daughter," he said, glancing at Maraly, "who would have been about your age, lass. But a year later the Black Carriage came and tore her from my arms. That day I swore I would serve Skree. I would do whatever it took to set my land free. Do you understand? I'll do *whatever it takes.*"

Janner stared at him with a confusion of sympathy and outrage.

"I don't know why Gnag the Nameless wants you." Gammon shrugged. "And I don't really care. I didn't even believe Anniera was real until you showed up here. But if I can use you to banish this evil from my country, then I will do so. At least this way your capture will mean something. Take heart in that."

He knelt in front of Maraly. "I'm sorry, lass, but sometimes things must be done whether you like it or not. You'll have to pass for the other boy." Gammon placed a hand on her shoulder. She thrashed like a wild animal, and Gammon recoiled. He straightened and said, "That's all. I'll send for you when the time comes. The Fangs will be here soon."

They sat for a long time, listening to the sputter of the torch and one another's breathing. They each took a turn twisting their arms to loosen the bonds, but it was no use. Soon the silence was broken by sniffles, and Janner saw Leeli was crying. Nia tried to talk to her through the gag, but it was no use.

When Leeli's tears ebbed, she began to hum. She had no whistleharp, and she could form no words, but the melody that emerged dripped with weariness and sorrow. The song filled the chamber, and all their hearts—even Maraly's—resonated with it. Janner looked at each of them in turn and saw their cheeks were wet. Janner closed his eyes—and saw bright colors.

His mind was vivid with swirls and bursts of movement. He soared across the steeps of the Stony Mountains, so close to a grimace of snickbuzzards that he saw the tiniest feathers on their rumpled necks. Then he swooped down, past a foraging bomnubble, across the foothills and south of the Barrier to the Mighty Blapp River. He felt the vision heading south toward Glipwood, but he remembered from the maps where the Phoob Islands lay, and he pressed his mind eastward. The image responded, and his view swung left. He skimmed the tops of the glipwood trees and caught glimpses of the river below, until the land fell away and he beheld the chaos of Fingap Falls.

He guided the image north and east over the Dark Sea of Darkness until he saw a cluster of brown islands just off the coast of Skree. Closer he flew to the islands, until he could make out the masts of ships and gray shapes moving on their decks. He wanted to move closer, and he pressed his mind that way, but the image seemed to resist, and he remembered his mother's words: *"That you can see these things when she plays is a gift. Never try to become its master, but serve it. Allow it to be what the Maker meant it to be."*

Janner let go and allowed the image to go where it wanted. He heard dimly the notes of Leeli's song, and he prayed she would keep humming. He sensed he was close to something.

The image sped past the islands, north along the coast, where the Stony Mountains spilled their giant crags into the sea, until the land whitened with snow. The flat nothingness of the Ice Prairies stretched away to the horizon, and Janner wondered what he was meant to see.

Then he detected a speck on the horizon. The image whooshed nearer with every note of Leeli's song, and the speck grew in size until Janner saw what it was. It was such a shocking, baffling sight that he cried out, and when he did, Leeli's song cut short and the spell was broken.

Janner opened his eyes and saw only the gray stones of the cell, but what he had seen in his vision was burned into his mind. It sent a violent shiver through his body and a jubilant cry out of his mouth. He sat on the bench in his bonds, bouncing up and down like a toddler throwing a happy fit.

"MMMT!" he said through the gag. "MMMK! MMMT!"

They looked at him like he was mad, half concerned and half amused by the joy on his face.

"MMMK!" he said again and again. They couldn't understand him, but he didn't care. He laughed and whooped and shook his head with wonder. Every time he calmed down enough to see the looks on his family's faces, their confusion was so delightful that it sent him into another fit of joy.

What is it? their faces asked. *What did you see?*

He could hardly wait to tell them.

59

The Transformation

Artham pressed his feet against the cage door and his back against the rear bars. He clenched his teeth, clamped his eyes shut, and pushed with all the strength in his heart. The eerie melody filled his ears, and above it he heard one of the Grey Fangs shout, "Eyes on the birdman! He's trying to break the cage!"

Artham felt hairy paws on his arms and legs, and more than once the butt of a spear smashed into his face, but he mustered his strength again and pressed. The bars of the cage were as thick, but Artham felt the tiniest give and it renewed his strength. Again and again pain flowered in his face as the Fangs tried to stop him. The bones in his knees and back throbbed and threatened to break if he pressed any harder. The melody from the chamber swelled, and even with his eyes closed he saw the bright flash of light.

"Esben!" he screeched, and in a loud voice he sang along with the melody that came from within the box, the melody he had tried so many years to quiet. He could run no more from his darkness.

The voices in his head that cried *coward* and *weakling* drew back into the shadows. He knew he was those things but feared them no longer. Then another voice spoke. It called him *throne warden* and *protector* and *uncle,* and at last he believed it.

A surge of power ran hot through his bones. With one final shove, the cage splintered into pieces. Grey Fangs tumbled backward. Bent steel littered the floor.

Artham P. Wingfeather stood in the center of the debris, bloodied and panting, eyes ablaze.

He was aware of an odd sensation in his back and wondered if he had broken some of his ribs. Children from the Carriage scattered to the corners of the cavern, while the Grey Fangs recoiled and whined like puppies.

Artham drew in a deep breath, spread his arms, and loosed a victorious scream. As he did, two graceful wings unfolded from his back, the feathers damp and glistening. They were dark gray, flecked with white and speckled eyelets of the brightest crimson. Though they were still sharp as knives, his talons had narrowed and lengthened enough that they felt more like hands and less like claws.

Artham felt lighter and stronger, and for the first time in nine years, his mind was clear and sure. The words to a hundred of his own poems scrolled across his memory; he saw faces of old friends, battles he had fought, and even the most terrible moments of his life—and yet he remained himself. The wild animal inside that he had struggled so long to kill pulsed with power, but it was no longer his master. He rode the pain like a knight rides a horse.

He spread his wings and leapt twenty feet into the air, over the heads of cowering Fangs, to the dais. He landed with sure feet and tore open the iron door.

"Tink! Kalmar!" he cried into the darkness.

Smoke wafted out. He folded his wings and entered the chamber.

"Kalmar!" he whispered.

He was answered by a whine from somewhere in the corner. Artham reached into the smoky blackness until he felt a furry arm. It trembled, damp and hot to the touch. The creature whined again.

"Hush, lad," said Artham. "I've got you. Your uncle Artham has got you. This story will end well. I don't know how, but things will be made right. Come on."

Artham lifted the trembling thing and held it in his arms. He moved to the doorway and peered outside. The Grey Fangs had found their feet, but none seemed ready to attack the wild man who had just broken a cage to bits. Then a voice came from deep in the box.

"You're too late, Throne Warden. The boy is gone and a new thing has come," the Stone Keeper said. "Sing the song of the ancient stones and the blood of the beast imbues your bones."

Artham paused at the door. He flexed his neck, shook the feathers of his mighty wings, and turned to the woman, barely visible at the back of the box.

"You call that poetry?" he said.

With Tink unconscious in his arms, Artham stepped to the edge of the dais and leapt into the air. His great wings beat the air and carried the two of them over the heads of the astounded Grey Fangs, even as the Stone Keeper emerged and ordered the Fangs to pursue. He landed lightly at the mouth of the tunnel from whence the Black Carriage had come, folded his wings, and sped toward the surface.

Many Grey Fangs had gathered at the mouth of the tunnel when they heard the frantic voice of the Stone Keeper from within. Artham saw their silhouettes clogging the exit, saw their wolf ears twitching. He lowered his head and slammed into them before they knew what they were seeing. He was running so fast that he had only to spread his wings and he lifted over the ferry, swooped high above the strait, and glided in a slow circle above the island.

The tiny figures of the Stone Keeper and her Grey Fangs emerged from the cavern and gathered quickly into companies. Artham realized his vision was clearer, more precise than it had ever been. He could see the Grey Fangs' yellow eyes, the flecks of seashell embedded in the stone walls of the fort. The turrets crawled with gray beasts, organizing themselves much faster than any green-scaled Fangs that Artham had ever seen. An arrow whizzed past, and he saw with alarm that a regiment of archers had him in their sights.

He clutched Tink's furry, trembling body close to his chest. "Let's go find your family, your highness," Artham said with a smile.

He drew in his wings and dove like a hawk, straight for the fort. The alarm on the Grey Fangs' faces was worth the risk. He spread his wings at the last moment and skimmed above their heads in a blur. The Grey Fangs ducked and scattered.

Artham's momentum carried him in a graceful arc over the strait to the rocky coast of Skree. He followed the mountainous coastline until the land flattened, white with the snow of the Ice Prairies.

An armada of warships lined the icy coast—a hundred at least. The trampled snow around the ships gathered into a wide path that scarred the perfect surface of the Ice Prairies. The path led northeast, and he knew the Grey Fangs marched on Kimera. Down he soared until he flew just a few feet above the snow, following the contour of the prairie as it rose and fell in gentle, pristine drifts.

Artham's eyes watered from the wind and from the speed and from the magnificent beauty of the land arrayed below him. Water streaked from the corners of his eyes toward his ears and, in the vicious cold, froze into silvery jewels.

He would have to write a poem about this.

60

Secrets in the Snow

The many hours Janner spent bound and gagged in the cell with his family were maddening. He pushed at the gag with his tongue, but it held fast no matter how hard he tried. They all looked at him with confusion and glimmers of hope, but they couldn't understand his grunts, and he couldn't understand theirs.

He still wasn't sure how the images worked. Had he seen things as they actually were or images that merely hinted at the truth? At the Fork Factory, when he had seen the vision of Leeli in the mountains, had that been a picture of where she was actually standing, or was it only a representation of her surroundings, as in a dream? The pictures swirled and moved, but they always had the look of a well-framed illustration in one of his picture books.

Could that explain the unbelievable thing he had just seen?

It was Peet—but it *wasn't* Peet. The Peet in his vision had great, feathered wings and soared like a lone fendril across wide drifts of snow. His face was handsome and bold, not like the haggard, jumpy Sock Man Janner had come to know. Maybe it was a metaphor. Maybe Peet was running—flying—to the Ice Prairies, and Janner's mind had added the wings.

Janner had seen something in Peet's arms, too, and though he didn't see it clearly, he was certain it was Tink. Again and again Janner closed his eyes and reconstructed the vision, willing himself to catch every detail, but he only saw a fuzzy blur in Peet's arms. Despite this, in the deepest part of his heart, he knew it was Tink.

After much grunting and head nodding, Janner communicated to Leeli that she should hum her song again. She tried several times, but as before, nothing happened.

The thrill of Janner's vision faded, and the hours slogged by, until heads drooped and some of them dozed.

At last, the door opened and Gammon looked them over.

"Brogman, loose them from the bench, but keep their hands bound. And keep them gagged."

Another bearded mountain of a man entered the room and untied their lashes from the bench. With a rope, he strung the seven of them together in a train with Podo at the front. He left one of Leeli's arms free so she could walk with her crutch and lashed her other wrist to the train.

"Tie the knot well, Brogman," said Gammon. When Brogman finished, Gammon looked the rope over and inspected each of the knots. When he was satisfied, he led them in single file through Kimera. The snow city was quiet as a tomb. Every room was empty.

They stopped at the foot of a graceful stairway that curved upward to a high ceiling, the same stairway Nia had ascended the night Janner arrived. A pile of furs lay at the foot of the stair. The two men guarding the staircase draped fine coats of fur over the company's shoulders and even wrapped scarves around the women's necks.

"It's cold outside," Gammon said with a smile.

Behind Brogman's yellow beard, his face twitched with apprehension.

"Fear not, Brogman," said Gammon, putting a hand on his shoulder.

"I'm not afraid, sir. Just eager." Brogman's smile was fierce.

Gammon looked the Igibys over one last time, and his gaze lingered on Maraly. "I'm sorry it's come to this, friends."

Janner glared at him. How could he call them friends when he was about to do this terrible thing? Maraly looked at Gammon with deepest hatred, and Janner's head spun with his treachery. He couldn't believe he would sacrifice her along with the rest of them. She had nothing to do with Anniera! And Gammon had spoken to her so kindly before.

"The army is gathered, and they await my delivery of the jewels. Brogman, be sure you lead them *exactly* to the place I showed you. That's where the Grey Fangs are expecting them, understand?"

Brogman nodded and said, "All right then, up you go."

Gammon stood at the foot of the stairs and watched them. Janner met his eyes, intending to give him a look of loathing he would never forget—but Gammon winked. Janner's anger faded to confusion. He studied Gammon's face but saw nothing but the same cold indifference, and he wondered if the wink had been nothing but a nervous tic.

Light flooded the stair as the trapdoor raised. Podo walked proudly into the bright day of their betrayal. From the back of the train, all Janner could see was light. Lumps of snow spilled into the tunnel and poofed on the steps. Sunlight blinded him, but with his hands bound to the train rope, he was unable to shield his eyes. He heard the wind howl and the crunch of their footsteps as Brogman led them through the snow to the place Gammon had designated.

When at last Janner could see, he wished he could not. Spread before them like a giant gray carpet was an army of wolves.

In Glipwood, when Janner was younger, Nugget and a stray dog had crossed paths and fought over a hogpig bone. Janner tried to separate them and was bitten. He never forgot the way the stray bared its long teeth, the way its lips curled back and its nose glistened. Thousands of Grey Fangs bared their teeth in the same savage manner.

And if that weren't enough, they also carried swords.

The Grey Fangs stood in ranks. They weren't the unruly, undisciplined Fangs Janner was used to; they had calm, intelligent eyes, and at the front of each company stood a Grey Fang that was clearly in command. To the southeast snaked a wide swath of tracks the army had made as it traversed the Ice Prairies from the Phoob Islands.

Between the Igibys and the Fangs stood no more than twenty Kimeran warriors. Janner recognized Olfin and Urland, the two men who had lost their families. Their weapons shone, and their beards whipped in the wind. Fierce as they appeared, the Kimerans were so few that Janner pitied them even though they meant to hand him and his family over. Did Gammon really believe the Fangs would evacuate Skree? Even Janner knew the beasts were not to be trusted. As soon as the Jewels of Anniera were in the keeping of the Grey Fangs, the wolves would turn on the Kimerans and the rebellion would be squashed. What little hope remained for Skree—and for Anniera, for that matter—would be extinguished.

Janner scanned the white horizon for any sign of Peet and Tink, but he only saw blinding snow. His vision had been clear—Peet was coming. But when? Would he come swooping in to save them as he had so many times before? Not with so many Fangs so near, not if these new beasts were as capable as they seemed. It would be better if Peet and Tink stayed far, far away until the battle was finished. At least that way they would remain free. And yet Janner ached to see his uncle and brother again. He couldn't keep his eyes from the snowy hills.

"We have them!" cried Brogman. "Into whose charge do we deliver the Jewels of Anniera?"

Where is Gammon? Janner wondered. *Why is this man Brogman doing all the talking?*

"Mine!" answered one of the Grey Fangs as it strode forward with a hooded figure at its side, struggling to keep up. They passed between the Kimeran men without even glancing at them and approached Janner and the others. The Grey Fang's voice was deep and husky, not the dry crackle of the snakemen, and its face was a terrible thing, yellow-eyed and unnatural. The nose at the end of the short snout was black and shiny; the ears stood at attention.

"My name is Timber," it said to Brogman. "I command these troops." It sniffed the air around Janner, Leeli, and Maraly. "These are the children, then?"

Maraly shook her head and grunted.

The Fang turned to the hooded figure. "Is it them, Zigrit?"

The figure raised its trembling arms and drew back the hood. Two black eyes set in a green, scaly face stared down at the children. Frost lined its mouth, and its long yellow fangs chattered in the cold.

"Y-y-y-esssss," it answered without looking twice at Maraly. The creature was miserable, and Janner saw that, indeed, ordinary Fangs would never have survived a battle in the Ice Prairies.

"The Jewels of Anniera," said Brogman, "safe and hale, as Gammon promised." Brogman's fingers twitched, and Janner thought of a cat about to spring. What was happening?

"And what of the girl?" asked Timber, narrowing his eyes.

"Er, girl?" Brogman faltered.

"This one," said Timber. The Fang placed a paw on the back of Maraly's neck and jerked her face toward Brogman. "This is not Kalmar Wingfeather, as promised."

Brogman's eyes shot nervously to the trapdoor.

"It's not as easy as you might think to fool the Grey Fangs," said Timber. "I received word by a crow just this morning that Gammon had only two of the jewels. Thank you, Urland."

The man called Urland edged away from the other Kimerans. The men growled at him as if they were Fangs themselves.

"You?" spat Brogman. "Gammon knew there were spies, but *you*?"

Urland looked like a mouse in a corner.

"It's not just Urland," said Timber. "There are several. Gnag has known the details of your rebellion for years. Gammon is not as shrewd a leader as he thinks he is."

Timber growled and bared his teeth at the warrior, then spun around and said, "Triffin! Bring two soldiers and seize these prisoners."

Three Grey Fangs pushed through the Kimerans.

Janner waited for Podo to break his bonds, or for Peet to appear, or even for a grimace of snickbuzzards to flap down and provide the distraction they needed to do *something*. But this time there would be no rescuer. This time they were caught—not just by one enemy but two.

Leeli leaned her head against Nia's side. Podo turned and looked at his family. He nodded at Oskar and Maraly and shrugged. He didn't seem sad, but he didn't seem ready to fight, either. The old pirate could see, Janner figured, that they were out of options and it was best to go without contest. That Tink at least would be free brought Janner some pleasure.

Three Grey Fangs marched straight to Podo and threw a sack over his head, then did the same to Oskar and Nia. Janner's heart raced. All the running, all the struggle and desperate clinging to the hope that they might one day escape—all of it came to this. They would be bound, gagged, and hooded in the company of those meant to protect them.

"Cease, I say!" said a voice from the stairway. "Proceed not in thy fur-fingered dealings! Forthwith!"

The Grey Fang about to place the sack over Leeli's head stopped cold. Its ears flattened, and it growled.

Janner turned to see a caped figure leap from the tunnel stairway. He was dressed in black from head to toe and whipped a sword about in the air like he was swatting flies.

"The F-f-f-lorid S-s-sword!" chattered the scaled Fang.

Brogman yanked a leather strap that dangled from Podo's wrists, and his bonds fell to the snow. Janner felt his own come untied as well and saw that each of their knots were loosed by the one strap. He and the others freed their hands and ripped the gags away.

"Aha!" said the Florid Sword. "'Tis I, 'tis I! And no sooner would I sprout fur and fangs than to allow thy flea-bitten hides to harm these, the Jewels of the Shining Isle! Now is the time of our mighty triumph! Now is the fruition of our many dazzling hopes in the yellowy sunlight of this bright and snowy day in the Ice Prairies of prairiness! Avast!"

When he finished speaking, there was no sound in all the Ice Prairies but the whistle of the wind. Thousands of Grey Fangs, a handful of Kimeran warriors, and the Igibys were busy sorting out in their minds what in the world the Florid Sword had just said.

"Gammon?" Janner said hesitantly.

"Aha!" The Florid Sword smiled.

"Who is this fool?" demanded Timber. "What's happening?"

"Kimerans!" bellowed the Florid Sword. "Make war! Loose the river!"

A thunderous crunch rang out, and the ground shook. Timber spun around, too frazzled to know whether to strike Gammon, seize the Jewels of Anniera, or command his troops.

Janner watched as the many columns of Grey Fangs broke formation and scattered. Enormous, jagged hunks of ice burst into the air and sent the wolves flying, hundreds of them disappearing beneath the surface. When the ice boulders fell, great plumes of water exploded and broke more of the ice away. Ear-shattering cracks appeared all about them, and soon Janner saw the shape of the great river snaking in a tight, graceful curve around Kimera.

Several trapdoors flew open, some directly beneath the Grey Fangs nearest the city. Out of the snow and into the ranks of the walking wolves streamed a thousand screaming Skreeans, young men and women, clad in shining silver armor and wielding swords. Among them appeared chorkneys, harnessed to boggans four at a time. Warriors crouched on the boggans with reins in one hand and swords in the other as the large birds pulled the warriors into the fray, snapping at the Grey Fangs as they ran.

The clash of steel split the air, and the Battle of Kimera began.

Timber growled at Gammon and pointed his sword at him. Several of the nearby Kimeran warriors rushed to their leader's side and leveled their blades at the Grey Fang. Urland stood between the Fangs and the Kimerans with his sword drawn, trembling with fear. He seemed as surprised as anyone that Gammon and the Florid Sword were one and the same.

Timber looked out at the chaos of his army, howled, and rushed away, bellowing orders as the Kimerans fought to drive his Fangs into the icy waters. Already many of the Grey Fangs had recovered from their shock, and it was clear that soon Timber would have them under his control to counterattack.

"Give me a blade!" Podo cried. The fever of war was upon him.

"Nay! Thou must make haste!" said the Florid Sword. "Away, friends, to yon haven!"

"Speak plainly, Gammon!" Nia snapped. "We don't have time!"

"Sorry," said Gammon with some embarrassment. He knelt before Janner and removed his mask. "Sorry about all the secrets, lad. I knew there were spies, and I needed the Fangs to believe I intended to hand you over. I didn't know whom to trust, and too much could go wrong if they found me out. Maraly, it's to you that I'm especially sorry. If you'd still like to stay, I'd like to take you in. There's a place for you here." Maraly's eyes were daggers. "If not, I wish you a fine journey across the Dark Sea of Darkness."

"What?" she said.

"That's where you're headed. A ship is waiting. These Annierans can't stay here. They'll bring me nothing but more trouble, and I've a feeling that once they're gone, Gnag's concern with Skree will go with it. I don't think the Fangs will leave without a fight, but I don't think they'll fight half so hard if the Jewels of Anniera have left. So I've arranged a crew and passage to wherever the old sailor wants to go."

"Are there enough supplies to get to the Green Hollows?" Nia asked.

"The ship is well stocked. All your things are there, too. I don't know how this battle will go, my lady, so I'd be off if I were you. Decide where to go once you hit the water."

"We'll stay and fight, Gammon!" Podo growled.

"No, he's right, Papa," said Nia. "This is no place for the children."

Howls filled the air. Timber and a company of Fangs charged at full speed for the little band of warriors that surrounded the Igibys.

"No time," said Gammon with a wink at Janner. "Have a good voyage. I trust you remember how to sail, old man?"

A warrior came forward, knelt just behind the Igibys, and fished two leather straps from the snow. "I'll be your driver," he said. It was Errol, the Kimeran who had led Janner to his cell.

"DRIVER? DRIVER OF WHAT?" bellowed Podo. "NO! I CAN'T!"

"Now!" cried Gammon, and a *thunk* sounded at Janner's feet. "Maraly?" Gammon held out his hand. She hesitated for a split second but took it. Janner smiled at her, and when she smiled back he saw not a Strander but a girl who had found a home.

"Gammon, give me a blade! I can't go to the sea!" cried Podo with real fear in his voice.

"In the words of—" began Oskar.

Then the ground fell away.

The nose of the boggan hidden in the snow beneath their feet dropped into a dark hole. Oskar toppled over, taking the Igibys with him, and they lay in a tangle of arms and legs on the boggan behind Errol as it zoomed down a slick tunnel toward the sea.

61

The Battle of Kimera

Long before Artham saw the battle, he heard it. The clash of steel and the thunder of the river ice carried across the prairie to his ears and made him beat his new wings even harder. Tink never moved. He slept as still and peaceful as a baby. Whenever Artham looked down at the boy in his arms, his heart nearly broke with love and pity. He knew well the journey that lay before his nephew but not how to spare him from it.

In the distance Artham detected a slight rise, the nearest thing to a hill he had seen during his flight. All around the hill the battle raged. Artham angled his wings and swooped high into the cold sky so he could survey the situation.

Like a curl of black ribbon on a white floor, an ice-fraught river curved around the rise of the hill, then disappeared again beneath the snow. It divided most of the Grey Fangs from the battle, and those left on the inside of the loop were locked in combat with the Kimerans. He saw bits of dust and fur whirling in the air where Grey Fangs had fallen, and he saw many fallen Kimerans too. The river was choked with hundreds of wolves clawing at ice floes and struggling to swim under the weight of their armor. Mounted chorkneys drove wedges into the ranks of Fangs, and wherever the line was breached, Kimerans appeared with sword and spear to drive the enemy back to the deadly waters. The Grey Fangs on the far side of the river had no way to cross, but their archers sent barrages of arrows into the battle.

Artham admired the Kimerans' strategy. The warriors would never have defeated the whole of the Fang army, but the river had divided the force in half. It was clear that the Kimerans would win the day.

But where were Janner and Leeli?

Artham held still in the gale and scanned the ground for Podo. To find the old man, he had only to look for a pile of slain Fangs. He saw a man in a black cape who seemed to dance on the heads of the wolves, swishing his blade so fast that he looked more like a stinging wasp than a warrior. Artham wondered who he was and wished he could meet such a fighter.

Chorkney

The common chorkney is a large, flightless bird found mainly in the Ice Prairies. The eating of chorkney meat is frowned upon, except in the event that the beast is killed in battle, in which case a chorkney feast is considered a way of honoring the animal's sacrifice. Though the chorkney is a creature of grace and power, it is malodorous. (Kimerans say they smell even worse on the inside.)

From Pembrick's *Creaturepedia*

But there was no sign of his family.

From his great height, he could see on the eastern edge of the horizon the Dark Sea of Darkness. He knew from his many wanderings that the Kimerans were a tunneling people and remembered they had courses that led to the sea.

Was that movement? He narrowed his new eyes and scanned the waters. Then he saw something terrible. Something moving faster than any ship.

In an instant Artham knew. He knew where his family was. He knew where Podo was, and his fury burst forth in a piercing screech. Tink stirred in his arms and whined.

It had been many years since Artham had thought about Podo Helmer's past. Long ago he had confronted Podo about his pirate days, and the old man had spurned him ever since for fear that he would reveal old secrets. Now Podo's past was about to catch up to him, quite literally, and Artham feared it would put an end to the dream of Anniera forever.

"Hold on, lad," Artham said, pulling Tink's furry body close.

With one last look at the battle below, he mustered his strength and soared toward the Dark Sea of Darkness, straight for the place where the waters roiled.

The boggan hissed down the ice tunnel at a sharp angle. The trapdoor clamped shut, and the bright opening above disappeared. They picked up so much speed so fast that Janner felt like he might choke on his stomach. No one spoke. Seconds ago they had been standing in the sun and snow amidst the noisy battle, and now the world was dark and quiet but for the hiss of the boggan on the ice.

Janner thought of the picture of his father as a boy, smiling at the prow of a sailboat, and a shiver of excitement ran up his spine. At last he would know the feel of a ship under his feet. He would taste the salt spray he had only read about. At the end of this tunnel, one of his wildest dreams would come true.

Then he remembered Peet and Tink. Where were they? What would they do when they arrived in Kimera to find a raging battle and their loved ones gone? But when he thought of the calm, brave look on Peet's face and the way he held Tink safe in his arms, Janner relaxed. Tink was probably safer now than the rest of them.

The angle of the slope lessened. Errol lit a lantern and tucked it under the nose of the boggan. Janner counted faces to be sure everyone was still there. The sides of the craft curved upward enough to match the shape of the tunnel, but there were no rails. What would they do if someone fell off? Oskar, for example, who because of his belly still flailed about, unable to sit up in the close quarters.

Janner's question was answered when Podo recovered from his shock and cried, "STOP!"

Errol looked at him and shrugged, then pulled a rope near his right leg, and a grinding sound came from the rear of the boggan. Ice sprayed in their wake, and the sled slowly came to a stop. Before and behind them was darkness. They sat in a bubble of yellow lamplight that reflected off the smooth surface of the tunnel.

"We're stopped, sir. What is it?" Errol asked.

"What is it?" Podo snapped. "Didn't ye hear me? We can't go to the sea. We can't, understand?"

"Grandpa, what's wrong?" Leeli said.

The old man's eyes were dark and troubled. The last time Janner had seen him look that way was that night in the tent when Podo had woken from a nightmare. *"There's things I done a long time ago,"* he had said. *"Things that ain't been paid for."*

"Leeli, I can't bring meself to tell you," their grandfather said after a pause. "Just know that I can't go to the sea."

"That's a problem, sir," said Errol.

"What do ye mean?" Podo asked.

"There's no turning back. You can't climb out. We're more than a mile from the surface by now, and it's much too steep. If you tried to crawl out, sooner or later you'd slip. Everyone in this tunnel will reach the bottom, one way or another."

"Then when we get to the port, let me out, and fast," he said. "There are ways back to Kimera. We have a chance if I'm fast enough."

"That's a problem, too," said Errol.

"What problem?" Podo growled. "I've been to the Kimeran port aplenty."

"This tunnel doesn't go to the port. It's an escape route—it empties right onto the deck of a ship in a hidden ice cove. It's what the old lords of Kimera used for escape whenever the city was under siege. Gammon figured that since you're an old sailor, you'd be happy with the situation. I'm afraid, sir," Errol said with a gulp, "that you don't have much choice in the matter. It's to the sea we go whether you want to or not. In fact," he added, "by now we're over the sea anyway."

Podo looked down instinctively, then back at Errol with wide eyes. "What have you done?" he screamed. He lunged forward and grabbed Errol by the beard.

Nia slapped Podo's hand. "Papa, that's enough! This man's trying to help us."

Podo let go of Errol and rounded on Nia. "I'm tryin' to help ye too! Can't you see that? I *can't* go back. Ever again. That's me punishment, lass! If ever they get a whiff of me near that water, it's the end, for me and for every poor creature in sight."

"What are you talking about?" Nia asked.

"Podo," said Oskar. "If you have something to say, now's the time."

Podo looked from Janner to Leeli to Nia, working his mouth, but nothing came out. He looked at Nia like a scared puppy and shook his head.

"I can't," he said, "I can't go to the sea."

Without turning her hard eyes from her father, Nia said, "Errol, carry on. It's to the ship we go."

Errol nodded and released the brake.

Podo leapt from the boggan as they slid away.

"Grandpa, no!" Leeli cried.

"Don't worry, ma'am," said Errol. "Watch."

He pulled the brake again, and the boggan stopped. Seconds later, from the darkness behind them, Podo slid into the lamplight, pawing at the ice in vain. He bumped into the rear of the boggan and lay staring at the ceiling. Leeli crawled over Oskar, took Podo by the hand, and drew him back onto the craft.

"Carry on," Nia said to Errol, and the boggan descended.

No one spoke a word.

Podo trembled, and Janner knew it wasn't because of the cold.

62

Ancient Anger

A faint glow appeared in the distance.

"Almost there," said Errol, and he snuffed the lantern.

Janner's eyes adjusted as the light grew stronger. The others sat up—all but Podo—and peered over Errol's shoulder. Moments later they saw a pale blue circle that grew as they sped nearer.

"Hold on," Errol said.

The boggan burst from the tunnel, flew through the air for a heart-lurching moment, and slammed into a pile of soft snow. Janner could see nothing but white. Cold, wet snow invaded every opening in his clothes, and he didn't know which way was up.

"Oh, sakes alive! Sakes alive!" said Oskar somewhere nearby.

Then strong hands pulled Janner sputtering from the snowbank. Several more of the big, bearded Kimerans helped Nia and Leeli to their feet. Podo crawled from the pile and dashed to the upper deck of the ship without a word.

"Welcome, Errol," said one of the crew. "Is everything going according to plan?"

"So far," said Errol as he climbed from the snow. "Gammon wants us out to sea as soon as possible in case things go badly. Clear the snow bed from the deck! Loose the moorings!"

The crew sprang into action.

Janner was too thrilled to wonder what was wrong with his grandfather. He was on a ship! He heard the muted splash of water, then the wonderful creak of timbers. On either side of the ship rose tall, smooth walls of ice. If the boat hadn't been there, the boggan would've splashed into the water. There was no shore, not even a stray ice floe. Beyond the prow, the corridor opened to the wild sea. Waves boomed against the ice cliffs and shot foam high into the air.

The sails unfurled, the crew hauled on fat ropes, oars churned, and the ship creaked forward toward open sea. Janner craned his neck and squinted upward at the fine sight of the mast and the mainsail unfolding in a spray of sunlight.

Then he saw something that caused his face to break into a wide smile. Far above the mast, a winged creature approached. Two human legs dangled behind the wings, and though it seemed impossible, Janner knew it was his uncle.

Peet's familiar screech cut through the sky, and Janner whooped with joy.

"Look!" he cried as the ship inched forward and the prow met the first waves of the sea. "It's Uncle Peet! And Tink! They made it!"

Janner waved at them and was thrilled to see Peet wave back. But as his uncle neared the mast of the ship, Janner realized he wasn't waving in greeting but in warning.

A mighty thunder shook the air, and cold water rained down on the ship. Nia screamed. Even some of the brave Kimeran warriors screamed.

Above it all rang Podo's strong voice.

"LORDS OF THE SEA! I'M PODO HELMER! SCALE RAKER, THEY CALL ME! YE KNOW MY NAME, AND YOU'VE JUSTLY CURSED IT THESE MANY YEARS! I BEG YOU! LET YOUR WRATH FALL ON ME AND ME ALONE!"

Janner tore his eyes from the sky and spun around.

Sea dragons erupted from the waves and towered over the ship. Their eyes glowed red as embers, and their mighty flanks trembled. The beasts dwarfed the ship; their fins churned beneath the water and rocked the boat like it was a toy.

Podo stood at the prow with his arms raised. The nearest dragon—the old one Janner had seen in his first vision, the one who had spoken in his mind—thrust its head forward, bared a thousand silvery teeth at Podo, and loosed a roar that tore the old man's coat from his shoulders and caused the ship to list to port. Podo stood firm, wet with sea spray and sweat.

Something thudded into the rear of the ship, and Janner turned, expecting to see another sea dragon. But it was no dragon. A Grey Fang climbed to its feet where it had slid across the rear deck and slammed against the stern rail. It drew its sword and growled as two more Grey Fangs shot from the hole in the ice wall and crashed to the deck of the ship. However the Kimerans fared in the battle far above, the Fangs had discovered the escape tunnel. Three more Grey Fangs thudded onto the rear deck in a tangle of fur and weapons and found their feet.

"Faster!" roared Errol. "Get the ship clear of the tunnel!"

By the time the ship's nose was into open sea—and into the throng of dragons— and the stern was clear of the tunnel mouth, fifteen Grey Fangs prowled the deck with teeth bared and swords slashing. Errol and the seven members of the crew not busy hauling ropes and oars engaged the Fangs with shouts and much bravery. Behind the ship, more Grey Fangs splashed into the water, and though they were bitter enemies,

Janner felt pity for them as they thrashed in the water and clawed futilely at the smooth walls of the cove.

Then the dragon's voice filled Janner's mind. It said the same words it had spoken that day at the cliffs, but now he knew whom it meant.

He is near you, young ones. Beware. He destroys what he touches and seeks the young ones to use them for his own ends. We have been watching, waiting for him. He sailed across the sea, and he is near you, child. We can smell him.

It wasn't Gnag. It wasn't Gammon.

The dragon's warning had been about Podo Helmer all along.

It was young dragons who were in danger, not he and his siblings. Janner was stunned. He knew Podo had been a pirate, and before that a Strander, but he had never stopped to consider the awful things his grandfather might have done—awful things that weren't just a part of some story but had actually happened.

But to slay the young of these magnificent creatures? Nia was right. Wicked people would do anything for money. He didn't want to think of Podo that way, but there was no escaping the brutal fact that his grandfather had done this terrible thing.

The dragon roared.

The crew battled the Fangs, but they were losing. Several of Errol's men already lay motionless on the deck of the ship. The Grey Fangs, unlike their scaly brothers, fought in silence, with precision and great skill. The rest of the crew scattered to protect the ship from the looming ice walls; others fetched bows and trained them on the sea dragons, though it was obvious arrows would be of no use.

Oskar lost his footing and sprawled on the deck, slipping to and fro like a dead fish. Nia's mouth hung open in a silent scream. Leeli, however, tucked her crutch under her arm, hopped up the stairs, and raced across the upper deck straight toward the dragon.

Janner snatched a sword from the hand of one of the fallen Kimerans and wondered whether he should hide, leap into the battle with the Grey Fangs, or follow Leeli to the forecastle where Podo faced the dragons.

The old dragon writhed in angry triumph, and its frenzy spread to the many dragons behind it. They roared and churned the waters until glaciers split and avalanches tumbled down from the sides of the Stony Mountains.

Podo stood like a statue at the prow, awaiting his death.

Dark wings suddenly blocked Janner's vision, and he found himself looking into Artham's eyes.

"Janner," he said.

His voice was strong and sure, and it cut through the clamor. His face was the same, though now colored with the same reddish tint as his forearms, and instead of wild, white hair, fine feathers shaded with subtle color and design covered his head and shoulders. He was beautiful.

"Uncle Artham—how did you—what happened?"

"I'm not sure I can explain it myself," Artham said. "Janner, there's no time. Take your brother."

In Artham's arms lay a Grey Fang, small and motionless. It wore no clothes, but its body was covered in long gray and white fur. Janner couldn't hide the disgust on his face. This wasn't Tink. This was a terrible mistake.

Then the Fang stirred and turned its head.

Janner's blood ran cold. Neither the fur, the pointed ears, the black nose, nor the sharp teeth could hide the fact that this was indeed Tink. Janner didn't want to touch him. He didn't want to believe this was his little brother.

"Drop your sword and take him," Artham said. "He needs you now more than ever, Throne Warden. The dragons will kill us all if we don't do something."

Janner nodded and took his brother into his arms. "What will you do?" he asked.

"I'll start by dealing with these wolves."

Artham snatched up the sword Janner had dropped, then spread his wings and leapt into the air. He dropped into the center of the fight and killed three Grey Fangs before his feet touched the deck. In seconds, the Kimerans had the advantage and backed the six remaining Grey Fangs into a corner.

Destroy them, said the dragon's voice in Janner's head. It was talking to the other sea dragons. *Destroy them all.*

"I can see that you're angry! Spare the others! It was me who took yer children!" Podo bellowed. He knelt in the prow and clenched his hands, and his big, broken voice rose above the chaos. *"Please!"*

The sea dragons would crush the ship and swallow every one of them. All because of Podo. All because of the wicked things he had done. It was no more use trying to stop the dragons than trying to stop a rack of dark clouds blowing in. Nothing in all of Aerwiar could stay such bitter vengeance.

Faster than Janner would have believed possible, the old dragon struck. Like a whip, the beast's head reared back and shot forward, straight at Podo and—

"Leeli!" Nia shrieked.

The little girl reached her grandfather and stood between him and the dragon.

63

Hulwen's Trophy

Stop!" Leeli said, and the dragon did.

It froze, so close to Leeli that she could have reached out and touched the tip of its nose.

And she did.

For the first time in an age, someone touched a living dragon.

Seawater washed down the sides of the dragon's slick face and puddled on the deck. Its mouth, full of teeth longer than Leeli was tall, was stretched open to eat Podo whole. The old pirate knelt with his eyes closed.

Janner sensed the dragon in his mind, who was speechless with surprise that this wavy-haired little creature would have such courage. The tips of her delicate fingers rested on the dragon's nose. She looked calmly into its eyes, though they were as big as wagon wheels and deep as the sea. A little burst of air from its nose blew back her hair.

It was your song that fell from the cliffs.

"Yes! It was her song!" Artham said, and Janner realized his uncle could hear the voice too. Artham broke away from the Kimerans at the stern, flew to the prow, and landed where Podo knelt. "Lords of the sea," he said with a bow, "before you stands the Song Maiden of Anniera."

The dragon blinked, and again its thoughts were spoken in Janner's mind.

Impossible.

"It's true, lords," said Artham.

Anniera has fallen. The dream is ended, and the world is dark.

"If the dream is ended," said Artham with a flap of his wings, "how do you explain these feathers? How do you explain Leeli's courage? How else could I hear your words if I were not a Throne Warden? It is true the Shining Isle is smoke and ashes and that darkness is wide over the land. But your long memory has failed you. Of all creatures, you should know that the darkness is seldom complete, and even when it is, the pinprick of light is not long in coming—and finer for the great shroud that surrounds it."

The dragon was silent.

Artham beckoned for Nia and Janner to approach. Nia took Tink from Janner's arms and rested his furry head on her shoulder, holding him close like she had a thousand times when he was very young.

Janner was ashamed to admit he was glad she took him. He didn't like the feel of the Fang fur or the eerie change in his brother's features; it was a reminder that the Throne Warden had failed. No matter what anyone said, though he knew it wasn't true, Janner would never escape the feeling of responsibility for what had happened to his brother. And then he began to understand something about his uncle: it was guilt that drove Artham P. Wingfeather mad.

Nia climbed the steps with Tink in her arms, and Janner followed. They stood beside Podo and Leeli, all of them wet and cold, shivering in the blustery sea wind.

"The heart of the kingdom stands before you. Behold," Artham said with a sweep of his hands, "the pinprick of light."

The dragon brought its head low and studied each of them in turn. When the giant eyes settled on Janner, he fought the urge to kneel as Podo had done. The beast was as old as mountains, and its gaze was heavy. When it looked at Leeli, she smiled and curtsied, and it bowed its head in return.

The dragon's eyes fell on Podo again, and a rumble issued from its chest. *Our anger is deep. However, for the sake of the old friendship with the Shining Isle, and for the Song Maiden's spirit, the ship may pass.*

"Our thanks, sea lord!" said Artham with a sigh of relief. He squeezed Podo's shoulder and whispered to the others, "They're letting us go. Thank the Maker, they're letting us go!"

The ship may pass, the dragon continued, *but Scale Raker is ours. His offense is great, and we will not so easily let him tread our waters. Long have I ached to foul his flesh.*

"No," Janner moaned.

"Please," Artham said.

"What did it say? Tell me!" Nia demanded.

"Hush, lass," said Podo. He looked up at Nia with a gentle smile. "Me voyage is over. I knew the sea held nothing but death and shame for me. Couldn't bear to lay me eyes on it all these years. I knew sooner or later me waters would carry me back here and there would be a reckoning."

"Quiet!" Nia said. "I'm too angry at you to let you die. This reckoning is nothing to what Mama would have said! To have kept this hidden from us, to have done these things—"

"She knew," Podo said quietly.

"What? Mama *despised* the dragon hunters. She hated what they did!" Nia sputtered.

"Aye," Podo said. "And so do I. Hate it more than you ever could. Many's the time I wished I could go back and fix it all, undo the things I done on the Strand and on the sea. But when yer mother gave me her heart, I left the old Podo behind and said good-bye to the sea. I never thought I'd see the ocean again once I married your ma in the Green Hollows, but then Esben chose you as his queen. Remember how I sent you and yer ma ahead and waited till winter before I crossed the strait to Anniera?"

"Yes, I remember," Nia said.

"I was scared silly that the dragons would rise up as they have now. The dragons took me leg, and they knew me scent. It was a miracle I made it across the strait to Anniera, and I made peace with never settin' foot on a ship again. Broke me heart, but I'd broken plenty of others and saw it as me just penance. Then Gnag the Nameless attacked, and that storm blew us across to Skree. I thought the dragons would gobble us up on the way, but I reckon the Maker had different plans. All those years I stayed at the cottage on Dragon Day because I couldn't bear to look out at that wide horizon and know I'd never sail it again.

"Listen, daughter. I'm glad beyond telling that it's just me they want. When we come out of that tunnel, I thought for certain that me deeds would be the end of you too. But they're lettin' you go. Nia dear, I'll go to the Deep happy knowing that."

"Enough!" said Nia. She rounded on Artham. "You tell these dragons I'm the Queen Mother, this is my father, and I pardon him for these crimes. They must let him pass!"

Artham hesitated.

"Tell them!" Nia snapped.

The dragon's chest rumbled again, and its eyes narrowed. Janner had the disturbing sense that its patience was wearing thin.

"I don't have to tell them," said Artham quietly. "You just did. They understand you."

"Nia, don't," said Podo. "I've done things that ain't been paid for, and it's time I stopped running from that."

Listen to the old man, said the dragon.

"It says—it says you should listen to Podo, Nia," Artham said.

"No!" she said with all the authority she could muster, clutching Tink so tight that he whined.

The dragon was finished listening to Nia. It reared its head and hissed at them. The other dragons writhed, the ship rocked, and it seemed they would break the vessel to pieces and swallow it whole.

"Please, sir," said Leeli to the dragon, "isn't there something that can be done?"

The dragon's answer was a name.

Hulwen! it said. *Come forth, daughter! Let these grovelers see what Scale Raker has done.*

A ruby red dragon rose from the waters at the old one's side. It was half the size of the others and swam in a graceless lurch. As it approached, the gray dragon drew back to allow it room. One of its eyes was missing. A long, twisted scar ran from the top of its head, past the missing eye, to the corner of its mouth. One of its fins hung limp, cut into shreds, and in several places its scales were twisted and corrupt where, Janner guessed, harpoons had pierced it long ago. Instead of a row of fine glimmering fangs, teeth were missing or stuck out at odd angles.

Podo shook his head like a child. "I beg ye, masters, please don't. I can't bear it."

The creature hung its mangled head over the deck of the ship, turned its good eye on Podo, and grunted. Janner waited for its words to fill his mind, but none came. Leeli and Nia hid their eyes.

My daughter, said the old dragon, *who was once as beautiful as the rising moon. My daughter, whose many scars came from Scale Raker's blade and the spears of his henchmen.*

Janner felt sick. It was one thing to learn his grandfather had done terrible things. It was another to see those terrible things with his own eyes. And this was only one of the dragons he had attacked. Janner tried to look at Podo but couldn't.

Do you remember her, old man?

"It wants to know if—if you remember her," Artham said. "It's the old one's daughter."

Podo shook his head.

Then remember this! said the old dragon. *Show him, Hulwen.*

The ruby red dragon sighed.

Show him!

The smaller dragon dipped her head into the water. When she emerged, she spat something at them. A clean, white bone clattered to the deck where Podo knelt.

"Me leg," he whispered. He looked up at the red dragon. "It was you. I remember. Oh Maker, I'm so sorry."

Hulwen, vengeance is yours, said the old gray dragon. *Kill the one who killed so many.*

64

And the Sea Turned Red

N o!" Janner screamed.

The ruby dragon grunted, reared back—and hesitated.

Do it! said the old dragon.

But the young dragon's eye fell on Leeli and her twisted leg. It looked at Podo, trembling and bent on his knees.

No, said Hulwen, a young, weary voice in Janner's mind.

What? said the old one.

Let them go, said Hulwen. *His scars run deeper than mine.*

Then she sank beneath the waves.

The old gray beast's fury shook the air. Its flanks rippled like a flag in a windstorm. The dragon's wordless cry stabbed Janner's mind, and he clamped his eyes shut and pressed both hands against his forehead. The other dragons shared the old one's rage until the water around the ship foamed like Fingap Falls.

Artham launched himself into the air and waved his sword at the great beast as it descended. With a flick of its nose, the dragon threw Artham against the glacier so hard that hunks of ice crashed into the sea. Artham was stunned, but his wings beat the air as he fell. The tips of his toes touched the water as he swooped up and circled the dragon again.

Janner no longer heard words in his mind. The creature had gone wild. He knew that if Artham hadn't distracted it, the dragon would have splintered the ship already and they would be dead.

"Janner!" Leeli said. "Get the First Book. Hurry!"

"Why? I don't know where it is!"

"Ask Errol. Gammon said our things are on the ship. Go!"

Janner had no idea what Leeli had in mind, but he was glad to do something other than wait to be eaten. He took the steps down from the foredeck in one leap. Out of the corner of his eye, he saw Oskar still flailing about on his back, unable to

find his feet on the rocking boat. Errol and the rest of the crew had subdued the Grey
Fangs and held them against the ship's rail at sword-point.

"Errol! Where are our packs?" Janner cried.

"In the captain's quarters, through that door!"

Janner burst into the room and saw his pack in a pile of bedrolls and furs beside
a large desk. He rummaged through it and yanked out the old book, wondering what
Leeli planned to do.

When he emerged from the cabin, he saw the great dragon wheeling about, snapping its teeth at Artham as he flew around its head like a gnat. The sound of the dragon's jaws closing on empty air was like lightning splitting an oak in two. Janner
wondered why Podo and the others hadn't sought cover, but he knew as well as they
did that it was futile. If the dragon wanted Podo, the dragon would have him. Even if
the old man hid in the ship's hold, the creature would have little trouble crushing the
ship with one bite.

Janner bounded up the steps and skidded to a halt in front of Leeli. She frantically flipped through the pages, thrust the book at Janner, and said, "Hold it open
where I can see it!"

Janner looked at the page but saw nothing but odd letters and lines.

Leeli reached inside her coat and removed the whistleharp. Light reflected from it
and glinted on the dragon's face. The dragon stilled.

Leeli raised the whistleharp to her lips with trembling hands and studied the
markings on the ancient paper. A great silence seemed to descend on the world. The
Kimerans, Artham, and even the Grey Fangs waited to see what would happen.

Then the melody broke on them like a sunrise.

After the first few notes, the dragon drew in a slow, deep breath and closed its eyes.
Leeli's song grew in strength and tension and beauty, and as she reached the first refrain,
the sea dragon exhaled a warm, mountainous note. Its voice was round and rich and
somehow fragrant, like the song a tree might sing when it blossoms in springtime.

"Yurgen's Tune," said Oskar, who stopped struggling and lay back on the deck
with a big smile on his face. "Good lass, Leeli."

The dragon raised its face to the sky with careful grace until its gleaming scales
caught the sun and the beast towered above them like a giant golden scepter. Soon the
other dragons joined it in song, and Janner felt that his heart might burst. He heard
the clatter of swords as they slipped from the Kimerans' limp hands while the big men
stood in awe. Artham spread his arms and wings wide and basked in the song as if it
were sunlight.

Podo knelt behind Leeli as still as a statue, unwilling or unable to raise his eyes to her or to the dragons. On his face was a look of insufferable shame, both for the killing of young dragons and for the way his treachery had nearly killed those whom he loved.

Leeli lowered the whistleharp when she had played all she could of "Yurgen's Tune," but the dragons continued.

"Grandpa," Leeli said gently. Podo lifted his eyes as if they weighed a thousand pounds. "Get up," she said. She took his old, crooked hand in her tiny, elegant one and raised him. Janner believed no other force in all of Aerwiar, not the finest words nor the strongest grip, would have been enough to lift the broken old pirate—only Leeli's voice and tender hand.

The Grey Fangs covered their ears. They howled with pain, but the sound was faint and distant and had no power to disrupt the dragons' music. Tink squirmed in Nia's arms. His eyes remained closed, but his claws dug into her skin and drew blood. She held him tighter and kissed his fur.

"Get these beasts below deck," Errol said. "And see to the wounded." He and his men bound the arms of the six remaining Fangs. The creatures, groggy and disoriented, were led to the ship's hold without protest. The dead Fangs had already turned to dust. Clumps of fur collected in the corners and lifted away on the breeze.

Janner hoped that when the song ended, the dragons would sink away as he had seen them do so many times before, but they did not. Instead, the old gray one arced its neck and looked down on them with a fierce stillness.

At last, said the dragon, *comes one who can ease our sorrow with song. We thought we would never again hear this music. How, little one, did you come to learn this melody? You sang something like it when the half moon rose, but it has been long since we have heard it as it was written.*[1]

"She learned it from this book," Janner said. "It's one of the First Books."

The First Books? the dragon said. *They have been lost for epochs.*

"And yet," said Artham, "the Song Maiden has just played 'Yurgen's Tune.' How else could she have learned it?"

Janner sensed the dragon remembering things from long ago, things the sea dragons had forgotten they ever knew, as if Leeli's whistleharp were a key that unlocked a secret chamber in the dragon's mind. He saw the ages turn like pages in a picture book. The old gray dragon glided backward through the waters of time with fins like wings, appeared younger by a day every hundred years, and led its herd a thousand times

---

1. See Book One, page 52, where Leeli sings with the sea dragons.

from Fingap Falls to the deep caverns of the Sunken Mountains, where stones gave light and the walls swirled with pictures.

He saw the dragons in pursuit of pirate ships, young dragons roped and hauled to the decks. He saw that in the days of the pirates, young dragons traveled the waters alone and were vulnerable. Only when they banded together as a herd did the pirates fear them and the hunting cease.

Then Janner sensed the dragon swimming back to an older time, when the world itself felt younger, when the sun was brighter and the waters warm. The old dragon saw itself wrecking ships, battering helpless sailors and their families. It remembered worming its way onto the shore to flatten villages and scar the land while the people wailed. Terror was in their eyes, and the dragon knew its own deeds were once dark.

It pushed further into memory but was met with a gray nothingness. No explanation for its fury, no cause for the killing. It would take another song to open those chambers. Janner felt a new emotion arise in the dragon's mind—contrition. The dragon had done evils of its own and regretted them.

Hulwen the ruby dragon raised her disfigured head from the water. The gray dragon closed its eyes and nuzzled her. Janner could tell they spoke with each other, but they had closed him off. He could hear nothing of what they said and wondered if the same were true of Artham. When the dragons finished, Hulwen looked into Janner's eyes and nodded.

A final passage, she said, and she sank away again.

Janner and Artham looked at each other with surprise.

There is no evil in justice, said the gray dragon. *The old man himself knows this. Though "Yurgen's Tune" has awakened pity in my ancient heart, yet the blood of our children cries out for justice. We will allow him the mercy of one last passage across the sea. Scale Raker may live out his last days in peace.*

But should he enter these waters again, the dragon said, *his days on Aerwiar will end. Without anger, without warning, we will rise from the deep and swallow him. So shall our dead be honored. Do you understand?*

Janner and Artham nodded gravely.

"Yes, lords," said Artham. "We thank you."

"They're letting him pass!" Janner ran to Podo and hugged him around the waist. "Grandpa, they're letting you go!"

"Eh?" The look on Podo's face alternated between disbelief and joy, which caused his bushy eyebrows to rise and fall like foamy waves. Nia raised her head to the heavens and mouthed a prayer while Leeli squealed and hopped into Podo's thick arms.

When the laughter and happy tears subsided, the dragons were gone. The ship rocked on the waves with the cliffs of the Ice Prairies behind and the wide horizon ahead.

Then a voice spoke that killed the smile on every face.

"Put me down," it said. It was an odd voice, raspy and deep as it was young.

Tink was awake, and he was growling.

He snapped at Nia and scratched her arms. She cried out and let him go, and the little Fang scurried away as soon as his paws hit the deck.

He squatted in a corner and panted like a dog. His eyes darted from his family to the crew of the ship to the sea spray that splashed onto the deck—and it was his eyes that sent a shiver down Janner's spine.

His brother was no taller than before, and even with the wolfish features he still somehow looked like Tink. But his eyes were yellow and wild. There was no depth or recognition, just a flat, shallow emptiness Janner had seen before. He had seen it when Slarb glared at him in the cell of the Glipwood jail; he had seen it when Commander Gnorm waggled his bejeweled fingers at him; he had seen it in the eyes of Timber, the leader of the Grey Fangs.

This creature might look like Tink, but it was no longer Tink. It was a Fang, through and through.

"Son," Nia said, her voice thick with sorrow. Streaks of blood colored her skin where he had scratched her. "It's me. It's your mama."

Tink growled.

She took a step nearer, but the wolf boy swiped a paw in the air and curled his lip.

"Don't come any closer," he said. "Where am I?" He looked around, desperate to escape. He turned and peeked over the railing at the waves as if he might jump overboard, and Janner noticed for the first time that his brother had a tail. Janner's stomach tightened, and he feared he might vomit or weep. He didn't know which.

"Don't scare him," Leeli said in the voice she used when she'd set her affection on an animal. "It's all right. We don't want to hurt you." The wolf ignored her and paced the railing, anxious for a place to run.

"What's your name?" asked Artham.

At this, Tink grew still. He cocked his head sideways like a dog. "I don't know. I don't know my name."

"Shall I tell you?" Artham said carefully. "You might not like it."

Tink studied the reddish man with wings. He shifted on his feet, licked his chops, and whined. "Tell me," he said in a small voice.

"Your true name is Kalmar Wingfeather."

The wolf boy's ears flattened against his head, and he howled at the sky. He flew into a fit of rage and darted about the deck. He snapped and clawed at his family. Nia and Leeli screamed. Janner and Podo put themselves between the women and the wild animal as Artham struggled to subdue him. Every time he laid a hand on the wolf, its teeth sank into his skin.

The Kimerans took up arms and raced to the prow at the commotion. Several of them trained their bows on Tink and drew back to shoot.

"Put down your weapons!" Artham commanded. "He's no Fang!" He flew across the deck and at the last moment knocked one of the bows upward so that the arrow whizzed harmlessly into the air.

But as soon as Artham turned his back, Tink leapt overboard into the icy sea.

That was the moment Janner truly became a Throne Warden.

Without a thought, Janner tore off his coat and ran. His heart's deepest instinct drove him forward and over the ship's rail to save his brother.

As soon as he hit the water, the world became a frigid, airless black. Too cold to think, he grabbed a handful of fur and pulled it near. Claws raked his skin. He felt Tink's teeth again and again, but he held his brother close. When every desperate gasp filled his lungs with water, he hugged the Fang to himself with all his strength. The sea turned red with Janner's blood.

The last thing he knew was Artham's strong taloned hands. He felt himself lifted on mighty wings from blackness to light, from silence to sound. And though his wounds were deep and bled freely, though Tink still fought to escape his embrace, in Janner's heart burned great joy.

65

The Final Voyage of Podo Helmer

And so Podo Helmer sailed the Dark Sea of Darkness for the last time.

The Wingfeathers traveled east to the Green Hollows, where many years before a rowdy pirate was tamed by the tender love of a woman named Wendolyn Igiby. Podo was often seen on the deck of the ship late at night while most of the crew slept. He gazed at the star-bright heavens and breathed deep the salty air, for he knew the night held a special beauty when one was far from land. He carried his leg bone wherever he went, and it brought him great pleasure to bang it on the mast to signal mealtimes. He moved through the days in peace and wonder, for his whole story had been told for the first time, and he found that he was still loved.

For days, Oskar N. Reteep was desperately seasick. His face was pale, and every few minutes he staggered like a drunkard to the ship's rail and provided the fish with rather unpleasant food. But soon the old man's pate became tanned and leathery. He learned the ropes with gusto and soon became as much a sailor as any of the crew. The Kimerans convinced him to shave his head, and in a fit of recklessness, he even allowed them to tattoo his arm with the somewhat unimpressive inscription, "I Like Books." Though he ate little and worked hard, at the end of the voyage he was as round and squishy as ever.

Nia and Leeli tended to the brothers.

When Janner woke, he ached from head to toe. He knew his wounds were severe because of the look on his mother's face when she changed his bandages. He lay in bed for days and listened to the creak of the ship and the thump of footsteps overhead. All his life he had dreamed of sailing, and now that he was finally on the open sea, he was confined to a bed. But he had plenty of time to reflect on his journey from Glipwood to Dugtown to the Ice Prairies to the bed where he now lay, and in the end he was grateful.

He also had plenty of time to talk to Tink.

The wolf lay on the bed next to Janner, strapped down with leather cords. He refused to eat soup or even cooked fish but devoured hunks of raw meat that Nia and Leeli tossed into his mouth. He snapped at anyone who came near, and whenever they tried to talk to him, he howled and snarled.

At first Nia tended to him with grief plain on her face. But soon a change came over her, and she kept her back straight and her chin high. She spoke to him firmly and told him, "I love you, Kalmar," whether or not he growled at her. And every day when she arrived and before she left, she looked him in the eye and asked him his name.

His answer was always violent: "I don't know," he would say, or "I have no name." His howls rattled the windows.

But at night, when moonlight passed through the small, round window and slid across the floor, Janner whispered stories to Kalmar, and Kalmar listened.

"You were fast," Janner said. "You could outrun me backward if you wanted to. In the summer when the days were long, we would run up the hill to the Blaggus boys' house and play zibzy until it got too dark to see."

"What's zibzy?" Tink whispered, and Janner told him.

"Once, you hid a thwap in Grandpa's underwear drawer," Janner said with a hiss of pain because it hurt to laugh.

"Then what happened?" asked the wolf.

"Grandpa jumped so high his head put a hole in the ceiling. You weren't allowed to play zibzy for a week, but we could tell Grandpa thought it was funny."

In the morning when Nia and Leeli arrived with breakfast, Nia would ask the Grey Fang his name, and Tink would be all teeth and howls again. His eyes stayed that awful, empty yellow. Janner began to ache for the nighttime so he wouldn't have to see those wolf eyes watching him. At night he could stare at the moon and tell his brother stories and pretend for a little while that the animal was gone.

More than once, Artham strode into the cabin and spoke to Tink, but whenever he appeared, the wolf was ferocious.

"Your name is Kalmar," Artham would say with impatience, and Kalmar would howl with pain. Soon, Artham stopped coming at all.

Then one night, something changed.

Janner told his brother of the Fork Factory and his escape through the streets of Dugtown. He told of his decision to rescue Tink from Claxton Weaver's cage and of the despair he felt when he was too late. There was no moon that night, so all Janner could see of his brother was an outline by the little window.

The wolf spoke, stopping Janner in midsentence.

"I remember," Tink whispered.

Janner didn't know what to say, so he lay in the dark for a long time, hardly daring to breathe. The seas were calm, so the waves made little sound against the hull. Then Janner heard, so soft that he thought it might be his imagination, the Grey Fang crying in the dark.

Janner fell asleep with hope in his heart.

In the morning, when Nia and Leeli entered the room, Janner lay still, afraid to open his eyes and find that Tink's tears had been but a dream, the little Grey Fang as wild and vicious as ever. Janner begged the Maker to answer his prayers.

And the Maker did.

"Good morning, Janner," Nia said. She sat on his bed and kissed his forehead. "Your grandfather spotted land this morning. He said we're only two days from the Green Hollows. And good morning to you," she said to Kalmar. The furry creature stirred. "What's your name?"

"My name," the creature said with its eyes still shut, "is Kalmar. My father was Esben Wingfeather, and I am his son, the High King of Anniera."

If an artist were asked to paint a picture of perfect joy and wonder, it would look exactly like Nia's face in that moment. She wept. Leeli covered her mouth with both hands and squealed. Janner leapt out of bed and ran to his brother's side in spite of the pain that shot through his body.

"Tink?" he said.

Kalmar opened his eyes, and they were clear and blue.

APPENDICES

A passage from the First Book, as translated in Kimera by Oskar N. Reteep and Nia Igiby Wingfeather:

It came to pass that Yurgen's son, Heir of the Dragon King, lay dying by Omer's hand.

Yurgen's son believed that Omer of Anyara, son of Dwayne, meant harm on the dragons and battled him on the shore of the great Southern Mountains. Omer bested the dragon but killed him not and raced up the mountain to the hall of Yurgen the Dragon King, for indeed he did not wish for the young dragon to die.

Omer feared for his life and did not tell Yurgen that it was he himself who wounded the son of the Dragon King. He told Yurgen of the secret of the healing stones at the Heart of the World, stones that warmed the days and opened the eyes, stones that the Maker lit with life when the world was made. A flinder of holoré might save the young dragon, Omer told him, and so Yurgen and his dragons burrowed. They clawed through layers of granite and marble, rimstone and brink, through rivers colder than ice, through stone so hot it bubbled, until at last, because their roots were hollowed and weak, the mountains fell.

Then rocks shook and land broke from land. Many waters filled the deep places, and cities moved like ships unmoored. Great waves swept across the continents and buried peoples and all their histories. Songs were silenced forever.

Unaware of the destruction above, Yurgen dug deeper, at last unto a cavern with a ceiling so tall that clouds rained and lightning flashed, yea, even in the cavern; jewels glittered in stone like stars in space. The walls shone with patterns of severe beauty, fanciful whirls and bold lines—loveliness that told of mysteries ancient and fine. And Yurgen knew that the Maker strode the deep places where the wells of the world began and the holoré and holoél spread underfoot like sunlit cobbles. There the Maker planted the power that blossoms the tree and rolls the tide; there He laughed into life the song that gathers the clouds to water the soil unto seed and cover with snow the mountain crowns; there lay the magic that beat the heart of Aerwiar, and it shall not be diminished until the last day, for so the Maker said and so shall it be done.

In the sight of his dragons, Yurgen the Dragon King sank his teeth into the bright stone and dislodged two pebbles, tiny sparkles of sun. He sped upward to save his wounded heir, but behold, Yurgen found him dead, and his mountain kingdom was crumbled. Yurgen folded his wings in sorrow at his folly, and the dragons diminished. There was a great wailing in Feruiar, for many bodies lay cold on the ocean floor. Even the behemoths, Dwellers of the Deep, filled the Dark Sea with sorrowful music, for they hovered wide over the ocean floor and knew evil in the death of so many.

So ended the First Epoch.

That is the story as it has always been told.

But that is not the truth.

Nay, treachery brought this evil on the world, and the treacher's name was Will, second son of Dwayne, brother of Omer.

It was Ouster Will who sought the power of the holoré and the holoél, and he knew his father Dwayne would never show him the way to the deep places where he walked in fellowship with the Maker. So Ouster Will disguised himself as Omer. When Omer was away, Will stole his brother's armor and carried his sword. He sailed to the Southern Mountains and sank Omer's blade into the young dragon, Yurgen's heir. Ouster Will sped to the Hall of the Dragon King and, pretending to be Omer, tricked Yurgen. He told Yurgen of the healing stones, for he planned to follow the Dragon King into the core of the world and learn many secrets.

But Ouster Will foresaw not that the mountains would crumble and the way would be forever sealed. It was Ouster Will who wasted the world, and Ouster Will who spread the lie that it was Omer's doing. The Maker knows this and shall mete vengeance.

That is my prayer, for I, even I, am Omer, Son of Dwayne, and I walk the world alone. It is my hand that writes this, and no other's.

A traditional Hollish children's rhyme about the infamous Will, son of Dwayne, from Fencher's *Scarytales and Spooks*

Ouster Will

Ouster Will, Ouster Will.
He breathes on your ankles beneath your bed,
Waits 'til you're sleeping and sneaks in your head,
Darkens your dreams 'til you wish you were dead
Under the ground on the graveyard hill

With Ouster Will, Ouster Will.
He tickles your neck like a spider's twine,
Smells like the sweat of a snorting swine,
Shivers your bones and rattles your spine,
Grins in the dark on the windowsill.

It's Ouster Will, Ouster Will!
Open the shutters and brighten the lamp!
Let in the light and wake up the camp!
Your heart is a panic, your forehead is damp!
He's there in the corner to frighten and kill—

You open the shade, the dark is distilled.
Your eyes roam the room for the wickedy smile,
For the form of the fiend in the laundry pile,
For the shadowy shape of the villain so vile.
Your voice is shrill: "Oh, Ouster Will!"

But it's only a chill, not Ouster Will!
'Tis the shade of the tree on the bedroom wall
And the creak of the boards in the basement hall
And the *skritch* of a mouse in the floor, that's all,
Not Ouster Will. Peace, be still.

Oskar's Map

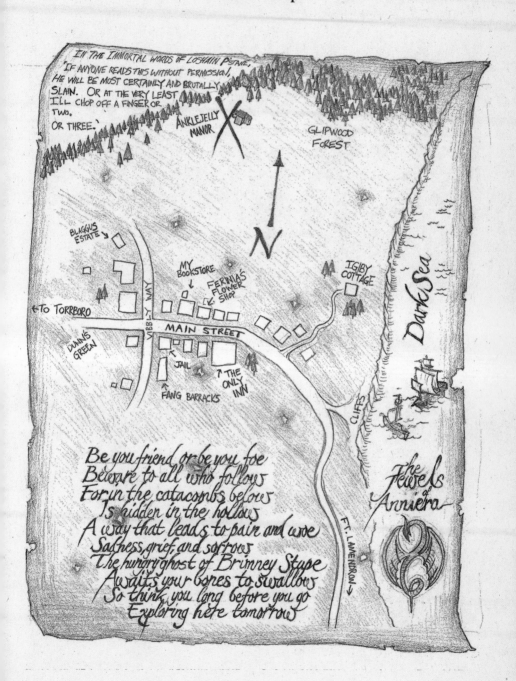

IN THE IMMORTAL WORDS OF LOSHAIN PSTWE,
'IF ANYONE READS THIS WITHOUT PERMISSION,
HE WILL BE MOST CERTAINLY AND BRUTALLY
SLAIN. OR AT THE VERY LEAST
ILL CHOP OFF A FINGER OR
TWO.

OR THREE.'

ANKLEJELLY MANOR

GLIPWOOD FOREST

N

BLAGGUS ESTATE

MY BOOKSTORE

FERNIA'S FLOWER SHOP

IGIBY COTTAGE

←TO TORRBORO

DUNN'S GREEN

VIBBLY WAY

MAIN STREET

JAIL

FANG BARRACKS

THE ONLY INN

Dark Sea

CLIFFS

FT. LAMENDRON↓

The Jewels of Anniera

Be you friend or be you foe
Beware to all who follow
For in the catacombs below
Is hidden in the hollow
A way that leads to pain and woe
Sadness, grief, and sorrow
The hungry ghost of Brimney Stupe
Awaits your bones to swallow
So think you long before you go
Exploring here tomorrow

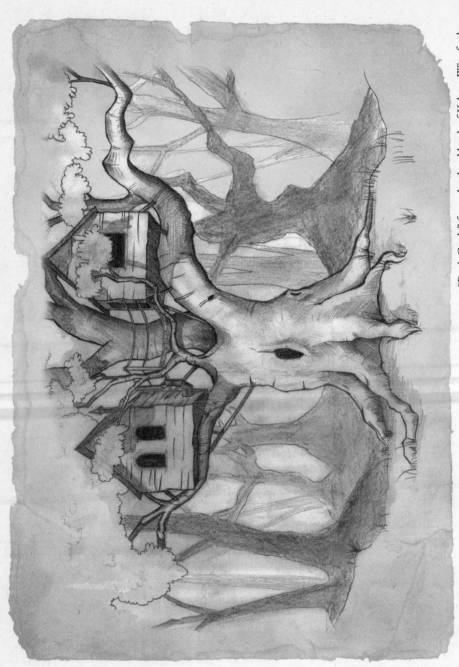

"Peet's Castle" from the sketchbook of Kalmar Wingfeather

A rendering of the whistleharp that belonged to Madia, Queen Sister of Anniera. The same whistleharp later came into the possession of Leeli Wingfeather, Song Maiden of the Shining Isle.

From the sketchbook of Kalmar Wingfeather

About the Author

ANDREW PETERSON is the author of *On the Edge of the Dark Sea of Darkness,* Book One in the Wingfeather Saga, and *The Ballad of Matthew's Begats.* He's also the critically acclaimed singer-songwriter and recording artist of ten albums, including *Resurrection Letters II.* He and his wife, Jamie, live with their two sons and one daughter in a little house they call The Warren near Nashville, Tennessee.

Visit wingfeathersaga.com for more information about Aerwiar
and its dangerous creatures.

Step into a World of **Wonder**

Get lost in a world where sea dragons sing, hidden treasure is unearthed, and surprises wait around every turn. Acclaimed singer-songwriter-storyteller Andrew Peterson takes readers of all ages on a dazzling journey through a world of stirring characters, creatures, and life lessons.